THE

WORKS OF BRET HARTE.

Riverside Edition.

COLLECTED AND REVISED BY THE AUTHOR.

GABRIEL CONROY

BY

BRET HARTE

BOSTON
HOUGHTON, MIFFLIN AND COMPANY
NEW YORK: 11 EAST SEVENTEENTH STREET
The Riverside Press, Cambridge
1882

CONTENTS.

BOOK I.—ON THE THRESHOLD.

BOOK II.—AFTER FIVE YEARS.

BOOK III.—THE LEAD.

BOOK IV.—DRIFTING.

BOOK V.—THE VEIN.

BOOK VI.—A DIP.

BOOK VII.—THE BED ROCK.

Contents.

GABRIEL CONROY.

BOOK I.

ON THE THRESHOLD.

CHAPTER I.

WITHOUT.

SNOW. Everywhere. As far as the eye could reach—fifty miles, looking southward from the highest white peak,—filling ravines and gulches, and dropping from the walls of cañons in white shroud-like drifts, fashioning the dividing ridge into the likeness of a monstrous grave, hiding the bases of giant pines, and completely covering young trees and larches, rimming with porcelain the bowl-like edges of still, cold lakes, and undulating in motionless white billows to the edge of the distant horizon. Snow lying everywhere over the California Sierras on the 15th day of March 1848, and still falling.

It had been snowing for ten days: snowing in finely granulated powder, in damp, spongy flakes, in thin, feathery plumes, snowing from a leaden sky steadily, snowing fiercely, shaken out of purple-black clouds in white flocculent masses, or dropping in long level lines, like white lances from the tumbled and broken heavens. But always silently! The woods were so choked with it—the branches were so laden with it—it had so permeated, filled and possessed earth and sky; it had so cushioned and muffled the ringing rocks and echoing hills, that all sound was deadened. The strongest gust, the fiercest blast, awoke no sigh or complaint from the snow-packed, rigid files of forest. There was no cracking of bough nor crackle of underbush; the overladen branches of pine and fir yielded and gave way without a sound. The silence was vast, measureless, complete! Nor could it be said that any outward sign of life or motion changed the fixed outlines of this stricken landscape. Above, there was no play of light and shadow, only the occasional deepening of storm or night. Below, no bird winged its flight across the white expanse, no beast haunted the confines of the black woods; whatever of brute nature might have once inhabited these solitudes had long since flown to the lowlands.

There was no track or imprint; whatever foot might have left its mark upon this waste, each succeeding snow-fall obliterated all trace or record. Every morning the solitude was virgin and unbroken; a million tiny feet had stepped into the track and filled it up. And yet, in the centre of this desolation, in the very stronghold of this grim fortress, there was the mark of human toil. A few trees had been felled at the entrance of the cañon, and the freshly-cut chips were but lightly covered with snow. They served, perhaps, to indicate another tree "blazed" with an axe, and bearing a rudely-shaped wooden effigy of a human hand, pointing to the cañon. Below the hand was a square strip of canvas, securely nailed against the bark, and bearing the following inscription—

"NOTICE.

CAPTAIN CONROY'S party of emigrants are lost in the snow, and camped up in this cañon. Out of provisions and starving!

Left St. Jo, October 8th, 1847.
Left Salt Lake, January 1st, 1848.

Arrived here, March 1st, 1848.
Lost half our stock on the Platte.
Abandoned our waggons, February 20th.

HELP!

Our names are:

Joel McCormick,	Jane Brackett,
Peter Dumphy,	Gabriel Conroy,
Paul Devarges,	John Walker,
Grace Conroy,	Henry March,
Olympia Conroy,	Philip Ashley,

Mary Dumphy.

(Then in smaller letters, in pencil:)

Mamie died, November 8th, Sweetwater.
Minnie died, December 1st, Echo Cañon.
Jane died, January 2nd, Salt Lake.
James Brackett, lost, February 3rd.

HELP!"

The language of suffering is not apt to be artistic or studied, but I think that rhetoric could not improve this actual record. So I let it stand, even as it stood this 15th day of March 1848, half-hidden by a thin film of damp snow, the snow-whitened hand stiffened and pointing rigidly to the fateful cañon like the finger of Death.

At noon there was a lull in the storm, and a slight brightening of the sky toward the east. The grim outlines of the distant hills returned, and the starved white flank of the mountain began to glisten. Across its gaunt hollow some black object was moving—moving slowly and laboriously; moving with such an uncertain mode of progression, that at first it was difficult to detect whether it was brute or human—sometimes on all fours, sometimes erect, again hurrying forward like a drunken man, but always with a certain definiteness of purpose, towards the cañon. As it approached nearer you saw that it was a man—a haggard man, ragged and enveloped in a tattered buffalo robe, but still a man, and a determined one. A young man despite his bent figure and wasted limbs—a young man despite the premature furrows that care and anxiety had set upon his brow and in the corners of his rigid mouth—a young man notwithstanding the expression of savage misanthropy with which suffering and famine had overlaid the frank impulsiveness of youth. When he reached the tree at the entrance of the cañon, he brushed the film of snow from the canvas placard, and then leant for a few moments exhaustedly against its trunk. There was something in the abandonment of his attitude that indicated even more pathetically than his face and figure his utter prostration—a prostration quite inconsistent with any visible cause. When he had rested himself, he again started forward with a nervous intensity, shambling, shuffling, falling, stooping to replace the rudely extemporised snow-shoes of fir bark that frequently slipped from his feet, but always starting on again with the feverishness of one who doubted even the sustaining power of his will.

A mile beyond the tree the cañon narrowed and turned gradually to the south, and at this point a thin curling cloud of smoke was visible that seemed to rise from some crevice in the snow. As he came nearer, the impression of recent footprints began to show; there was some displacement of the snow around a low mound from which the smoke now plainly issued. Here he stopped, or rather lay down, before an opening or cavern in the snow, and uttered a feeble shout. It was responded to still more feebly. Presently a face appeared above the opening, and a ragged figure like his own, then another, and then another, until eight human creatures, men and women, surrounded him in the snow, squatting like animals, and like animals lost to all sense of decency and shame.

They were so haggard, so faded, so forlorn, so wan,—so

piteous in their human aspect, or rather all that was left of a human aspect,—that they might have been wept over as they sat there; they were so brutal, so imbecile, unreasoning and grotesque in these newer animal attributes, that they might have provoked a smile. They were originally country people, mainly of that social class whose self-respect is apt to be dependent rather on their circumstances, position and surroundings, than upon any individual moral power or intellectual force. They had lost the sense of shame in the sense of equality of suffering; there was nothing within them to take the place of the material enjoyments they were losing. They were childish without the ambition or emulation of childhood; they were men and women without the dignity or simplicity of man and womanhood. All that had raised them above the level of the brute was lost in the snow. Even the characteristics of sex were gone; an old woman of sixty quarrelled, fought, and swore with the harsh utterance and ungainly gestures of a man; a young man of scorbutic temperament wept, sighed, and fainted with the hysteria of a woman. So profound was their degradation that the stranger who had thus evoked them from the earth, even in his very rags and sadness, seemed of another race.

They were all intellectually weak and helpless, but one, a woman, appeared to have completely lost her mind. She carried a small blanket wrapped up to represent a child—the tangible memory of one that had starved to death in her arms a few days before—and rocked it from side to side as she sat, with a faith that was piteous. But even more piteous was the fact that none of her companions took the east notice, either by sympathy or complaint, of her aberration. When, a few moments later, she called upon them to be quiet, for that "baby" was asleep, they glared at her indifferently and went on. A red-haired man, who was chewing a piece of buffalo hide, cast a single murderous glance at her, but the next moment seemed to have forgotten her presence in his more absorbing occupation.

The stranger paused a moment rather to regain his breath than to wait for their more orderly and undivided attention. Then he uttered the single word:

"Nothing!"

"Nothing!" They all echoed the word simultaneously, but with different inflection and significance—one fiercely, another gloomily, another stupidly, another mechanically. The woman with the blanket baby explained to it, "he says 'nothing,'" and laughed.

"No—nothing," repeated the speaker. "Yesterday's snow blocked up the old trail again. The beacon on the summit's burnt out. I left a notice at the Divide. Do that again, Dumphy, and I'll knock the top of your ugly head off."

Dumphy, the red-haired man, had rudely shoved and stricken the woman with the baby—she was his wife, and this conjugal act may have been partly habit—as she was crawling nearer the speaker. She did not seem to notice the blow or its giver—the apathy with which these people received blows or slights was more terrible than wrangling—but said assuringly, when she had reached the side of the young man—

"To-morrow, then?"

The face of the young man softened as he made the same reply he had made for the last eight days to the same question—

"To-morrow, surely!"

She crawled away, still holding the effigy of her dead baby very carefully, and retreated down the opening.

"'Pears to me you don't do much ennyway, out scouting! 'Pears to me you ain't worth shucks!" said the harsh-voiced woman, glancing at the speaker. "Why don't some on ye take his place? Why do you trust your lives and the lives of women to that thar Ashley?" she continued, with her voice raised to a strident bark.

The hysterical young man, Henry March, who sat next to her, turned a wild scared face upon her, and then, as if fearful of being dragged into the conversation, disappeared hastily after Mrs. Dumphy.

Ashley shrugged his shoulders, and, replying to the group, rather than any individual speaker, said curtly—

"There's but one chance—equal for all—open to all. You know what it is. To stay here is death; to go cannot be worse than that."

He rose and walked slowly away up the cañon a few rods to where another mound was visible, and disappeared from their view. When he had gone, a querulous chatter went around the squatting circle.

"Gone to see the old Doctor and the gal. We're no account."

"Thar's two too many in this yer party."

"Yes—the crazy Doctor and Ashley."

"They're both interlopers, any way."

"Jonahs."

"Said no good could come of it, ever since we picked him up."

"But the Cap'n invited the ol' Doctor, and took all his stock at Sweetwater, and Ashley put in his provisions with the rest."

The speaker was McCormick. Somewhere in the feeble depths of his consciousness there was still a lingering sense of justice. He was hungry, but not unreasonable. Besides, he remembered with a tender regret the excellent quality of provision that Ashley had furnished.

"What's that got to do with it?" screamed Mrs. Brackett. "He brought the bad luck with him. Ain't my husband dead, and isn't that skunk—an entire stranger—still livin'?"

The voice was masculine, but the logic was feminine. In cases of great prostration with mental debility, in the hopeless vacuity that precedes death by inanition or starvation, it is sometimes very effective. They all assented to it, and, by a singular intellectual harmony, the expression of each was the same. It was simply an awful curse.

"What are you goin' to do?"

"If I was a man, I'd know!"

"Knife him!"

"Kill him, and"——

The remainder of this sentence was lost to the others in a confidential whisper between Mrs. Brackett and Dumphy. After this confidence they sat and wagged their heads together, like two unmatched but hideous Chinese idols.

"Look at his strength! and he not a workin' man like us," said Dumphy. "Don't tell me he don't get suthin' reg'lar."

"Suthin' what?"

"Suthin' TO EAT!"

But it is impossible to convey, even by capitals, the intense emphasis put upon this verb. It was followed by a horrible pause.

"Let's go and see."

"And kill him?" suggested the gentle Mrs. Brackett.

They all rose with a common interest almost like enthusiasm. But after they had tottered a few steps, they fell. Yet even then there was not enough self-respect left among them to feel any sense of shame or mortification in their baffled design. They stopped—all except Dumphy.

"Wot's that dream you was talkin' 'bout jess now?" said Mr. McCormick, sitting down and abandoning the enterprise with the most shameless indifference.

"'Bout the dinner at St. Jo?" asked the person addressed—a gentleman whose faculty of alimentary imagination had been at once the bliss and torment of his present social circle.

"Yes."

They all gathered eagerly around Mr. McCormick; even Mr. Dumphy, who was still moving away, stopped.

"Well," said Mr. March, "it began with beefsteak and injins—beefsteak, you know, juicy and cut very thick, and jess squashy with gravy and injins." There was a very perceptible watering of the mouth in the party, and Mr. March, with the genius of a true narrator, under the plausible disguise of having forgotten his story, repeated the last sentence —"jess squashy with gravy and injins. And taters—baked."

"You said fried before!—and dripping with fat!" interposed Mrs. Brackett, hastily.

"For them as likes fried—but baked goes furder—skins and all—and sassage and coffee and flapjacks!"

At this magical word they laughed, not mirthfully perhaps, but eagerly and expectantly, and said, "Go on!"

"And flapjacks!"

"You said that afore," said Mrs Brackett, with a burst of passion. "Go on!" with an oath.

The giver of this Barmecide feast saw his dangerous position, and looked around for Dumphy, but he had disappeared.

CHAPTER II.

WITHIN.

The hut into which Ashley descended was like a Greenlander's "iglook," below the surface of the snow. Accident rather than design had given it this Arctic resemblance. As snow upon snow had blocked up its entrance, and reared its white ladders against its walls, and as the strength of its exhausted inmates slowly declined, communication with the outward world was kept up only by a single narrow passage. Excluded from the air, it was close and stifling, but it had a warmth that perhaps the thin blood of its occupants craved more than light or ventilation.

A smouldering fire in a wooden chimney threw a faint flicker on the walls. By its light, lying on the floor, were discernible four figures—a young woman and a child of three or four years wrapped in a single blanket, near the fire; nearer the door two men, separately enwrapped, lay apart. They might have been dead, so deep and motionless were their slumbers.

Perhaps some fear of this filled the mind of Ashley as he entered, for after a moment's hesitation, without saying a word, he passed quickly to the side of the young woman, and, kneeling beside her, placed his hand upon her face. Slight as was the touch, it awakened her. I know not what subtle magnetism was in that contact, but she caught the hand in her own, sat up, and before the eyes were scarcely opened, uttered the single word—

"Philip!"

"Grace—hush!"

He took her hand, kissed it, and pointed warningly toward the other sleepers.

"Speak low. I have much to say to you."

The young girl seemed to be content to devour the speaker with her eyes.

"You have come back," she whispered, with a faint smile, and a look that showed too plainly the predominance of that fact above all others in her mind. "I dreamt of you, Philip."

"Dear Grace"—he kissed her hand again. "Listen to me, darling! I have come back, but only with the old story—no signs of succour, no indications of help from without! My belief is, Grace," he added, in a voice so low as to be audible only to the quick ear to which it was addressed, "that we have blundered far south of the usual travelled trail. Nothing but a miracle or a misfortune like our own would bring another train this way. We are alone and helpless—in an unknown region that even the savage and brute have abandoned. The only aid we can calculate upon is from within—from ourselves. What that aid amounts to," he continued, turning a cynical eye towards the sleepers, "you know as well as I."

She pressed his hand, apologetically, as if accepting the reproach herself, but did not speak.

"As a party we have no strength—no discipline," he went on. "Since your father died we have had no leader. I know what you would say, Grace dear," he continued, answering the mute protest of the girl's hand, "but even if it were true—if I were capable of leading them, they would not take my counsels. Perhaps it is as well. If we kept together, the greatest peril of our situation would be ever present—the peril from *ourselves!*"

He looked intently at her as he spoke, but she evidently did not take his meaning. "Grace," he said, desperately, "when starving men are thrown together, they are capable of any sacrifice—of any crime, to keep the miserable life that they hold so dear just in proportion as it becomes valueless. You have read in books—Grace! good God, what is the matter?"

If she had not read his meaning in books, she might have read it at that moment in the face that was peering in at the door—a face with so much of animal suggestion in its horrible wistfulness that she needed no further revelation; a face full of inhuman ferocity and watchful eagerness, and yet a face familiar in its outlines—the face of Dumphy! Even with her danger came the swifter instinct of feminine tact and concealment, and without betraying the real cause of her momentary horror, she dropped her head upon Philip's shoulder and whispered, "I understand." When she raised her head again the face was gone.

"Enough, I did not mean to frighten you, Grace, but only to show you what we must avoid—what we have still strength left to avoid. There is but one chance of escape; you know what it is—a desperate one, but no more desperate than this passive waiting for a certain end. I ask you again—will you share it with me? When I first spoke I was less sanguine than now. Since then I have explored the ground carefully, and studied the trend of these mountains. It is *possible.* I say no more."

"But my sister and brother?"

"The child would be a hopeless impediment, even if she could survive the fatigue and exposure. Your brother must stay with her; she will need all his remaining strength and all the hopefulness that keeps him up. No, Grace, we must go alone. Remember, our safety means theirs. Their strength will last until we can send relief; while they would sink in the attempt to reach it with us. I would go alone, but I cannot bear, dear Grace, to leave you here."

"I should die if you left me," she said, simply.

"I believe you would, Grace," he said as simply.

"But can we not wait? Help may come at any moment —to-morrow."

"To-morrow will find us weaker. I should not trust your strength nor my own a day longer."

"But the old man—the Doctor?"

"He will soon be beyond the reach of help," said the young man, sadly. "Hush, he is moving."

One of the blanketed figures had rolled over. Philip walked to the fire, threw on a fresh stick, and stirred the embers. The upspringing flash showed the face of an old man whose eyes were fixed with feverish intensity upon him.

"What are you doing with the fire?" he asked querulously, with a slight foreign accent.

"Stirring it!"

"Leave it alone!"

Philip listlessly turned away.

"Come here," said the old man.

Philip approached.

"You need say nothing," said the old man after a pause, in which he examined Philip's face keenly. "I read your news in your face—the old story—I know it by heart."

"Well?" said Philip.

"Well!" said the old man, stolidly.

Philip again turned away.

"You buried the case and papers?" asked the old man.

"Yes."

"Through the snow—in the earth?"

"Yes."

"Securely?"

"Securely."

"How do you indicate it?"

"By a cairn of stones."

"And the notices—in German and French?"

"I nailed them up wherever I could, near the old trail."

"Good."

The cynical look on Philip's face deepened as he once more turned away. But before he reached the door he paused, and drawing from his breast a faded flower, with a few limp leaves, handed it to the old man.

"I found the duplicate of the plant you were looking for."

The old man half rose on his elbow, breathless with excitement as he clutched and eagerly examined the plant.

"It is the same," he said, with a sigh of relief, "and yet you said there was no news!"

"May I ask what it means?" said Philip, with a slight smile.

"It means that I am right, and Linnæus, Darwin, and Eschscholtz are wrong. It means a discovery. It means that this which you call an Alpine flower is not one, but a new species."

"An important fact to starving men," said Philip, bitterly.

"It means more," continued the old man, without heeding Philip's tone. "It means that this flower is not developed in perpetual snow. It means that it is first germinated in a warm soil and under a kindly sun. It means that if you had not plucked it, it would have fulfilled its destiny under those conditions. It means that in two months grass will be springing where you found it—even where we now lie. We are below the limit of perpetual snow."

"In two months!" said the young girl, eagerly, clasping her hands.

"In two months," said the young man, bitterly. "In two months we shall be far from here, or dead."

"Probably!" said the old man, coolly; "but if you have fulfilled my injunctions in regard to my papers and the collection, they will in good time be discovered and saved."

Ashley turned away with an impatient gesture, and the old man's head again sank exhaustedly upon his arm. Under the pretext of caressing the child, Ashley crossed over to Grace, uttered a few hurried and almost inaudible words, and disappeared through the door. When he had gone, the old man raised his head again and called feebly—

"Grace!"

"Dr. Devarges!"

"Come here!"

She rose and crossed over to his side.

"Why did he stir the fire, Grace?" said Devarges, with a suspicious glance.

"I don't know."

"You tell him everything—did you tell him that?"

"I did not, sir."

Devarges looked as if he would read the inmost thoughts of the girl, and then, as if reassured, said—

"Take it from the fire, and let it cool in the snow."

The young girl raked away the embers of the dying fire, and disclosed what seemed to be a stone of the size of a hen's egg incandescent and glowing. With the aid of two half-burnt sticks she managed to extract it, and deposited it in a convenient snow-drift near the door, and then returned to the side of the old man.

"Grace!"

"Sir!"

"You are going away!"

Grace did not speak.

"Don't deny it. I overheard you. Perhaps it is the best that you can do. But whether it is or not you will do it—of course. Grace, what do you know of that man?"

Neither the contact of daily familiarity, the quality of suffering, nor the presence of approaching death, could subdue the woman's nature in Grace. She instantly raised her shield. From behind it she began to fence feebly with the dying man.

"Why, what we all know of him, sir,—a true friend; a man to whose courage, intellect, and endurance we owe so much. And so unselfish, sir!"

"Humph!—what else?"

"Nothing—except that he has always been your devoted friend—and I thought you were his. You brought him to us," she said a little viciously.

"Yes—I picked him up at Sweetwater. But what do you know of his history? What has he told you?"

"He ran away from a wicked stepfather and relations

whom he hated. He came out West to live alone—among the Indians—or to seek his fortune in Oregon. He is very proud—you know, sir. He is as unlike us as you are, sir,—he is a gentleman. He is educated."

"Yes, I believe that's what they call it here, and he doesn't know the petals of a flower from the stamens," muttered Devarges. "Well! After you run away with him does he propose to marry you?"

For an instant a faint flush deepened the wan cheek of the girl, and she lost her guard. But the next moment she recovered it.

"Oh, sir," said this arch hypocrite, sweetly, "how can you jest so cruelly at such a moment? The life of my dear brother and sister, the lives of the poor women in yonder hut, depend upon our going. He and I are the only ones left who have strength enough to make the trial. I can assist him, for, although strong, I require less to support my strength than he. Something tells me we shall be successful; we shall return soon with help. Oh, sir,—it is no time for trifling now; our lives—even your own is at stake!"

"My own life," said the old man, impassively, "is already spent. Before you return, if you return at all, I shall be beyond your help."

A spasm of pain appeared to pass over his face. He lay still for a moment as if to concentrate his strength for a further effort. But when he again spoke his voice was much lower, and he seemed to articulate with difficulty.

"Grace," he said at last, "come nearer, girl,—I have something to tell you."

Grace hesitated. Within the last few moments a shy, nervous dread of the man which she could not account for had taken possession of her. She looked toward her sleeping brother.

"He will not waken," said Devarges, following the direction of her eyes. "The anodyne still holds its effect. Bring me what you took from the fire."

Grace brought the stone—a dull bluish-grey slag. The old man took it, examined it, and then said to Grace—

"Rub it briskly on your blanket."

Grace did so. After a few moments it began to exhibit a faint white lustre on its polished surface.

"It looks like silver," said Grace, doubtfully.

"It *is* silver!" replied Devarges.

Grace put it down quickly and moved slightly away.

"Take it," said the old man,—"it is yours. A year ago I found it in a ledge of the mountain range far west of this. I know where it lies in bulk—a fortune, Grace, do you hear?—hidden in the bluish stone you put in the fire for me last night. I can tell you where and how to find it. I can give you the title to it—the right of discovery. Take it—it is yours."

"No, no," said the girl, hurriedly, "keep it yourself. You will live to enjoy it."

"Never, Grace! even were I to live I should not make use of it. I have in my life had more than my share of it, and it brought me no happiness. It has no value to me—the rankest weed that grows above it is worth more in my eyes. Take it. To the world it means everything—wealth and position. Take it. It will make you as proud and independent as your lover—it will make you always gracious in his eyes;—it will be a setting to your beauty,—it will be a pedestal to your virtue. Take it—it is yours."

"But you have relatives—friends," said the girl, drawing away from the shining stone with a half superstitious awe. "There are others whose claims"——

"None greater than yours," interrupted the old man, with the nervous haste of failing breath. "Call it a reward if you choose. Look upon it as a bribe to keep your lover to the fulfilment of his promise to preserve my manuscripts and collection. Think, if you like, that it is an act of retribution—that once in my life I might have known a young girl whose future would have been blest by such a gift. Think—think what you like—but take it!"

His voice had sunk to a whisper. A greyish pallor had overspread his face, and his breath came with difficulty. Grace would have called her brother, but with a motion of his hand Devarges restrained her. With a desperate effort he raised himself upon his elbow, and drawing an envelope from his pocket, put it in her hand.

"It contains—map—description of mine and locality—yours—say you will take it—Grace, quick, say"——

His head had again sunk to the floor. She stooped to raise it. As she did so a slight shadow darkened the opening by the door. She raised her eyes quickly and saw the face of Dumphy!

She did not shrink this time; but, with a sudden instinct, she turned to Devarges, and said—

"I will!"

She raised her eyes again defiantly, but the face had disappeared.

"Thank you," said the old man. His lips moved again, but without a sound. A strange film had begun to gather in his eyes.

"Dr. Devarges," whispered Grace.

He did not speak. "He is dying," thought the young girl as a new and sudden fear overcame her. She rose quickly and crossed hurriedly to her brother and shook him. A prolonged inspiration, like a moan, was the only response. For a moment she glanced wildly around the room and then ran to the door.

"Philip!"

There was no response. She climbed up through the tunnel-like opening. It was already quite dark, and a few feet beyona the hut nothing was distinguishable. She cast a rapid backward glance, and then, with a sudden desperation, darted forward into the darkness. At the same moment two figures raised themselves from behind the shadow of the mound and slipped down the tunnel into the hut—Mrs. Brackett and Mr. Dumphy. They might have been the meanest predatory animals—so stealthy, so eager, so timorous, so crouching, and yet so agile were their motions. They ran sometimes upright, and sometimes on all fours, hither and thither. They fell over each other in their eagerness, and struck and spat savagely at each other in the half darkness. They peered into corners, they rooted in the dying embers and among the ashes, they groped among the skins and blankets, they smelt and sniffed at every article. They paused at last apparently unsuccessful, and glared at each other.

"They must have eaten it," said Mrs. Brackett, in a hoarse whisper.

"It didn't look like suthin' to eat," said Dumphy.

"You saw 'em take it from the fire?"

"Yes!"

"And rub it?"

"Yes!"

"Fool. Don't you see"——

"What?"

"It was a baked potato."

Dumphy sat dumfounded.

"Why should they rub it? it takes off the cracklin' skins," he said.

"They've got such fine stomachs!" answered Mrs. Brackett, with an oath.

Dumphy was still aghast with the importance of his discovery.

"He said he knew where there was more!" he whispered eagerly.

"Where?"

"I didn't get to hear."

"Fool! Why didn't ye rush in and grip his throat until he told yer?" hissed Mrs Brackett, in a tempest of baffled rage and disappointment. "Ye ain't got the spunk of a flea. Let me get hold of that gal—Hush! what's that?"

"He's moving!" said Dumphy.

In an instant they had both changed again into slinking, crouching, baffled animals, eager only for escape. Yet they dared not move.

The old man had turned over, and his lips were moving in the mutterings of delirium. Presently he called "Grace!"

With a sign of caution to her companion, the woman leaned over him.

"Yes, deary, I'm here."

"Tell him not to forget. Make him keep his promise. Ask him where it is buried!"

"Yes, deary!"

"He'll tell you. He knows!"

"Yes, deary!"

"At the head of Monument Cañon. A hundred feet north of the lone pine. Dig two feet down below the surface of the cairn."

"Yes!"

"Where the wolves can't get it."

"Yes!"

"The stones keep it from ravenous beasts."

"Yes, in course."

"That might tear it up."

"Yes!"

"Starving beasts!"

"Yes, deary!"

The fire of his wandering eyes went out suddenly, like a candle; his jaw dropped; he was dead. And over him the man and woman crouched in fearful joy, looking at each other with the first smile that had been upon their lips since they had entered the fateful cañon.

CHAPTER III.

GABRIEL.

It was found the next morning that the party was diminished by five. Philip Ashley and Grace Conroy, Peter Dumphy and Mrs. Brackett, were missing; Dr. Paul Devarges was dead. The death of the old man caused but little excitement and no sorrow; the absconding of the others was attributed to some information which they had selfishly withheld from the remaining ones, and produced a spasm of impotent rage. In five minutes their fury knew no bounds. The lives and property of the fugitives were instantly declared forfeit. Steps were taken—about twenty, I think—in the direction of their flight, but finally abandoned.

Only one person knew that Philip and Grace had gone together—Gabriel Conroy. On awakening early that morning he had found pinned to his blanket a paper with these words in pencil—

"God bless dear brother and sister, and keep them until Philip and I come back with help."

With it were a few scraps of provisions, evidently saved by Grace from her scant rations, and left as a parting gift. These Gabriel instantly turned into the common stock. Then he began to comfort the child. Added to his natural hopefulness, he had a sympathetic instinct with the pains and penalties of childhood, not so much a quality of his intellect as of his nature. He had all the physical adaptabilities of a nurse—a large, tender touch, a low persuasive voice, pliant yet unhesitating limbs, and broad, well-cushioned surfaces. During the weary journey women had instinctively entrusted babies to his charge; most of the dead had died in his arms; all forms and conditions of helplessness had availed themselves of his easy capacity. No one thought of thanking him. I do not think he ever expected it; he always appeared morally irresponsible and quite unconscious of his own importance, and, as is frequent in such cases, there was a tendency to accept his services at his own valuation. Nay more, there was a slight consciousness of superiority in those who thus gave him an opportunity of exhibiting his special faculty.

"Olly," he said, after an airy preliminary toss, "would ye like to have a nice dolly?"

Olly opened her wide hungry eyes in hopeful anticipation and nodded assent.

"A nice dolly, with real mamma," he continued, "who plays with it like a true baby. Would ye like to help her play with it?"

The idea of a joint partnership of this kind evidently pleased Olly by its novelty.

"Well then, brother Gabe will get you one. But Gracie will have to go away, so that the doll's mamma kin come."

Olly at first resented this, but eventually succumbed to novelty, after the fashion of her sex, starving or otherwise. Yet she prudently asked—

"Is it ever hungry?"

"It is never hungry," replied Gabriel, confidently.

"Oh!" said Olly, with an air of relief.

Then Gabriel, the cunning, sought Mrs. Dumphy, the mentally alienated.

"You are jest killin' of yourself with the tendin' o' that

child," he said, after bestowing a caress on the blanket and slightly pinching an imaginary cheek of the effigy. "It would be likelier and stronger fur a playmate. Good gracious ! how thin it is gettin'. A change will do it good; fetch it to Olly, and let her help you to tend it until—until—to-morrow." To-morrow was the extreme limit of Mrs. Dumphy's future.

So Mrs. Dumphy and her effigy were installed in Gracie's place, and Olly was made happy. A finer nature or a more active imagination than Gabriel's would have revolted at this monstrous combination; but Gabriel only saw that they appeared contented, and the first pressing difficulty of Gracie's absence was overcome. So alternately they took care of the effigy, the child simulating the cares of the future and losing the present in them, the mother living in the memories of the past. Perhaps it might have been pathetic to have seen Olly and Mrs. Dumphy both saving the infinitesimal remnants of their provisions for the doll, but the only spectator was one of the actors, Gabriel, who lent himself to the deception; and pathos, to be effective, must be viewed from the outside.

At noon that day the hysterical young man, Gabriel's cousin, died. Gabriel went over to the other hut and endeavoured to cheer the survivors. He succeeded in infecting them so far with his hopefulness as to loosen the tongue and imagination of the story-teller, but at four o'clock the body had not yet been buried. It was evening, and the three were sitting over the embers, when a singular change came over Mrs. Dumphy. The effigy suddenly slipped from her hands, and looking up, Gabriel perceived that her arms had dropped to her side, and that her eyes were fixed on vacancy. He spoke to her, but she made no sign nor response of any kind. He touched her and found her limbs rigid and motionless. Olly began to cry.

The sound seemed to agitate Mrs. Dumphy. Without moving a limb, she said, in a changed, unnatural voice, "Hark!"

Olly choked her sobs at a sign from Gabriel.

"They're coming!" said Mrs. Dumphy.

"Which?" said Gabriel.

"The relief party."

"Where?"

"Far, far away. They re jest setting out. I see 'em—a dozen men with pack horses and provisions. The leader is an American—the others are strangers. They're coming—but far, oh, so far away!"

Gabriel fixed his eyes upon her, but did not speak. After a death-like pause, she went on—

"The sun is shining, the birds are singing, the grass is springing where they ride—but, oh, so far—too far away!"

"Do you know them?" asked Gabriel.

"No."

"Do they know us?"

"No."

"Why do they come, and how do they know where we are?" asked Gabriel.

"Their leader has seen us."

"Where?"

"In a dream." *

Gabriel whistled and looked at the rag baby. He was

* I fear I must task the incredulous reader's further patience by calling attention to what may perhaps prove the most literal and thoroughly-attested fact of this otherwise fanciful chronicle. The condition and situation of the ill-famed "Donner Party"—then an unknown, unheralded cavalcade of emigrants—starving in an unfrequented pass of the Sierras, was first made known to Captain Yount of Napa, *in a dream*. The Spanish records of California show that the relief party which succoured the survivors was projected upon this *spiritual* information.

willing to recognise something abnormal, and perhaps even prophetic, in this insane woman; but a coincident exaltation in a stranger who was not suffering from the illusions produced by starvation was beyond his credulity. Nevertheless, the instincts of good humour and hopefulness were stronger, and he presently asked—

"How will they come?"

"Up through a beautiful valley and a broad shining river. Then they will cross a mountain until they come to another beautiful valley with steep sides, and a rushing river that runs so near us that I can almost hear it now. Don't you see it? It is just beyond the snow peak there; a green valley, with the rain falling upon it. Look! it is there."

She pointed directly north, toward the region of inhospitable snow.

"Could you get to it?" asked the practical Gabriel.

"No."

"Why not?"

"I must wait here for my baby. She is coming for us. She will find me here."

"When?"

"To-morrow."

It was the last time that she uttered that well-worn sentence; for it was only a little past midnight that her baby came to her—came to her with a sudden light, that might have been invisible to Gabriel, but that it was reflected in her own lack-lustre eyes—came to this poor half-witted creature with such distinctness that she half rose, stretched out her thin yearning arms, and received it—a corpse! Gabriel placed the effigy in her arms and folded them over it. Then he ran swiftly to the other hut. For some unexplained reason he did not get further than the door. What he saw there he has never told; but when he groped his fainting way back to his own hut again, his face was white and bloodless, and his eyes wild and staring. Only one impulse remained—to fly for ever from the cursed spot. He stopped only long enough to snatch up the sobbing and frightened Olly, and then, with a loud cry to God to help him—to help *them*—he dashed out, and was lost in the darkness.

CHAPTER IV

NATURE SHOWS THEM THE WAY.

It was a spur of the long grave-like ridge that lay to the north of the cañon. Up its gaunt white flank two figures had been slowly crawling since noon, until at sunset they at last stood upon its outer verge outlined against the sky—Philip and Grace.

For all the fatigues of the journey, the want of nourishing food and the haunting shadow of the suffering she had left, the face of Grace, flushed with the dying sun, was very pretty. The boy's dress she had borrowed was ill-fitting, and made her exquisite little figure still more diminutive, but it could not entirely hide its graceful curves. Here in this rosy light the swooning fringes of her dark eyes were no longer hidden; the perfect oval of her face, even the few freckles on her short upper lip, were visible to Philip. Partly as a physical support, partly to reassure her, he put his arm tenderly around her waist. Then he kissed her. It is possible that this last act was purely gratuitous.

Howbeit Grace first asked, with the characteristic prudence of her sex, the question she had already asked many days before that day, "Do you love me, Philip?" And Philip, with the ready frankness of our sex on such occasions, had invariably replied, "I do."

Nevertheless the young man was pre-occupied, anxious,

and hungry. It was the fourth day since they had left the hut. On the second day they had found some pine cones with the nuts still intact and fresh beneath the snow, and later a squirrel's hoard. On the third day Philip had killed the proprietor and eaten him. The same evening Philip had espied a duck winging his way up the cañon. Philip, strong in the belief that some inland lake was the immediate object of its flight, had first marked its course, and then brought it down with a long shot. Then having altered their course in accordance with its suggestion, they ate their guide next morning for breakfast.

Philip was also disappointed. The summit of the spur so laboriously attained only showed him the same endless succession of white snow billows stretching rigidly to the horizon's edge. There was no break—no glimpse of water-course or lake. There was nothing to indicate whence the bird had come or the probable point it was endeavouring to reach. He was beginning to consider the feasibility of again changing their course, when an unlooked-for accident took that volition from his hands.

Grace had ventured out to the extreme limit of the rocky cliff, and with straining eyes was trying to peer beyond the snow fields, when the treacherous ledge on which she was standing began to give way. In an instant Philip was at her side and had caught her hand, but at the same moment a large rock of the ledge dropped from beneath her feet, and left her with no support but his grasp. The sudden shock loosened also the insecure granite on which Philip stood. Before he could gain secure foothold it also trembled, tottered, slipped, and then fell, carrying Philip and Grace with it. Luckily this immense mass of stone and ice got fairly away before them, and ploughed down the steep bank of the cliff, breaking off the projecting rocks and protuberances, and cutting a clean, though almost perpendicular, path down the mountain side. Even in falling Philip had presence of mind enough to forbear clutching at the crumbling ledge, and so precipitating the rock that might crush them. Before he lost his senses he remembered tightening his grip of Grace's arm, and drawing her face and head forward to his breast, and even in his unconsciousness it seemed that he instinctively guided her into the smooth passage or "shoot" made by the plunging rock below them; and even then he was half conscious of dashing into sudden material darkness and out again into light, and of the crashing and crackling of branches around him, and even the brushing of the stiff pine needles against his face and limbs. Then he felt himself stopped, and then, and then only, everything whirled confusedly by him, and his brain seemed to partake of the motion, and then—the relief of utter blankness and oblivion. When he regained his senses, it was with a burning heat in his throat, and the sensation of strangling. When he opened his eyes he saw Grace bending over him, pale and anxious, and chafing his hands and temples with snow. There was a spot of blood upon her round cheek.

"You are hurt, Grace!" were the first words that Philip gasped.

"No!—dear, brave Philip—but only so thankful and happy for your escape." Yet, at the same moment the colour faded from her cheek, and even the sun-kissed line of her upper lip grew bloodless, as she leaned back against a tree.

But Philip did not see her. His eyes were rapidly taking in his strange surroundings. He was lying among the broken fragments of pine branches and the débris of the cliff above. In his ears was the sound of hurrying water, and before him, scarce a hundred feet, a rushing river! He looked up; the red glow of sunset was streaming through the broken limbs and shattered branches of the snow-thatched roof that he had broken through in his descent. Here and there along the river the same light was penetrating the interstices and openings of this strange vault that arched above this sunless stream.

He knew now whence the duck had flown! He knew now why he had not seen the water-course before! He knew now where the birds and beasts had betaken themselves—why the woods and cañons were trackless! Here was at last the open road! He staggered to his feet with a cry of delight.

"Grace, we are saved."

Grace looked at him with eyes that perhaps spoke more eloquently of joy at his recovery than of comprehension of his delight.

"Look, Grace! this is Nature's own road—only a lane, perhaps—but a clue to our way out of this wilderness. As we descend the stream it will open into a broader valley."

"I know it," she said, simply.

Philip looked at her inquiringly.

"When I dragged you out of the way of the falling rocks and snow above, I had a glimpse of the valley you speak of. I saw it from there."

She pointed to a ledge of rock above the opening where the great stone that had fallen had lodged.

"When you dragged me, my child?"

Grace smiled faintly.

"You don't know how strong I am," she said, and then proved it by fainting dead away.

Philip started to his feet and ran to her side. Then he felt for the precious flask that he had preserved so sacredly through all their hardships, but it was gone. He glanced around him; it was lying on the snow, empty! For the first time in their weary pilgrimage Philip uttered a groan.

At the sound Grace opened her sweet eyes. She saw her lover with the empty flask in his hand, and smiled faintly.

"I poured it all down your throat, dear," she said. "You looked so faint—I thought you were dying—forgive me!"

"But I was only stunned; and you, Grace, you"——

"Am better now," she said, as she strove to rise. But she uttered a weak little cry and fell back again.

Philip did not hear her. He was already climbing the ledge she had spoken of. When he returned his face was joyous.

"I see it, Grace; it is only a few miles away. It is still light, and we shall camp there to-night."

"I am afraid—not—dear Philip," said Grace, doubtfully.

"Why not?" asked Philip, a little impatiently.

"Because—I—think—my leg is broken!"

"Grace!"

But she had fainted.

CHAPTER V.

OUT OF THE WOODS—INTO THE SHADOW.

HAPPILY Grace was wrong. Her ankle was severely sprained, and she could not stand. Philip tore up his shirt, and, with bandages dipped in snow water, wrapped up the swollen limb. Then he knocked over a quail in the bushes and another duck, and clearing away the brush for a camping spot, built a fire, and tempted the young girl with a hot supper. The peril of starvation passed, their greatest danger was over—a few days longer of enforced rest and inactivity was the worst to be feared.

The air had grown singularly milder with the last few hours. At midnight a damp breeze stirred the pine needles above their heads, and an ominous muffled beating was heard upon the snow-packed vault. It was rain.

"It is the reveille of spring!" whispered Philip.

But Grace was in no mood for poetry—even a lover's. She let her head drop upon his shoulder, and then said—

"You must go on, dear, and leave me here."

"Grace!"

"Yes, Philip! I can live till you come back. I fear no danger now. I am so much better off than *they* are!"

A few tears dropped on his hand. Philip winced. Perhaps it was his conscience; perhaps there was something in the girl's tone, perhaps because she had once before spoken in the same way, but it jarred upon a certain quality in his nature which he was pleased to call his "common sense." Philip really believed himself a high-souled, thoughtless, ardent, impetuous temperament, saved only from destruction by the occasional dominance of this quality.

For a moment he did not speak. He thought how, at the risk of his own safety, he had snatched this girl from terrible death; he thought how he had guarded her through their perilous journey, taking all the burdens upon himself; he thought how happy he had made her—how she had even admitted her happiness to him; he thought of her present helplessness, and how willing he was to delay the journey on her account; he dwelt even upon a certain mysterious, ill-defined but blissful future with him to which he was taking her; and yet here, at the moment of their possible deliverance, she was fretting about two dying people, who, without miraculous interference, would be dead before she could reach them. It was part of Philip's equitable self-examination—a fact of which he was very proud—that he always put himself in the position of the person with whom he differed, and imagined how *he* would act under the like circumstances. Perhaps it is hardly necessary to say that Philip always found that his conduct under those conditions would be totally different. In the present instance, putting himself in Grace's position, he felt that he would have abandoned all and everything for a love and future like hers. That she did not was evidence of a moral deficiency or a blood taint. Logic of this kind is easy and irrefutable. It has been known to obtain even beyond the Sierras, and with people who were not physically exhausted. After a pause he said to Grace, in a changed voice—

"Let us talk plainly for a few moments, Grace, and understand each other before we go forward or backward. It is five days since we left the hut; were we even certain of finding our wandering way back again, we could not reach there before another five days had elapsed; by that time all will be over. They have either been saved or are beyond the reach of help. This sounds harsh, Grace, but it is no harsher than the fact. Had we stayed, we would, without helping them, have only shared their fate. I might have been in your brother's place, you in your sister's. It is our fortune, not our fault, that we are not dying with them. It has been willed that you and I should be saved. It might have been willed that we should have perished in our attempts to succour them, and that relief which came to *them* would have never reached *us.*"

Grace was no logician, and could not help thinking that if Philip had said this before, she would not have left the hut. But the masculine reader will, I trust, at once detect the irrelevance of the feminine suggestion, and observe that it did not refute Philip's argument. She looked at him with a half frightened air. Perhaps it was the tears that dimmed her eyes, but his few words seemed to have removed him to a great distance, and for the first time a strange sense of loneliness came over her. She longed to reach her yearning arms to him again, but with this feeling came a sense of shame that she had not felt before.

Philip noticed her hesitation, and half interpreted it. He let her passive head fall.

"Perhaps we had better wait until we are ourselves out of danger before we talk of helping others," he said with something of his old bitterness. "This accident may keep us here some days, and we know not as yet where we are. Go to sleep now," he said more kindly, "and in the morning we will see what can be done."

Grace sobbed herself to sleep! Poor, poor Grace! She had been looking for this opportunity of speaking about herself—about their future. This was to have been the beginning of her confidence about Dr. Devarges's secret; she would have told him frankly all the doctor had said, even his suspicions of Philip himself. And then Philip would have been sure to have told her his plans, and they would have gone back with help, and Philip would have been a hero whom Gabriel would have instantly recognised as the proper husband for Grace, and they would have all been very happy. And now they were all dead, and had died, perhaps, cursing her, and—Philip—Philip had not kissed her good-night, and was sitting gloomily under a tree!

The dim light of a leaden morning broke through the snow vault above their heads. It was raining heavily, the river had risen, and was still rising. It was filled with drift and branches, and snow and ice, the waste and ware of many a mile. Occasionally a large uprooted tree with a gaunt forked root like a mast sailed by. Suddenly Philip, who had been sitting with his chin upon his hands, rose with a shout. Grace looked up languidly. He pointed to a tree that, floating by, had struck the bank where they sat, and then drifted broadside against it, where for a moment it lay motionless.

"Grace," he said, with his old spirits, "Nature has taken us in hand herself. If we are to be saved, it is by her methods. She brought us here to the water's edge, and now she sends a boat to take us off again. Come!"

Before Grace could reply, Philip had lifted her gaily in his arms, and deposited her between two upright roots of the tree. Then he placed beside her his rifle and provisions, and leaping himself on the bow of this strange craft, shoved it off with a broken branch that he had found. For a moment it still clung to the bank, and then suddenly catching the impulse of the current, darted away like a living creature.

The river was very narrow and rapid where they had embarked, and for a few moments it took all of Philip's energy and undivided attention to keep the tree in the centre of the current. Grace sat silent, admiring her lover, alert, forceful, and glowing with excitement. Presently Philip called to her—

"Do you see that log? We are near a settlement."

A freshly-hewn log of pine was floating in the current beside them. A ray of hope shot through Grace's sad fancies; if they were so near help, might not it have already reached the sufferers? But she forbore to speak to Philip again upon that subject, and in his new occupation he seemed to have forgotten her. It was with a little thrill of joy that at last she saw him turn, and balancing himself with his bough upon their crank craft, walk down slowly toward her. When he reached her side he sat down, and, taking her hand in his, for the first time since the previous night, he said gently—

"Grace, my child, I have something to tell you."

Grace's little heart throbbed quickly; for a moment she did not dare to lift her long lashes toward his. Without noticing her embarrassment he went on—

"In a few hours we shall be no longer in the wilderness, but in the world again—in a settlement perhaps, among men and—perhaps women. Strangers certainly—not the relatives you have known, and who know you—not the people with whom we have been familiar for so many weeks and days—but people who know nothing of us, or our sufferings."

Grace looked at him, but did not speak.

"You understand, Grace, that, not knowing this, they might put their own construction upon our flight.

"To speak plainly, my child, you are a young woman, and I am a young man. Your beauty, dear Grace, offers an explanation of our companionship that the world will accept more readily than any other, and the truth to many would seem scarcely as natural. For this reason it must not be told. I will go back alone with relief, and leave you here in some safe hands until I return. But I leave you here not as Grace Conroy—you shall take my own name!"

A hot flush mounted to Grace's throat and cheek, and for an instant, with parted lips, she hung breathless upon his next word. He continued quietly—

"You shall be my sister—Grace Ashley."

The blood fell from her cheek, her eyelids dropped, and she buried her face in her hands. Philip waited patiently for her reply. When she lifted her face again, it was quiet and calm—there was even a slight flush of proud colour in her cheek as she met his gaze, and with the faintest curl of her upper lip said—

"You are right!"

At the same moment there was a sudden breaking of light and warmth and sunshine over their heads; the tree swiftly swung round a sharp curve in the river, and then drifted slowly into a broad, overflowed valley, sparkling with the emerald of gently sloping hillsides, and dazzling with the glow of the noonday sun. And beyond, from a cluster of willows scarcely a mile away, the smoke of a cabin chimney curled in the still air.

CHAPTER VI.

FOOTPRINTS.

FOR two weeks an unclouded sun rose and set on the rigid outlines of Monument Point. For two weeks there had been no apparent change in the ghastly whiteness of the snow-flanked rocks; in the white billows that rose rank on rank beyond, in the deathlike stillness that reigned above and below. It was the first day of April; there was the mildness of early spring in the air that blew over this gaunt waste, and yet awoke no sound or motion. And yet a nearer approach showed that a slow insidious change had been taking place. The white flanks of the mountain were more hollow; the snow had shrunk visibly away in places, leaving the grey rocks naked and protuberant; the rigid outlines were there, but less full and rounded; the skeleton was beginning to show through the wasting flesh; there were great patches of snow that had sloughed away, leaving the gleaming granite bare below. It was the last change of the Hippocratic face that Nature turned toward the spectator. And yet this change had been noiseless—the solitude unbroken.

And then one day there suddenly drifted across the deathlike valley the chime of jingling spurs and the sound of human voices. Down the long defile a cavalcade of mounted men and pack mules made their way, plunging through drifts and clattering over rocks. The unwonted sound awoke the long slumbering echoes of the mountain, brought down small avalanches from cliff and tree, and at last brought from some cavern of the rocks to the surface of the snow a figure so wild, haggard, dishevelled and monstrous, that it was scarcely human. It crawled upon the snow, dodging behind rocks with the timidity of a frightened animal, and at last, squatting behind a tree, awaited in ambush the approach of the party.

Two men rode ahead; one grave, preoccupied, and reticent. The other alert, active, and voluble. At last the reticent man spoke, but slowly, and as if recalling a memory rather than recording a present impression.

"They cannot be far away from us now. It was in some such spot that I first saw them. The place is familiar."

"Heaven send that it may be!" said the other hastily, "for to tell you the truth, I doubt if we will be able to keep the men together a day longer in this crazy quest, unless we discover something."

"It was here," continued the other dreamily, not heeding his companion, "that I saw the figures of a man and woman. If there is not a cairn of stone somewhere about this spot, I shall believe my dream false, and confess myself an old fool."

"Well—as I said before," rejoined the other, laughing, "anything—a scrap of paper, an old blanket, or a broken waggon-tongue will do. Columbus helped his course and kept up his crew on a fragment of seaweed. But what are the men looking at? Great God! There *is* something moving by yonder rock!"

By one common superstitious instinct the whole party had crowded together—those who, a few moments before, had been loudest in their scepticism, held their breath with awe, and trembled with excitement—as the shambling figure that had watched them enter the cañon rose from its lair, and taking upon itself a human semblance, with uncouth gestures and a strange hoarse cry made towards them. It was Dumphy!

The leader was the first to recover himself. He advanced from the rest and met Dumphy half-way.

"Who are you?"

"A man."

"What's the matter?"

"Starving."

"Where are the others?"

Dumphy cast a suspicious glance at him and said—

"Who?"

"The others. You are not alone?"

"Yes, I am!"

"How did you get here?"

"What's that to you? I'm here and starving. Gimme suthin' to eat and drink."

He sank exhaustedly on all fours again.

There was a murmur of sympathy from the men.

"Give him suthin'. Don't you see he can't stand—much less talk? Where's the doctor?"

And then the younger of the leaders thus adjured—"Leave him to me—he wants my help just now more than yours."

He poured some brandy down his throat. Dumphy gasped, and then staggered to his feet.

"What did you say your name was?" asked the young surgeon kindly.

"Jackson," said Dumphy, with a defiantly blank look.

"Where from?"

"Missouri."

"How did you get here?"

"Strayed from my party."

"And they are ——"

"Gone on. Gimme suthin' to eat!"

"Take him back to camp and hand him over to Sanchez. He'll know what to do," said the surgeon to one of the men. "Well, Blunt," he continued, addressing the leader, "you're saved—but your nine men in buckram have dwindled down to one, and not a very creditable specimen at that," he said, as his eyes followed the retreating Dumphy.

"I wish it were all, doctor," said Blunt simply; "I would be willing to go back now, but something tells me we have only begun. This one makes everything else possible. What have you there?"

One of the men was approaching, holding a slip of paper with ragged edges, as if torn from some position where it had been nailed.

"A notiss—from a tree. Me no sabe," said the ex-vaquero.

"Nor I," said Blunt, looking at it; "it seems to be in German. Call Glohr."

A tall Swiss came forward. Blunt handed him the paper. The man examined it.

"It is a direction to find property—important and valuable property—buried."

"Where?"

"Under a cairn of stones."

The surgeon and Blunt exchanged glances.

"Lead us there!" said Blunt.

It was a muffled monotonous tramp of about an hour. At the end of that time they reached a spur of the mountain around which the cañon turned abruptly. Blunt uttered a cry. Before them was a ruin—a rude heap of stones originally symmetrical and elevated, but now thrown down and dismantled. The snow and earth were torn up around and beneath it. On the snow lay some scattered papers, a portfolio of drawings of birds and flowers: a glass case of insects broken and demolished, and the scattered feathers of a few stuffed birds. At a little distance lay what seemed to be a heap of ragged clothing. At the sight of it the nearest horseman uttered a shout and leaped to the ground. It was Mrs. Brackett, dead.

CHAPTER VII.

IN WHICH THE FOOTPRINTS BEGIN TO FADE.

SHE had been dead about a week. The features and clothing were scarcely recognizable; the limbs were drawn up convulsively. The young surgeon bent over her attentively.

"Starved to death?" said Blunt interrogatively.

The surgeon did not reply, but rose and examined the scattered specimens. One of them he picked up and placed first to his nose and then to his lips. After a pause he replied quietly—

"No. Poisoned."

The men fell back from the body.

"Accidentally, I think," continued the surgeon coolly; "the poor creature has been driven by starvation to attack the specimens. They have been covered with a strong solution of arsenic to preserve them from the ravages of insects, and this starving woman has been the first to fall a victim to the collector's caution."

There was a general movement of horror and indignation among the men. "Shoost to keep dem birds," said the irate Swiss. "Killing women to save his cussed game," said another. The surgeon smiled. It was an inauspicious moment for Dr. Devarges to have introduced himself in person.

"If this enthusiastic naturalist is still living, I hope he'll keep away from the men for some hours," said the surgeon to Blunt, privately.

"Who is he?" asked the other.

"A foreigner—a *savant* of some note, I should say, in his own country. I think I have heard the name before—'Devarges,'" replied the surgeon, looking over some papers that he had picked up. "He speaks of some surprising discoveries he has made, and evidently valued his collection very highly."

"Are they worth re-collecting and preserving?" asked Blunt.

"Not now!" said the surgeon. "Every moment is precious. Humanity first, science afterward," he added lightly, and they rode on.

And so the papers and collections preserved with such care, the evidence of many months of patient study, privation, and hardship, the records of triumph and discovery were left lying upon the snow. The wind came down the flanks of the mountain and tossed them hither and thither as if in scorn, and the sun, already fervid, heating the metallic surfaces of the box and portfolio, sank them deeper in the snow, as if to bury them from the sight for ever.

By skirting the edge of the valley where the snow had fallen away from the mountain-side, they reached in a few hours the blazed tree at the entrance of the fateful cañon. The placard was still there, but the wooden hand that once pointed in the direction of the buried huts had, through some mischance of wind or weather, dropped slightly, and was ominously pointing to the snow below. This was still so deep in drifts that the party were obliged to leave their horses and enter the cañon a-foot. Almost unconsciously, this was done in perfect silence, walking in single file, occasionally climbing up the sides of the cañon where the rocks offered a better foothold than the damp snow, until they reached a wooden chimney and part of a roof that now reared itself above the snow. Here they paused and looked at each other. The leader approached the chimney, and leaning over it called within.

There was no response. Presently, however, the cañon took up the shout and repeated it, and then there was a silence broken only by the falling of an icicle from a rock, or a snow slide from the hill above. Then all was quiet again, until Blunt, after a moment's hesitation, walked around to the opening and descended into the hut. He had scarcely disappeared, as it seemed, before he returned, looking very white and grave, and beckoned to the surgeon. He instantly followed. After a little, the rest of the party, one after another, went down. They stayed some time, and then came slowly to the surface bearing three dead bodies. They returned again quickly, and then brought up the *dissevered* members of a fourth. This done they looked at each other in silence.

"There should be another cabin here," said Blunt after a pause.

"Here it is!" said one of the men, pointing to the chimney of the second hut.

There was no preliminary "hallo!" or hesitation now. The worst was known. They all passed rapidly to the opening, and disappeared within. When they returned to the surface they huddled together—a whispering but excited group. They were so much preoccupied that they did not see that their party was suddenly increased by the presence of a stranger.

CHAPTER VIII.

THE FOOTPRINTS GROW FAINTER.

It was Philip Ashley! Philip Ashley—faded, travel-worn, hollow-eyed, but nervously energetic and eager. Philip, who four days before had left Grace the guest of a hospitable trapper's half-breed family in the California Valley. Philip—gloomy, discontented, hateful of the quest he had undertaken, but still fulfilling his promise to Grace and the savage dictates of his own conscience. It was Philip Ashley, who now standing beside the hut, turned half-cynically, half-indifferently toward the party.

The surgeon was first to discover him. He darted forward with a cry of recognition, "Poinsett! Arthur!—what are you doing here?"

Ashley's face flushed crimson at the sight of the stranger. "Hush!" he said almost involuntarily. He glanced rapidly around the group, and then in some embarrassment replied with awkward literalness, "I left my horse with the others at the entrance of the cañon."

"I see," said the surgeon briskly, "you have come with relief like ourselves; but you are too late! too late!"

"Too late!" echoed Ashley.

"Yes, they are all dead or gone!"

A singular expression crossed Ashley's face. It was unnoticed by the surgeon, who was whispering to Blunt. Presently he came forward.

"Captain Blunt, this is Lieutenant Poinsett of the Fifth Infantry, an old messmate of mine, whom I have not met before for two years. He is here, like ourselves, on an errand of mercy. It is like him!"

The unmistakable air of high breeding and intelligence

which distinguished Philip always, and the cordial endorsement of the young surgeon, prepossessed the party instantly in his favour. With that recognition, something of his singular embarrassment dropped away.

"Who are those people?" he ventured at last to say.

"Their names are on this paper, which we found nailed to a tree. Of course, with no survivor present, we are unable to identify them all. The hut occupied by Dr. Devarges, whose body, buried in the snow, we have identified by his clothing, and the young girl Grace Conroy and her child-sister, are the only ones we are positive about."

Philip looked at the doctor.

"How have you identified the young girl?"

"By her clothing, which was marked."

Philip remembered that Grace had changed her clothes for the suit of a younger brother who was dead.

"Only by that?" he asked.

"No. Dr. Devarges in his papers gives the names of the occupants of the hut. We have accounted for all but her brother, and a fellow by the name of Ashley."

"How do you account for them?" asked Philip with a dark face.

"Ran away! What can you expect from that class of people?" said the surgeon with a contemptuous shrug.

"What class?" asked Philip almost savagely.

"My dear boy," said the surgeon, "you know them as well as I. Didn't they always pass the Fort where we were stationed? Didn't they beg what they could, and steal what they otherwise couldn't get, and then report to Washington the incompetency of the military? Weren't they always getting up rows with the Indians and then sneaking away to let us settle the bill? Don't you remember them—the men gaunt, sickly, vulgar, low-toned; the women dirty, snuffy, prematurely old and prematurely prolific?"

Philip tried to combat this picture with his recollection of Grace's youthful features, but somehow failed. Within the last half-hour his instinctive fastidiousness had increased a hundredfold. He looked at the doctor, and said "Yes."

"Of course," said the surgeon. "It was the old lot. What could you expect? People who could be strong only in proportion to their physical strength, and losing everything with the loss of that? There have been selfishness, cruelty—God knows—perhaps murder done here!"

"Yes, yes," said Philip, hastily; "but you were speaking of this girl, Grace Conroy; what do you know of her?"

"Nothing, except that she was found lying there dead with her name on her clothes and her sister's blanket in her arms, as if the wretches had stolen the dying child from the dead girl's arms. But you, Arthur, how chanced you to be here in this vicinity? Are you stationed here?"

"No, I have resigned from the army."

"Good! and you are here"——

"Alone!"

"Come, we will talk this over as we return. You will help me make out my report. This you know, is an official inquiry, based upon the alleged clairvoyant quality of our friend Blunt. I must say we have established that fact, if we have been able to do nothing more."

The surgeon then lightly sketched an account of the expedition, from its inception in a dream of Blunt (who was distinctly impressed with the fact that a number of emigrants were perishing from hunger in the Sierras) to his meeting with Philip, with such deftness of cynical humour and playful satire—qualities that had lightened the weariness of the mess-table of Fort Bobadil—that the young men were both presently laughing. Two or three of the party who had been engaged in laying out the unburied bodies, and talking in whispers, hearing these fine gentlemen make light of the calamity, in well-chosen epithets, were somewhat ashamed of their own awe, and less elegantly, and I fear less grammatically, began to be jocose too. Whereat the fastidious Philip frowned, the surgeon laughed, and the two friends returned to the entrance of the cañon, and thence rode out of the valley together.

Philip's reticence regarding his own immediate past was too characteristic to excite any suspicion or surprise in the mind of his friend. In truth, the doctor was too well pleased with his presence, and the undoubted support which he should have in Philip's sympathetic tastes and congenial habits, to think of much else. He was proud of his friend —proud of the impression he had made among the rude unlettered men with whom he was forced by the conditions of frontier democracy to associate on terms of equality. And Philip, though young, was accustomed to have his friends proud of him. Indeed, he always felt some complacency with himself that he seldom took advantage of this fact. Satisfied that he might have confided to the doctor the truth of his connection with the ill-fated party and his flight with Grace, and that the doctor would probably have regarded him as a hero, he felt less compunction at his suppression of the fact.

Their way lay by Monument Point and the dismantled cairn. Philip had already passed it on his way to the cañon, and had felt a thankfulness for the unexpected tragedy that had, as he believed, conscientiously relieved him of a duty to the departed naturalist, yet he could not forego a question.

"Is there anything among these papers and collections worth our preserving?" he asked the surgeon.

The doctor, who had not for many months had an opportunity to air his general scepticism, was nothing if not derogatory.

"No," he answered, shortly. "If there were any way that we might restore them to the living Dr. Devarges, they might minister to his vanity, and please the poor fellow. I see nothing in them that should make them worthy to survive him."

The tone was so like Dr. Devarges' own manner, as Philip remembered it, that he smiled grimly and felt relieved. When they reached the spot Nature seemed to have already taken the same cynical view; the metallic case was already deeply sunken in the snow, the wind had scattered the papers far and wide, and even the cairn itself had tumbled into a shapeless, meaningless ruin.

CHAPTER IX.

IN WHICH THE FOOTPRINTS ARE LOST FOR EVER.

A FERVID May sun had been baking the adobe walls of the Presidio of San Ramon, firing the red tiles, scorching the black courtyard, and driving the mules and vaqueros of a train that had just arrived into the shade of the long galleries of the quadrangle, when the *Comandante*, who was taking his noonday *siesta* in a low, studded chamber beside the guard-room, was gently awakened by his secretary. For thirty years the noonday slumbers of the Commander had never been broken; his first thought was the heathen!—his first impulse to reach for his trusty Toledo. But, as it so happened, the cook had borrowed it that morning to rake *tortillas* from the Presidio oven, and Don Juan Salvatierra contented himself with sternly demanding the reason for this unwonted intrusion.

"A senorita—an American—desires an immediate audience."

Don Juan removed the black silk handkerchief which he had tied round his grizzled brows, and sat up. Before he could assume a more formal attitude, the door was timidly opened, and a young girl entered. For all the disfigurement of scant, coarse, ill-fitting clothing, or the hollowness of her sweet eyes, and even the tears that dimmed their long lashes; for all the sorrow that had pinched her young cheek and straightened the corners of her childlike mouth, she was still so fair, so frank, so youthful, so innocent and helpless, that the *Comandante* stood erect, and then bent forward in a salutation that almost swept the floor. Apparently the prepossession was mutual. The young girl took a quick survey of the gaunt but gentlemanlike figure before her, cast a rapid glance at the serious but kindly eyes that shone above the Commander's iron-grey mustachios, dropped her hesitating, timid manner, and, with an impulsive gesture and a little cry, ran forward and fell upon her knees at his feet. The Commander would have raised her gently, but she restrained his hand.

"No, no, listen! I am only a poor, poor girl, without friends or home. A month ago, I left my family starving in the mountains, and came away to get them help. My brother came with me. God was good to us, Señor, and after a weary tramp of many days we found a trapper's hut, and food and shelter. Philip, my brother, went back alone to succour them. He has not returned. Oh, sir, he may be dead; they all may be dead—God only knows! It is three weeks ago since he left me; three weeks! It is a long time to be alone, Señor, a stranger in a strange land. The trapper was kind, and sent me here to you for assistance. You will help me? I know you will. You will find them, my friends, my little sister, my brother!"

The Commander waited until she had finished, and then gently lifted her to a seat by his side. Then he turned to his secretary, who, with a few hurried words in Spanish, answered the mute inquiry of the Commander's eyes. The young girl felt a thrill of disappointment as she saw that her personal appeal had been lost and unintelligible; it was with a slight touch of defiance that was new to her nature that she turned to the secretary who advanced as interpreter.

"You are an American?"

"Yes," said the girl, curtly, who had taken one of the strange, swift, instinctive dislikes of her sex to the man.

"How many years?"

"Fifteen."

The Commander, almost unconsciously, laid his brown hand on her clustering curls.

"Name?"

She hesitated and looked at the Commander.

"Grace," she said.

Then she hesitated; and, with a defiant glance at the secretary, added—

"Grace Ashley!"

"Give to me the names of some of your company, Mees Graziashly."

Grace hesitated.

"Philip Ashley, Gabriel Conroy, Peter Dumphy, Mrs. Jane Dumphy," she said at last.

The secretary opened a desk, took out a printed document, unfolded it, and glanced over its contents. Presently he handed it to the Commander with the comment "*Bueno.*" The Commander said "*Bueno*" also, and glanced kindly and reassuringly at Grace.

"An expedition from the upper Presidio has found traces of a party of Americans in the Sierra," said the secretary, monotonously. "There are names like these."

"It is the same—it is our party!" said Grace, joyously.

"You say so?" said the secretary, cautiously.

"Yes," said Grace, defiantly.

The secretary glanced at the paper again, and then said, looking at Grace intently—

"There is no name of Mees Graziashly."

The hot blood suddenly dyed the cheek of Grace and her eyelids dropped. She raised her eyes imploringly to the Commander. If she could have reached him directly, she would have thrown herself at his feet and confessed her innocent deceit, but she shrank from a confidence that first filtered through the consciousness of the secretary. So she began to fence feebly with the issue.

"It is a mistake," she said. "But the name of Philip, my brother, is there?"

"The name of Philip Ashley is here," said the secretary, grimly.

"And he is alive and safe!" cried Grace, forgetting in her relief and joy her previous shame and mortification.

"He is not found," said the secretary.

"Not found?" said Grace, with widely opened eyes.

"He is not there."

"No, of course," said Grace, with a nervous hysterical laugh; "he was with me; but he came back—he returned."

"On the 30th of April there is no record of the finding of Philip Ashley."

Grace groaned and clasped her hands. In her greater anxiety now, all lesser fears were forgotten. She turned and threw herself before the Commander.

"Oh, forgive me, Señor, but I swear to you I meant no harm! Philip is not my brother, but a friend, so kind, so good. He asked me to take his name, poor boy, God knows if he will ever claim it again, and I did. My name is not Ashley. I know not what is in that paper, but it must tell of my brother, Gabriel, my sister, of all! O,

Señor, are they living or dead? Answer me you must—for —I am—I am Grace Conroy!"

The secretary had refolded the paper. He opened it again, glanced over it, fixed his eyes upon Grace, and, pointing to a paragraph, handed it to the Commander. The two men exchanged glances, the Commander coughed, rose, and averted his face from the beseeching eyes of Grace. A sudden death-like chill ran through her limbs as, at a word from the Commander, the secretary rose and placed the paper in her hands.

Grace took it with trembling fingers. It seemed to be a proclamation in Spanish.

"I cannot read it," she said, stamping her little foot with passionate vehemence. "Tell me what it says."

At a sign from the Commander, the secretary opened the paper and arose. The Commander, with his face averted, looked through the open window. The light streaming through its deep, tunnel-like embrasure, fell upon the central figure of Grace, with her shapely head slightly bent forward, her lips apart, and her eager, passionate eyes fixed upon the Commander. The secretary cleared his throat in a perfunctory manner; and, with the conscious pride of an irreproachable linguist, began—

"NOTICE.

"TO HIS EXCELLENCY THE COMANDANTE OF THE PRESIDIO OF SAN FELIPE.

"I have the honour to report that the expedition sent out to relieve certain distressed emigrants in the fastnesses of the Sierra Nevadas, said expedition being sent on the information of Don Jose Bluent of San Geronimo, found in a cañon east of the Canada del Diablo the evidences of the recent existence of such emigrants buried in the snow, and the melancholy and deeply-to-be-deplored record of their sufferings, abandonment, and death. A written record preserved by these miserable and most infelicitous ones gives the names and history of their organisation, known as 'Captain Conroy's Party,' a copy of which is annexed below.

"The remains of five of these unfortunates were recovered from the snow, but it was impossible to identify but two, who were buried with sacred and reverential rites.

"Our soldiers behaved with that gallantry, coolness, patriotism, inflexible hardihood, and high-principled devotion which ever animate the swelling heart of the Mexican warrior. Nor can too much praise be given to the voluntary efforts of one Don Arthur Poinsett, late Lieutenant of the Army of the United States of America, who, though himself a voyager and stranger, assisted our commander in the efforts of humanity.

"The wretched dead appeared to have expired from hunger, although one was evidently a victim "——

The tongue of the translator hesitated a moment, and then with an air of proud superiority to the difficulties of the English language, he resumed—

"A victim to fly poison. It is to be regretted that among the victims was the famous Doctor Paul Devarges, a Natural, and collector of the stuffed Bird and Beast, a name most illustrious in science."

The secretary paused, his voice dropped its pretentious pitch, he lifted his eyes from the paper, and fixing them on Grace, repeated, deliberately—

"The bodies who were identified were those of Paul Devarges and Grace Conroy."

"Oh, no! no!" said Grace, clasping her hands, wildly; "it is a mistake! You are trying to frighten me, a poor, helpless, friendless girl! You are punishing me, gentlemen, because you know I have done wrong, because you think I have lied! Oh, have pity, gentlemen. My God—save me—Philip!"

And with a loud, despairing cry, she rose to her feet, caught at the clustering tendrils of her hair, raised her little hands, palms upward, high in air, and then sank perpendicularly, as if crushed and beaten flat, a pale and senseless heap upon the floor.

The Commander stooped over the prostrate girl. "Send Manuela here," he said quickly, waving aside the proffered aid of the secretary, with an impatient gesture quite unlike his usual gravity, as he lifted the unconscious Grace in his arms.

An Indian waiting-woman hurriedly appeared, and assisted the Commander to lay the fainting girl upon a couch.

"Poor child!" said the Commander, as Manuela, bending over Grace, unloosed her garments with sympathetic feminine hands. "Poor little one, and without a father!"

"Poor woman!" said Manuela to herself, half aloud; "and without a husband."

BOOK II.

AFTER FIVE YEARS.

CHAPTER I.

ONE HORSE GULCH.

It was a season of unexampled prosperity in One Horse Gulch. Even the despondent original locator, who, in a fit of depressed alcoholism, had given it that infelicitous title, would have admitted its injustice, but that he fell a victim to the "craftily qualified" cups of San Francisco long before the Gulch had become prosperous. "Hed Jim stuck to straight whisky he might hev got his pile outer the very ledge whar his cabin stood," said a local critic. But Jim did not; after taking a thousand dollars from his claim, he had flown to San Franciscos, where, gorgeously arrayed, he had flitted from champagne to cognac, and from gin to lager beer, until he brought his gilded and ephemeral existence to a close in the country hospital.

Howbeit, One Horse Gulch survived not only its godfather, but the baleful promise of its unhallowed christening. It had its Hotel and its Temperance House, its Express office, its saloons, its two squares of low wooden buildings in the main street, its clustering nests of cabins on the hill-sides, its freshly-hewn stumps, and its lately-cleared lots. Young in years, it still had its memories, experiences, and antiquities. The first tent pitched by Jim White was still standing, the bullet holes were yet to be seen in the shutters of the Cachucha saloon, where the great fight took place between Boston Joe, Harry Worth, and Thompson of Angel's; from the upper loft of Watson's "Emporium" a beam still projected from which a year ago a noted citizen had been suspended, after an informal inquiry into the ownership of some mules that he was found possessed of. Near it was a small unpretentious square shed, where the famous caucus had met that had selected the delegates who chose the celebrated and Honourable Blank to represent California in the councils of the nation.

It was raining. Not in the usual direct, honest, perpendicular fashion of that mountain region, but only suggestively, and in a vague, uncertain sort of way, as if it might at any time prove to be fog or mist, and any money wagered upon it would be hazardous. It was raining as much from below as above, and the lower limbs of the loungers who gathered around the square box stove that stood in Briggs's warehouse, exhaled a cloud of steam. The loungers in Briggs's were those who from deficiency of taste or the requisite capital avoided the gambling and drinking saloons, and quietly appropriated biscuits from the convenient barrel of the generous Briggs, or filled their pipes from his open tobacco canisters, with the general suggestion in their manner that their company fully compensated for any waste of his material.

They had been smoking silently—a silence only broken by the occasional hiss of expectoration against the hot stove, when the door of a back room opened softly, and Gabriel Conroy entered.

"How is he gettin' on, Gabe?" asked one of the loungers.

"So, so," said Gabriel. "You'll want to shift those

bandages again," he said, turning to Briggs, "afore the doctor comes. I'd come back in an hour, but I've got to drop in and see how Steve's gettin' on, and it's a matter of two miles from home."

"But he says he won't let anybody tech him but you," said Mr. Briggs.

"I know he *says* so," said Gabriel, soothingly; "but he'll get over that. That's what Stimson sed when he was took worse, but he got over that, and I never got to see him except in time to lay him out."

The justice of this was admitted even by Briggs, although evidently disappointed. Gabriel was walking to the door, when another voice from the stove stopped him.

"Oh, Gabe! you mind that emigrant family with the sick baby camped down the gulch! Well, the baby up and died last night."

"I want to know," said Gabriel, with thoughtful gravity.

"Yes, and that woman's in a heap of trouble. Couldn't you kinder drop in in passing and look after things?"

"I will," said Gabriel thoughtfully.

"I thought you'd like to know it, and I thought she'd like me to tell you," said the speaker, settling himself back again over the stove with the air of a man who had just fulfilled, at great personal sacrifice and labour, a work of supererogation.

"You're always thoughtful of other folks, Johnson," said Briggs, admiringly.

"Well, yes," said Johnson, with a modest serenity; "I allers allow that men in Californy ought to think of others besides themselves. A little keer and a little *sabe* on my part, and there's that family in the gulch made comfortable with Gabe around 'em."

Meanwhile this homely inciter of the unselfish virtues of One Horse Gulch had passed out into the rain and darkness. So conscientiously did he fulfil his various obligations, that it was nearly one o'clock before he reached his rude hut on the hill-side, a rough cabin of pine logs, so unpretentious and wild in exterior as to be but a slight improvement on nature. The vines clambered unrestrainedly over the bark-thatched roof; the birds occupied the crevices of the walls, the squirrel ate his acorns on the ridge pole without fear and without reproach.

Softly drawing the wooden peg that served as a bolt, Gabriel entered with that noiselessness and caution that were habitual to him. Lighting a candle by the embers of a dying fire, he carefully looked around him. The cabin was divided into two compartments by the aid of a canvas stretched between the walls, with a flap for the door-way. On a pine table lay several garments apparently belonging to a girl of seven or eight—a frock grievously rent and torn, a frayed petticoat of white flannel already patched with material taken from a red shirt, and a pair of stockings so excessively and sincerely darned, as to have lost nearly all of their original fabric in repeated bits of relief that covered almost the entire structure. Gabriel looked at these articles ruefully, and, slowly picking them up, examined each with the greatest gravity and concern. Then he took off his coat and boots, and having in this way settled himself into an easy dishabille, he took a box from the shelf, and proceeded to lay out thread and needles, when he was interrupted by a child's voice from behind the canvas screen.

"Is that you, Gabe?"—"Yes."

"Oh, Gabe, I got tired and went to bed."

"I see you did," said Gabriel, drily, picking up a needle and thread that had apparently been abandoned after a slight excursion into the neighbourhood of a rent and left hopelessly sticking in the petticoat.

"Yes, Gabe; they're so awfully old!"

"Old!" repeated Gabe, reproachfully. "Old! Lettin' on a little wear and tear, they're as good as they ever were. That petticoat is stronger," said Gabriel, holding up the garment and eyeing the patches with a slight glow of artistic pride—"stronger, Olly, than the first day you put it on."

"But that's five years ago, Gabe."

"Well," said Gabriel, turning round and addressing himself impatiently to the screen, "wot if it is?"

"And I've growed."

"Growed!" said Gabriel, scornfully. "And haven't I let out the tucks, and didn't I put three fingers of the best sacking around the waist? You'll just ruin me in clothes."

Olly laughed from behind the screen. Finding, however, no response from the grim worker, presently there appeared a curly head at the flap, and then a slim little girl, in the scantiest of nightgowns, ran, and began to nestle at his side, and to endeavour to inwrap herself in his waistcoat.

"Oh, go 'way!" said Gabriel, with a severe voice and the most shameless signs of relenting in his face. "Go away! What do you care? Here I might slave myself to death to dress you in silks and satins, and you'd dip into the first ditch or waltz through the first underbush that you kem across. You haven't got no *sabe* in dress, Olly. It ain't ten days ago as I iron-bound and copper-fastened that dress, so to speak, and look at it now! Olly, look at it now!" And he held it up indignantly before the maiden.

Olly placed the top of her head against the breast of her brother as a *point d'appui*, and began to revolve around him as if she wished to bore a way into his inmost feelings.

"Oh, you ain't mad, Gabe!" she said, leaping first over one knee and then over the other without lifting her head. "You ain't mad!"

Gabriel did not deign to reply, but continued mending the frayed petticoat in dignified silence.

"Who did you see down town?" said Olly, not at all rebuffed.

"No one," said Gabriel, shortly.

"You did! You smell of linnyments and peppermint," said Olly, with a positive shake of the head. "You've been to Briggs's and the new family up the gulch."

"Yes," said Gabriel, "that Mexican's legs is better, but the baby's dead. Jest remind me, to-morrow, to look through mother's things for suthin' for that poor woman."

"Gabe, do you know what Mrs. Markle says of you?" said Olly, suddenly raising her head.

"No," replied Gabriel, with an affectation of indifference that, like all his affectations, was a perfect failure.

"She says," said Olly, "that you want to be looked after yourself more'n all these people. She says you're just throwing yourself away on other folks. She says I ought to have a woman to look after me."

Gabriel stopped his work, laid down the petticoat, and taking the curly head of Olly between his knees, with one hand beneath her chin and the other on the top of her head, turned her mischievous face towards his. "Olly," he said, seriously, "when I got you outer the snow at Starvation Camp; when I toted you on my back for miles till we got into the valley; when we lay by thar for two weeks, and me a felling trees and picking up provisions here and thar, in the wood or the river, wharever thar was bird or fish, I reckon you got along as well—I won't say better—ez if you had a woman to look arter you. When at last we kem here to this camp, and I built this yer house, I don't think any woman could hev done better. If they could, I'm wrong, and Mrs. Markle's right."

Olly began to be uncomfortable. Then the quick instincts of her sex came to her relief, and she archly assumed the aggressive.

"I think Mrs. Markle likes you, Gabe."

Gabriel looked down at the little figure in alarm. There are some subjects whereof the youngest of womankind has an instinctive knowledge that makes the wisest of us tremble.

"Go to bed, Olly," said the cowardly Gabriel.

But Olly wanted to sit up, so she changed the subject.

"The Mexican you're tendin' isn't a Mexican, he's a Chileno; Mrs. Markle says so."

"May be; it's all the same. *I* call him a Mexican. He talks too straight, anyway," said Gabriel, indifferently.

"Did he ask you any more questions about—about old times?" continued the girl.

"Yes; he wanted to know everything that happened in Starvation Camp. He was rek'larly took with poor Gracie; asked a heap o' questions about her—how she acted, and seemed to feel as bad as we did about never hearing anything from her. I never met a man, Olly, afore, as seemed to take such an interest in other folks' sorrers as he did. You'd have tho't he'd been one of the party. And he made me tell him all about Dr. Devarges."

"And Philip?" queried Olly.

"No," said Gabriel, somewhat curtly.

"Gabriel," said Olly, sullenly, "I wish you didn't talk so to people about those days."

"Why?" asked Gabriel, wonderingly.

"Because it ain't good to talk about. Gabriel dear," she continued, with a slight quivering of the upper lip, "sometimes I think the people round yer look upon us sorter queer. That little boy that came here with the emigrant family wouldn't play with me, and Mrs. Markle's little girl said that we did dreadful things up there in the snow. He said I was a cannon-ball."

"A what?" asked Gabriel.

"A cannon-ball! He said that you and I"——

"Hush," interrupted Gabriel, sternly, as an angry flush came into his sunburnt cheek, "I'll jest bust that boy if I see him round yer agin."

"But, Gabriel," persisted Olly, "nobody"——

"Will you go to bed, Olly, and not catch your death yer on this cold floor asking ornery and perfectly ridickulus questions?" said Gabriel, briskly, lifting her to her feet. "Thet Markle girl ain't got no sense anyway—she's allers leading you round in ditches, ruinin' your best clothes, and keepin' me up half the night mendin' on 'em."

Thus admonished, Olly retreated behind the canvas screen, and Gabriel resumed his needle and thread. But the thread became entangled, and was often snappishly broken, and Gabriel sewed imaginary, vindictive stitches in the imaginary calves of an imaginary youthful emigrant, until Olly's voice again broke the silence.

"Oh, Gabe!"

"Yes," said Gabriel, putting down his work despairingly.

"Do you think—that Philip—ate Grace?"

Gabriel rose swiftly, and disappeared behind the screen. As he did so, the door softly opened, and a man stepped into the cabin. The new-comer cast a rapid glance around the dimly-lighted room, and then remained motionless in the door-way. From behind the screen came the sound of voices. The stranger hesitated, and then uttered a slight cough.

In an instant Gabriel reappeared. The look of angry concern at the intrusion turned to one of absolute stupefaction as he examined the stranger more attentively. The new-comer smiled faintly, yet politely, and then, with a slight halt in his step, moved towards a chair, into which he dropped with a deprecating gesture.

"I shall sit—and you shall pardon me. You have surprise! Yes? Five, six hour ago you leave me very sick on a bed—where you are so kind—so good. Yes? Ah? You see me here now, and you say crazy! Mad!"

He raised his right hand with the fingers upward, twirled them to signify Gabriel's supposed idea of a whirling brain, and smiled again.

"Listen. Comes to me an hour ago a message most important. Most necessary it is I go to-night—now, to Marysville. You see. Yes? I rise and dress myself. Ha! I have great strength for the effort. I am better. But I say to myself, 'Victor, you shall first pay your respects to the good Pike who have been so kind, so good. You shall press the hand of the noble grand miner who have recover you. *Bueno*, I am here!"

He extended a thin, nervous brown hand, and for the first time since his entrance concentrated his keen black eyes, which had roved over the apartment and taken in its minutest details, upon his host. Gabriel, lost in bewilderment, could only gasp—"But you ain't well enough, you know. You can't walk yet. You'll kill yourself!"

The stranger smiled.

"Yes?—you think—you think? Look now! Waits me, outside, the horse of the livery-stable man. How many miles you think to the stage town? Fifteen." (He emphasized them with his five uplifted fingers.) "It is nothing. Two hour comes the stage and I am there. Ha!"

Even as he spoke, with a gesture, as if brushing away all difficulties, his keen eyes were resting upon a little shelf above the chimney, whereon stood an old-fashioned daguerreotype case open. He rose, and, with a slight halting step and an expression of pain, limped across the room to the shelf, and took up the daguerreotype.

"What have we?" he asked.

"It is Gracie," said Gabriel, brightening up. "Taken the day we started from St. Jo."

"How long?"

"Six years ago. She was fourteen then," said Gabriel, taking the case in his hand and brushing the glass fondly with his palm. "Thar warn't no puttier gal in all Missouri," he added, with fraternal pride, looking down upon the picture with moistened eyes. "Eh—what did you say?"

The stranger had uttered a few words hastily in a foreign tongue. But they were apparently complimentary, for when Gabriel looked up at him with an inquiring glance, he was smiling and saying, "Beautiful! Angelic! Very pretty!" with eyes still fixed upon the picture. "And it is like—ah, I see the brother's face, too," he said, gravely, comparing Gabriel's face with the picture. Gabriel looked pleased. Any nature less simple than his would have detected the polite fiction. In the square, honest face of the brother there was not the faintest suggestion of the delicate, girlish, poetical oval before him.

"It is precious," said the stranger: "and it is all, ha?"

"All?" echoed Gabriel, inquiringly.

"You have nothing more?"

"No."

"A line of her writing, a letter, her private papers would be a treasure, eh?"

"She left nothing," said Gabriel, simply, "but her clothes. You know she put on a boy's suit—Johnny's clothes—when she left. Thet's how it allus puzzles me thet they knew *who* she was, when they came across the poor child dead."

The stranger did not speak, and Gabriel went on—

"It was nigh on a month afore I got back. When I did, the snow was gone, and there warn't no track or trace of anybody. Then I heerd the story I told ye—thet a relief party had found 'em all dead—and thet among the dead was Grace. How that poor child ever got back thar alone (for thar warn't no trace or mention of the man she went away with) is what gets me. And that there's my trouble, Mr. Ramirez! To think of thet pooty darlin' climbing back to the old nest, and finding no one thar! To think of her coming back, as she allowed, to Olly and me, and findin' all her own blood gone, is suthin' thet, at times, drives me almost mad. She didn't die of starvation; she didn't die of cold. Her heart was broke, Mr. Ramirez; her little heart was broke!"

The stranger looked at him curiously, but did not speak. After a moment's pause, he lifted his bowed head from his hands, wiped his eyes with Olly's flannel petticoat, and went on—

"For more than a year I tried to get sight o' that report. Then I tried to find the Mission or the Presidio that the relief party started from, and may be see some of that party. But then kem the gold excitement, and the Americans took possession of the Missions and Presidios, and when I got to San—San—San——"

"Geronimo," interrupted Ramirez, hastily.

"Did I tell?" asked Gabriel, simply; "I don't remember that."

Ramirez showed all his teeth in quick assent, and motioned him with his finger to go on.

"When I got to San Geronimo, there was nobody, and no records left. Then I put a notiss in the San Francisco paper for Philip Ashley—that was the man as helped her away—to communicate with me. But thar weren't no answer."

Ramirez rose.

"You are not rich, friend Gabriel?"

"No," said Gabriel.

"But you expect—ah—you expect?"

"Well, I reckon some day to make a strike like the rest."

"Anywhere, my friend?"

"Anywhere," repeated Gabriel, smiling.

"*Adios*," said the stranger, going to the door.

"*Adios*," repeated Gabriel. "Must you go to-night? What's your hurry? You're sure you feel better now?"

"Better?" answered Ramirez, with a singular smile. "Better! Look, I am so strong!"

He stretched out his arms, and expanded his chest, and walked erect to the door.

"You have cured my rheumatism, friend Gabriel. Good night."

The door closed behind him. In another moment he was in the saddle, and speeding so swiftly that, in spite of mud and darkness, in two hours he had reached the mining town where the Wingdam and Sacramento stage-coach changed horses. The next morning, while Olly and Gabriel were eating breakfast, Mr. Victor Ramirez stepped briskly from the stage that drew up at Marysville Hotel, and entered the hotel office. As the clerk looked up inquiringly, Mr. Ramirez handed him a card—

"Send that, if you please, to Miss Grace Conroy."

CHAPTER II.

MADAME DEVARGES.

MR. RAMIREZ followed the porter upstairs, and along a narrow passage, until he reached a larger hall. Here the porter indicated that he should wait until he returned, and then disappeared down the darkened vista of another passage. Mr. Ramirez had ample time to observe the freshness of the boarded partitions and scant details of the interior of the International Hotel; he even had time to attempt to grapple the foreign mystery of the notice conspicuously on the wall,

"Gentlemen are requested not to sleep on the stairs," before his companion reappeared. Beckoning to Mr. Ramirez, with an air of surly suspicion, the porter led him along the darkened passage until he paused before a door at its farther extremity and knocked gently. Slight as was the knock, it had the mysterious effect of causing all the other doors along the passage to open, and a masculine head to appear at each opening. Mr. Ramirez's brow darkened quickly. He was sufficiently conversant with the conditions of that early civilization to know that, as a visitor to a lady, he was the object of every man's curious envy and aggressive suspicion. There was the sound of light footsteps within, and the door opened. The porter lingered long enough to be able to decide upon the character and propriety of the greeting, and then sullenly retired. The door closed, and Mr. Ramirez found himself face to face with the occupant of the room. She was a small, slight blonde, who, when the smile that had lit her mouth and eyes as she opened the door faded suddenly as she closed it, might have passed for a plain, indistinctive woman. But for a certain dangerous submissiveness of manner—which I here humbly submit is always to be feared in an all-powerful sex—and an address that was rather more deprecatory than occasion called for, she would hardly have awakened the admiration of our sex or the fears of her own.

As Ramirez advanced, with both hands impulsively extended, she drew back shyly, and, pointing to the ceiling and walls, said quietly, "Cloth and paper!"

Ramirez's dark face grew darker. There was a long pause. Suddenly the lady lightened the shadow that seemed to have fallen upon their interview with both her teeth and eyes, and, pointing to a chair, said—

"Sit down, Victor, and tell me why you have returned so soon."

Victor sat sullenly down. The lady looked all deprecation and submissiveness, but said nothing.

Ramirez would, in his sullenness, have imitated her, but his natural impulsiveness was too strong, and he broke out—

"Look! From the book of the hotel it is better you should erase the name of Grace Conroy, and put down your own!"

"And why, Victor?"

"She asks why," said Victor, appealing to the ceiling. "My God! Because one hundred miles from here live the brother and sister of Grace Conroy. I have seen him!"

"Well."

"Well," echoed Victor. "Is it well? Listen. You shall hear if it is well."

He drew his chair beside her, and went on in a low, earnest voice—

"I have at last located the mine. I followed the *deseno*—the description of the spot, and all its surroundings—which was in the paper that I—I—found. Good! It is true!—ah, you begin to be interested!—it is true, all true of the locality. See! Of the spot I do not know. Of the mine it has not yet been discovered!

"It is called 'One Horse Gulch;' why—who knows? It is a rich mining camp. All around are valuable claims; but the mine on the top of the little hill is unknown, unclaimed! For why? You understand, it promises not as much as the other claims on the surface. It is the same—all as described here."

He took from his pocket an envelope, and drew out a folded paper (the papers given to Grace Conroy by Dr. Devarges), and pointed to the map.

"The description here leads me to the head waters of the American River. I followed the range of foot-hills, for I know every foot, every step, and I came one day last week to 'One Horse Gulch.' See, it is the gulch described here —all the same."

He held the paper before her, and her thin, long fingers closed like a bird's claw over its corners.

"It is necessary I should stay there four or five days to inquire. And yet how? I am a stranger, a foreigner; the miners have suspicion of all such, and to me they do not talk easily. But I hear of one Gabriel Conroy, a good man, very kind with the sick. Good! I have sickness—very sudden, very strong! My rheumatism takes me here." He pointed to his knee. "I am helpless as a child. I have to be taken care of at the house of Mr. Briggs. Comes to me here Gabriel Conroy, sits by me, talks to me, tells me everything. He brings to me his little sister. I go to his cabin on the hill. I see the picture of his sister. Good. You understand? It is all over!"

"Why?"

"Eh? She asks why, this woman," said Victor, appealing to the ceiling. "Is it more you ask? Then listen. The house of Gabriel Conroy is upon the land, the very land, you understand? of the grant made by the Governor to Dr. Devarges. He is this Gabriel, look! he is in possession!"

"How? Does he know of the mine?"

"No! It is accident—what you call Fate!"

She walked to the window, and stood for a few moments looking out upon the falling rain. The face that looked out was so old, so haggard, so hard and set in its outlines, that one of the loungers on the side-walk, glancing at the window to catch a glimpse of the pretty French stranger, did not recognise her. Possibly the incident recalled her to herself, for she presently turned with a smile of ineffable sweetness, and returning to the side of Ramirez, said, in the gentlest of voices, "Then you abandon me?"

Victor did not dare to meet her eyes. He looked

straight before him, shrugged his shoulders, and said—"It is Fate!"

She clasped her thin fingers lightly before her, and, standing in front of her companion, so as to be level with his eyes, said—"You have a good memory, Victor."

He did not reply.

"Let me assist it. It is a year ago that I received a letter in Berlin, signed by a Mr. Peter Dumphy, of San Francisco, saying that he was in possession of important papers regarding property of my late husband, Dr. Paul Devarges, and asking me to communicate with him. I did not answer his letter; I came. It is not my way to deliberate or hesitate—perhaps a wise man would. I am only a poor, weak woman, so I came. I know it was all wrong. You sharp, bold, cautious men would have written first. Well, I came!"

Victor winced slightly, but did not speak.

"I saw Mr. Dumphy in San Francisco. He showed me some papers that he said he had found in a place of deposit which Dr. Devarges had evidently wished preserved. One was a record of a Spanish grant, others indicated some valuable discoveries. He referred me to the Mission and Presidio of San Ysabel that had sent out the relief party for further information. He was a trader—a mere man of business—it was a question of money with him; he agreed to assist me for a *percentage!* Is it not so?"

Victor raised his dark eyes to hers, and nodded.

"I came to the Mission. I saw *you*—the Secretary of the former Comandante—the only one left who remembered the expedition, and the custodian of the Presidio records. You showed me the only copy of the report; *you*, too, would have been cold and business-like, until I told you my story. You seemed interested. You told me about the young girl, this mysterious Grace Conroy, whose name appeared among the dead, who you said you thought was an impostor! Did you not?"

Victor nodded.

"You told me of her agony on reading the report! Of her fainting, of the discovery of her condition by the women, of the Comandante's pity, of her mysterious disappearance, of the Comandante's reticence, of your own suspicions of the birth of a child! Did you not, Victor?"

He endeavoured to take her hand. Without altering her gentle manner, she withdrew her hand quietly, and went on—

"And then you told me of your finding that paper on the floor where they loosened her dress—the paper you now hold in your hand. You told me of your reasons for concealing and withholding it. And then, Victor, you proposed to me a plan to secure my own again—to personate this girl—to out-imposture this imposture. You did not ask me for a percentage! You did not seek to make money out of my needs; you asked only for my love! Well, well! perhaps I was a fool, a weak woman. It was a tempting bribe; possibly I listened more to the promptings of my heart than my interest. I promised you my hand and my fortune when we succeeded. You come to me now, and ask to be relieved of that obligation. No! no! you have said enough."

The now frightened man had seized her by the hand, and thrown himself on his knees before her in passionate contrition; but, with a powerful effort, she had wrested herself free.

"No, no!" she continued, in the same deprecatory voice. "Go to this brother, whom the chief end of your labours seems to have been to discover. Go to him now. Restore to him the paper you hold in your hand. Say that you stole it from his sister, whom you suspected to have been an impostor, and that you knew to be the mother of an illegitimate child! Say that in doing this, you took the last hope from the wronged and cast-off wife who came thousands of miles to claim something from the man who should have supported her. Say this, and that brother, if he is the good and kind man you represent him to be, he will rise up and bless you! You have only to tell him further, that this paper cannot be of any use to him, as this property legally belongs to his sister's child, if living. You have only to hand him the report which declares both of his sisters to be dead, and leaves his own identity in doubt, to show him what a blessing has fallen upon him."

"Forgive me," gasped Victor, with a painful blending of shame and awesome admiration of the woman before him; "forgive me, Julie! I am a coward! a slave! an ingrate! I will do anything, Julie; anything you say."

Madame Devarges was too sagacious to press her victory further; perhaps she was too cautious to exasperate the already incautiously demonstrative man before her. She said "Hush," and permitted him at the same time, as if unconsciously, to draw her beside him.

"Listen, Victor. What have you to fear from this man?" she asked, after a pause. "What would his evidence weigh against me, when he is in unlawful possession of my property, my legally declared property, if I choose to deny his relationship? Who will identify him as Gabriel Conroy, when his only surviving relative dare not come forward to recognise him; when, if she did, you could swear that she came to you under another name? What would this brother's self-interested evidence amount to opposed to yours, that I was the Grace Conroy who came to the Mission, to the proof of my identity offered by one of the survivors, Peter Dumphy?"

"Dumphy!" echoed Ramirez, in amazement.

"Yes, Dumphy!" repeated Madame Devarges. "When

he found that, as the divorced wife of Dr. Devarges, I could make no legal claim, and I told him of your plan, he offered himself as witness of my identity. Ah, Victor! I have not been idle while you have found only obstacles."

"Forgive me!" He caught and kissed her hands passionately. "I fly now. Good-bye."

"Where are you going?" she asked, rising.

"To 'One Horse Gulch,'" he answered.

"No! Sit down. Listen. You must go to San Francisco, and inform Dumphy of your discovery. It will be necessary, perhaps, to have a lawyer; but we must first see how strong we stand. You must find out the whereabouts of this girl Grace, at once. Go to San Francisco, see Dumphy, and return to me here!"

"But you are alone here, and unprotected. These men!"

The quick suspicions of a jealous nature flashed in his eyes.

"Believe me, they are less dangerous to our plans than women! Do you not trust me, Victor?" she said, with a dazzling smile.

He would have thrown himself at her feet, but she restrained him with an arch look at the wall, and a precautionary uplifted finger.

"Good; go now. Stay. This Gabriel—is he married?"

"No."

"Good-bye."

The door closed upon his dark, eager face, and he was gone. A moment later there was a sharp ringing of the bell of No. 92, the next room to that occupied by Mme. Devarges.

The truculent porter knocked at the door, and entered this room respectfully. There was no suspicion attached to the character of *its* occupant. *He* was well known as Mr. Jack Hamlin, a gambler.

"Why the devil did you keep me waiting?" said Jack,

reaching from the bed, and wrathfully clutching his boot-jack.

The man murmured some apology.

"Bring me some hot water."

The porter was about to hurriedly withdraw, when Jack stopped him with an oath.

"You've been long enough coming without shooting off like that. Who was that man that just left the next room?"

"I don't know, sir."

"Find out, and let me know."

He flung a gold piece at the man, beat up his pillow, and turned his face to the wall. The porter still lingered, and Jack faced sharply round.

"Not gone yet? What the devil"——

"Beg your pardon, sir; do you know anything about her?"

"No," said Jack, raising himself on his elbow; "but if I catch you hanging round that door, as you were five minutes ago, I'll"—— .

Here Mr. Hamlin dropped his voice, and intimated that he would forcibly dislodge certain vital and necessary organs from the porter's body.

"Go."

After the door closed again, Mr. Hamlin lay silent for an hour. At the end of that time he got up and began to dress himself slowly, singing softly to himself the while, as was his invariable custom, in that sweet tenor for which he was famous. When he had thus warbled through his toilet, replacing a small ivory-handled pistol in his waistcoat-pocket to one of his most heart-breaking notes, he put his hat on his handsome head, perhaps a trifle more on one side than usual, and stepped into the hall. As he sharply shut his door and locked it, the slight concussion of the thin partitions caused the door of his fair neighbour's room to start ajar, and Mr. Hamlin, looking up mechanically, saw the lady standing by the bureau, with her handkerchief to her eyes. Mr. Hamlin instantly stopped his warbling, and walked gravely downstairs. At the foot of the steps he met the porter. The man touched his hat.

"He doesn't belong here, sir."

"Who doesn't belong here?" asked Mr. Hamlin, coldly.

"That man."

"What man?"

"The man you asked about."

Mr. Hamlin quietly took out a cigar, lit it, and after one or two puffs, looked fixedly in the man's eyes, and said—

"I haven't asked you about any man."

"I thought, sir"——

"You shouldn't begin to drink so early in the day, Michael," said Mr. Hamlin, quietly, without withdrawing his black eyes from the man's face. "You can't stand it on an empty stomach. Take my advice and wait till after dinner."

CHAPTER III.

MRS. MARKLE.

Olly's allusion to Mrs. Markle and her criticism had recurred to Gabriel more or less uneasily through the night, and as he rose betimes the next morning and stood by the table on which lay his handiwork, a grim doubt of his proficiency in that branch of domestic economy began to oppress him.

"Like as not I ain't doin' my duty to that child," he said softly to himself, as he picked up the garments one by one, and deposited them beside the bedside of the still sleeping Olly. "Them clothes are—leavin' out the strength and sayin' nothin' o' durability as material—a trifle old-fashioned and onbecomin'. Not as you requires anything o' the kind, bless your pooty face," he said, apostrophising the dewy curls and slumber-flushed cheek of the unconscious child; "but mebbe it does sorter provoke remarks from the other children. And the settlement's gettin' crowded. Three new families in six months is rather too—too——" considered Gabriel, hesitating for a word; "rather too popylating! And Mrs. Markle"—Gabriel flushed even in the stillness and solitude of his own cabin—"to think of that little gal, not nine years old, speaking o' that widder in that way. It beats everything. And to think I've kept clar of that sort o' thing jest on Olly's account, jest that she shouldn't have any woman around to boss her."

Nevertheless, when he and Olly sat down to their frugal breakfast, he was uneasily conscious of several oddities of her dress, not before noticeable, and even some peculiarities of manner.

"Ez a gineral thing, Olly," he pointed out with cautious generalisation, "ez a gineral thing, in perlite society, young gals don't sit down a-straddle of their chairs, and don't reach down every five minnits to heave away at their boot-straps."

"As a general thing, Gabe, girls don't wear boots," said Olly, leaning forward to dip her bread in the frying-pan.

Artfully evading the question whether high india-rubber boots were an indispensable feature of a girl's clothing, Gabriel continued with easy indifference—"I think I'll drop in on Mrs. Markle on my way to the Gulch this morning."

He glanced under his eyelids at as much of his sister's face as was visible behind the slice of bread she was consuming.

"Take me with you, Gabe?"

"No," said Gabriel, "you must stay here and do up the house; and mind you keep out o' the woods until your work's done. Besides," he added, loftily, "I've got some business with Mrs. Markle."

"Oh, Gabe!" said Olly, shining all over her face with gravy and archness.

"I'd like to know what's the matter with you, Olly," said Gabriel, with dignified composure.

"Ain't you ashamed, Gabe?"

Gabriel did not stop to reply, but rose, gathered up his tools, and took his hat from the corner. He walked to the door, but suddenly turned and came back to Olly.

"Olly," he said, taking her face in both hands, after his old fashion, "ef anything at any time should happen to me, I want ye to think, my darling, ez I always did my best for you, Olly, for you. Wotever I did was always for the best."

Olly thought instantly of the river.

"You ain't goin' into deep water to-day, Gabe, are you?" she asked, with a slight premonitory quiver of her short upper lip.

"Pooty deep for me, Olly; but," he added, hastily, with a glance at her alarmed face, "don't you mind, I'll come out all safe. Good-bye." He kissed her tenderly. She ran her fingers through his sandy curls, deftly smoothed his beard, and reknotted his neckerchief.

"You oughter hev put on your other shirt, Gabe; that ain't clean; and you a-goin' to Mrs. Markle's! Let me get your straw hat, Gabe. Wait." She ran in behind the screen, but when she returned he was gone.

It had been raining the night before, but on the earth beneath there was a dewy freshness, and in the sky above the beauty of cloud scenery—a beauty rare to California except during the rainy season. Gabriel, although not usually affected by meteorological influences, nor peculiarly susceptible to the charms of Nature, felt that the morning was a fine one, and was for that reason, I imagine, more than usually accessible to the blandishments of the fair. From admiring a tree, a flower, or a gleam of sunshine, to the entertainment of a dangerous sentimentalism in regard to the other sex, is, I fear, but a facile step to some natures, whose only safety is in continuous practicality. Wherefore, Gabriel, as he approached the cottage of Mrs. Markle, was induced to look from Nature up to—Nature's goddess—Mrs. Markle, as her strong bright face appeared above the dishes she was washing by the kitchen window. And here occurred one of those feminine inconsistencies that are charming to the average man, but are occasionally inefficient with an exceptional character. Mrs. Markle, who had always been exceedingly genial, gentle, and natural with Gabriel during his shyness, seeing him coming with a certain fell intent of cheerfulness in his face, instantly assumed an aggressive manner, which, for the sake of its probable warning to the rest of her sex, I venture to transcribe.

"Ef you want to see me, Gabriel Conroy," said Mrs. Markle, stopping to wipe the suds from her brown but handsomely shaped arms, "you must come up to the sink, for I can't leave the dishes. Joe Markle always used to say to me, 'Sue, when you've got work to do, you don't let your mind wander round much on anything else.' Sal, bring a cheer here for Gabriel—he don't come often enough to stand up for a change. We're hard-working women, you and me, Sal, and we don't get time to be sick—and sick folks is about the only kind as Mr. Conroy cares to see."

Thoroughly astonished as Gabriel was with this sarcastic reception, there was still a certain relief that it brought to him. "Olly was wrong," he said to himself; "that woman only thinks of washin' dishes and lookin' after her boarders. Ef she was allus like this—and would leave a man alone, never foolin' around him, but kinder standin' off and 'tendin' strictly to the business of the house, why, it wouldn't be such a bad thing to marry her. But like as not she'd change—you can't trust them critters. Howsomever I can set Olly's mind at rest."

Happily unconscious of the heresies that were being entertained by the silent man before her, Mrs. Markle briskly continued her washing and her monologue, occasionally sprinkling Gabriel with the overflow of each.

"When I say hard-workin' women, Sal," said Mrs. Markle, still addressing a gaunt female companion, whose sole functions were confined to chuckling at Gabriel over the dishes she was wiping, and standing with her back to her mistress —"when I say hard-workin' women, Sal, I don't forget ez there are men ez is capable of doin' all that, and more—men ez looks down on you and me." Here Mistress Markle broke a plate, and then, after a pause, sighed, faced around with a little colour in her cheek and a sharp snap in her black eyes, and declared that she was "that narvous" this morning that she couldn't go on.

There was an embarrassing silence. Luckily for Gabriel, at this moment the gaunt Sal picked up the dropped thread of conversation, and with her back to her mistress, and profoundly ignoring his presence, addressed herself to the wall.

"Narvous you well may be, Susan, and you slavin' for forty boarders, with transitory meals for travellers, and nobody to help you. If you was flat on your back with rheumatiz, ez you well might be, perhaps you might get a hand. A death in the family might be of sarvice to you in callin' round you friends az couldn't otherwise leave their business. That cough that little Manty had on to her for the last five weeks would frighten some mothers into a narvous consumption."

Gabriel at this moment had a vivid and guilty recollection

of noticing Manty Markle wading in the ditch below the house as he entered, and of having observed her with the interest of possible paternal relationship. That relationship seemed so preposterous and indefensible on all moral grounds, now that he began to feel himself in the light of an impostor, and was proportionally embarrassed. His confusion was shown in a manner peculiarly characteristic of himself. Drawing a small pocket comb from his pocket, he began combing out his sandy curls, softly, with a perplexed smile on his face. The widow had often noticed this action, divined its cause, and accepted it as a tribute. She began to relent. By some occult feminine sympathy, this relenting was indicated by the other woman.

"You're out of sorts this morning, Susan, 'nd if ye'll take a fool's advice, ye'll jest quit work, and make yourself comfortable in the settin'-room, and kinder pass the time o' day with Gabriel; onless he's after waitin' to pick up some hints about housework. I never could work with a man around. I'll do up the dishes ef you'll excuse my kempany, which two is and three's none. Yer give me this apron. You don't hev time, I declare, Sue, to tidy yourself up. And your hair's comin' down."

The gaunt Sal, having recognised Gabriel's presence to this extent, attempted to reorganise Mrs. Markle's coiffure, but was playfully put aside by that lady, with the remark, that "she had too much to do to think of them things."

"And it's only a mop, anyway," she added, with severe self-depreciation; "let it alone, will you, Sal! Thar! I told you; now you've done it." And she had. The infamous Sal, by some deft trick well known to her deceitful sex, had suddenly tumbled the whole wealth of Mrs. Markle's black mane over her plump shoulders. Mrs. Markle, with a laugh, would have flown to the chaste recesses of the sitting-room; but Sal, like a true artist, restrained her, until the full effect of this poetic picture should be impressed upon the unsuspecting Gabriel's memory.

"Mop, indeed!" said Sal. "It's well that many folks is of many minds, and self-praise is open disgrace; but when a man like Lawyer Maxwell sez to me only yesterday sittin' at this very table, lookin' kinder up at you, Sue, as you was passin' soup, unconscious like, and one o' 'em braids droppin' down, and jest missin' the plate, when Lawyer Maxwell sez to me, 'Sal, thar's many a fine lady in Frisco ez would give her pile to have Susan Markle's hair'"——

But here Sal was interrupted by the bashful escape of Mrs. Markle to the sitting-room. "Ye don't know whether Lawyer Maxwell has any bisness up this way, Gabriel, do ye?" said Sal, resuming her work.

"No," said the unconscious Gabriel, happily as oblivious of the artful drift of the question as he had been of the dangerous suggestiveness of Mrs. Markle's hair.

"Because he *does* kinder pass here more frequent than he used, and hez taken ez menny ez five meals in one day. I declare, I thought that was him when you kem just now! I don't think thet Sue notices it, not keering much for that kind of build in a man," continued Sal, glancing at Gabriel's passively powerful shoulders, and the placid strength of his long limbs. "How do you think Sue's looking now—ez a friend interested in the family—how does she look to you?"

Gabriel hastened to assure Sal of the healthful appearance of Mrs. Markle, but only extracted from his gaunt companion a long sigh and a shake of the head.

"It's deceitful, Gabriel! No one knows what that poor critter goes through. Her mind's kinder onsettled o' late, and in that onsettled state, she breaks things. You see her break that plate just now? Well, perhaps I oughtn't to say it—but you being a friend and in confidence, for she'd kill me, being a proud kind o' nater, suthin' like my own, and it may not amount to nothin' arter all—but I kin always tell when you've been around by the breakages. You was here, let's see, the week afore last, and there wasn't cups enough left to go round that night for supper!"

"Maybe it's chills," said the horror-stricken Gabriel, his worst fears realised, rising from his chair; "I've got some Indian cholagogue over to the cabin, and I'll jest run over and get it, or send it back." Intent only upon retreat, he would have shamelessly flown; but Sal intercepted him with a face of mysterious awe.

"Ef she should kem in here and find you gone, Gabriel, in that weak state of hers—narvous you may call it, but so it is—I wouldn't be answerable for that poor critter's life. Ef she should think you'd gone, arter what has happened, arter what has passed between you and her to-day, it would jest kill her."

"But what has passed?" said Gabriel, in vague alarm.

"It ain't for me," said the gaunt Sal, loftily, "to pass my opinion on other folks' conduct, or to let on what this means, or what thet means, or to give my say about people callin' on other people, and broken crockery, hair combs"—Gabriel winced—"and people ez is too nice and keerful to open their mouths afore folks! It ain't for me to get up and say that, when a woman is ever so little out of sorts, and a man is so far gone ez he allows to rush off like a madman to get her medicines, what ez or what ezn't in it. I keep my own counsel, and thet's my way. Many's the time Sue hez said to me: 'Ef thar ever was a woman ez knowed how to lock herself up and throw away the key, it's you, Sal.' And there you are, ma'am, and it's high time ez plain help like me stopped talkin' while ladies and gentlemen exchanged the time o' day."

It is hardly necessary to say that the latter part of this speech was addressed to the widow, who at that moment appeared at the door of the sitting-room, in a new calico gown that showed her plump figure to advantage, or that the gaunt Sal intended to indicate the serious character of the performance by a show of increased respect to the actors.

"I hope I ain't intrudin' on your conversation," said the widow, archly, stopping, with a show of consideration, on the threshold. "Ef you and Sal ain't done private matters yet—I'll wait."

"I don't think ez Gabriel hez anything more to say thet you shouldn't hear, Mrs. Markle," said Sal, strongly implying a recent confidential disclosure from Gabriel, which delicacy to Gabriel alone prevented her from giving. "But it ain't for me to hear confidence in matters of the feelin's."

It is difficult to say whether Mrs. Markle's archness, or Sal's woeful perspicuity, was most alarming to Gabriel. He rose; he would have flown, even with the terrible contingency of Mrs. Markle's hysterics before his eyes; he would have faced even that forcible opposition from Sal of which he fully believed her capable, but that a dreadful suspicion that he was already hopelessly involved, that something would yet transpire that would enable him to explain himself, and perhaps an awful fascination of his very danger, turned his irresolute feet into Mrs. Markle's sitting-room. Mrs. Markle offered him a chair; he sank helplessly into it, while, from the other room, Sal, violently clattering her dishes, burst into shrill song, so palpably done for the purpose of assuring the bashful couple of her inability to overhear their tender confidences, that Gabriel coloured to the roots of his hair.

That evening Gabriel returned from his work in the gulch more than usually grave. To Olly's inquiries he replied shortly and evasively. It was not, however, Gabriel's custom to remain uncommunicative on even disagreeable topics, and Olly bided her time. It came after their frugal supper was over—which, unlike the morning meal, passed without any fastidious criticism on Gabriel's . part—and Olly had drawn a small box, her favourite seat, between her brother's legs, and rested the back of her head comfortably against his waistcoat. When Gabriel had lighted his pipe at the solitary candle, he gave one or two preliminary puffs, and then, taking his pipe from his mouth, said gently, "Olly, it can't be done."

"What can't be done, Gabe?" queried the artful Olly, with a swift preconception of the answer, expanding her little mouth into a thoughtful smile.

"Thet thing."—"What thing, Gabe?"

"This yer marryin' o' Mrs. Markle," said Gabriel, with an assumption of easy, business-like indifference.

"Why?" asked Olly.

"She wouldn't hev me."

"What?" said Olly, facing swiftly round.

Gabriel evaded his sister's eyes, and looking in the fire, repeated slowly, but with great firmness—

"No; not fur—fur—fur a gift!"

"She's a mean, stuck-up, horrid old thing!" said Olly, fiercely. "I'd jest like to—why, there ain't a man az kin compare with you, Gabe! Like her impudence!"

Gabriel waved his pipe in the air deprecatingly, yet with such an evident air of cheerful resignation, that Olly faced upon him again suspiciously, and asked—"What did she say?"

"She said," replied Gabe, slowly, "thet her heart was given to another. I think she struck into poetry, and said—

"'My heart it is another's,
And it never can be thine.

"Thet is, I think so. I disremember her special remark,

Olly; but you know women allers spout poetry at sech times. Ennyhow, that's about the way the thing panned out."

"Who was it?" said Olly, suddenly.

"She didn't let on who," said Gabriel, uneasily. "I didn't think it the square thing to inquire."

"Well," said Olly.

Gabriel looked down still more embarrassed, and shifted his position. "Well," he repeated.

"What did *you* say?" said Olly.—"Then?"

"No, afore. How did you do it, Gabe?" said Olly, comfortably fixing her chin in her hands, and looking up in her brother's face.

"Oh, the usual way!" said Gabriel, with a motion of his pipe, to indicate vague and glittering generalities of courtship.

"But how? Gabe, tell me all about it."

"Well," said Gabriel, looking up at the roof, "wimmen is bashful ez a general thing, and thar's about only one way ez a man can get at 'em, and that ez, by being kinder keerless and bold. Ye see, Olly, when I kem inter the house, I sorter jest chucked Sal under the chin—thet way, you know—and then went up and put my arm around the widder's waist, and kissed her two or three times, you know, jest to be sociable and familiar like."

"And to think, Gabe, thet after all that she wouldn't hev ye," said Olly.

"Not at any price," said Gabriel, positively.

"The disgustin' creature!" said Olly. "I'd jest like to ketch that Manty hangin' round yer after that!" she continued, savagely, with a vicious shake of her little fist. "And just to think, only to-day we give her her pick o' them pups!"

"Hush, Olly, ye mustn't do anythin' o' the sort," said

Gabriel, hastily. "Ye must never let on to any one anything. It's confidence, Olly, confidence, ez these sort o' things allus is—atween you and me. Besides," he went on, reassuringly, "that's nothin'. Lord, afore a man's married he hez to go through this kind o' thing a dozen times. It's expected. There was a man as I once knowed," continued Gabriel, with shameless mendacity, "ez went through it fifty times, and he was a better man nor me, and could shake a thousand dollars in the face of any woman. Why, bless your eyes, Olly, some men jest likes it—it's excitement—like perspectin'."

"But what did you say, Gabe?" said Olly, returning with fresh curiosity to the central fact, and ignoring the Pleasures of Rejection as expounded by Gabriel.

"Well, I just up, and sez this: Susan Markle, sez I, the case is just this. Here's Olly and me up there on the hill, and jess you and Manty down there on the Gulch, and mountings wild and valleys deep two loving hearts do now divide, and there's no reason why it shouldn't be one family and one house, and that family and that house mine. And it's for you to say when. And then I kinder slung in a little more poetry, and sorter fooled around with that ring," said Gabriel, showing a heavy plain gold ring on his powerful little finger, "and jest kissed her agin, and chucked Sally under the chin, and that's all."

"And she wouldn't hev ye, Gabe," said Olly, thoughtfully, "after all that? Well, who wants her to? I don't."

"I'm glad to hear you say that, Olly," said Gabriel. "But ye mustn't let on a word of it to her. She talks o' coming up on the hill to build, and wants to buy that part of the old claim where I perspected last summer, so's to be near us, and look arter you. And, Olly," continued Gabriel, gravely, "ef she comes round yer foolin' around me ez she used to do, ye mustn't mind that—it's women's ways."

"I'd like to catch her at it," said Olly.

Gabriel looked at Olly with a guilty satisfaction, and drew her toward him. "And now that it's all over, Olly," said he, "it's all the better ez it is. You and me'll get along together ez comfortable as we kin. I talked with some of the boys the other day about sendin' for a school-marm from Marysville, and Mrs. Markle thinks it's a good idee. And you'll go to school, Olly. I'll run up to Marysville next week and get you some better clothes, and we'll be just ez happy ez ever. And then some day, Olly, afore you know it—them things come always suddent—I'll jest make a strike outer that ledge, and we'll be rich. Thar's money in that ledge, Olly, I've allus allowed that. And then we'll go—you and me—to San Francisco, and we'll hev a big house, and I'll jest invite a lot of little girls, the best they is in Frisco, to play with you, and you'll hev all the teachers you want, and women ez will be glad to look arter ye. And then maybe I might make it up with Mrs. Markle"——

"Never!" said Olly, passionately.

"Never it is!" said the artful Gabriel, with a glow of pleasure in his eyes, and a slight stirring of remorse in his breast. "But it's time that small gals like you was abed."

Thus admonished, Olly retired behind the screen, taking the solitary candle, and leaving her brother smoking his pipe by the light of the slowly dying fire. But Olly did not go to sleep, and half an hour later, peering out of the screen, she saw her brother still sitting by the fire, his pipe extinguished, and his head resting on his hand. She went up to him so softly that she startled him, shaking a drop of water on the hand that she suddenly threw round his neck.

"You ain't worrying about that woman, Gabe?"

"No," said Gabriel, with a laugh.

Olly looked down at her hand. Gabriel looked up at the roof. "There's a leak thar that's got to be stopped to-morrow. Go to bed, Olly, or you'll take your death."

CHAPTER IV.

IN WHICH THE ARTFUL GABRIEL IS DISCOVERED.

NOTWITHSTANDING his assumed ease and a certain relief, which was real, Gabriel was far from being satisfied with the result of his visit to Mrs. Markle. Whatever may have actually occurred, not known to the reader except through Gabriel's own disclosure to Olly, Gabriel's manner hardly bore out the boldness and conclusiveness of his statement. For a day or two afterward he resented any allusion to the subject from Olly, but on the third day he held a conversation with one of the Eureka Bar miners, which seemed to bear some remote reference to his experience.

"Thar's a good deal said lately in the papers," began Gabriel, cautiously, "in regard to breach o' promise trials. Lookin' at it, by and large, thar don't seem to be much show for a fellow ez hez been in enny ways kind to a gal, is thar?"

The person addressed, whom rumour declared to have sought One Horse Gulch as a place of refuge from his wife, remarked with an oath that women were blank fools anyway, and that on general principles they were not to be trusted.

"But thar must be a kind o' gin'ral law on the subject," urged Gabriel. "Now what would be your opinion if you was on a jury onto a case like this? It happened to a friend o' mine in Frisco," said Gabriel, with a marked parenthesis, "a man ez you don't know. Thar was a woman—we'll say a widder—ez had been kinder hangin' round him off and on for two or three year, and he hadn't allowed anything to her about marryin.' One day he goes down thar to her house, kinder easy-like, jest to pass the time o' day, and be sociable "——

"That's bad," interrupted the cynic.

"Yes," said Gabriel, doubtingly, "p'r'aps it does look bad, but you see he didn't mean anythin'."

"Well?" said the adviser.

"Well! thet's all," said Gabriel.

"All!" exclaimed his companion, indignantly.

"Yes, all. Now this woman kinder allows she'll bring a suit agin him to make him marry her."

"My opinion is," said the adviser, bluntly, "my opinion is, that the man was a fool, and didn't tell ye the truth nuther, and I'd give damages agin him, for being such a fool."

This opinion was so crushing to Gabriel that he turned hopelessly away. Nevertheless, in his present state of mind, he could not refrain from pushing his inquiries further, and in a general conversation which took place at Briggs's store, in the afternoon, among a group of smokers, Gabriel artfully introduced the subject of courtship and marriage.

"Thar's different ways of getting at the feelin's of a woman," said the oracular Johnson, after a graphic statement of his own method of ensnaring the affections of a former sweetheart, "thar's different ways jest as thar's different men and women in the world. One man's way won't do with some wimmen. But thar's one way ez is pretty sure to fetch 'em allers. That is, to play off indifferent—to never let on ye like 'em! To kinder look arter them in a gin'ral sort o' way, pretty much as Gabe thar looks arter the sick!—but not to say anythin' particler. To make them understand that they've got to do all the courtin', ef thar's enny to be done. What's the matter, Gabe, ye ain't goin'?"

Gabriel, who had risen in great uneasiness, muttered something about "its being time to go home," and then sat down again, looking at Johnson in fearful fascination.

"That kind o' thing is pretty sure to fetch almost enny woman," continued Johnson, "and a man ez does it orter be looked arter. It orter be put down by law. It's tamperin', don't yer see, with the holiest affections. Sich a man orter be spotted wharever found."

"But mebbe the man don't mean anythin'—mebbe it's jest his way," suggested Gabriel, ruefully, looking around in the faces of the party, "mebbe he don't take to wimmen and marriage nat'ral, and it's jest his way."

"Way be blowed!" said the irate Johnson, scornfully. "Ketch him, indeed! It's jest the artfullest kind o' artfulness. It's jest begging on a full hand."

Gabriel rose slowly, and, resisting any further attempts to detain him, walked to the door, and, after a remark on the threatening nature of the weather, delivered in a manner calculated to impress his audience with his general indifference to the subject then under discussion, melted dejectedly away into the driving rain that had all day swept over One Horse Gulch, and converted its one long narrow street into a ditch of turbulent yellow water.

"Thet Gabe seems to be out o' sorts to-day," said Johnson. "I heerd Lawyer Maxwell asking arter him this morning; I reckon thar's suthin' up! Gabe ain't a bad sort of chap. Hezen't got enny too much *sabe* about him, but he's mighty good at looking arter sick folks, and thet kind o' man's a power o' use in this camp. Hope thar ain't anything ez will interfere with his sphere o' usefulness."

"May be a woman scrape," suggested Briggs. "He seemed sort o' bound up in what you was saying about women jest now. Thar is folks round yer," said Briggs, dropping his voice and looking about him, "ez believes that that yer Olly, which he lets on to be his sister, to be actooally his own child. No man would tote round a child like that, and jest bind himself up in her, and give up wimmen and whisky, and keerds, and kempeny, ef it wasn't his own. Thet ain't like brothers in my part of the country."

"It's a mighty queer story he tells, ennyways—all this yer stuff about Starvation Camp and escapin'," suggested another. "I never did, somehow, take enny stock in that."

"Well, it's his own look out," concluded Johnson. "It's nothin' to me. Ef I've been any service to him pintin' out sick people, and kinder makin' suggestions here and thar, how he should look arter them, he's welcome to it. I don't go back on my record, if he hez got into trouble."

"And I'm sure," said Briggs, "if I did allow him to come in here and look arter thet sick Mexican, it ain't for me to be expected to look arter his moril character too." But here the entrance of a customer put a stop to further criticism.

Meanwhile the unfortunate subject of this discussion, by clinging close to the walls of houses, had avoided the keen blast that descended from the mountain, and had at last reached the little trail that led through the gulch to his cabin on the opposite hill-side. Here Gabriel hesitated. To follow that trail would lead him past the boarding-house of Mrs. Markle. In the light of the baleful counsel he had just received, to place himself as soon again in the way of danger seemed to him to be only a provocation of fate. That the widow and Sal might swoop down upon him as he passed, and compel him to enter; that the spectacle of his passing without a visit might superinduce instant hysterics on the part of the widow, appeared to his terror-stricken fancy as almost a certainty. The only other way home was by a circuitous road along the ridge of the hill, at least three miles farther. Gabriel did not hesitate long, but began promptly to ascend the hill. This was no easy task in the face of a strong gale and torrents of beating rain, but the overcoming of physical difficulties by the exercise of his all-conquering muscles, and the fact that he was doing something, relieved his mind of its absurd terrors. When he had reached the summit he noticed for the first time the full power of those subtle agencies that had been silently at work during the last week's steady rain. A thin trickling mountain rill where he had two weeks before slaked his thirst during a ramble with Olly, was now transformed into a roaring cataract; the brook that they had leaped across was now a swollen river. There were slowly widening pools in the valleys, darkly glancing sheets of water on the distant plains, and a monotonous rush and gurgle always in the air. It was half an hour later, and two miles farther on his rough road, that he came in view of the narrow precipitous gorge through which the Wingdam stage passed on its way from Marysville. As he approached nearer he could see that the little mountain stream which ran beside the stage road had already slightly encroached upon the road-bed, and that here and there the stage road itself was lost in drifts of standing water. "It will be pretty rough drivin' up that cañon," said Gabriel to himself as he thought of the incoming Wingdam stage, now nearly due; "mighty onpleasant and risky with narvous leaders, but thar's worse things than that in this yer world," he meditated, as his mind reverted again to Mrs. Markle, "and ef I could change places with Yuba Bill, and get on that box and Olly inside—I'd do it!"

But just then the reservoir of the Wingdam ditch came in view on the hill beside him, and with it a revelation that in a twinkling displaced Mrs. Markle, and seemed almost to change the man's entire nature! What was it? Apparently nothing to the eye of the ordinary traveller. The dam was full, and through a cut-off the overplus water was escaping with a roar. Nothing more? Yes—to an experienced eye the escaping water was not abating the quantity in the dam. Was that all? No! Halfway down the rudely constructed *adobe* bank of the dam, the water was slowly oozing and trickling through a slowly-widening crevice, over the rocks above the gorge and stage road below! The wall of the dam was giving way! To tear off coat and all impeding garments, to leap from rock to rock, and boulder to boulder, hanging on by slippery chimisal and the decayed roots of trees; to reach at the risk of life and limb the cañon below, and then to run at the highest speed to warn the incoming stage of the danger before it should enter the narrow gorge, was only the resolve and action of a brave man. But to do this without the smallest waste of strength that ought to be preserved, to do this with the greatest economy of force, to do this with the agility and skill of a mountaineer, and the reserved power of a giant; to do this with a will so simple, direct, and unhesitating, that the action appeared to have been planned and rehearsed days before, instead of being the resolution of the instant,—this belonged to Gabriel Conroy! And to have seen him settle into a long swinging trot, and to have observed his calm, grave, earnest, but unexcited face, and quiet, steadfast eye, you would have believed him some healthy giant simply exercising himself.

He had not gone half a mile before his quick ear caught a dull sound and roar of advancing water. Yet even then he only slightly increased his steady stride, as if he had been quickened and followed by his trainer rather than by approaching Death. At the same moment there was a quick rattle and clatter in the road ahead—a halt, and turning back, for Gabriel's warning shout had run before him like a bullet. But it was too late. The roaring water behind him struck him and bore him down, and the next instant swept the coach and horses a confused, struggling, black mass, against the rocky walls of the cañon. And then it was that the immense reserved strength of Gabriel came into play. Set upon by the almost irresistible volume of water, he did not waste his power in useless opposition, but allowed himself to be swept hither and thither until he touched a branch of chimisal that depended from the cañon side. Seizing it with one sudden and mighty effort, he raised himself above the sweep and suction of the boiling flood. The coach was gone; where it had stood a few black figures struggled, swirled, and circled. One of them was a woman. In an instant Gabriel plunged into the yellow water. A few strokes brought him to her side; in another moment he had encircled her waist with his powerful arm and lifted her head above the surface, when he was seized by two despairing arms from the other side. Gabriel did not shake them off. "Take hold of me lower down and I'll help ye both," he shouted, as he struck out with his only free arm for the chimisal. He reached it; drew himself up so that he could grasp it with his teeth, and then, hanging on by his jaw, raised his two clinging companions beside him. They had barely grasped it, when another ominous roar was heard below, and another wall of yellow water swept swiftly up the cañon. The chimisal began to yield to their weight. Gabriel dug his fingers into the soil about its roots, clutched the jagged edges of a rock beneath, and threw his arm about the woman, pressing her closely to the face of the wall. As the wave swept over them, there was a sudden despairing cry, a splash, and the man was gone. Only Gabriel and the woman remained. They were safe, but for the moment only. Gabriel's left hand grasping an insecure projection, was all that sustained their united weight. Gabriel, for the first time, looked down upon the woman. Then he said hesitatingly—

"Kin ye hold yourself a minnit?"—"Yes."

Even at that critical moment some occult quality of sweetness in her voice thrilled him.

"Lock your hands together hard, and sling 'em over my neck." She did so. Gabriel freed his right hand. He scarcely felt the weight thus suddenly thrown upon his shoulders, but cautiously groped for a projection on the rock above. He found it, raised himself by a supreme effort, until he secured a foothold in the hole left by the uprooted chimisal bush. Here he paused.

"Kin ye hang on a minnit longer?"

"Go on," she said.

Gabriel went on. He found another projection, and another, and gradually at last reached a ledge a foot wide, near the top of the cliff. Here he paused. It was the woman's turn to speak.

"Can you climb to the top?" she asked.

"Yes—if you"——

"Go on," she said, simply.

Gabriel continued the ascent cautiously. In a few minutes he had reached the top. Here her hands suddenly relaxed their grasp; she would have slipped to the ground had not Gabriel caught her by the waist, lifted her in his arms, and borne her to a spot where a fallen pine-tree had carpeted and cushioned the damp ground with its withered tassels. Here he laid her down with that exquisite delicacy and tenderness of touch which was so habitual to him in his treatment of all helplessness as to be almost unconscious. But she thanked him, with such a graceful revelation of small white teeth, and such a singular look out of her dark grey eyes, that he could not help looking at her again. She was a small light-haired woman, tastefully and neatly dressed, and of a type and class unknown to him. But for her smile, he would not have thought her pretty. But even with that smile on her face, she presently paled and fainted. At the same moment Gabriel heard the sound of voices, and, looking up, saw two of the passengers, who had evidently escaped by climbing the cliff, coming towards them. And then—I know not how to tell it—but a sudden and awe-inspiring sense of his ambiguous and peculiar situation took possession of him. What would they think of it? Would they believe his statement? A sickening recollection of the late conversation at Briggs's returned to him; the indignant faces of the gaunt Sal and the plump Mrs. Markle were before him; even the questioning eyes of little Olly seemed to pierce his inmost soul, and, alas! this hero, the victorious giant, turned and fled.

CHAPTER V.

SIMPLICITY *versus* SAGACITY.

WHEN Gabriel reached his home it was after dark, and Olly was anxiously waiting to receive him.

"You're wet all through, you awful Gabe, and covered with mud into the bargain. Go and change your clothes, or you'll get your death, as sure as you're a born sinner!"

The tone and manner in which this was uttered was something unusual with Olly, but Gabriel was too glad to escape further questioning to criticise or rebuke it. But when he had reappeared from behind the screen with dry clothes, he was surprised to observe by the light of the newly-lit candle that Olly herself had undergone since morning a decided change in her external appearance. Not to speak alone of an unusual cleanliness of face and hands, and a certain attempt at confining her yellow curls with a vivid pink ribbon, there was an unwonted neatness in her attire, and some essay at adornment in a faded thread-lace collar which she had found among her mother's "things" in the family bag, and a purple neck-ribbon.

"It seems to me," said the delighted Gabriel, "that somebody else hez been dressin' up and makin' a toylit, sence I've been away. Hev you been in the ditches agin, Olly?"

"No," said Olly, with some dignity of manner, as she busied herself in setting the table for supper.

"But I reckon I never seen ye look so peart afore, Olly; who's been here?" he added, with a sudden alarm.

"Nobody," said Olly; "I reckon some folks kin get along and look decent without the help of other folks, leastways of Susan Markle."

At this barbed arrow Gabriel winced slightly. "See yer, Olly," said Gabriel, "ye mustn't talk thet way about thet woman. You're only a chile—and ef yer brother did let on to ye, in confidence, certing things ez a brother may say to his sister, ye oughtn't say anythin' about it."

"Say anythin'!" echoed Olly, scornfully; "do you think I'd ever let on to thet woman ennything? Ketch me!"

Gabriel looked up at his sister in awful admiration, and felt at the depths of his conscience-stricken and self-deprecatory nature that he didn't deserve so brave a little defender. For a moment he resolved to tell her the truth, but a fear of Olly's scorn and a desire to bask in the sunshine of her active sympathy withheld him. "Besides," he added to himself, in a single flash of self-satisfaction, "this yer thing may be the makin' o' thet gal yet. Look at thet collar, Gabriel! look at thet hair, Gabriel! all your truth-tellin' never fetched outer thet purty child what thet one yarn did."

Nevertheless, as Gabriel sat down to his supper he was still haunted by the ominous advice and counsel he had heard that day. When Olly had finished her meal, he noticed that she had forborne, evidently at great personal sacrifice, to sop the frying-pan with her bread. He turned to her gravely—

"Ef you wus ever asked, Olly, ef I had been sweet upon Mrs. Markle, wot would ye say?"

"Say," said Olly savagely, "I'd say that if there ever was a woman ez had run arter a man with less call to do it—it was Mrs. Markle—that same old disgustin' Susan Markle. Thet's wot I'd say, and I'd say it—to her face! Gabe, see here!"

"Well," said the delighted Gabriel.

"Ef that school-ma'am comes up here, do you jest make up to her!"

"Olly!" ejaculated the alarmed Gabriel.

"You jest go for her! You jest do for her what you did for that Susan Markle. And jest you do it, if you can, Gabe—when Mrs. Markle's around—or afore little Manty—she'll go and tell her mother—she tells her everything. I've heerd, Gabe, that some o' them school-ma'ams is nice."

In his desire to please Olly, Gabriel would have imparted to her the story of his adventure in the cañon, but a vague fear that Olly might demand from him an instant offer of his hand and heart to the woman he had saved, checked the disclosure. And the next moment there was a rap at the door of the cabin.

"I forgot to say, Gabe, that Lawyer Maxwell was here to-day to see ye," said Olly, "and I bet you thet's him. If he wants you to nuss anybody, Gabe, don't ye do it! You got enough to do to look arter me!"

Gabriel rose with a perplexed face and opened the door. A tall dark man, with a beard heavily streaked with grey, entered. There was something in his manner and dress, although both conformed to local prejudices and customs, that denoted a type of man a little above the average social condition of One Horse Gulch. Unlike Gabriel's previous evening visitor, he did not glance around him, but fixed a pair of keen, half-humorous, half-interrogating grey eyes upon his host's face, and kept them there. The habitual expression of his features was serious, except for a certain half-nervous twitching at the left corner of his mouth, which continued usually, until he stopped and passed his hand softly across it. The impression always left on the spectator was, that he had wiped away a smile, as some people do a tear.

"I don't think I ever before met you, Gabriel," he said, advancing and offering his hand. "My name is Maxwell. I think you've heard of me. I have come for a little talk on a matter of business."

The blank dismay of Gabriel's face did not escape him, nor the gesture with which he motioned to Olly to retire.

"It's quite evident," he said to himself, "that the child knows nothing of this, or is unprepared. I have taken him by surprise."

"If I mistake not, Gabriel," said Maxwell aloud, "your little—er—girl—is as much concerned in this matter as yourself. Why not let her remain?"

"No, no;" said Gabriel, now feeling perfectly convinced in the depths of his conscience-stricken soul that Maxwell was here as the legal adviser of the indignant Mrs. Markle. "No! Olly, run out and get some chips in the wood-house agin to-morrow morning's fire. Run!"

Olly ran. Maxwell cast a look after the child, wiped his mouth, and leaning his elbow on the table, fixed his eyes on Gabriel. "I have called to-night, Gabriel, to see if we can arrange a certain matter without trouble, and even—as I am employed against you—with as little talk as possible To be frank, I am entrusted with the papers in a legal proceeding against you. Now, see here! is it necessary for me to say what these proceedings are? Is it even necessary for me to give the name of my client?"

Gabriel dropped his eyes, but even then the frank honesty of his nature spoke for him. He raised his head and said simply—"No!"

Lawyer Maxwell was for a moment staggered, but only for a moment. "Good," he said thoughtfully; "you are frank. Let me ask you now if, to avoid legal proceedings, publicity, and scandal—and allow me to add, the almost absolute certainty of losing in any suit that might be brought against you—would you be willing to abandon this house and claim at once, allowing it to go for damages in the past? If you would, I think I could accept it for such. I think I could promise that even this question of a closer relationship would not come up. Briefly, *she* might keep her name, and *you* might keep yours, and you would remain to each other as strangers. What do you say?"

Gabriel rose quickly and took the lawyer's hands with a tremulous grasp. "You're a kind man, Mr. Maxwell," he said, shaking the lawyer's hand vigorously; "a good man. It's a bad business, and you've made the best of it. Ef you'd been my own lawyer instead o' hers, you couldn't hev treated me better. I'll leave here at once. I've been thinking o' doing it ever since this yer thing troubled me; but I'll go to-morrow. Ye can hev the house, and all it contains. If I had anything else in a way of a fee to offer ye, I'd do it. She kin hev the house and all that they is of it. And then nothing will be said?"

"Not a word," said Maxwell, examining Gabriel curiously.

"No talk—nothin' in the newspapers?" continued Gabriel.

"Your conduct toward her and your attitude in this whole affair will be kept a profound secret, unless you happen to betray it yourself; and that is my one reason for advising you to leave here."

"I'll do it—to-morrow," said Gabriel, rubbing his hands. "Wouldn't you like to have me sign some bit o' paper?"

"No, no," said the lawyer, wiping his mouth with his hand, and looking at Gabriel as if he belonged to some entirely new species. "Let me advise you, as a friend, to sign no paper that might be brought against you hereafter. Your simple abandonment of the claim and house is sufficient for our purposes. I will make out no papers in the case until Thursday; by that time I expect to find no one to serve them on. You understand?"

Gabriel nodded, and wrung the lawyer's hand warmly.

Maxwell walked toward the door, still keeping his glance fixed on Gabriel's clear, honest eyes. On the threshold he paused, and leaning against it, wiped his mouth with a slow gesture, and said—"From all I can hear, Gabriel, you are a simple, honest fellow, and I frankly confess to you, but for the admission you have made to me, I would have thought you incapable of attempting to wrong a woman. I should have supposed it some mistake. I am not a judge of the motives of men; I am too old a lawyer, and too familiar with things of this kind to be surprised at men's motives, or even to judge their rights or wrongs by my own. But now that we understand each other, would you mind telling me what was your motive for this peculiar and monstrous form of deception? Understand me; it will not alter my opinion of you, which is, that you are not a bad man. But I am curious to know how you could deliberately set about to wrong this woman; what was the motive?"

Gabriel's face flushed deeply. Then he lifted his eyes and pointed to the screen. The lawyer followed the direction of his finger, and saw Olly standing in the doorway.

Lawyer Maxwell smiled. "It is the sex, anyway," he said to himself; "perhaps a little younger than I supposed; of course, his own child." He nodded again, smiled at Olly, and with the consciousness of a professional triumph, blent with a certain moral satisfaction that did not always necessarily accompany his professional success, he passed out into the night.

Gabriel avoided conversation with Olly until late in the evening. When she had taken her accustomed seat at his feet before the fire, she came directly to the point. "What did he want, Gabe?"

"Nothing partickler," said Gabriel, with an affectation of supreme indifference. "I was thinking, Olly, that I'd tell you a story. It's a long time since I told one." It had been Gabriel's habit to improve these precious moments by relating the news of the camp, or the current topics of the day, artfully imparted as pure fiction; but since his preoccupation with Mrs. Markle, he had lately omitted it.

Olly nodded her head, and Gabriel went on—

"Once upon a time they lived a man ez hed lived and would live—for thet was wot was so sing'ler about him—all alone, 'cept for a little sister ez this man hed, wot he loved very dearly. They was no one ez this man would ever let ring in, so to speak, between him and this little sister, and the heaps o' private confidence, and the private talks about this and thet, thet this yer man hed with this little sister, was wonderful to behold."

"Was it a real man—a pure man?" queried Olly.

"The man was a real man, but the little sister, I oughter say, was a kind o' fairy, you know, Olly, ez hed a heap o' power to do good to this yer man, unbeknownst to him and afore his face. They lived in a sorter paliss in the woods, this yer man and his sister. And one day this yer man hed a heap o' troubil come upon him that was sich ez would make him leave this beautiful paliss, and he didn't know how to let on to his little sister about it; and so he up, and he sez to her, sez he, 'Gloriana'—thet was her name—'Gloriana,' sez he, 'we must quit this beautiful paliss and wander into furrin parts, and the reason why is a secret ez I can't tell ye.' And this yer little sister jest ups and sez, 'Wot's agreeable to you, brother, is agreeable to me, for we is everything to each other the wide world over, and variety is the spice o' life, and I'll pack my traps to-morrow.' And she did. For why, Olly? Why, don't ye see, this yer little sister was a fairy, and knowed it all without bein' told. And they went away to furrin parts and strange places, war they built a more beautiful paliss than the other was, and they lived thar peaceful like and happy all the days o' their life."

"And thar wasn't any old witch of a Mrs. Markle to bother them. When are ye goin', Gabe?" asked the practical Olly.

"I thought to-morrow," said Gabriel, helplessly abandoning all allegory, and looking at his sister in respectful awe, "thet ez, I reckoned, Olly, to get to Casey's in time to take the arternoon stage up to Marysville."

"Well," said Olly, "then I'm goin' to bed now."

"Olly," said Gabriel reproachfully, as he watched the little figure disappear behind the canvas, "ye didn't kiss me fur good-night."

Olly came back. "You ole Gabe—you!" she said patronisingly, as she ran her fingers through his tangled curls, and stooped to bestow a kiss on his forehead from an apparently immeasurable moral and intellectual height—"You old big Gabe, what would you do without me, I'd like to know?"

The next morning Gabriel was somewhat surprised at observing Olly, immediately after the morning meal, proceed gravely to array herself in the few more respectable garments that belonged to her wardrobe. Over a white muslin frock, yellow and scant with age, she had tied a scarf of glaring cheap pink ribbon, and over this again she had secured, by the aid of an enormous tortoiseshell brooch, a large black and white check shawl of her mother's, that even repeated folding could not reduce in size. She then tied over her yellow curls a large straw hat trimmed with white and yellow daisies and pale-green ribbon, and completed her toilet by unfurling over her shoulder a small yellow parasol. Gabriel, who had been watching these preparations in great concern, at last ventured to address the *bizarre* but pretty little figure before him.

"War you goin', Olly?"

"Down the gulch to say good-bye to the Reed gals. 'Tain't the square thing to vamose the ranch without lettin' on to folks."

"Ye ain't goin' near Mrs. Markle's, are ye?" queried Gabriel, in deprecatory alarm.

Olly turned a scornful flash of her clear blue eye upon her brother, and said curtly, "Ketch me!"

There was something so appalling in her quickness, such a sudden revelation of quaint determination in the lines of her mouth and eyebrows, that Gabriel could say no more. Without a word he watched the yellow sunshade and flapping straw hat with its streaming ribbons slowly disappear down the winding descent of the hill. And then a sudden and grotesque sense of dependence upon the child—an appreciation of some reserved quality in her nature hitherto unsuspected by him—something that separated them now, and in the years to come would slowly widen the rift between them—came upon him with such a desolating sense of loneliness that it seemed unendurable. He did not dare to re-enter or look back upon the cabin, but pushed on vaguely toward his claim on the hillside. On his way thither he had to pass a solitary red-wood tree that he had often noticed, whose enormous bulk belittled the rest of the forest; yet, also, by reason of its very isolation had acquired a certain lonely pathos that was far beyond the suggestion of its heroic size. It seemed so imbecile, so gratuitously large, so unproductive of the good that might be expected of its bulk, so unlike the smart spruces and pert young firs and larches that stood beside it, that Gabriel instantly accepted it as a symbol of himself, and could not help wondering if there were not some other locality where everything else might be on its own plane of existence. "If I war to go thar," said Gabriel to himself, "I wonder if I might not suit better than I do yer, and be of some sarvice to thet child." He pushed his way through the underbrush, and stood upon the ledge that he had first claimed on his arrival at One Horse Gulch. It was dreary—it was unpromising—a vast stony field high up in air, covered with scattered boulders of dark iron-grey rock. Gabriel smiled bitterly. "Any other man but me couldn't hev bin sich a fool as to preëmpt sich a claim fur gold. P'r'aps it's all for the best that I'm short of it now," said Gabriel, as he turned away, and descended the hill to his later claim in the gulch, which yielded him that pittance known in the mining dialect as "grub."

It was nearly three o'clock before he returned to the cabin with the few tools that he had gathered. When he did so, he found Olly awaiting him, with a slight flush of excitement on her cheek, but no visible evidences of any late employment to be seen in the cabin.

"Ye don't seem to have been doin' much packin', Olly," said Gabriel—"tho' thar ain't, so to speak, much to pack up."

"Thar ain't no use in packin', Gabe," replied Olly, looking directly into the giant's bashful eyes.

"No use?" echoed Gabriel.

"No sort o' use," said Olly decidedly. "We ain't goin',

Gabe, and that's the end on't. I've been over to see Lawyer Maxwell, and I've made it all right!"

Gabriel dropped speechless into a chair, and gazed, open-mouthed, at his sister. "I've made it all right, Gabe," continued Olly coolly, "you'll see. I jest went over thar this morning, and hed a little talk with the lawyer, and gin him a piece o' my mind about Mrs. Markle—and jest settled the whole thing."

"Good Lord! Olly, what did you say?"

"Say?" echoed Olly. "I jest up and told him everythin' I knew about thet woman, and I never told you, Gabe, the half of it. I jest sed ez how she'd been runnin' round arter you ever sence she first set eyes on you, when you was nussin' her husband wot died. How you never ez much ez looked at her ontil I set you up to it! How she used to come round yer, and sit and sit and look at you, Gabe, and kinder do this et ye over her shoulder."—(Here Olly achieved an admirable imitation of certain arch glances of Mrs. Markle that would have driven that estimable lady frantic with rage, and even at this moment caused the bashful blood of Gabriel to fly into his very eyes.) "And how she used to let on all sorts of excuses to get you over thar, and how you refoosed! And wot a deceitful, old, mean, disgustin' critter she was enny way!" and here Olly paused for want of breath.

"And wot did he say?" said the equally breathless Gabriel.

"Nothin' at first! Then he laughed and laughed, and laughed till I thought he'd bust! And then—let me see," reflected the conscientious Olly, "he said thar was some 'absurd blunder and mistake'—that's jest what he called thet Mrs. Markle, Gabe—those was his very words! And then he set up another yell o' laughin', and somehow, Gabe, I got to laughin', and she got to laughin' too!" And Olly laughed at the recollection.

"Who's *she?*" asked Gabriel, with a most lugubrious face.

"O Gabe! you think everybody's Mrs. Markle," said Olly swiftly. "*She* was a lady ez was with thet Lawyer Maxwell, ez heerd it all. Why, Lord! she seemed to take ez much interest in it as the lawyer. P'r'aps," said Olly, with a slight degree of conscious pride as *raconteur*, "p'r'aps it was the way I told it. I was *thet* mad, Gabe, and sassy!"

"And what did he say?" continued Gabriel, still ruefully, for to him, as to most simple, serious natures devoid of any sense of humour, all this inconsequent hilarity looked suspicious.

"Why, he was fur puttin' right over here 'to explain,' ez he called it, but the lady stopped him, and sed somethin' low I didn't get to hear. Oh, she must be a partickler friend o' his, Gabe—for he did everythin' thet she said. And she said I was to go back and say thet we needn't hurry ourselves to git away at all. And thet's the end of it, Gabe."

"But didn't he say anythin' more, Olly?" said Gabriel anxiously.

"No. He begin to ask me some questions about old times and Starvation Camp, and I'd made up my mind to disremember all them things ez I told you, Gabe, fur I'm jest sick of being called a cannon-ball, so I jest disremembered everything ez fast ez he asked it, until he sez, sez he to this lady, 'she evidently knows nothin' o' the whole thing.' But the lady had been tryin' to stop his askin' questions, and he'd been kinder signin' to me not to answer too. Oh, she's cute, Gabe; I could see thet ez soon ez I set down."

"What did she look like, Olly?" said Gabriel, with an affectation of carelessness, but still by no means yet entirely relieved in his mind.

"Oh, she didn't look like Mrs. Markle, Gabe, or any o' thet kind. A kinder short woman, with white teeth, and a small waist, and good clo'es. I didn't sort o' take to her much, Gabe, though she was very kind to me. I don't know ez I could say ezackly what she did look like; I reckon thar ain't anybody about yer looks like she. Saints and goodness! Gabe, that's her now; thar she is!"

Something darkened the doorway. Gabriel, looking up, beheld the woman he had saved in the cañon. It was Madame Devarges!

BOOK III.

THE LEAD.

CHAPTER I.

AN OLD PIONEER OF '49.

A THICK fog, dense, impenetrable, bluish-grey and raw, marked the advent of the gentle summer of 1854 on the California coast. The brief immature spring was scarcely yet over; there were flowers still to be seen on the outlying hills around San Francisco, and the wild oats were yet green on the Contra Costa mountains. But the wild oats were hidden under a dim India-inky veil, and the wild flowers accepted the joyless embraces of the fog with a staring waxen rigidity. In short, the weather was so uncomfortable that the average Californian was more than ever inclined to impress the stranger aggressively with the fact that fogs were healthy, and that it was the "finest climate on the earth."

Perhaps no one was better calculated or more accustomed to impress the stranger with this belief than Mr. Peter Dumphy, banker and capitalist. His outspoken faith in the present and future of California was unbounded. His sincere convictions that no country or climate was ever before so signally favoured, his intoleration of any criticism or belief to the contrary, made him a representative man.

So positive and unmistakable was his habitual expression on these subjects, that it was impossible to remain long in his presence without becoming impressed with the idea that any other condition of society, climate, or civilization than that which obtained in California, was a mistake. Strangers were brought early to imbibe from this fountain; timid and weak Californians, in danger of a relapse, had their faith renewed and their eyesight restored by bathing in this pool that Mr. Dumphy kept always replenished. Unconsciously, people at last got to echoing Mr. Dumphy's views as their own, and much of the large praise that appeared in newspapers, public speeches, and correspondence, was first voiced by Dumphy. It must not be supposed that Mr. Dumphy's positiveness of statement and peremptory manner were at all injurious to his social reputation. Owing to that suspicion with which most frontier communities regard polite concession and suavity of method, Mr. Dumphy's brusque frankness was always accepted as genuine. "You always know what Pete Dumphy means," was the average criticism. "He ain't goin' to lie to please any man." To a conceit that was so outspoken as to be courageous, to an ignorance that was so freely and shamelessly expressed as to make hesitating and cautious wisdom appear weak and unmanly beside it, Mr. Dumphy added the rare quality of perfect unconscientiousness unmixed with any adulterating virtue. It was with such rare combative qualities as these that Mr. Dumphy sat that morning in his private office and generally opposed the fog without, or rather its influence upon his patrons and society at large. The face he offered to it was a strong one, although superficially smooth, for since the reader had the honour of his acquaintance, he had shaved off his beard, as a probably unnecessary indication of character. It was still early, but he had already despatched much business with that prompt decision which made even an occasional blunder seem heroic. He was signing a letter that one of his clerks had brought him, when he said briskly, without looking up—"Send Mr. Ramirez in."

Mr. Ramirez, who had already called for three successive days without obtaining an audience of Dumphy, entered the private room with an excited sense of having been wronged, which, however, instantly disappeared, as far as external manifestation was concerned, on his contact with the hard-headed, aggressive, and prompt Dumphy.

"How do?" said Dumphy, without looking up from his desk. Mr. Ramirez uttered some objection to the weather, and then took a seat uneasily near Dumphy. "Go on," said Dumphy, "I can listen."

"It is I who came to listen," said Mr. Ramirez, with great suavity. "It is of the news I would hear."

"Yes," said Mr. Dumphy, signing his name rapidly to several documents, "Yes, *Yes*, YES." He finished them, turned rapidly upon Ramirez, and said "Yes!" again, in such a positive manner as to utterly shipwreck that gentleman's self-control. "Ramirez!" said Dumphy abruptly, "how much have you got in that thing?"

Mr. Ramirez, still floating on a sea of conjecture, could only say, "Eh! Ah! It is what?"

"How *deep* are you? How much would you *lose?*"

Mr. Ramirez endeavoured to fix his eyes upon Dumphy's. "How—much—would I lose?—if how? If what?"

"What—money—have—you—got—in—it?" said Mr. Dumphy, emphasising each word sharply with the blunt end of his pen on the desk.

"No money! I have much interest in the success of Madame Devarges!"

"Then you're not 'in' much! That's lucky for you. Read that letter.—Show him in!"

The last remark was in reply to a mumbled interrogatory

of the clerk, who had just entered. Perhaps it was lucky for Mr. Ramirez that Mr. Dumphy's absorption with his new visitor prevented his observation of his previous visitor's face. As he read the letter, Ramirez's face first turned to an ashen-grey hue, then to a livid purple, then he smacked his dry lips thrice, and said "*Carámba!*" then with burning eyes he turned towards Dumphy.

"You have read this?" he asked, shaking the letter towards Dumphy.

"One moment," interrupted Dumphy, finishing the conversation with his latest visitor, and following him to the door. "Yes," he continued, returning to his desk and facing Ramirez. "Yes!" Mr. Ramirez could only shake the letter and smile in a ghastly way at Dumphy. "Yes," said Dumphy, reaching forward and coolly taking the letter out of Ramirez's hand. "Yes. Seems she is going to get married," he continued, consulting the letter. "Going to marry the brother, the man in possession. That puts you all right; any way, the cat jumps; and it lets *you* out." With the air of having finished the interview, Mr. Dumphy quietly returned the letter, followed by Ramirez's glaring eyes, to a pigeon-hole in his desk, and tapped his desk with his penholder.

"And you—you?" gasped Ramirez hoarsely, "you?"

"Oh, *I* didn't go into it a dollar. Yet it was a good investment. She could have made out a strong case. You had possession of the deed or will, hadn't you? There was no evidence of the existence of the other woman," continued Mr. Dumphy, in his usually loud voice, overlooking the cautionary gestures of Mr. Ramirez with perfect indifference. "Hello! How do?" he added to another visitor. "I was sending you a note." Mr. Ramirez rose. His long finger nails were buried in the yellow flesh of his palms. His face was quite bloodless, and his lips were dry. "What's your hurry?" said Dumphy, looking up. "Come in again; there's another matter I want you to look into, Ramirez! We've got some money out on a claim that ought to have one or two essential papers to make it right. I daresay they're lying round somewhere where you can find 'em. Draw on me for the expense." Mr. Dumphy did not say this slyly, nor with any dark significance, but with perfect frankness. Virtually it said—"You're a scamp, so am I; whether or not this other man who overhears us is one likewise, it matters not." He took his seat again, turned to the latest comer, and became oblivious of his previous companion.

Luckily for Mr. Ramirez, when he reached the street he had recovered the control of his features, if not his natural colour. At least the fog, which seemed to lend a bluish-grey shade to all complexions, allowed his own livid cheek to pass unnoticed. He walked quickly, and it appeared almost unconsciously, towards the water, for it was not until he reached the steamboat wharf that he knew where he was. He seemed to have taken one step from Mr. Dumphy's office to the pier. There was nothing between these two objects in his consciousness. The interval was utterly annihilated. The steamboat did not leave for Sacramento until eight that evening, and it was only ten o'clock now. He had been conscious of this as he walked, but he could not have resisted this one movement, even if a futile one, towards the object of his revengeful frenzy. Ten hours to wait—ten hours to be passive, inactive—to be doing nothing! How could he pass the time? He could sharpen his knife. He could buy a new one. He could purchase a better pistol. He remembered passing a gunsmith's shop with a display of glittering weapons in its window. He retraced his steps, and entered the shop, spending some moments in turning over the gunsmith's various wares. Especially was he fascinated by a long broad-bladed bowie-knife. "My own make," said the tradesman, with professional pride, passing a broad, leathery thumb along the keen edge of the blade. "It'll split a half-dollar. See!"

He threw a half-dollar on the counter, and with a quick, straight, down-darting stab pierced it in halves. Mr. Ramirez was pleased, and professed a desire to make the experiment himself. But the point slipped, sending the half-dollar across the shop and cutting a long splintering furrow in the counter. "Yer narves ain't steady. And ye try too hard," said the man, coolly. "Thet's the way it's apt to be with you gents. Ye jest work yourself up into a fever 'bout a little thing like thet, ez if everything depended on it. Don't make sich a big thing of it. Take it easy like this," and with a quick, firm, workmanlike stroke the tradesman repeated the act successfully. Mr. Ramirez bought the knife. As the man wrapped it up in paper, he remarked with philosophic kindness—"I wouldn't try to do it agin this mornin'. It's early in the day, and I've noticed thet gents ez hez been runnin' free all night ain't apt to do theirselves justice next mornin'. Take it quietly alone by yourself, this arternoon; don't think you're goin' to do anythin' big, and you'll fetch it, sure!"

When Mr. Ramirez was in the street again he looked at his watch. Eleven o'clock! Only one hour gone. He buttoned his coat tightly over the knife in his breast pocket, and started on again feverishly. Twelve o'clock found him rambling over the sand hills near the Mission Dolores. In one of the by-streets he came upon a woman looking so like the one that filled all his thoughts, that he turned to look at her again with a glance so full of malevolence that she turned from him in terror. This circumstance, his agitation, and the continual dryness of his lips sent him into a saloon, where he drank freely, without, however, increasing or abating his excitement. When he returned to the crowded streets again he walked quickly, imagining that his manner was noticed by others, in such intervals as he snatched from the contemplation of a single intention. There were several ways of doing it. One was to tax her with her deceit and then kill her in the tempest of his indignation. Another and a more favourable thought was to surprise her and her new accomplice—for Mr. Ramirez, after the manner of most jealous reasoners, never gave her credit for any higher motive than that she had shown to him—and kill them both. Another and a later idea was to spend the strength of his murderous passion upon the man, and then to enjoy her discomfiture, the failure of her plans, and perhaps her appeals for forgiveness. But it would still be two days before he could reach them. Perhaps they were already married. Perhaps they would be gone! In all this wild, passionate, and tumultuous contemplation of an effect, there never had been for a single moment in his mind the least doubt of the adequacy of the cause. That he was a *dupe*,—a hopeless, helpless dupe,—was sufficient. Since he had read the letter, his self-consciousness had centred upon a single thought, expressed to him in a single native word, "Bobo." It was continually before his eyes. He spelled it on the signs in the street. It kept up a dull monotonous echo in his ears. "Bobo." Ah! she should see!

It was past noon, and the fog had deepened. Afar from the bay came the sounds of bells and whistles. If the steamer should not go? If she should be delayed, as often happened, for several hours? He would go down to the wharf and inquire. In the meantime, let the devil seize the fog! Might the Holy St. Bartholomew damn for ever the cowardly dog of a captain and the cayote crew who would refuse to go! He came sharply enough down

Commercial Street, and then, when opposite the Arcade Saloon, with the instinct that leads desperate men into desperate places, he entered and glared vindictively around him. The immense room, bright with lights and glittering with gilding and mirrors, seemed quiet and grave in contrast with the busy thoroughfare without. It was still too early for the usual *habitués* of the place; only a few of the long gambling tables were occupied. There was only a single *monte* bank "open," and to this Ramirez bent his steps with the peculiar predilections of his race. It so chanced that Mr. Jack Hamlin was temporarily in charge of the interests of this bank, and was dealing in a listless, perfunctory manner. It may be parenthetically remarked that his own game was faro. His present position was one of pure friendliness to the absent dealer, who was taking his dinner above stairs. Ramirez flung a piece of gold on the table and lost. Again he attempted fortune and lost. He lost the third time. Then his pent-up feelings found vent in the characteristic "*Carámba!*" Mr. Jack Hamlin looked up. It was not the oath, it was not the expression of ill-humour, both of which were common enough in Mr. Hamlin's experience, but a certain distinguishing quality in the voice which awoke Jack's peculiarly retentive memory. He looked up, and, to borrow his own dialect, at once "spotted" the owner of the voice. He made no outward sign of his recognition, but quietly pursued the game. In the next deal Mr. Ramirez won! Mr. Hamlin quietly extended his *croupe* and raked down Mr. Ramirez's money with the losers'.

As Mr. Hamlin doubtless had fully expected, Mr. Ramirez rose with a passionate scream of rage. Whereat Mr. Hamlin coolly pushed back Mr. Ramirez's stake and winnings without looking up. Leaving it upon the table, Ramirez leaped to the gambler's side.

"You would insult me, so! You would ch—ee—at! eh? You would take my money, so!" he said, hoarsely, gesticulating passionately with one hand, while with the other he grasped as wildly in his breast.

Mr. Jack Hamlin turned a pair of dark eyes on the speaker, and said, quietly, "Sit down, Johnny!"

With the pent-up passion of the last few hours boiling in his blood, with the murderous intent of the morning still darkling in his mind, with the passionate sense of a new insult stinging him to madness, Mr. Ramirez should have struck the gambler to the earth. Possibly that was his intention as he crossed to his side; possibly that was his conviction as he heard himself—*he*—Victor Ramirez! whose presence in two days should strike terror to two hearts in One Horse Gulch!—addressed as Johnny! But he looked into the eyes of Mr. Hamlin and hesitated. What he saw there I cannot say. They were handsome eyes, clear and well opened, and had been considered by several members of a fond and confiding sex as peculiarly arch and tender. But, it must be confessed, Mr. Ramirez returned to his seat without doing anything.

"Ye don't know that man," said Mr. Hamlin to the two players nearest him, in a tone of the deepest confidence, which was, however, singularly enough, to be heard distinctly by every one at the table, including Ramirez. "You don't know him, but I do! He's a desprit character," continued Mr. Hamlin, glancing at him and quietly shuffling the cards, "a very desprit character! Make your game, gentlemen! Keeps a cattle ranch in Sonoma, and a private graveyard whar he buries his own dead. They call him the 'Yaller Hawk of Sonoma.' He's outer sorts jest now: probably jest killed some one up thar, and smells blood." Mr. Ramirez smiled a ghastly smile, and affected to examine the game minutely and critically as Mr. Hamlin paused to rake in the gold. "He's artful—is Johnny!" continued Mr. Hamlin, in the interval of shuffling, "artful and sly! Partikerly when he's after blood! See him sittin' thar and smilin'. He doesn't want to interrupt the game. He knows, gentlemen, thet in five minutes from now, Jim will be back here and I'll be free. Thet's what he's waitin' for! Thet's what's the matter with the 'Yaller Slaughterer of Sonoma!' Got his knife ready in his breast, too. Done up in brown paper to keep it clean. He's mighty pertikler 'bout his weppins is Johnny. Hez a knife for every new man." Ramirez rose with an attempt at jocularity, and pocketed his gains. Mr. Hamlin affected not to notice him until he was about to leave the table. "He's goin' to wait for me outside," he exclaimed. "In five minutes, Johnny," he called to Ramirez's retreating figure. "If you can't wait, I'll expect to see you at the Marysville Hotel next week, Room No. 95, the next room, Johnny, the next room!"

The Mr. Ramirez who reached the busy thoroughfare again was so different from the Mr. Ramirez who twenty minutes before had entered the Arcade that his identity might have easily been doubted. He did not even breathe in the same way; his cheek, although haggard, had resumed its colour; his eyes, which hitherto had been fixed and contemplative, had returned to their usual restless vivacity. With the exception that at first he walked quickly on leaving the saloon, and once or twice hurriedly turned to see if anybody were following him, his manner was totally changed. And this without effusion of blood, or the indulgence of an insatiable desire for revenge! As I prefer to deal with Mr. Ramirez without affecting to know any more of that gentleman than he did himself, I am unable to explain any more clearly than he did to himself the reason for this change in his manner, or the utter subjection of his murderous passion. When it is remembered that for several hours he had had unlimited indulgence, without opposition, in his own instincts, but that for the last twenty minutes he had some reason to doubt their omnipotence, perhaps some explanation may be adduced. I only know that by half-past six Mr. Ramirez had settled in his mind that physical punishment of his enemies was not the most efficacious means of revenge, and that at half-past seven he had concluded *not* to take the Sacramento boat. And yet for the previous six hours I have reason to believe that Mr. Ramirez was as sincere a murderer as ever suffered the penalty of his act, or to whom circumstances had not offered a Mr. Hamlin to act upon a constitutional cowardice.

Mr. Ramirez proceeded leisurely down Montgomery Street until he came to Pacific Street. At the corner of the street his way was for a moment stopped by a rattling team and waggon that dashed off through the fog in the direction of the wharf. Mr. Ramirez recognised the express and mail for the Sacramento boat. But Mr. Ramirez did not know that the express contained a letter which ran as follows—

"DEAR MADAM,—Yours of the 10th received, and contents noted. Am willing to make our services contingent upon your success. We believe your present course will be quite as satisfactory as the plan you first proposed. Would advise you not to give a personal interview to Mr. Ramirez, but refer him to Mr. Gabriel Conroy. Mr. Ramirez's manner is such as to lead us to suppose that he might offer violence, unless withheld by the presence of a third party.—Yours respectfully,

"PETER DUMPHY."

CHAPTER II.

A CLOUD OF WITNESSES.

THE street into which Ramirez plunged at first sight appeared almost impassable, and but for a certain regularity in the parallels of irregular, oddly-built houses, its original intention as a thoroughfare might have been open to grave doubt. It was dirty, it was muddy, it was ill-lighted; it was rocky and precipitous in some places, and sandy and monotonous in others. The grade had been changed two or three times, and each time apparently for the worse, but always with a noble disregard for the dwellings, which were invariably treated as an accident in the original design, or as obstacles to be overcome at any hazard. The near result of this large intent was to isolate some houses completely, to render others utterly inaccessible except by scaling ladders, and to produce the general impression that they were begun at the top and built down. The remoter effect was to place the locality under a social ban, and work a kind of outlawry among the inhabitants. Several of the houses were originally occupied by the Spanish native Californians, who, with the conservative instincts of their race, still clung to their *casas* after the Americans had flown to pastures new and less rocky and inaccessible beyond. Their vacant places were again filled by other native Californians, through that social law which draws the members of an inferior and politically degraded race into gregarious solitude and isolation, and the locality became known as the Spanish Quarter. That they lived in houses utterly inconsistent with their habits and tastes, that they affected a locality utterly foreign to their inclinations or customs, was not the least pathetic and grotesque element to a contemplative observer.

Before, or rather beneath one of these structures, Mr. Ramirez stopped, and began the ascent of a long flight of wooden steps, that at last brought him to the foundations of the dwelling. Another equally long exterior staircase brought him at last to the verandah or gallery of the second story, the first being partly hidden by an embankment. Here Mr. Ramirez discovered another flight of narrower steps leading down to a platform before the front door. It was open. In the hall-way two or three dark-faced men were lounging, smoking *cigaritos*, and enjoying, in spite of the fog, the apparently unseasonable *négligé* of shirt sleeves and no collars. At the open front windows of the parlour two or three women were sitting, clad in the lightest and whitest of flounced muslin skirts, with heavy shawls over their heads and shoulders, as if summer had stopped at their waists, like an equator.

The house was feebly lighted, or rather the gloom of yellowish-browned walls and dark furniture, from which all lustre and polish had been smoked, made it seem darker. Nearly every room and all the piazzas were dim with the yellow haze of burning *cigaritos*. There were light brown stains on the shirt sleeves of the men, there were yellowish streaks on the otherwise spotless skirts of the women; every masculine and feminine forefinger and thumb was steeped to its first joint with yellow. The fumes of burnt paper and tobacco permeated the whole house like some religious incense, through which occasionally struggled an inspiration of red peppers and garlic.

Two or three of the loungers addressed Ramirez in terms of grave recognition. One of the women—the stoutest—appeared at the doorway, holding her shawl tightly over her shoulders with one hand, as if to conceal a dangerous dishabille above the waist, and playfully shaking a black fan at the young man with the other hand, applied to him the various epithets of "Ingrate," "Traitor," and "Judas," with great vivacity and volubility. Then she faced him coquettishly. "And after so long, whence now, thou little blackguard?"

"It is of business, my heart and soul," exclaimed Ramirez, with hasty and somewhat perfunctory gallantry. "Who is above?"—"Those who testify."

"And Don Pedro?"

"He is there, and the Señor Perkins."

"Good. I will go on after a little," he nodded apologetically, as he hastily ascended the staircase. On the first landing above he paused, turned doubtfully toward the nearest door, and knocked hesitatingly. There was no response. Ramirez knocked again more sharply and decidedly. This resulted in a quick rattling of the lock, the sudden opening of the door, and the abrupt appearance of a man in ragged alpaca coat and frayed trousers. He stared fiercely at Ramirez, said in English, "What in h—— ! next door!" and as abruptly slammed the door in Ramirez's face. Ramirez entered hastily the room indicated by the savage stranger, and was at once greeted by a dense cloud of smoke and the sound of welcoming voices.

Around a long table covered with quaint-looking legal papers, maps, and parchments, a half-dozen men were seated. The greater number were past the middle age, dark-featured and grizzle-haired, and one, whose wrinkled face was the colour and texture of redwood bark, was bowed with decrepitude.

"He had one hundred and two years day before yesterday. He is the principal witness to Micheltorrena's signature in the Castro claim," exclaimed Don Pedro.

"Is he able to remember?" asked Ramirez.

"Who knows?" said Don Pedro, shrugging his shoulder. "He will swear; it is enough!"

"What animal have we in the next room?" asked Ramirez. "Is it wolf or bear?"

"The Señor Perkins," said Don Pedro.

"Why is he?"

"He translates."

Here Ramirez related, with some vehemence, how he mistook the room, and the stranger's brusque salutation.

The company listened attentively and even respectfully. An American audience would have laughed. The present company did not alter their serious demeanour ; a breach of politeness to a stranger was a matter of grave importance even to these doubtful characters. Don Pedro explained—

"Ah, so it is believed that God has visited him here." He tapped his forehead. "He is not of their country fashion at all. He has punctuality, he has secrecy, he has the habitude. When strikes the clock three he is here ; when it strikes nine he is gone. Six hours to work in that room ! Ah, heavens ! The quantity of work—it is astounding ! Folios ! Volumes ! Good ! it is done. Punctually at nine of the night he takes up a paper left on his desk by his *padrone*, in which is enwrapped ten dollars —the golden eagle, and he departs for that day. They tell to me that five dollars is gone at the gambling table, but no more ! then five dollars for subsistence—always the same. Always ! Always ! He is a scholar—so profound, so admirable ! He has the Spanish, the French, perfect. He is worth his weight in gold to the lawyers—you understand— but they cannot use him. To them he says—'I translate, lies or what not ! Who knows ? I care not—but no more.' He is wonderful ! "

The allusion to the gaming-table revived Victor's recollection, and his intention in his present visit. "Thou hast told me, Don Pedro," he said, lowering his voice in confidence, "how much is fashioned the testimony of the witnesses in regard of the old land grants by the Governors and Alcaldes. Good. Is it so ?"

Don Pedro glanced around the room. "Of those that are here to-night five will swear as they are prepared by me— you comprehend—and there is a Governor, a Military Secretary, an Alcalde, a Comandante, and saints preserve us ! an Archbishop ! They are respectable *caballeros ;* but they have been robbed, you comprehend, by the *Americanos.* What matters? They have been taught a lesson. They will get the best price for their memory. Eh? They will sell it where it pays best. Believe me, Victor; it is so."

"Good," said Victor. "Listen; if there was a man—a brigand, a devil—an American!—who had extorted from Pico a grant—you comprehend—a grant, formal, and regular, and recorded—accepted of the Land Commission—and some one, eh?—even myself, should say to you it is all wrong, my friend, my brother—ah!"

"From Pico?" asked Don Pedro.

"*Si*, from Pico, in '47," responded Victor,—"a grant."

Don Pedro rose, opened a secretary in the corner, and took out some badly-printed, yellowish blanks, with a seal in the right hand lower corner.

"Custom House paper from Monterey," explained Don Pedro, "blank with Governor Pico's signature and rubric. Comprehendest thou, Victor, my friend? A second grant is simple enough!"

Victor's eyes sparkled.

"But two for the same land, my brother?"

Don Pedro shrugged his shoulders, and rolled a fresh *cigarito*.

"There are two for nearly every grant of his late Excellency. Art thou certain, my brave friend, there are not *three* to this of which thou speakest? If there be but one—Holy Mother! it is nothing. Surely the land has no value. Where is this modest property? How many leagues square? Come, we will retire in this room, and thou mayest talk undisturbed. There is excellent *aguardiente* too, my Victor, come," and Don Pedro rose, conducted Victor into a smaller apartment, and closed the door.

Nearly an hour elapsed. During that interval the sound of Victor's voice, raised in passionate recital, might have been heard by the occupants of the larger room but that they were completely involved in their own smoky atmosphere, and were perhaps politely oblivious of the stranger's business. They chatted, compared notes, and examined legal documents with the excited and pleased curiosity of men to whom business and the present importance of its results was a novelty. At a few minutes before nine Don Pedro reappeared with Victor. I grieve to say that either from the reaction of the intense excitement of the morning, from the active sympathy of his friend, or from the equally soothing anodyne of *aguardiente*, he was somewhat incoherent, interjectional, and effusive. The effect of excessive stimulation on passionate natures like Victor's is to render them either maudlin or affectionate. Mr. Ramirez was both. He demanded with tears in his eyes to be led to the ladies. He would seek in the company of Manuela, the stout female before introduced to the reader, that sympathy which an injured, deceived, and confiding nature like his own so deeply craved.

On the staircase he ran against a stranger, precise, dignified, accurately clothed and fitted—the "Señor Perkins" just released from his slavery, a very different person from the one accidentally disclosed to him an hour before, on his probable way to the gaming table, and his habitual enjoyment on the evening of the day. In his maudlin condition, Victor would have fain exchanged views with him in regard to the general deceitfulness of the fair, and the misfortunes that attend a sincere passion, but Don Pedro hurried him below into the parlour, and out of the reach of the serenely contemptuous observation of the Señor Perkins's eye. Once in the parlour, and in the presence of the coquettish Manuela, who was still closely shawled, as if yet uncertain and doubtful in regard to the propriety of her garments above the waist, Victor, after a few vague remarks upon the general inability of the sex to understand a nature so profoundly deep and so wildly passionate as his own, eventually succumbed in a large black haircloth arm-chair, and became helplessly and hopelessly comatose.

"We must find a bed here for him to-night," said the sympathising, but practical Manuela; "he is not fit, poor imbecile, to be sent to his hotel. Mother of God! what is this?"

In lifting him out of the chair into which he had subsided with a fatal tendency to slide to the floor, unless held by main force, something had fallen from his breast pocket, and Manuela had picked it up. It was the bowie-knife he had purchased that morning.

"Ah!" said Manuela, "desperate little brigand: he has been among the *Americanos!* Look, my uncle!"

Don Pedro took the weapon quietly from the brown hands of Manuela and examined it coolly.

"It is new, my niece," he responded, with a slight shrug of his shoulders. "The gloss is still upon its blade. We will take him to bed."

CHAPTER III.

THE CHARMING MRS. SEPULVIDA.

If there was a spot on earth of which the usual dead monotony of the Californian seasons seemed a perfectly consistent and natural expression, that spot was the ancient and time-honoured *pueblo* and Mission of the blessed St. Anthony. The changeless, cloudless, expressionless skies of summer seemed to symbolise that aristocratic conservatism which repelled all innovation, and was its distinguishing mark. The stranger who rode into the *pueblo*, in his own conveyance,—for the instincts of San Antonio refused to sanction the introduction of a stage-coach or diligence that might bring into the town irresponsible and vagabond travellers,—read in the faces of the idle, lounging *peons* the fact that the great *rancheros* who occupied the outlying grants had refused to sell their lands, long before he entered the one short walled street and open plaza, and found that he was in a town where there was no hotel or tavern, and that he was dependent entirely upon the hospitality of some courteous resident for a meal or a night's lodging.

As he drew rein in the courtyard of the first large adobe dwelling, and received the grave welcome of a strange but kindly face, he saw around him everywhere the past unchanged. The sun shone as brightly and fiercely on the long red tiles of the low roofs, that looked as if they had been thatched with longitudinal slips of cinnamon, even as it had shone for the last hundred years; the gaunt wolf-like dogs ran out and barked at him as their fathers and mothers had barked at the preceding stranger of twenty years before. There were the few wild half-broken mustangs tethered by strong riatas before the verandah of the long low *Fonda*, with the sunlight glittering on their silver trappings; there were the broad, blank expanses of whitewashed adobe walls, as barren and guiltless of record as the uneventful days, as monotonous and expressionless as the staring sky above; there were the white, dome-shaped towers of the Mission rising above the green of olives and pear-trees, twisted, gnarled, and knotted with the rheumatism of age; there was the unchanged strip of narrow white beach, and beyond, the sea—vast, illimitable, and always the same. The steamers that crept slowly up the darkening coast line were something remote, unreal, and phantasmal; since the Philippine galleon had left its bleached and broken ribs in the sand in 1640, no vessel had, in the memory of man, dropped anchor in the open roadstead below the curving Point of

Pines, and the white walls, and dismounted bronze cannon of the Presidio, that looked blankly and hopelessly seaward.

For all this, the *pueblo* of San Antonio was the cynosure of the covetous American eye. Its vast leagues of fertile soil, its countless herds of cattle, the semi-tropical luxuriance of its vegetation, the salubrity of its climate, and the existence of miraculous mineral springs, were at once a temptation and an exasperation to greedy speculators of San Francisco. Happily for San Antonio, its square leagues were held by only a few of the wealthiest native gentry. The ranchos of the "Bear," of the "Holy Fisherman," of the "Blessed Trinity," comprised all of the outlying lands, and their titles were patented and secured to their native owners in the earlier days of the American occupation, while their comparative remoteness from the populous centres had protected them from the advances of foreign cupidity. But one American had ever entered upon the possession and enjoyment of this Californian Arcadia, and that was the widow of Don José Sepulvida. Eighteen months ago the excellent Sepulvida had died at the age of eighty-four, and left his charming young American wife the sole mistress of his vast estate. Attractive, of a pleasant, social temperament, that the Donna Maria should eventually bestow her hand and the estate upon some losel *Americano*, who would bring ruin in the hollow disguise of "improvements" to the established and conservative life of San Antonio, was an event to be expected, feared, and, if possible, estopped by fasting and prayer.

When the Donna Maria returned from a month's visit to San Francisco after her year's widowhood, alone, and to all appearances as yet unattached, it is said that a *Te Deum* was sung at the Mission church. The possible defection of the widow became still more important to San Antonio, when it was remembered that the largest estate in the valley, the "Rancho of the Holy Trinity," was held by another member of this deceitful sex—the alleged natural half-breed daughter of a deceased Governor—but happily preserved from the possible fate of the widow by religious preoccupation and the habits of a recluse. That the irony of Providence should leave the fate and future of San Antonio so largely dependent upon the results of levity, and the caprice of a susceptible sex, gave a sombre tinge to the gossip of the little *pueblo*—if the grave, decorous discussion of Señores and Señoras could deserve that name. Nevertheless it was believed by the more devout that a miraculous interposition would eventually save San Antonio from the *Americanos* and destruction, and it was alleged that the patron saint, himself accomplished in the art of resisting a peculiar form of temptation, would not scruple to oppose personally any undue weakness of vanity or the flesh in helpless widowhood. Yet, even the most devout and trustful believers, as they slyly slipped aside veil or *manta*, to peep furtively at the Donna Maria entering chapel, in the heathenish abominations of a Parisian dress and bonnet, and a face rosy with self-consciousness and innocent satisfaction, felt their hearts sink within them, and turned their eyes in mute supplication to the gaunt, austere patron saint pictured on the chancel wall above them, who, clutching a skull and crucifix as if for support, seemed to glare upon the pretty stranger with some trepidation and a possible doubt of his being able to resist the newer temptation.

As far as was consistent with Spanish courtesy, the Donna Maria was subject to a certain mild espionage. It was even hinted by some of the more conservative that a *duenna* was absolutely essential to the proper decorum of a lady representing such large social interests as the widow Sepulvida, although certain husbands, who had already suffered from the imperfect protection of this safeguard, offered some objection. But the pretty widow, when this proposition was gravely offered by her ghostly confessor, only shook her head and laughed. "A husband is the best *duenna*, Father Felipe," she said, archly, and the conversation ended.

Perhaps it was as well that the gossips of San Antonio did not know how imminent was their danger, or how closely imperilled were the vast social interests of the *pueblo* on the 3rd day of June 1854.

It was a bright, clear morning—so clear that the distant peaks of the San Bruno mountains seemed to have encroached upon the San Antonio valley overnight—so clear that the horizon line of the vast Pacific seemed to take in half the globe beyond. It was a morning, cold, hard, and material as granite, yet with a certain mica sparkle in its quality—a morning full of practical animal life, in which bodily exercise was absolutely essential to its perfect understanding and enjoyment. It was scarcely to be wondered that the Donna Maria Sepulvida, who was returning from a visit to her steward and major-domo, attended by a single *vaquero*, should have thrown the reins forward on the neck of her yellow mare, "Tita," and dashed at a wild gallop down the white strip of beach that curved from the garden wall of the Mission to the Point of Pines, a league beyond. "Concho," the venerable *vaquero*, after vainly endeavouring to keep pace with his mistress's fiery steed, and still more capricious fancy, shrugged his shoulders, and subsided into a trot, and was soon lost among the shifting sand dunes. Completely carried away by the exhilarating air and intoxication of the exercise, the Donna Maria—with her brown hair shaken loose from the confinement of her little velvet hat, the whole of a pretty foot, and at times, I fear, part of a symmetrical ankle visible below the flying folds of her grey riding-skirt, flecked here and there with the racing spume of those Homeric seas—at last reached the Point of Pines which defined the limits of the peninsula.

But when the gentle Mistress Sepulvida was within a hundred yards of the Point she expected to round, she saw with some chagrin that the tide was up, and that each dash of the breaking seas sent a thin, reaching film of shining water up to the very roots of the pines. To her still further discomfiture, she saw also that a smart-looking cavalier had likewise reined in his horse on the other side of the Point, and was evidently watching her movements with great interest, and, as she feared, with some amusement. To go back would be to be followed by this stranger, and to meet the cynical but respectful observation of Concho; to go forward, at the worst, could only be a slight wetting, and a canter beyond the reach of observation of the stranger, who could not in decency turn back after her. All this Donna Maria saw with the swiftness of feminine intuition, and, without apparently any hesitation in her face of her intent, dashed into the surf below the Point.

Alas for feminine logic! Mistress Sepulvida's reasoning was perfect, but her premises were wrong. Tita's first dash was a brave one, and carried her half round the Point, the next was a simple flounder; the next struggle sunk her to her knees, the next to her haunches. She was in a quicksand!

"Let the horse go. Don't struggle! Take the end of your riata. Throw yourself flat on the next wave, and let it take you out to sea!"

Donna Maria mechanically loosed the coil of hair rope which hung over the pommel of her saddle. Then she looked around in the direction of the voice. But she saw only a riderless horse, moving slowly along the Point.

"Quick! Now then!" The voice was seaward now; where, to her frightened fancy, some one appeared to be swimming. Donna Maria hesitated no longer; with the recoil of the next wave, she threw herself forward and was carried floating a few yards, and dropped again on the treacherous sand.

"Don't move, but keep your grip on the riata!"

The next wave would have carried her back, but she began to comprehend, and, assisted by the yielding sand, held her own and her breath until the under-tow sucked her a few yards seaward; the sand was firmer now; she floated a few yards farther, when her arm was seized; she was conscious of being impelled swiftly through the water, of being dragged out of the surge, of all her back hair coming down, that she had left her boots behind her in the quicksand, that her rescuer was a stranger, and a young man—and then she fainted.

When she opened her brown eyes again she was lying on the dry sand beyond the Point, and the young man was on the beach below her, holding both the horses—his own and Tita!

"I took the opportunity of getting your horse out. Relieved of your weight, and loosened by the tide, he got his foot over the riata, and Charley and I pulled him out. If I am not mistaken, this is Mrs. Sepulvida?"

Donna Maria assented in surprise.

"And I imagine this is your man coming to look for you." He pointed to Concho, who was slowly making his way among the sand dunes towards the Point. "Let me assist you on your horse again. He need not know—nobody need know—the extent of your disaster."

Donna Maria, still bewildered, permitted herself to be assisted to her saddle again, despite the consequent terrible revelation of her shoeless feet. Then she became conscious that she had not thanked her deliverer, and proceeded to do so with such embarrassment that the stranger's laughing interruption was a positive relief.

"You would thank me better if you were to set off in a swinging gallop over those sun-baked, oven-like sand-hills, and so stave off a chill! For the rest, I am Mr. Poinsett, one of your late husband's legal advisers, here on business that will most likely bring us together—I trust much more pleasantly to you than this. Good morning!"

He had already mounted his horse, and was lifting his hat. Donna Maria was not a very clever woman, but she was bright enough to see that his business *brusquerie* was either the concealment of a man shy of women, or the impertinence of one too familiar with them. In either case it was to be resented.

How did she do it? Ah me! She took the most favourable hypothesis. She pouted, I regret to say. Then she said—

"It was all your fault!"

"How?"

"Why, if you hadn't stood there, looking at me and criticising, I shouldn't have tried to go round."

With this Parthian arrow she dashed off, leaving her rescuer halting between a bow and a smile.

CHAPTER IV.

FATHER FELIPE.

WHEN Arthur Poinsett, after an hour's rapid riding over the scorching sand-hills, finally drew up at the door of the Mission Refectory, he had so far profited by his own advice to Donna Maria as to be quite dry, and to exhibit very little external trace of his late adventure. It is more remarkable perhaps that there was very little internal evidence either. No one who did not know the peculiar self-sufficiency of Poinsett's individuality would be able to understand the singular mental and moral adjustment of a man keenly alive to all new and present impressions, and yet able to dismiss them entirely, without a sense of responsibility or inconsistency. That Poinsett thought twice of the woman he had rescued—that he ever reflected again on the possibilities or natural logic of his act—during his ride, no one who thoroughly knew him would believe. When he first saw Mrs. Sepulvida at the Point of Pines, he was considering the possible evils or advantages of a change in the conservative element of San Antonio ; when he left her, he returned to the subject again, and it fully occupied his thoughts until Father Felipe stood before him in the door of the refectory. I do not mean to say that he at all ignored a certain sense of self-gratulation in the act, but I wish to convey the idea that all other considerations were subordinate to this sense. And possibly also the feeling, unexpressed, however, by any look or manner, that if *he* was satisfied, everybody else ought to be.

If Donna Maria had thought his general address a little too irreverent, she would have been surprised at his greeting with Father Felipe. His whole manner was changed to one of courteous and even reverential consideration, of a boyish faith and trustfulness, of perfect confidence and self-forgetfulness, and moreover was perfectly sincere. She would have been more surprised to have noted that the object of Arthur's earnestness was an old man, and that beyond a certain gentle and courteous manner and refined bearing, he was unpicturesque and odd-fashioned in dress, snuffy in the sleeves, and possessed and inhabited a pair of shoes so large, shapeless, and inconsistent with the usual requirements of that article as to be grotesque.

It was evident that Arthur's manner had previously predisposed the old man in his favour. He held out two soft brown hands to the young man, addressed him with a pleasant smile as "My son," and welcomed him to the Mission.

"And why not this visit before?" asked Father Felipe, when they were seated upon the little verandah that overlooked the Mission garden, before their chocolate and *cigaritos*.

"I did not know I was coming until the day before yesterday. It seems that some new grants of the old ex-Governor's have been discovered, and that a patent is to be applied for. My partners being busy, I was deputed to come here and look up the matter. To tell the truth, I was glad of an excuse to see our fair client, or, at least, be disappointed, as my partners have been, in obtaining a glimpse of the mysterious Donna Dolores."

"Ah, my dear Don Arturo," said the Padre, with a slightly deprecatory movement of his brown hands, "I fear you will be no more fortunate than others. It is a penitential week with the poor child, and at such times she refuses to see any one, even on business. Believe me, my dear boy, you, like the others—more than the others—permit your imagination to run away with your judgment. Donna Dolores' concealment of her face is not to heighten or tempt the masculine curiosity, but alas!—poor child—is only to hide the heathenish tattooings that deface her cheek. You know she is a half-breed. Believe me, you are all wrong. It is foolish, perhaps—vanity—who knows? but she is a *woman*—what would you?" continued the sagacious Padre, emphasising the substantive with a slight shrug worthy of his patron saint.

"But they say, for all that, she is very beautiful," continued Arthur, with that mischievousness which was his habitual method of entertaining the earnestness of others, and which he could not entirely forego, even with the Padre.

"So! so! Don Arturo—it is idle gossip!" said Father Felipe, impatiently,—"a brown Indian girl with a cheek as tawny as the summer fields."

Arthur made a grimace that might have been either of assent or deprecation.

"Well, I suppose this means that I am to look over the papers with *you* alone. *Bueno!* Have them out, and let us get over this business as soon as possible."

"*Poco tiempo,*" said Father Felipe, with a smile. Then more gravely, "But what is this? You do not seem to have that interest in your profession that one might expect of the rising young advocate—the junior partner of the great firm you represent. Your heart is not in your work—eh?"

Arthur laughed.

"Why not? It is as good as any."

"But to right the oppressed? To do justice to the unjustly accused, eh? To redress wrongs—ah, my son! *that* is noble. That, Don Arturo—it is *that* has made you and your colleagues dear to me—dear to those who have been the helpless victims of your courts—your *corregidores.*"

"Yes, yes," interrupted Arthur, hastily, shedding the Father's praise with an habitual deft ease that was not so much the result of modesty as a certain conscious pride that resented any imperfect tribute. "Yes, I suppose it pays as well, if not better, in the long run. 'Honesty is the best policy,' as our earliest philosophers say."

"Pardon?" queried the Padre.

Arthur, intensely amused, made a purposely severe and literal translation of Franklin's famous apothegm, and then watched Father Felipe raise his eyes and hands to the ceiling in pious protest and mute consternation.

"And these are your American ethics?" he said at last.

"They are, and in conjunction with manifest destiny, and the star of Empire, they have brought us here, and—have given me the honour of your acquaintance," said Arthur in English.

Father Felipe looked at his friend in hopeless bewilderment. Arthur instantly became respectful and Spanish. To change the subject and relieve the old man's evident embarrassment, he at once plunged into a humorous description of his adventure of the morning. The diversion was only partially successful. Father Felipe became at once interested, but did not laugh. When the young man had concluded he approached him, and laying his soft hand on Arthur's curls, turned his face upward toward him with a parental gesture that was at once habitual and professional, and said—

"Look at me here. I am an old man, Don Arturo. Pardon me if I think I have some advice to give you that may be worthy your hearing. Listen, then! You are one of those men capable of peculiarly affecting and being affected by women. So! Pardon," he continued, gently, as a slight flush rose into Arthur's cheek, despite the smile that came as quickly to his face. "Is it not so? Be not ashamed, Don Arturo! It is not here," he added, with a poetical gesture toward the wall of the refectory, where hung the painted effigy of the blessed St. Anthony; "it is not here that I would undervalue or speak lightly of their influence. The widow is rich, eh?—handsome, eh? impulsive? You have no heart in the profession you have chosen. What then? You have some in the instincts—what shall I say—the accomplishments and graces you have not considered worthy of a practical end! You are a natural lover. Pardon! You have the four S's—'*Sáno, solo, solicito, y secreto.*' Good! Take an old man's advice, and make good use of them. Turn your weaknesses—eh? perhaps it *is* too strong a word!—the frivolities and vanities of your youth into a power for your old age! Eh?"

Arthur smiled a superior smile. He was thinking of the horror with which the old man had received the axiom he had recently quoted. He threw himself back in his chair in an attitude of burlesque sentiment, and said, with simulated heroics—

"But what, O my Father! what if a devoted, exhausting passion for somebody else already filled my heart? You would not advise me to be false to that? Perish the thought!"

Father Felipe did not smile. A peculiar expression passed over his broad, brown, smoothly shaven face, and the habitual look of childlike simplicity and deferential courtesy faded from it. He turned his small black eyes on Arthur, and said—

"Do you think you are capable of such a passion, my son? Have you had an attachment that was superior to novelty or self-interest?"

Arthur rose a little stiffly.

"As we are talking of one of my clients and one of your parishioners, are we not getting a little too serious, Father? At all events, save me from assuming a bashful attitude towards the lady with whom I am to have a business interview to-morrow. And now about the papers, Father," continued Arthur, recovering his former ease. "I suppose the invisible fair one has supplied you with all the necessary documents and the fullest material for a brief. Go on. I am all attention."

"You are wrong again, son," said Father Felipe. "It is a matter in which she has shown even more than her usual disinclination to talk. I believe but for my interference, she would have even refused to press the claim. As it is,

I imagine she wishes to make some compromise with the thief—pardon me !—the what do you say ? eh ? the pre-emptor ! But I have nothing to do with it. All the papers, all the facts are in the possession of your friend, Mrs. Sepulvida. You are to see her. Believe me, my friend, if you have been disappointed in not finding your Indian client, you will have a charming substitute—and one of your own race and colour—in the Donna Maria. Forget, if you can, what I have said—but you will not. Ah, Don Arturo ! I know you better than yourself ! Come. Let us walk in the garden. You have not seen the vines. I have a new variety of grape since you were here before."

"I find nothing better than the old Mission grape, Father," said Arthur, as they passed down the branching avenue of olives.

"Ah ! Yet the aborigines knew it not, and only valued it when found wild, for the colouring matter contained in its skin. From this, with some mordant that still remains a secret with them, they made a dye to stain their bodies and heighten their copper hue. You are not listening, Don Arturo, yet it should interest you, for it is the colour of your mysterious client, the Donna Dolores."

Thus chatting, and pointing out the various objects that might interest Arthur, from the overflowing boughs of a venerable fig tree to the crack made in the adobe wall of the church by the last earthquake, Father Felipe, with characteristic courteous formality, led his young friend through the ancient garden of the Mission. By degrees, the former ease and mutual confidence of the two friends returned, and by the time that Father Felipe excused himself for a few moments to attend to certain domestic arrangements on behalf of his new guest perfect sympathy had been restored.

Left to himself, Arthur strolled back until opposite the

open chancel door of the church. Here he paused, and, in obedience to a sudden impulse, entered. The old church was unchanged—like all things in San Antonio—since the last hundred years; perhaps there was little about it that Arthur had not seen at the other Missions. There were the old rafters painted in barbaric splendour of red and brown stripes; there were the hideous, waxen, glass-eyed saints, leaning forward helplessly and rigidly from their niches; there was the Virgin Mary in a white dress and satin slippers, carrying the infant Saviour in the opulence of lace long-clothes; there was the Magdalen in the fashionable costume of a Spanish lady of the last century. There was the usual quantity of bad pictures; the portrait, full length, of the patron saint himself, so hideously and gratuitously old and ugly that his temptation by any self-respecting woman appeared more miraculous than his resistance; the usual martyrdoms in terrible realism; the usual "Last Judgments" in frightful accuracy of detail.

But there was one picture under the nave which attracted Arthur's listless eyes. It was a fanciful representation of Junipero Serra preaching to the heathen. I am afraid that it was not the figure of that most admirable and heroic missionary which drew Arthur's gaze; I am quite certain that it was not the moral sentiment of the subject, but rather the slim, graceful, girlish, half-nude figure of one of the Indian converts who knelt at Father Junipero Serra's feet, in childlike but touching awe and contrition. There was such a depth of penitential supplication in the young girl's eyes—a penitence so pathetically inconsistent with the absolute virgin innocence and helplessness of the exquisite little figure, that Arthur felt his heart beat quickly as he gazed. He turned quickly to the other picture—look where he would, the eyes of the little acolyte seemed to follow and subdue him.

I think I have already intimated that his was not a reverential nature. With a quick imagination and great poetic sensibility nevertheless, the evident intent of the picture, or even the sentiment of the place, did not touch his heart or brain. But he still half-unconsciously dropped into a seat, and, leaning both arms over the screen before him, bowed his head against the oaken panel. A soft hand laid upon his shoulder suddenly aroused him.

He looked up sharply and met the eyes of the Padre looking down on him with a tenderness that both touched and exasperated him.

"Pardon!" said Padre Felipe, gently. "I have broken in upon your thoughts, child!"

A little more brusquely than was his habit with the Padre, Arthur explained that he had been studying up a difficult case.

"So!" said the Padre, softly, in response. "With tears in your eyes, Don Arturo? Not so!" he added to himself, as he drew the young man's arm in his own and the two passed slowly out once more into the sunlight.

CHAPTER V.

IN WHICH THE DONNA MARIA MAKES AN IMPRESSION.

THE Rancho of the Blessed Fisherman looked seaward as became its title. If the founder of the rancho had shown a religious taste in the selection of the site of the dwelling, his charming widow had certainly shown equal practical taste, and indeed a profitable availing of some advantages that the founder did not contemplate, in the adornment of the house. The low-walled square adobe dwelling had been relieved of much of its hard practical outline by several feminine additions and suggestions. The tiled roof had been carried over a very broad verandah, supported by vine-clad columns, and the lounging corridor had been, in defiance of all Spanish custom, transferred from the inside of the house to the outside. The interior courtyard no longer existed. The sombreness of the heavy Mexican architecture was relieved by bright French chintzes, delicate lace curtains, and fresh-coloured hangings. The broad verandah was filled with the latest novelties of Chinese bamboo chairs and settees, and a striped Venetian awning shaded the glare of the seaward front. Nevertheless, Donna Maria, out of respect to the local opinion, which regarded these changes as ominous of, if not a symbolical putting off the weeds of widowhood, still clung to a few of the local traditions. It is true that a piano occupied one side of her drawing-room, but a harp stood in the corner. If a freshly-cut novel lay open on the piano, a breviary was conspicuous on the marble centre-table. If, on the mantel, an elaborate French clock with bronze shepherdesses trifled with Time, on the wall above it an iron crucifix spoke of Eternity.

Mrs. Sepulvida was at home that morning expecting a guest. She was lying in a Manilla hammock, swung between two posts of the verandah, with her face partially hidden by the netting, and the toe of a little shoe just peeping beyond. Not that Donna Maria expected to receive her guest thus ; on the contrary, she had given orders to her servants that the moment a stranger *caballero* appeared on the road she was to be apprised of the fact. For I grieve to say that, far from taking Arthur's advice, the details of the adventure at the Point of Pines had been imparted by her own lips to most of her female friends, and even to the domestics of her household. In the earlier stages of a woman's interest in a man she is apt to be exceedingly communicative ; it is only when she becomes fully aware of the gravity of the stake involved that she begins to hedge before the public. The morning after her adventure Donna Maria was innocently full of its hero and unreservedly voluble.

I have forgotten whether I have described her. Certainly I could not have a better opportunity than the present. In the hammock she looked a little smaller, as women are apt to when their length is rigidly defined. She had the average quantity of brown hair, a little badly treated by her habit of wearing it flat over her temples—a tradition of her boarding-school days, fifteen years ago. She had soft brown eyes, with a slight redness of the eyelid not inconsistent nor entirely unbecoming to widowhood; a small mouth depressed at the corners with a charming, childlike discontent; white regular teeth, and the eloquence of a complexion that followed unvaryingly the spirits of her physical condition. She appeared to be about thirty, and had that unmistakable "married" look which even the most amiable and considerate of us, my dear sir, are apt to impress upon the one woman whom we choose to elect to years of exclusive intimacy and attention. The late Don José Sepulvida's private mark—as well defined as the brand upon his cattle—was a certain rigid line, like a grave accent, from the angle of this little woman's nostril to the corners of her mouth, and possibly to an increased peevishness of depression at those corners. It bore witness to the fondness of the deceased for bear-baiting and bull-fighting, and a possible weakness for a certain Señora X. of San Francisco, whose reputation was none of the best, and was not increased by her distance from San Antonio and the surveillance of Donna Maria.

When an hour later "Pepe" appeared to his mistress, bearing a salver with Arthur Poinsett's business card and a formal request for an interview, I am afraid Donna Maria was a little disappointed. If he had suddenly scaled the verandah, evaded her servants, and appeared before her in an impulsive, forgivable way, it would have seemed consistent with his character as a hero, and perhaps more in keeping with the general tenor of her reveries when the servitor entered. Howbeit, after heaving an impatient little sigh, and bidding "Pepe" show the gentleman into the drawing-room, she slipped quietly down from the hammock in a deft womanish way, and whisked herself into her dressing-room.

"He couldn't have been more formal if Don José had been alive," she said to herself as she walked to her glass and dressing-table.

Arthur Poinsett entered the vacant drawing-room not in the best of his many humours. He had read in the eyes of the lounging *vaqueros*, in the covert glances of the women servants, that the story of his adventure was known to the household. Habitually petted and spoiled as he had been by the women of his acquaintance, he was half inclined to attribute this reference and assignment of his client's business to the hands of Mrs. Sepulvida, as the result of a plan of Father Felipe's, or absolute collusion between the parties. A little sore yet, and irritated by his recollection of the Padre's counsel, and more impatient of the imputation of a weakness than anything else, Arthur had resolved to limit the interview to the practical business on hand, and in so doing had, for a moment, I fear, forgotten his native courtesy. It did not tend to lessen his irritation and self-consciousness when Mrs. Sepulvida entered the room without the slightest evidence of her recent disappointment visible in her perfectly easy, frank self-possession, and after a conventional, half Spanish solicitousness regarding his health since their last interview, without any further allusions to their adventure, begged him to be seated. She herself took an easy chair on the opposite side of the table, and assumed at once an air of respectful but somewhat indifferent attention.

"I believe," said Arthur, plunging at once into his subject to get rid of his embarrassment and the slight instinct of antagonism he was beginning to feel toward the woman before him, "I believe—that is, I am told—that besides your own business, you are intrusted with some documents and facts regarding a claim of the Donna Dolores Salvatierra. Which shall we have first? I am entirely at your service for the next two hours, but we shall proceed faster and with less confusion by taking up one thing at a time."

"Then let us begin with Donna Dolores, by all means," said Donna Maria; "my own affairs can wait. Indeed," she added, languidly, "I daresay one of your clerks could attend to it as well as yourself. If your time is valuable—as indeed it must be—I can put the papers in his hands and make him listen to all my foolish, irrelevant talk. He can sift it for you, Don Arturo. I really am a child about business, really."

Arthur smiled, and made a slight gesture of deprecation. In spite of his previous resolution, Donna Maria's tone of slight pique pleased him. Yet he gravely opened his notebook, and took up his pencil without a word. Donna Maria observed the movements, and said more seriously—

"Ah yes! how foolish! Here I am talking about my own affairs, when I should be speaking of Donna Dolores! Well, to begin. Let me first explain why she has put this matter in my hands. My husband and her father were friends, and had many business interests in common. As you have doubtless heard, she has always been very quiet, very reserved, very religious—almost a nun. I daresay she was driven into this isolation by reason of the delicacy of her position here, for you know—do you not?—that her mother was an Indian. It is only a few years ago that the old Governor, becoming a widower and childless, bethought himself of this Indian child, Dolores. He found the mother dead, and the girl living somewhere at a distant Mission as an acolyte. He brought her to San Antonio, had her christened, and made legally his daughter and heiress. She was a mere slip of a thing, about fourteen or fifteen. She might have had a pretty complexion, for some of these half-breeds are nearly white, but she had been stained when an infant with some barbarous and indelible dye, after the savage custom of her race. She is now a light copper colour, not unlike those bronze shepherdesses on yonder clock. In spite of all this I call her pretty. Perhaps it is because I love her and am prejudiced. But you gentlemen are so critical about complexion and colour—no wonder that the poor child refuses to see anybody, and never goes into society at all. It is a shame! But—pardon, Mr. Poinsett, here am I gossiping about your client's looks, when I should be stating her grievances."

"No, no!" said Arthur, hastily, "go on—in your own way."

Mrs Sepulvida lifted her forefinger archly.

"Ah! is it so, Don Arturo? I thought so! Well, it is a great shame that she is not here for you to judge for yourself."

Angry with himself for his embarrassment, and for the rising colour on his cheek, Arthur would have explained himself, but the lady, with feminine tact, did not permit him.

"To proceed: Partly because I did not participate in the prejudices with which the old families here regarded her race and colour, partly, perhaps, because we were both strangers here, we became friends. At first she resisted all my advances—indeed, I think she was more shy of me than the others, but I triumphed in time, and we became good friends. Friends, you understand, Mr. Poinsett, not *confidants*. You men, I know, deem this impossible, but Donna

Dolores is a singular girl, and I have never, except upon the most general topics, won her from her habitual reserve. And I possess perhaps her only friendship."

"Except Father Felipe, her confessor?"

Mrs. Sepulvida shrugged her shoulders, and then borrowed the habitual sceptical formula of San Antonio.

"*Quien sabe?* But I am rambling again. Now for the case."

She rose, and taking from the drawer of the secretary an envelope, drew out some papers it contained, and referred to them as she went on.

"It appears that a grant of Micheltorena to Salvatierra was discovered recently at Monterey, a grant of which there was no record among Salvatierra's papers. The explanation given is that it was placed some five years ago in trust with a Don Pedro Ruiz, of San Francisco, as security for a lease now expired. The grant is apparently regular, properly witnessed, and attested. Don Pedro has written that some of the witnesses are still alive, and remember it."

"Then why not make the proper application for a patent?"

"True, but if that were all, Don Arturo would not have been summoned from San Francisco for consultation. There is something else. Don Pedro writes that another grant for the same land has been discovered recorded to another party."

"That is, I am sorry to say, not a singular experience in our profession," said Arthur, with a smile. "But Salvatierra's known reputation and probity would probably be sufficient to outweigh equal documentary evidence on the other side. It's unfortunate he's dead, and the grant was discovered after his death."

"But the holder of the other grant is dead too!" said the widow.

"That makes it about equal again. But who is he?"

Mrs. Sepulvida referred to her papers, and then said—

"Dr. Devarges."

"Who?"

"Devarges," said Mrs. Sepulvida, referring to her notes. "A singular name—a foreigner, I suppose. No, really Mr. Poinsett, you shall not look at the paper until I have copied it—it's written horribly—you can't understand it! I'm really ashamed of my writing, but I was in such a hurry, expecting you every moment! Why, la! Mr. Poinsett, how cold your hands are!"

Arthur Poinsett had risen hurriedly, and reached out almost brusquely for the paper that she held. But the widow had coquettishly resisted him with a mischievous show of force, and had caught and—dropped his hand!

"And you are pale, too. Dear me! I'm afraid you took cold that morning," said Mrs. Sepulvida. "I should never forgive myself if you did. I should cry my eyes out!" and Donna Maria cast a dangerous look from under her slightly swollen lids that looked as if they might threaten a deluge.

"Nothing, nothing, I have ridden far this morning, and rose early," said Arthur, chafing his hands with a slightly embarrassed smile. "But I interrupted you. Pray go on. Has Dr. Devarges any heirs to contest the grant?"

But the widow did not seem inclined to go on. She was positive that Arthur wanted some wine. Would he not let her order some slight repast before they proceeded further in this horrid business? She was tired. She was quite sure that Arthur must be so too.

"It is my business," said Arthur, a little stiffly, but, recovering himself again in a sudden and new alarm of the widow, he smiled and suggested the sooner the business was over, the sooner he would be able to partake of her hospitality.

The widow beamed prospectively.

"There are no heirs that we can find. But there is a—what do you call it?—a something or other—in possession!"

"A squatter?" said Poinsett, shortly.

"Yes," continued the widow, with a light laugh; "a 'squatter,' by the name of—of—my writing is so horrid—let me see, oh, yes! 'Gabriel Conroy.'"

Arthur made an involuntary gesture toward the paper with his hand, but the widow mischievously skipped toward the window, and, luckily for the spectacle of his bloodless face, held the paper before her dimpled face and laughing eyes, as she did so.

"Gabriel Conroy," repeated Mrs. Sepulvida, "and—and—and—his"——

"His sister?" said Arthur, with an effort.

"No, sir!" responded Mrs. Sepulvida, with a slight pout, "his *wife!* Sister indeed! As if we married women are always to be ignored by you legal gentlemen!"

Arthur remained silent, with his face turned toward the sea. When he did speak his voice was quite natural.

"Might I change my mind regarding your offer of a moment ago, and take a glass of wine and a biscuit now?"

Mrs. Sepulvida ran to the door.

"Let me look over your notes while you are gone," said Arthur.

"You won't laugh at my writing?"

"No!"

Donna Maria tossed him the envelope gaily and flew out of the room. Arthur hurried to the window with the coveted memoranda. There were the names she had given him—but nothing more! At least this was some slight relief.

The suddenness of the shock, rather than any moral sentiment or fear, had upset him. Like most imaginative men, he was a trifle superstitious, and with the first mention of Devarges's name came a swift recollection of Padre Felipe's analysis of his own character, his sad, ominous reverie in the chapel, the trifling circumstance that brought him instead of his partner to San Antonio, and the remoter chance that had discovered the forgotten grant and selected him to prosecute its recovery. This conviction entertained and forgotten, all the resources of his combative nature returned. Of course he could not prosecute this claim ; of course he ought to prevent others from doing it. There was every probability that the grant of Devarges was a true one—and Gabriel was in possession! Had he really become Devarges's heir, and if so, why had he not claimed the grant boldly? And where was Grace?

In this last question there was a slight tinge of sentimental recollection, but no remorse or shame. That he might in some way be of service to her, he fervently hoped. That, time having blotted out the romantic quality of their early acquaintance, there would really be something fine and loyal in so doing, he did not for a moment doubt. He would suggest a compromise to his fair client, himself seek out and confer with Grace and Gabriel, and all should be made right. His nervousness and his agitation was, he was satisfied, only the result of a conscientiousness and a delicately honourable nature, perhaps too fine and spiritual for the exigencies of his profession. Of one thing he was convinced: he really ought to carefully consider Father Felipe's advice; he ought to put himself beyond the reach of these romantic relapses.

In this self-sustained, self-satisfied mood, Mrs. Sepulvida found him on her return. Since she had been gone, he said, he had been able to see his way quite clearly into this case, and he had no doubt his perspicacity was greatly aided by the admirable manner in which she had indicated the various points on the paper she had given him. He was now ready to take up her own matters, only he begged as clear and concise a brief as she had already made for her friend. He was so cheerful and gallant that by the time luncheon was announced the widow found him quite charming, and was inclined to forgive him for the disappointment of the morning. And when, after luncheon, he challenged her to a sharp canter with him along the beach, by way, as he said, of keeping her memory from taking cold, and to satisfy herself that the Point of Pines could be doubled without going out to sea, I fear that, without a prudent consideration of the gossips of San Antonio before her eyes, she assented. There could be no harm in riding with her late husband's legal adviser, who had called, as everybody knew, on business, and whose time was so precious that he must return even before the business was concluded. And then "Pepe" could follow them, to return with her!

It did not, of course, occur to either Arthur or Donna Maria that they might outrun "Pepe," who was fat and indisposed to violent exertion; nor that they should find other things to talk about than the details of business; nor that the afternoon should be so marvellously beautiful as to cause them to frequently stop and admire the stretch of glittering sea beyond; nor that the roar of the waves was so deafening as to oblige them to keep so near each other for the purposes of conversation that the widow's soft breath was continually upon Arthur's cheek; nor that Donna Maria's saddle girth should become so loose that she was forced to dismount while Arthur tightened it, and that he should be obliged to lift her in his arms to restore her to her seat again. But finally, when the Point of Pines was safely rounded, and Arthur was delivering a few parting words of legal counsel, holding one of her hands in his, while with the other he was untwisting a long tress of her blown down hair, that, after buffeting his check into colour, had suddenly twined itself around his neck, an old-fashioned family carriage, drawn by four black mules with silver harness, passed them suddenly on the road.

Donna Maria drew her head and her hand away with a quick blush and laugh, and then gaily kissed her finger-tips to the retreating carriage. Arthur laughed also—but a little foolishly—and looked as if expecting some explanation.

"You should have your wits about you, sir. Did you know who that was?"

Arthur sincerely confessed ignorance. He had not noticed the carriage until it had passed.

"Think what you have lost! That was your fair young client."

"I did not even see her," laughed Arthur.

"But she saw you! She never took her eyes off you. Adios!"

CHAPTER VI.

THE LADY OF GRIEF.

"You will not go to-day," said Father Felipe to Arthur, as he entered the Mission refectory early the next morning to breakfast.

"I shall be on the road in an hour, Father," replied Arthur, gaily.

"But not toward San Francisco," said the Padre. "Listen! Your wish of yesterday has been attained. You are to have your desired interview with the fair invisible. Do you comprehend? Donna Dolores has sent for you."

Arthur looked up in surprise. Perhaps his face did not express as much pleasure as Father Felipe expected, who lifted his eyes to the ceiling, took a philosophical pinch of snuff, and muttered—

"*Ah, lo que es el mudo!*—Now that he has his wish—it is nothing, Mother of God!"

"This is *your* kindness, Father."

"God forbid!" returned Padre Felipe, hastily. "Believe me, my son, I know nothing. When the Donna left here before the *Angelus* yesterday, she said nothing of this. Perhaps it is the office of your friend, Mrs. Sepulvida."

"Hardly, I think," said Arthur; "she was so well prepared with all the facts as to render an interview with Donna Dolores unnecessary. *Bueno*, be it so! I will go."

Nevertheless, he was ill at ease. He ate little, he was silent. All the fears he had argued away with such self-satisfied logic the day before, returned to him again with greater anxiety. Could there have been any further facts regarding this inopportune grant that Mrs. Sepulvida had not disclosed? Was there any particular reason why this strange recluse, who had hitherto avoided his necessary professional presence, should now desire a personal interview which was not apparently necessary? Could it be possible that communication had already been established with Gabriel or Grace, and that the history of their previous life had become known to his client? Had his connexion with it been in any way revealed to the Donna Dolores?

If he had been able to contemplate this last possibility with calmness and courage yesterday when Mrs. Sepulvida first repeated the name of Gabriel Conroy, was he capable of equal resignation now? Had anything occurred since then?—had any new resolution entered his head to which such a revelation would be fatal? Nonsense! And yet he could not help commenting, with more or less vague uneasiness of mind, on his chance meeting of Donna Dolores at the Point of Pines yesterday and the summons of this morning. Would not his foolish attitude with Donna Maria, aided, perhaps, by some indiscreet expression from the well-meaning but senile Padre Felipe, be sufficient to exasperate his fair client had she been cognizant of his first relations with Grace? It is not mean natures alone that are the most suspicious. A quick, generous imagination, feverishly excited, will project theories of character and intention far more ridiculous and uncomplimentary to humanity than the lowest surmises of ignorance and imbecility. Arthur was feverish and excited; with all the instincts of a contradictory nature, his easy sentimentalism dreaded, while his combative principles longed for, this interview. Within an hour of the time appointed by Donna Dolores, he had thrown himself on his horse, and was galloping furiously toward the "Rancho of the Holy Trinity."

It was inland and three leagues away under the foot-hills. But as he entered upon the level plain, unrelieved by any watercourse; and baked and cracked by the fierce sun into narrow gaping chasms and yawning fissures, he unconsciously began to slacken his pace. Nothing could be more dreary, passionless, and resigned than the vast, sunlit, yet joyless waste. It seemed as if it might be some illimitable, desolate sea, beaten flat by the north-westerly gales that spent their impotent fury on its unopposing levels. As far as the eye could reach, its dead monotony was unbroken; even the black cattle that in the clear distance seemed to crawl over its surface, did not animate it; rather by contrast brought into relief its fixed rigidity of outline. Neither wind, sky, nor sun wrought any change over its blank, expressionless face. It was the symbol of Patience—a hopeless, weary, helpless patience—but a patience that was Eternal.

He had ridden for nearly an hour, when suddenly there seemed to spring up from the earth, a mile away, a dark line of wall, terminating in an irregular, broken outline against the sky. His first impression was that it was the *valda* or a break of the stiff skirt of the mountain as it struck the level plain. But he presently saw the dull red of tiled roofs over the dark adobe wall, and as he dashed down into the dry bed of a vanished stream and up again on the opposite bank, he passed the low walls of a *corral*, until then unnoticed, and a few crows, in a rusty, half-Spanish, half-clerical suit, uttered a croaking welcome to the Rancho of the Holy Trinity, as they rose from the ground before him. It was the first sound that for an hour had interrupted the monotonous jingle of his spurs or the hollow beat of his horse's hoofs. And then, after the fashion of the country, he rose slightly in his stirrups, dashed his spurs into the sides of his mustang, swung the long, horsehair, braided thong of his bridle-rein, and charged at headlong speed upon the dozen lounging, apparently listless *vaqueros*, who, for the past hour, had nevertheless been watching and waiting for him at the courtyard gate. As he rode toward them, they separated, drew up each side of the gate, doffed their glazed, stiff-brimmed, black *sombreros*, wheeled, put spurs to their horses, and in another instant were scattered to the four winds. When Arthur leaped to the brick pavement of the courtyard, there was not one in sight.

An Indian servant noiselessly led away his horse. Another *peon* as mutely led the way along a corridor over whose low railings *serapes* and saddle blankets were hung in a barbaric confusion of colouring, and entered a bare-walled ante-room, where another Indian—old, grey-headed, with a face like a wrinkled tobacco leaf—was seated on a low wooden settle in an attitude of patient expectancy. To Arthur's active fancy he seemed to have been sitting there since the establishment of the Mission, and to have grown grey in waiting for him. As Arthur entered he rose, and with a few grave Spanish courtesies, ushered him into a larger and more elaborately furnished apartment, and again retired with a bow. Familiar as Arthur was with these various formalities, at present they seemed to have an undue significance, and he turned somewhat impatiently as a door opened at the other end of the apartment. At the same moment a subtle strange perfume—not unlike some barbaric spice or odorous Indian herb—stole through the door, and an old woman, brown-faced, murky-eyed, and decrepit, entered with a respectful curtsey.

"It is Don Arturo Poinsett?" Arthur bowed.

"The Donna Dolores has a little indisposition, and claims your indulgence if she receives you in her own room."

Arthur bowed assent.

"*Bueno!* This way."

She pointed to the open door. Arthur entered by a narrow passage cut through the thickness of the adobe wall into another room beyond, and paused on the threshold.

Even the gradual change from the glaring sunshine of the courtyard to the heavy shadows of the two rooms he had passed through was not sufficient to accustom his eyes to the twilight of the apartment he now entered. For several seconds he could not distinguish anything but a few dimly outlined objects. By degrees he saw that there were a bed, a *prie-dieu*, and a sofa against the opposite wall. The scant light of two windows—mere longitudinal slits in the deep walls—at first permitted him only this. Later he saw that the sofa was occupied by a half-reclining figure, whose face was partly hidden by a fan, and the white folds of whose skirt fell in graceful curves to the floor.

"You speak Spanish, Don Arturo?" said an exquisitely modulated voice from behind the fan, in perfect Castilian.

Arthur turned quickly toward the voice with an indescribable thrill of pleasure in his nerves.

"A little."

He was usually rather proud of his Spanish, but for once the conventional polite disclaimer was quite sincere.

"Be seated, Don Arturo!"

He advanced to a chair indicated by the old woman within a few feet of the sofa and sat down. At the same instant the reclining figure, by a quick, dexterous movement, folded the large black fan that had partly hidden her features, and turned her face toward him.

Arthur's heart leaped with a sudden throb, and then, as it seemed to him, for a few seconds stopped beating. The eyes that met his were large, lustrous, and singularly beautiful; the features were small, European, and perfectly modelled; the outline of the small face was a perfect oval, but the complexion was of burnished copper! Yet even the next moment he found himself halting among a dozen comparisons—a golden sherry, a faintly dyed meerschaum, an autumn leaf, the inner bark of the *madroño*. Of only one thing was he certain—she was the most beautiful woman he had ever seen!

It is possible that the Donna read this in his eyes, for she opened her fan again quietly, and raised it slowly before her face. Arthur's eager glance swept down the long curves of her graceful figure to the little foot in the white satin slipper below. Yet her quaint dress, except for its colour, might have been taken for a religious habit, and had a hood or cape descending over her shoulders not unlike a nun's.

"You have surprise, Don Arturo," she said, after a pause, "that I have sent for you, after having before consulted you by proxy. Good! But I have changed my mind since then! I have concluded to take no steps for the present toward perfecting the grant."

In an instant Arthur was himself again—and completely

on his guard. The Donna's few words had recalled the past that he had been rapidly forgetting; even the perfectly delicious cadence of the tones in which it was uttered had now no power to fascinate him or lull his nervous anxiety. He felt a presentiment that the worst was coming. He turned toward her, outwardly calm, but alert, eager, and watchful.

"Have you any newly discovered evidence that makes the issue doubtful?" he asked.

"No," said Donna Dolores.

"Is there anything?—any fact that Mrs. Sepulvida has forgotten?" continued Arthur. "Here are, I believe, the points she gave me," he added, and, with the habit of a well-trained intelligence, he put before Donna Dolores, in a few well-chosen words, the substance of Mrs. Sepulvida's story. Nor did his manner in the least betray a fact of which he was perpetually cognisant—namely, that his fair client, between the sticks of her fan, was studying his face with more than feminine curiosity. When he paused she said—

"*Bueno!* That is what I told her."

"Is there anything more?"—"Perhaps!"

Arthur folded his arms and looked attentive. Donna Dolores began to go over the sticks of her fan one by one, as if it were a rosary.

"I have become acquainted with some facts in this case which may not interest you as a lawyer, Don Arturo, but which affect me as a woman. When I have told you them, you will tell me—who knows?—that they do not alter the legal aspect of my—my father's claim. You will perhaps laugh at me for my resolution. But I have given you so much trouble, that it is only fair you should know it is not merely caprice that governs me—that you should know why your visit here is a barren one; why you—the great advocate—have been obliged to waste your valuable time with my poor friend, Donna Maria, for nothing."

Arthur was too much pre-occupied to notice the peculiarly feminine significance with which the Donna dwelt upon this latter sentence—a fact that would not otherwise have escaped his keen observation. He slightly stroked his brown moustache, and looked out of the window with masculine patience.

"It is not caprice, Don Arturo. But I am a woman and an orphan! You know my history! The only friend I had has left me here alone the custodian of these vast estates. Listen to me, Don Arturo, and you will understand, or at least forgive, my foolish interest in the people who contest this claim. For what has happened to them, to *her*, might have happened to me, but for the blessed Virgin's mediation."

"To *her*—who is *she?*" asked Arthur, quietly.

"Pardon! I had forgotten you do not know. Listen. You have heard that this grant is occupied by a man and his wife—a certain Gabriel Conroy. Good! You have heard that they have made no claim to a legal title to the land, except through pre-emption. Good. That is not true, Don Arturo!"

Arthur turned to her in undisguised surprise.

"This is new matter; this *is* a legal point of some importance."

"Who knows?" said Donna Dolores, indifferently. "It is not in regard of that that I speak. The claim is this. The Dr. Devarges, who also possesses a grant for the same land, made a gift of it to the sister of this Gabriel. Do you comprehend?" She paused, and fixed her eyes on Arthur.

"Perfectly," said Arthur, with his gaze still fixed on the window; "it accounts for the presence of this Gabriel on the land. But is she living? Or, if not, is he her legally constituted heir? That is the question, and—pardon me if I suggest again—a purely legal and not a sentimental question. Was this woman who has disappeared—this sister—this sole and only legatee—a married woman—had she a child? Because that is the heir."

The silence that followed this question was so protracted that Arthur turned towards Donna Dolores. She had apparently made some sign to her aged waiting-woman, who was bending over her, between Arthur and the sofa. In a moment, however, the venerable handmaid withdrew, leaving them alone.

"You are right, Don Arturo," continued Donna Dolores, behind her fan. "You see that, after all, your advice is necessary, and what I began as an explanation of my folly may be of business importance; who knows? It is good of you to recall me to that. We women are foolish. You are sagacious and prudent. It was well that I saw you!"

Arthur nodded assent, and resumed his professional attitude of patient toleration—that attitude which the world over has been at once the exasperation and awful admiration of the largely injured client.

"And the sister, the real heiress, is gone—disappeared! No one knows where! All trace of her is lost. But now comes to the surface an impostor! a woman who assumes the character and name of Grace Conroy, the sister!"

"One moment," said Arthur, quietly, "how do you know that it is an impostor?"

"How—do—I—know—it?"

"Yes, what are the proofs?"

"I am told so!"

"Oh!" said Arthur, relapsing into his professional attitude again.

"Proofs," repeated Donna Dolores, hurriedly. "Is it not enough that she has married this Gabriel, her brother?"

"That is certainly strong moral proof—and perhaps legal corroborative evidence," said Arthur, coolly; "but it will not legally estop her proving that she is his sister—if she can do so. But I ask your pardon—go on!"

"That is all," said Donna Dolores, sitting up, with a slight gesture of impatience.

"Very well. Then, as I understand, the case is simply this: You hold a grant to a piece of land, actually possessed by a squatter, who claims it through his wife or sister—legally it doesn't matter which—by virtue of a bequest made by one Dr. Devarges, who also held a grant to the same property?"

"Yes," said Donna Dolores, hesitatingly.

"Well, the matter lies between you and Dr. Devarges only. It is simply a question of the validity of the original grants. All that you have told me does not alter that radical fact. Stay! One moment! May I ask how you have acquired these later details?"

"By letter."

"From whom?"

"There was no signature. The writer offered to prove all he said. It was anonymous."

Arthur rose with a superior smile.

"May I ask you further, without impertinence, if it is upon this evidence that you propose to abandon your claim to a valuable property?"

"I have told you before that it is not a legal question, Don Arturo," said Donna Dolores, waving her fan a little more rapidly.

"Good! let us take it in the moral or sentimental aspect—since you have purposed to honour me with a request for my counsel. To begin, you have a sympathy for the orphan, who does not apparently exist."

"But her brother?"

"Has already struck hands with the impostor, and married her to secure the claim. And this brother—what proof is there that he is not an impostor too?"

"True," said Donna Dolores, musingly.

"He will certainly have to settle that trifling question with Dr. Devarges's heirs, whoever they may be."

"True," said Donna Dolores.

"In short, I see no reason, even from your own view-point, why you should not fight this claim. The orphan you sympathise with is not an active party. You have only a brother opposed to you, who seems to have been willing to barter away a sister's birthright. And, as I said before, your sympathies, however kind and commendable they may be, will be of no avail unless the courts decide against Dr. Devarges. My advice is to fight. If the right does not always succeed, my experience is that the Right, at least, is apt to play its best card, and put forward its best skill. And until it does that, it might as well be the Wrong, you know."

"You are wise, Don Arturo. But you lawyers are so often only advocates. Pardon, I mean no wrong. But if it were Grace—the sister, you understand—what would be your advice?

"The same. Fight it out! If I could overthrow your grant, I should do it. The struggle, understand me, is there, and not with this wife and sister. But how does it come that a patent for this has not been applied for before by Gabriel? Did your anonymous correspondent explain that fact? It is a point in our favour."

"You forget—*our* grant was only recently discovered."

"True! it is about equal, then, *ab initio.* And the absence of this actual legatee is in our favour."

"Why?"

"Because there is a certain human sympathy in juries with a pretty orphan—particularly if poor."

"How do you know she was pretty?" asked Donna Dolores, quickly.

"I presume so. It is the privilege of orphanage," he said, with a bow of cold gallantry.

"You are wise, Don Arturo. May you live a thousand years."

This time it was impossible but Arthur should notice the irony of Donna Dolores's manner. All his strong combative instincts rose. The mysterious power of her beauty, which he could not help acknowledging, her tone of superiority, whether attributable to a consciousness of this power over him, or some knowledge of his past—all aroused his cold pride. He remembered the reputation that Donna Dolores bore as a religious devotee and rigid moralist. If he had been taxed with his abandonment of Grace, with his half-formed designs upon Mrs. Sepulvida, he would have coldly admitted them without excuse or argument. In doing so, he would have been perfectly conscious that he should lose the esteem of Donna Dolores, of whose value he had become, within the last few moments, equally conscious. But it was a part of this young man's singular nature that he would have experienced a certain self-satisfaction in the act, that would have outweighed all other considerations. In the ethics of his own consciousness he called this "being true to himself." In a certain sense he was right.

He rose, and, standing respectfully before his fair client, said—

"Have you decided fully? Do I understand that I am to press this claim with a view of ousting these parties? or will you leave them for the present in undisturbed possession of the land?"

"But what do *you* say?" continued Donna Dolores, with her eyes fixed upon his face.

"I have said already," returned Arthur, with a patient smile. "Morally and legally, my advice is to press the claim!"

Donna Dolores turned her eyes away with the slightest shade of annoyance.

"*Bueno!* We shall see. There is time enough. Be seated, Don Arturo. What is this? Surely you will not refuse our hospitality to-night?"

"I fear," said Arthur, with grave politeness, "that I must return to the Mission at once. I have already delayed my departure a day. They expect me in San Francisco to-morrow."

"Let them wait. You shall write that important business keeps you here, and Diego shall ride my own horse to reach the *embarcadero* for the steamer to-night. To-morrow he will be in San Francisco."

Before he could stay her hand she had rung a small bronze bell that stood beside her.

"But, Donna Dolores" —— Arthur began, hastily.

"I understand," interrupted Donna Dolores. "Diego," she continued rapidly, as a servant entered the room, "saddle Jovita instantly and make ready for a journey. Then return here. Pardon!" she turned to Arthur. "You would say your time is valuable. A large sum depends upon your presence! Good! Write to your partners that I will pay all—that no one else can afford to give as large a sum for your services as myself. Write that here you must stay."

Annoyed and insulted as Arthur felt, he could not help gazing upon her with an admiring fascination. The imperious habit of command; an almost despotic control of a hundred servants; a certain barbaric contempt for the unlimited revenues at her disposal that prompted the act, became her wonderfully. In her impatience the quick blood glanced through her bronzed cheek, her little slipper tapped the floor imperiously, and her eyes flashed in the darkness. Suddenly she stopped, looked at Arthur, and hesitated.

"Pardon me; I have done wrong. Forgive me, Don Arturo. I am a spoiled woman who for five years has had her own way. I am apt to forget there is any world beyond my little kingdom here. Go, since it must be so, go at once."

She sank back on the sofa, half veiled her face with her fan, and dropped the long fringes of her eyes with a deprecating and half languid movement.

Arthur stood for a moment irresolute and hesitating, but only for a moment.

"Let me thank you for enabling me to fulfil a duty without foregoing a pleasure. If your messenger is trustworthy and fleet it can be done. I will stay."

She turned towards him suddenly and smiled. A smile apparently so rare to that proud little mouth and those dark, melancholy eyes; a smile that disclosed the smallest and whitest of teeth in such dazzling contrast to the shadow of her face; a smile that even after its brightness had passed still left its memory in a dimple in either nut-brown cheek, and a glistening moisture in the dark eyes—that Arthur felt the warm blood rise to his face.

"There are writing materials in the other room. Diego will find you there," said Donna Dolores, "and I will rejoin you soon. Thanks."

She held out the smallest and brownest of hands. Arthur bent over it for a single moment, and then withdrew with a quickened pulse to the outer room. As the door closed upon him, Donna Dolores folded her fan, threw herself back upon the sofa, and called, in a quick whisper—

"Manuela!"

The old woman reappeared with an anxious face and ran towards the sofa. But she was too late; her mistress had fainted.

CHAPTER VII.

A LEAF OUT OF THE PAST.

ARTHUR'S letter to his partners was a brief explanation of his delay, and closed with the following sentence—

"Search the records for any deed or transfer of the grant from Dr. Devarges."

He had scarcely concluded before Diego entered ready for the journey. When he had gone, Arthur waited with some impatience the reappearance of Donna Dolores. To his disappointment, however, only the solemn major-domo strode grimly into the room like a dark-complexioned ghost, and, as it seemed to Arthur, with a strong suggestion of the Commander in "Don Giovanni" in his manner, silently beckoned him to follow to the apartment set aside for his reception. In keeping with the sun-evading instincts of Spanish Californian architecture the room was long, low, and half lighted; the two barred windows on either side of the doorway gave upon the corridor and courtyard below; the opposite wall held only a small narrow, deeply-embrasured loop-hole, through which Arthur could see the vast, glittering, sun-illumined plain beyond. The hard, monotonous, unwinking glare without did not penetrate the monastic gloom of this chamber; even the insane, incessant restlessness of the wind that perpetually beset the bleak walls was unheard and unfelt in the grave, contemplative solitude of this religious cell.

Mingled with this grateful asceticism was the quaint contrast of a peculiar Spanish luxuriousness. In a curtained recess an immense mahogany bedstead displayed a yellow satin coverlet profusely embroidered with pink and purple silk flowers. The borders of the sheets and cases of the satin pillows were deeply edged with the finest lace. Beside the bed and before a large armchair heavy rugs of barbaric colours covered the dark wooden floor, and in front of the deep oven-like hearth lay an immense bear-skin. About the hearth hung an ebony and gold crucifix, and, mingled with a few modern engravings, the usual Catholic saints and martyrs occupied the walls. It struck Arthur's observation oddly that the subjects of the secular engravings were snow landscapes. The Hospice of St. Bernard in winter, a pass in the Austrian Tyrol, the Steppes of Russia, a Norwegian plain, all to Arthur's fancy brought the temperature of the room down considerably. A small water-colour of an Alpine flower touched him so closely that it might have blossomed from his recollection.

Dinner, which was prefaced by a message from Donna Dolores excusing herself through indisposition, was served in solemn silence. A cousin of the late Don José Salvatierra represented the family, and pervaded the meal with a mild flavour of stale cigaritos and dignified criticism of remote events. Arthur, disappointed at the absence of the Donna, found himself regarding this gentleman with some degree of asperity, and a disposition to resent any reference to his client's business as an unwarrantable impertinence. But when the dinner was over, and he had smoked a cigar on the corridor without further communication with Donna Dolores, he began to be angry with himself for accepting her invitation, and savagely critical of the motives that impelled him to it. He was meditating an early retreat—even a visit to Mrs. Sepulvida—when Manuela entered.

Would Don Arturo grant the Donna his further counsel and presence?

Don Arturo was conscious that his cheek was flushing, and that his counsel at the present moment would not have been eminently remarkable for coolness or judiciousness, but he followed the Indian woman with a slight inclination of the head. They entered the room where he had first met the Donna. She might not have moved from the position she had occupied that morning on the couch, so like was her attitude and manner. As he approached her respectfully, he was conscious of the same fragrance, and the same mysterious magnetism that seemed to leap from her dark eyes, and draw his own resisting and unwilling gaze toward her.

"You will despise me, Don Arturo—you, whose country-women are so strong and active—because I am so little and weak, and,—Mother of God!—so lazy! But I am an invalid, and am not yet quite recovered. But then I am accustomed to it. I have lain here for days, Don Arturo, doing nothing. It is weary—eh? You think? This watching, this waiting!—day after day—always the same!"

There was something so delicately plaintive and tender in the cadence of her speech—a cadence that might, perhaps, have been attributed to the characteristic intonation of the Castilian feminine speech, but which Arthur could not help thinking was peculiar to herself, that at the moment he dared not lift his eyes to her, although he was conscious she was looking at him. But by an impulse of safety he addressed himself to the fan.

"You have been an invalid then—Donna Dolores?"

"A sufferer, Don Arturo."

"Have you ever tried the benefit of change of scene—of habits of life? Your ample means, your freedom from the cares of family or kinship, offer you such opportunities," he continued, still addressing the fan.

But the fan, as if magnetised by his gaze, became coquettishly conscious; fluttered, faltered, drooped, and then languidly folded its wings. Arthur was left helpless.

"Perhaps," said Donna Dolores: "who knows?"

She paused for an instant, and then made a sign to Manuela. The Indian woman rose and left the room.

"I have something to tell you, Don Arturo," she continued, "something I should have told you this morning. It is not too late now. But it is a secret. It is only that I have questioned my right to tell it—not that I have doubted your honour, Don Arturo, that I withheld it then."

Arthur raised his eyes to hers. It was her turn to evade his glance. With her long lashes drooped, she went on—

"It is five years ago, and my father—whom may the Saints assoil—was alive. Came to us then at the Presidio of San Geronimo, a young girl—an American, a stranger and helpless. She had escaped from a lost camp in the snowy mountains where her family and friends were starving. That was the story she told my father. It was a probable one—was it not?"

Arthur bowed his head, but did not reply.

"But the name that she gave was not a true one, as it appeared. My father had sent an *Expedicion* to relieve these people, and they had found among the dead the person whom this young girl—the stranger—assumed to be. That was their report. The name of the young girl who was found dead and the name of the young girl who came to us was the same. It was Grace Conroy."

Arthur's face did not move a muscle, nor did he once take his eyes from the drooping lids of his companion.

"It was a grave matter—a very grave matter. And it was the more surprising because the young girl had at first given another name—the name of Grace Ashley—which she afterwards explained was the name of the young man who helped her to escape, and whose sister she at first assumed to be. My father was a good man, a kind man—a saint, Don Arturo. It was not for him to know if she were Grace Ashley or Grace Conroy—it was enough for him to know that she was alive, weak, helpless, suffering. Against the advice of his officers, he took her into his own house, into his own family, into his own fatherly heart, to wait until her brother, or this Philip Ashley, should return. He never returned. In six months she was taken ill—very ill—a little child was born—Don Arturo—but in the same moment it died and the mother died—both, you comprehend—both died—in my arms!"

"That was bad," said Arthur, curtly.

"I do not comprehend," said Donna Dolores.

"Pardon. Do not misunderstand me. I say it was bad, for I really believe that this girl, the mysterious stranger, with the *alias*, was really Grace Conroy."

Donna Dolores raised her eyes and stared at Arthur.

"And why?"

"Because the identification of the bodies by the *Expedicion* was hurried and imperfect."

"How know you this?"

Arthur arose and drew his chair a little nearer his fair client.

"You have been good enough to intrust me with an important and honourable secret. Let me show my appreciation of that confidence by intrusting you with one equally important. I know that the identification was imperfect and hurried, because *I* was present. In the report of the *Expedicion* you will find the name, if you have not already read it, of Lieutenant Arthur Poinsett. That was myself."

Donna Dolores raised herself to a sitting posture.

"But why did you not tell me this before?"

"Because, first, I believed that you knew that I was Lieutenant Poinsett. Because, secondly, I did *not* believe that you knew that Arthur Poinsett and Philip Ashley were one and the same person."

"I do not understand," said Donna Dolores slowly, in a hard metallic voice.

"I am Lieutenant Arthur Poinsett, formerly of the army, who, under the assumed name of Philip Ashley, brought Grace Conroy out of Starvation Camp. I am the person who afterwards abandoned her—the father of her child."

He had not the slightest intention of saying this when he first entered the room, but something in his nature, which he had never tried to control, brought it out. He was neither ashamed of it nor apprehensive of its results; but, having said it, leaned back in his chair, proud, self-reliant, and self-sustained. If he had been uttering a moral sentiment he could not have been externally more calm or inwardly less agitated. More than that, there was a certain injured dignity in his manner, as he rose, without giving the speechless and astonished woman before him a chance to recover herself, and said—

"You will be able now to know whether your confidence has been misplaced. You will be able now to determine what you wish done, and whether I am the person best calculated to assist you. I can only say, Donna Dolores, that I am ready to act either as your witness to the identification of the real Grace Conroy, or as your legal adviser, or both. When you have decided which, you shall give me your further commands, or dismiss me. Until then, *adios!*"

He bowed, waved his hand with a certain grand courtesy, and withdrew. When Donna Dolores raised her stupified head, the door had closed upon him.

When this conceited young gentleman reached his own room, he was, I grieve to say, to some extent mentally, and, if I may use the word, morally exalted by the interview. More than that, he was in better spirits that he had been since his arrival. From his room he strode out into the corridor. If his horse had been saddled, he would have taken a sharp canter over the low hills for exercise, pending the decision of his fair client, but it was the hour of the noonday *siesta*, and the courtyard was deserted. He walked to the gate, and looked across the plain. A fierce wind held uninterrupted possession of earth and sky. Something of its restlessness, just at that instant, was in Arthur's breast, and, with a glance around the corridor, and a momentary hesitation, as an opening door, in a distant part of the building, suggested the possibility of another summons from Donna Dolores, he stepped beyond the walls.

CHAPTER VIII.

THE BULLS OF THE BLESSED TRINITY.

THE absolute freedom of illimitable space, the exhilaration of the sparkling sunlight, and the excitement of the opposing wind, which was strong enough to oblige him to exert a certain degree of physical strength to overcome it, so wrought upon Arthur, that in a few moments he had thrown off the mysterious spell which the Rancho of the Blessed Trinity appeared to have cast over his spirits, and had placed a material distance between himself and its gloomy towers. The landscape, which had hitherto seemed monotonous and uninspiring, now became suggestive; in the low dome-shaped hills beyond, that were huddled together like half-blown earth bubbles raised by the fiery breath of some long-dead volcano, he fancied he saw the origin of the mission architecture. In the long sweep of the level plain, he recognised the calm, uneventful life that had left its expression in the patient gravity of the people. In the fierce, restless wind that blew over it—a wind so persistent and perpetual that all umbrage, except a narrow fringe of dwarfed willows defining the line of an extinct watercourse, was hidden in sheltered cañons and the leeward slopes of the hills—he recognised something of his own restless race, and no longer wondered at the barrenness of the life that was turned towards the invader. "I daresay," he muttered to himself, "somewhere in the leeward of these people's natures may exist a luxurious growth that we shall never know. I wonder if the Donna has not"—but here he stopped; angry, and, if the truth must be told, a little frightened at the persistency with which Donna Dolores obtruded herself into his abstract philosophy and sentiment.

Possibly something else caused him for the moment to dismiss her from his mind. During his rapid walk he had noticed, as an accidental, and by no means an essential feature of the bleak landscape, the vast herds of crawling, purposeless cattle. An entirely new and distinct impression was now forming itself in his consciousness—namely, that they no longer were purposeless, vagrant, and wandering, but were actually obeying a certain definite law of attraction, and were moving deliberately toward an equally definite object. And that object was himself!

Look where he would; before, behind, on either side, north, east, south, west,—on the bleak hill-tops, on the slope of the *falda*, across the dried-up *arroyo*, there were the same converging lines of slowly moving objects towards a single focus—himself! Although walking briskly, and with a certain definiteness of purpose, he was apparently the only unchanging, fixed, and limited point in the now active landscape. Everything that rose above the dead, barren level was now moving slowly, irresistibly, instinctively, but unmistakably, towards one common centre—himself! Alone and unsupported, he was the helpless, unconscious nucleus of a slowly gathering force, almost immeasurable in its immensity and power!

At first the idea was amusing and grotesque. Then it became picturesque. Then it became something for practical consideration. And then—but no!—with the quick and unerring instincts of a powerful will, he choked down the next consideration before it had time to fasten upon or paralyse his strength. He stopped and turned. The Rancho of the Blessed Trinity was gone! Had it suddenly sank in the earth, or had he diverged from his path? Neither; he had simply walked over the little elevation in the plain beside the *arroyo* and *corral*, and had already left the Rancho two miles behind him.

It was not the only surprise that came upon him suddenly like a blow between the eyes. The same mysterious attraction had been operating in his rear, and when he turned to retrace his steps towards the Mission, he faced the staring eyes of a hundred bulls not fifty yards away. As he faced them, the nearest turned, the next rank followed their example, the next the same, and the next, until in the distance he could see the movement repeated with military precision and sequence. With a sense of relief, that he put aside as quickly as he had the sense of fear, he quickened his pace, until the nearest bull ahead broke into a gentle trot, which was communicated line by line to the cattle beyond, until the whole herd before him undulated like a vast monotonous sea. He continued on across the *arroyo* and past the *corral* until the blinding and penetrating cloud of dust, raised by the plunging hoofs of the moving mass before him, caused him to stop. A dull reverberation of the plain—a sound that at first might have been attributed to a passing earthquake—now became so distinct that he turned. Not twenty yards behind him rose the advance wall of another vast, tumultuous sea of tossing horns and undulating backs that had been slowly following his retreat! He had forgotten that he was surrounded.

The nearest were now so close upon him that he could observe them separately. They were neither large, powerful, vindictive, nor ferocious. On the contrary, they were thin, wasted, haggard, anxious beasts, economically equipped and gotten up, the better to wrestle with a six months' drought, occasional famine, and the incessant buffeting of the wind—wild and untamable, but their staring eyes and nervous limbs expressed only wonder and curiosity. And when he ran toward them with a shout, they turned, as had the others, file by file, and rank by rank, and in a moment were, like the others, in full retreat. Rather, let me say, retreated as the others *had* retreated, for when he faced about again to retrace his steps toward the Mission, he fronted the bossy bucklers and inextricable horns of those he had driven only a few moments ago before him. They had availed themselves of his diversion with the rear-guard to return.

With the rapidity of a quick intellect and swift perceptions, Arthur saw at once the resistless logic and utter hopelessness of his situation. The inevitable culmination of all this was only a question of time—and a very brief period. Would it be sufficient to enable him to reach the *casa?* No! Could he regain the *corral?* Perhaps. Between it and himself already were a thousand cattle. Would they continue to retreat as he advanced? Possibly. But would he be overtaken meanwhile by those in his rear?

He answered the question himself by drawing from his waistcoat pocket his only weapon, a small "Derringer," and taking aim at the foremost bull. The shot took effect in the animal's shoulder, and he fell upon his knees. As Arthur had expected, his nearer comrades stopped and sniffed at their helpless companion. But, as Arthur had not expected, the eager crowd pressing behind overbore them and their wounded brother, and in another instant the unfortunate animal was prostrate and his life beaten out by the trampling hoofs of the resistless, blind, and eager crowd that followed. With a terrible intuition that it was a foreshadowing of his own fate, Arthur turned in the direction of the *corral*, and ran for his very life!

As he ran he was conscious that the act precipitated the inevitable catastrophe—but he could think of nothing better. As he ran, he felt, from the shaking of the earth beneath his feet, that the act had once more put the whole herd in equally active motion behind him. As he ran, he noticed that the cattle before him retreated with something of his own precipitation. But as he ran, he thought of nothing but the awful fate that was following him, and the thought spurred him to an almost frantic effort. I have tried to make the reader understand that Arthur was quite inaccessible to any of those weaknesses which mankind regard as physical cowardice. In the defence of what he believed to be an intellectual truth, in the interests of his pride or his self-love, or in a moment of passion, he would have faced death with unbroken fortitude and calmness. But to be the victim of an accident; to be the lamentable sequel of a logical succession of chances, without motive or purpose; to be sacrificed for nothing—without proving or disproving anything; to be trampled to death by idiotic beasts, who had not even the instincts of passion or revenge to justify them; to die the death of an ignorant tramp, or any negligent clown—a death that had a ghastly ludicrousness in its method, a death that would leave his body a shapeless, indistinguishable, unrecognisable clod, which affection could not idealise nor friendship reverence,—all this brought a horror with it so keen, so exquisite, so excruciating, that the fastidious, proud, intellectual being fleeing from it might have been the veriest dastard that ever turned his back on danger. And superadded to it was a superstitious thought that for its very horror, perhaps, it was a retribution for something that he dared not contemplate!

And it was then that his strength suddenly flagged. His senses began to reel. His breath, which had kept pace with the quick beating of his heart, intermitted, hesitated, was lost! Above the advancing thunder of hoofs behind him, he thought he heard a woman's voice. He knew now he was going crazy; he shouted and fell; he rose again and staggered forward a few steps and fell again. It was over now! A sudden sense of some strange, subtle perfume, beating up through the acrid, smarting dust of the plain, that choked his mouth and blinded his eyes, came swooning over him. And then the blessed interposition of unconsciousness and peace.

He struggled back to life again with the word "Philip" in his ears, a throbbing brow, and the sensation of an effort to do something that was required of him. Of all his experience of the last few moments only the perfume remained. He was lying alone in the dry bed of the *arroyo;* on the bank a horse was standing, and above him bent the dark face and darker eyes of Donna Dolores.

"Try to recover sufficient strength to mount that horse," she said, after a pause.

It was a woman before him. With that innate dread which all masculine nature has of exhibiting physical weakness before a weaker sex, Arthur struggled to rise without the assistance offered by the small hand of his friend. That, however, even at that crucial moment, he so far availed himself of it, as to press it, I fear was the fact.

"You came to my assistance alone?" asked Arthur, as he struggled to his feet.

"Why not? We are equal now, Don Arturo," said

Donna Dolores, with a dazzling smile. "I saw you from my window. You were rash—pardon me—foolish! The oldest vaquero never ventures a foot upon these plains. But come; you shall ride with me. There was no time to saddle another horse, and I thought you would not care to let others know of your adventure. Am I right?"

There was a slight dimple of mischief in her cheek, and a quaint sparkle in her dark eye, as she turned her questioning gaze on Arthur. He caught her hand and raised it respectfully to his lips.

"You are wise as you are brave, Donna Dolores."

"We shall see. But at present you must believe that I am right, and do as I say. Mount that horse—I will help you if you are too weak—and—leave a space for me behind you!"

Thus adjured, Arthur leaped into the saddle. If his bones had been broken instead of being bruised, he would still have found strength for that effort. In another instant Donna Dolores' little foot rested on his, and she lightly mounted behind him.

"Home now. Hasten; we will be there before any one will know it," she said, as she threw one arm around his waist, with superb unconsciousness.

Arthur lifted the rein and dropped his heels into the flanks of the horse. In five minutes—the briefest, as it seemed to him, he had ever passed—they were once more within the walls of the Blessed Trinity.

BOOK IV.

DRIFTING.

CHAPTER I.

MR. AND MRS. CONROY AT HOME.

THE manner in which One Horse Gulch received the news of Gabriel Conroy's marriage was characteristic of that frank and outspoken community. Without entering upon the question of his previous shameless flirtation with Mrs. Markle—the baleful extent of which was generally unknown to the camp—the nearer objections were based upon the fact that the bride was a stranger and consequently an object of suspicion, and that Gabriel's sphere of usefulness in a public philanthropic capacity would be seriously impaired and limited. His very brief courtship did not excite any surprise in a climate where the harvest so promptly followed the sowing, and the fact, now generally known, that it was he who saved the woman's life after the breaking of the dam at Black Cañon, was accepted as a sufficient reason for his success in that courtship. It may be remarked here that a certain grim disbelief in feminine coyness obtained at One Horse Gulch. That the conditions of life there were as near the perfect and original condition of mankind as could be found anywhere, and that the hollow shams of society and weak artifices of conventionalism could not exist in that sincere atmosphere, were two beliefs that One Horse Gulch never doubted.

Possibly there was also some little envy of Gabriel's success, an envy not based upon any evidence of his superior courage, skill, or strength, but only of the peculiar "luck," opportunity, or providence, that had enabled him to turn certain qualities very common to One Horse Gulch to such favourable account.

"Toe think," said Jo. Briggs, "thet I was allowin'—only thet very afternoon—to go up that cañon arter game, and didn't go from some derned foolishness or other, and yer's Gabe, hevin' no call to go thar, jest comes along, accidental like, and, dern my skin! but he strikes onto a purty gal and a wife the first lick!"

"Thet's so," responded Barker, "it's all luck. Thar's thet Cy. Dudley, with plenty o' money and wantin' a wife bad, and ez is goin' to Sacramento to-morrow to prospect fur one, and he hez been up and down that cañon time outer mind, and no dam ever said 'break' to him! No, sir! Or take my own case; on'y last week when the Fiddletown coach went over the bank at Dry Creek, wasn't I the fust man thar ez cut the leaders adrift and bruk open the coach-door and helped out the passengers? And wot passengers? Six Chinymen by Jinks—and a Greaser! Thet's my luck."

There were few preliminaries to the marriage. The consent of Olly was easily gained. As an act of aggression and provocation towards Mrs. Markle, nothing could offer greater inducements. The superior gentility of the stranger, the fact of her being a stranger, and the expeditiousness of the courtship coming so hard upon Mrs. Markle's fickleness commended itself to the child's sense of justice and feminine retaliation. For herself, Olly hardly knew if she liked her prospective sister; she was gentle, she was kind, she seemed to love Gabriel—but Olly was often haunted by a vague instinct that Mrs. Markle would have been a better match—and with true feminine inconsistency she hated her the more for it. Possibly she tasted also something of the disappointment of the baffled match-maker in the depths of her childish consciousness.

It may be fairly presumed that the former Mrs. Devarges had confided to no one but her lawyer the secret of her assumption of the character of Grace Conroy. How far or how much more she had confided to that gentleman was known only to himself; he kept her secret, whatever might have been its extent, and received the announcement of her intended marriage to Gabriel with the superior smile of one to whom all things are possible from the unprofessional sex.

"Now that you are about to enter into actual possession," said Mr. Maxwell, quietly buttoning up his pocket again, "I suppose you will not require my services immediately."

It is said, upon what authority I know not, that Madame Devarges blushed slightly, heaved the least possible sigh as she shook her head and said, "I hope not," with an evident sincerity that left her legal adviser in some slight astonishment.

How far her intended husband participated in this confidence I do not know. He was evidently proud of alluding to her in the few brief days of his courtship as the widow of the "great Doctor Devarges," and his knowledge of her former husband to some extent mitigated in the public mind the apparent want of premeditation in the courtship.

"To think of the artfulness of that man," said Sal, confidentially, to Mrs. Markle, "and he a-gettin' up sympathy about his sufferin's at Starvation Camp, and all the while a-carryin' on with the widder of one o' them onfortunets. No wonder that man was queer! Wot you allowed in the innocents o' yer heart was bashfulness was jest conscience. I never let on to ye, Mrs. Markle, but I allus noticed thet thet Gabe never could meet my eye."

The flippant mind might have suggested that as both of Miss Sarah's eyes were afflicted with a cast, there might have been a physical impediment to this exchange of frankness, but then the flippant mind never enjoyed the confidence of this powerful young woman.

It was a month after the wedding, and Mrs. Markle was sitting alone in her parlour, whither she had retired after the professional duties of supper were over, when the front door opened, and Sal entered. It was Sunday evening, and Sal had been enjoying the brief recreation of gossip with the neighbours, and, as was alleged by the flippant mind before alluded to, some coquettish conversation and dalliance with certain youth of One Horse Gulch.

Mrs. Markle watched her handmaid slowly remove an immense straw "flat" trimmed with tropical flowers, and then proceed to fold away an enormous plaid shawl which represented quite another zone, and then her curiosity got the better of her prudence.

"Well, and how did ye find the young couple gettin' on, Sal?"

Sal too well understood the value of coyly-withheld information to answer at once, and with the instincts of a true artist, she affected to misunderstand her mistress. When Mrs. Markle had repeated her question Sal replied, with a sarcastic laugh—

"Axin yer pardin fur manners, but you let on about the *young* couple, and *she* forty if she's anythin'."

"Oh, no, Sal," remonstrated Mrs. Markle, with reproachful accents, and yet a certain self-satisfaction; "you're mistaken, sure."

"Well," said Sal, breathlessly slapping her hands on her lap, "if pearl powder and another woman's har and fancy doin's beggiles folks, it ain't Sal ez is among the folks fooled. No, Sue Markle. Ef I ain't lived long enough with a woman ez owns to thirty-three and hez—ef it wuz my last words and God is my jedge—the neck and arms of a gal of sixteen, not to know when a woman is trying to warm over the scraps of forty year with a kind o' hash o' twenty, then Sal Clark ain't got no eyes, thet's all."

Mrs. Markle blushed slightly under the direct flattery of Sal, and continued—

"Some folks says she's purty."

"Some men's meat is other men's pizen," responded Sal, sententiously, unfastening an enormous black velvet zone, and apparently permitting her figure to fall into instant ruin.

"How did they look?" said Mrs. Markle, after a pause, recommencing her darning, which she had put down.

"Well, purty much as I allowed they would from the first. Thar ain't any love wasted over thar. My opinion is thet he's sick of his bargin. She runs the house and ev'ry thing that's in it. Jest look at the critter! She's just put that thar Gabe up to prospecting all along the ledge here, and that fool's left his diggin's and hez been running hither and yon, making ridiklus holes all over the hill jest to satisfy thet woman, and she ain't satisfied neither. Take my word for it, Sue Markle, thar's suthin' wrong thar. And then thar's thet Olly"——

Mrs. Markle raised her eyes quickly, and put down her work. "Olly," she repeated, with great animation—"poor little Olly! what's gone of her?"

"Well," said Sal, with an impatient toss of her head, "I

never did see what thar wuz in that peart and sassy piece for any one to take to—leastwise a woman with a child of her own. The airs and graces thet thet Olly would put on wuz too much. Why, she hedn't been nigh us for a month, and the day afore the wedding what does that limb do but meet me and sez, sez she, 'Sal, ye kin tell Mrs. Markle as my brother Gabe ez goin' to marry a lady—a lady,' sez she. 'Thar ain't goin' to be enny Pikes about our cabin.' And thet child only eight years! Oh, git out thar! I ain't no patience!"

To the infinite credit of a much abused sex, be it recorded that Mrs. Markle overlooked the implied slur, and asked—

"But what about Olly?"

"I mean to say," said Sal, "thet thet child hain't no place in thet house, and thet Gabe is jest thet weak and mean spirited ez to let thet woman have her own way. No wonder thet the child was crying when I met her out in the woods yonder."

Mrs. Markle instantly flushed, and her black eyes snapped ominously. "I should jest like to ketch—" she began quickly, and then stopped and looked at her companion. "Sal," she said, with swift vehemence, "I must see thet child."

"How?"

The word in Sal's dialect had a various, large, and catholic significance. Mrs. Markle understood it, and repeated briefly—

"Olly—I must see her—right off!"

"Which?" continued Sal.

"Here," replied Mrs. Markle; "anywhere. Fetch her when ye kin."

"She won't come."

"Then I'll go to her," said Mrs. Markle, with a sudden and characteristic determination that closed the conversation and sent Sal back viciously to her unwashed dishes.

Whatever might have been the truth of Sal's report, there was certainly no general external indication of the facts. The newly-married couple were, to all appearances, as happy and contented, and as enviable to the masculine inhabitants of One Horse Gulch, as any who had ever built a nest within its pastoral close. If a majority of Gabriel's visitors were gentlemen, it was easily attributed to the preponderance of males in the settlement. If these gentlemen were unanimously extravagant in their praise of Mrs. Conroy, it was as easily attributable to the same cause. That Gabriel should dig purposeless holes over the hill-side, that he should for the time abandon his regular occupation in his little modest claim in the cañon, was quite consistent with the ambition of a newly-married man.

A few evenings after this, Gabriel Conroy was sitting alone by the hearth of that new house, which popular opinion and the tastes of Mrs. Conroy seemed to think was essential to his new condition. It was a larger, more ambitious, more expensive, and perhaps less comfortable dwelling than the one in which he has been introduced to the reader. It was projected upon that credit which a man of family was sure to obtain in One Horse Gulch, where the immigration and establishment of families and household centres were fostered even at pecuniary risks. It contained, beside the chambers, the gratuitous addition of a parlour, which at this moment was adorned and made attractive by the presence of Mrs. Conroy, who was entertaining a few visitors that, under her attractions, had prolonged their sitting until late. When the laugh had ceased and the door closed on the last lingering imbecile, Mrs. Conroy returned to the sitting-room. It was dark, for Gabriel had not lighted a candle yet, and he was occupying his favourite seat and attitude before the fire.

"Why! are *you* there?" said Mrs. Conroy, gaily.

Gabriel looked up, and with that seriousness which was habitual to him, replied—

"Yes."

Mrs. Conroy approached her lord and master, and ran her thin, claw-like fingers through his hair with married audacity. He caught them, held them for a moment with a kindly, caressing, and yet slightly embarrassed air that the lady did not like. She withdrew them quickly.

"Why didn't you come into the parlour?" she said, examining him curiously.

"I didn't admire to to-night," returned Gabriel, with grave simplicity, "and I reckoned you'd get on as well without me."

There was not the slightest trace of bitterness nor aggrieved sensitiveness in his tone or manner, and although Mrs. Conroy eyed him sharply for any latent spark of jealousy, she was forced to admit to herself that it did not exist in the quiet, serious man before her. Vaguely aware of some annoyance in his wife's face, Gabriel reached out his arm, and, lightly taking her around her waist, drew her to his knee. But the very act was so evidently a recognition of a certain kind of physical and moral weakness in the creature before him—so professional—so, as Mrs. Conroy put it to herself,—"like as if I were a sick man," that her irritation was not soothed. She rose quickly and seated herself on the other side of the fireplace. With the same implied toleration Gabriel had already displayed, he now made no attempt to restrain her.

Mrs. Conroy did not pout as another woman might have done. She only smiled a haggard smile that deepened the line of her nostril into her cheek, and pinched her thin, straight nose. Then she said, looking at the fire—

"Ain't you well?"

"I reckon not—not overly well."

There was a silence, both looking at the fire.

"You don't get anything out of that hill-side?" asked Mrs. Conroy at last, pettishly.

"No," said Gabriel.

"You have prospected all over the ridge?" continued the woman, impatiently.

"All over!"

"And you don't find anything?

"Nothin'," said Gabriel. "Nary. Thet is," he added with his usual cautious deliberation, "thet is, nothin' o' any account. The gold, ef there is any, lies lower down in the gulch, whar I used to dig. But I kept at it jest to satisfy your whim. You know, July, it *was* a whim of yours," he continued, with a certain gentle deprecatoriness of manner.

A terrible thought flashed suddenly upon Mrs. Conroy. Could Dr. Devarges have made a mistake? Might he not have been delirious or insane when he wrote of the treasure? Or had the Secretary deceived her as to its location? A swift and sickening sense that all she had gained, or was to gain, from her scheme, was the man before her—and that *he* did not love her as other men had—asserted itself through her trembling consciousness. Mrs. Conroy had already begun to fear that she loved this husband, and it was with a new sense of yearning and dependence that she in her turn looked deprecatingly and submissively into his face and said—

"It *was* only a whim, dear—I dare say a foolish one. It's gone now. Don't mind it!"

"I don't," said Gabriel, simply.

Mrs. Conroy winced.

"I thought you looked disappointed," she said after a pause.

"It ain't that I was thinkin' on, July; it's Olly," said Gabriel.

There is a limit even to a frightened woman's submission.

"Of course," she said, sharply; "Olly, Olly again and always. I ought to have remembered that."

"Thet's so," said Gabriel with the same exasperating quiet. "I was reckonin' jest now, ez there don't seem to be any likeliness of you and Olly's gettin' on together, you'd better separate. Thar ain't no sense goin' on this way, July—no sense et all. And the worst o' the hull thing ez thet Olly ain't gettin' no kinder good outer it, no way!"

Mrs. Conroy was very pale and dangerously quiet as Mr. Conroy went on.

"I've allers allowed to send that child to school, but she don't keer to go. She's thet foolish, thet Olly is, thet she doesn't like to leave me, and I reckon I'm thet foolish too thet I don't like to hev her go. The only way to put things square ez this"——

Mrs. Conroy turned and fixed her grey eyes upon her husband, but she did not speak.

"You'd better go away," continued Gabriel, quietly, "for a while. I've heerd afore now that it's the reg'lar thing fur a bride to go away and visit her mother. You hain't got no mother," said Gabriel thoughtfully, "hev ye?—that's bad. But you was a sayin' the other day suthin' about some business you had down at 'Frisco. Now it would be about the nateral sort o' thing for ye to go thar fur two or three months, jest till things get round square with Olly and me."

It is probable that Gabriel was the only man from whom Mrs. Conroy could have received this humiliating proposition without interrupting him with a burst of indignation. Yet she only turned a rigid face towards the fire again with a hysterical laugh.

"Why limit my stay to two or three months?" she said.

"Well, it might be four," said Gabriel, simply—"it would give me and Olly a longer time to get things in shape."

Mrs. Conroy rose and walked rigidly to her husband's side.

"What," she said huskily, "what if I were to refuse?"

Gabriel looked as if this suggestion would not have been startling or inconsistent as an abstract possibility in woman, but said nothing.

"What," continued Mrs. Conroy, more rapidly and huskily, "what if I were to tell *you* and that brat to go! What," she said, suddenly raising her voice to a thin high soprano, "what if I were to turn you both out of this house—*my* house! off this land—*my* land! Eh? eh? eh?" she almost screamed, emphasising each interrogatory with her thin hand on Gabriel's shoulder, in a desperate but impotent attempt to shake him.

"Certingly, certingly," said Gabriel calmly. "But thar's somebody at the door, July," he continued quietly, as he rose slowly and walked into the hall.

His quick ear had detected a knocking without, above the truculent pitch of Mrs. Conroy's voice. He threw open the door, and disclosed Olly and Sal standing upon the threshold.

It is scarcely necessary to say that Sal was first to recover the use of that noble organ, the tongue.

"With chills and ager in every breath—it's an hour if it's five minutes that we've stood here," she began, "pounding at that door. 'You're interrupting the young couple, Sal,' sez I, 'comin' yer this time o' night, breakin' in, so to speak, on the holiest confidences,' sez I; 'but it's business, and onless you hev thet to back you, Sarah Clark,' I sez, 'and you ain't a woman ez ever turned her back on thet or them, you ain't no call there.' But I was to fetch this child home, Mrs. Conroy," continued Sal, pushing her way into the little sitting-room, "and"——

She paused, for the room was vacant. Mrs. Conroy had disappeared.

"I thought I heerd"—— said Sal, completely taken aback.

"It was only Gabe," said Olly, with the ready mendacity of swift feminine tact. "I told you so. Thank you, Sal, for seeing me home. Good night, Sal," and, with a dexterity that smote Gabriel into awesome and admiring silence, she absolutely led the breathless Sal to the door and closed it upon her before that astonished female could recover her speech.

Then she returned quietly, took off her hat and shawl, and taking the unresisting hand of her brother, led him back to his former seat by the fire. Drawing a low stool in front of him, she proceeded to nestle between his knees—an old trick of hers—and once more taking his hand, stroked it between her brown fingers, looked up into his face, and said—

"Dear old Gabe!"

The sudden smile that irradiated Gabriel's serious face would have been even worse provocation to Mrs. Conroy than his previous conduct.

"What was the matter, Gabe?" said Olly; "what was she saying when we came in?"

Gabriel had not, since the entrance of his sister, thought of Mrs. Conroy's parting speech and manner. Even now its full significance did not appear to have reached him.

"I disremember, Olly," he replied, looking down into Olly's earnest eyes, "suthin' or other; she was techy, thet's all."

"But wot did she mean by saying that the house and lands vas hers?" persisted the child.

"Married folks, Olly," said Gabriel, with the lazy, easy manner of vast matrimonial experience, "married folks hev little jokes and ways o' thar own. Bein' onmarried yourself, ye don't know. 'With all my worldly goods I thee endow,' thet's all—thet's what she meant, Olly. 'With all my worldly goods I thee endow.' Did you hev a good time down there?"

"Yes," said Olly.

"You'll hev a nice time here soon, Olly," said Gabriel.

Olly looked incredulously across the hall toward the door of Mrs. Conroy's chamber.

"Thet's it, Olly," said Gabriel, "Mrs. Conroy's goin' to 'Frisco to see some friends. She's thet bent on goin' thet nothin' 'il stop her. Ye see, Olly, it's the fashion fur new married folks to kinder go way and visit absent and sufferin' friends. Thar's them little ways about the married state, that, bein' onmarried yourself, you don't sabe. But it's all right, she's goin'. Bein' a lady, and raised, so to speak, 'mong fashi'n'ble people, she's got to folly the fashin. She's goin' for three months, mebbe four. I disremember now wot's the fashi'n'ble time. But she'll do it, Olly."

Olly cast a penetrating look at her brother.

"She ain't goin' on my account, Gabe?"

"Lord love the child, no! Wot put thet into your head, Olly? Why," said Gabriel with cheerful mendacity, "she's been takin' a shine to ye o' late. On'y to-night she was wonderin' whar you be."

As if to give credence to his words, and much to his inward astonishment, the door of Mrs. Conroy's room opened, and the lady herself, with a gracious smile on her lips and a brightly beaming eye, albeit somewhat reddened around the lids, crossed the hall, and, going up to Olly, kissed her round cheek.

"I thought it was your voice, and although I was just going to bed," she added gaily, with a slightly apologetic look at her charming dishabille, "I had to come in and be sure it was you. And where have you been, you naughty girl? Do you know I shall be dreadfully jealous of this Mrs. Markle. Come and tell me all about her. Come. You shall stay with me to-night, and we won't let brother Gabe hear our little secrets—shall we? Come!"

And before the awe-struck Gabriel could believe his own senses she had actually whisked the half-pleased, half-frightened child into her own room, and he was left standing alone. Nor was he the less amazed, although relieved of a certain undefined anxiety for the child, when, a moment later, Olly herself thrust her curly head out of the door, and, calling out, "Good-night, old Gabe," with a mischievous accent, shut and locked the door in his face. For a moment Gabriel stood petrified on his own hearthstone. Was he mistaken, and had Mrs. Conroy's anger actually been nothing but a joke? Was Olly really sincere in her dislike of his wife? There was but one apparent solution to these various and perplexing problems, and that was the general incomprehensibility of the sex.

"The ways o' woman is awful onsartin," said Gabriel, as he sought the solitary little room which had been set apart for Olly, "and somehow I ain't the man ez hez the gift o' findin' them out."

And with these reflections he went apologetically, yet, to a certain extent, contentedly, as was his usual habit, to bed.

CHAPTER II.

IN WHICH THE TREASURE IS FOUND—AND LOST.

As no word has been handed down of the conversation that night between Olly and her sister-in-law, I fear the masculine reader must view their subsequent conduct in the light of Gabriel's abstract proposition. The feminine reader—to whose well-known sense of justice and readiness to acknowledge a characteristic weakness, I chiefly commend these pages—will of course require no further explanation, and will be quite ready to believe that the next morning Olly and Mrs. Conroy were apparently firm friends, and that Gabriel was incontinently snubbed by both of these ladies as he deserved.

"You don't treat July right," said Olly, one morning, to Gabriel, during five minutes that she had snatched from the inseparable company of Mrs. Conroy.

Gabriel opened his eyes in wonder. "I hain't been 'round the house much, because I allowed you and July didn't want my kempany," he began apologetically, "and ef it's shortness of provisions, I've fooled away so much time, Olly, in prospectin' that ledge that I had no time to clar up and get any dust. I reckon, may be the pork bar'l *is* low. But I'll fix thet straight soon, Olly, soon."

"But it ain't thet, Gabe—it ain't provisions—it's—it's—O! you ain't got no sabe ez a husband—thar!" burst out the direct Olly at last.

Without the least sign of resentment, Gabriel looked thoughtfully at his sister.

"Thet's so—I reckon thet *is* the thing. Not hevin' been married afore, and bein', so to speak, strange and green-handed, like as not I don't exactly come up to the views of a woman ez hez hed thet experience. And her husband a savang! a savang! Olly, and a larned man."

"You're as good as him!" ejaculated Olly, hastily, whose parts of speech were less accurately placed than her feelings, "and I reckon she loves you a heap better, Gabe. But you ain't quite lovin' enough," she added, as Gabriel started. "Why, thar was thet young couple thet came up from Simpson's last week, and stayed over at Mrs. Markle's.

Thar was no end of the attentions thet thet man paid to thet thar woman—fixin' her shawl, histin' the winder and puttin' it down, and askin' after her health every five minnits—and they'd sit and sit, just like this"——here Olly, in the interests of domestic felicity, improvised the favourite attitude of the bridegroom, as far as the great girth of Gabriel's waist and chest could be "clipped" by her small arms.

"Wot! afore folks?" asked Gabriel, looking down a little shamefully on the twining arms of his sister.

"Yes—in course—afore folks. Why, they want it to be known thet they're married."

"Olly," broke out Gabriel desperately, "your sister-in-law ain't thet kind of a woman. She'd reckon thet kind o' thing was low."

But Olly only replied by casting a mischievous look at her brother, shaking her curls, and with the mysterious admonition, "Try it!" left him, and went back to Mrs. Conroy.

Happily for Gabriel, Mrs. Conroy did not offer an opportunity for the exhibition of any tenderness on Gabriel's part. Although she did not make any allusion to the past, and even utterly ignored any previous quarrel, she still preserved a certain coy demeanour toward him, that, while it relieved him of an onerous duty, very greatly weakened his faith in the infallibility of Olly's judgment. When, out of respect to that judgment, he went so far as to throw his arms ostentatiously around his wife's waist one Sunday, while perambulating the single long public street of One Horse Gulch, and that lady, with great decision, quietly slipped out of his embrace, he doubted still more.

"I did it on account o' wot you said, Olly, and darn my skin if she seemed to like it at all, and even the boys hangin' around seemed to think it was queer. Jo Hobson snickered right out."

"When was it?" said Olly.

"Sunday."

Olly, sharply—"Where?"

Gabriel—"On Main Street.

Olly, apostrophising heaven with her blue eyes—"Ef thar ever was a blunderin' mule, Gabe, it's YOU!"

Gabriel, mildly and thoughtfully—"Thet's so."

Howbeit, some kind of a hollow truce was patched up between these three belligerents, and Mrs. Conroy did not go to San Francisco on business. It is presumed that the urgency of her affairs there was relieved by correspondence, for during the next two weeks she expressed much anxiety on the arrival of the regular tri-weekly mails. And one day it brought her not only a letter, but an individual of some importance in this history.

He got down from the Wingdam coach amid considerable local enthusiasm. Apart from the fact that it was well known that he was a rich San Francisco banker and capitalist, his brusque, sharp energy, his easy, sceptical familiarity and general contempt for and ignoring of everything but the practical and material, and, above all, his reputation for success, which seemed to make that success a wholesome business principle rather than good fortune, had already fascinated the passengers who had listened to his curt speech and half oracular axioms. They had forgiven dogmatisms voiced in such a hearty manner, and emphasised possibly with a slap on the back of the listener. He had already converted them to his broad materialism—less, perhaps, by his curt rhetoric than by the logic of his habitual business success, and the respectability that it commanded. It was easy to accept scepticism from a man who evidently had not suffered by it. Radicalism and democracy are much more fascinating to us when the apostle is in comfortable case and easy circumstances, than when he is clad in fustian, and consistently out of a situation. Human nature thirsts for the fruit of the tree of the knowledge of good and evil, but would prefer to receive it from the happy owner of a latch-key to the Garden of Eden, rather than from the pilferer who had just been ejected from the premises.

It is probable, however, that the possessor of these admirable qualities had none of that fine scorn for a mankind accessible to this weakness which at present fills the breast of the writer, and, I trust, the reader, of these pages. If he had, I doubt if he would have been successful. Like a true hero, he was quite unconscious of the quality of his heroism, and utterly unable to analyse it. So that, without any previous calculations or pre-arranged plan, he managed to get rid of his admirers, and apply himself to the business he had in hand without either wilfully misleading the public of One Horse Gulch, or giving the slightest intimation of what that real business was. That the general interests of One Horse Gulch had attracted the attention of this powerful capitalist—that he intended to erect a new Hotel, or "start" an independent line of stage-coaches from Sacramento, were among the accepted theories. Everybody offered him vast and gratuitous information, and out of the various facts and theories submitted to him he gained the particular knowledge he required without asking for it. Given a reputation for business shrewdness and omnipresence in any one individual, and the world will speedily place him beyond the necessity of using them.

And so in a casual, general way, the stranger was shown over the length and breadth and thickness and present and future of One Horse Gulch. When he had reached the farther extremity of the Gulch he turned to his escort —"I'll make the inquiry you ask now."

"How?"

"By telegraph—if you'll take it."

He tore a leaf from a memorandum-book and wrote a few lines.

And you?"

"Oh, I'll look around here—I suppose there's not much beyond this?"

"No; the next claim is Gabriel Conroy's."

"Not much account, I reckon?"

"No? It pays him grub!"

"Well, dine with me at three o'clock, when and where you choose—you know best. Invite whom you like. Good-bye!" And the great man's escort, thus dismissed, departed, lost in admiration of the decisive promptitude and liberality of his guest.

Left to himself, the stranger turned his footsteps in the direction of Gabriel Conroy's claim. Had he been an admirer of Nature, or accessible to any of those influences which a contemplation of wild scenery is apt to produce in weaker humanity, he would have been awed by the gradual transition of a pastoral landscape to one of uncouth heroics. In a few minutes he had left the belt of sheltering pines and entered upon the ascent of a shadowless, scorched, and blistered mountain, that here and there in places of vegetation had put on the excrescences of scoria, or a singular eruption of crust, that, breaking beneath his feet in slippery grey powder, made his footing difficult and uncertain. Had he been possessed of a scientific eye, he would have noted here and there the evidences of volcanic action, in the sudden depressions, the abrupt elevations, the marks of disruption and upheaval, and the river-like flow of debris that protruded a black tongue into the valley below. But I am constrained to believe the stranger's dominant impression was simply one of heat. Half-way up the ascent he took off his coat and wiped his forehead with his handkerchief. Nevertheless, certain peculiarities in his modes of progression showed him to be not unfamiliar with mountain travel. Two or three times during the ascent he stopped, and, facing about, carefully resurveyed the path beneath him. Slight as was the action, it was the unfailing sign of the mountaineer, who recognised that the other side of a mountain was as yet an undetermined quantity, and was prepared to retrace his steps if necessary. At the summit he paused and looked around him.

Immediately at his feet the Gulch which gave its name to the settlement, and from which the golden harvest was gathered, broadened into a thickly wooded valley. Its quivering depths were suffused by the incense of odorous gums and balms liberated by the fierce heat of the noonday sun that rose to his face in soft, tremulous waves, and filled the air with its heated spices. Through a gap in the cañon to the west, a faint, scarcely-distinguishable line of cloud indicated the coast range. North and south, higher hills arose heavily terraced with straight colonnades of pines, that made the vast black monolith on which he stood appear blacker and barer by contrast. Higher hills to the east—one or two peaks—and between them in the sunlight odd-looking, indistinct, vacant intervals—blanks in the landscape as yet not filled in with colour or expression. Yet the stranger knew them to be snow, and for a few moments seemed fascinated—gazing at them with a fixed eye and rigid mouth, until, with an effort, he tore himself away.

Scattered over the summit were numerous holes that appeared to have been recently sunk. In one of them the stranger picked up a fragment of the crumbled rock, and examined it carelessly. Then he slowly descended the gentler slope towards the west, in the direction of a claim wherein his quick eye had discovered a man at work. A walk of a few moments brought him to the bank of red clay, the heap of tailings, the wooden sluice-box, and the pan and shovel which constituted the appurtenances of an ordinary claim. As he approached nearer, the workman rose from the bank over which he was bending, and leaning on his pick, turned his face to the new-comer. His broad, athletic figure, his heavy blonde beard, and serious, perplexed eyes, were unmistakable. It was Gabriel Conroy.

"How are ye?" said the stranger, briskly extending a hand, which Gabriel took mechanically. "You're looking well! Recollect *you*, but you don't recollect me. Eh?" He laughed curtly, in a fashion as short and businesslike as his speech, and then fixed his eyes rather impatiently on the hesitating Gabriel.

Gabriel could only stare, and struggle with a tide of thick-coming remembrances. He looked around him; the sun was beating down on the old familiar objects, everything was unchanged—and yet this face, this voice.

"I am here on a matter of business," continued the stranger briskly, dismissing the question of recognition as one unessential to the business on hand—"and—what have you got to propose?" He leaned lightly against the bank and supported himself by thrusting Gabriel's pickaxe against the bank, as he waited a reply.

"It's Peter Dumphy," said Gabriel, in a awe-stricken voice.

"Yes. You recollect me now! Thought you would. It's five years and over—ain't it? Rough times them, Gabriel—warn't they? Eh! But *you're* lookin' well—doin' well, too. Hey? Well—what do you propose to do about this claim? Haven't made up your mind—hey? Come then—I'll make a proposition. First, I suppose your title's all right, hey?"

It was so evident from Gabriel's dazed manner that, apart from his astonishment at meeting Peter Dumphy, he did not know what he was talking about, that Dumphy paused.

"It's about these specimens," he added, eyeing Gabriel keenly, "the specimens you sent me."

"Wot specimens?" said Gabriel vaguely, still lost in the past.

"The ones your wife sent me—all the same thing, you know."

"But it ain't," said Gabriel, with his old truthful directness. "You better talk to her 'bout thet. Thet's her lookout. I reckon now she *did* say suthin'," continued Gabriel, meditatively, "about sendin' rock to Frisco to be tested, but I didn't somehow get to take an interest in it. Leastways, it's her funeral. You'd better see her.

It was Mr. Dumphy's turn to be perplexed. In his perfect misapprehension of the character of the man before him, he saw only skilful business evasion under the guise of simplicity. He remembered, moreover, that in the earlier days of his prosperity as Dumphy and Jenkins, Commission Merchants, he was himself in the habit of referring customers with whom he was not ready to treat, to Jenkins, very much as he had just now been referred to Mrs. Conroy.

"Of course," he said briskly; "only I thought I'd save time, which is short with me to-day, by coming directly to you. May not have time to see her. But you can write."

"Thet's so," said Gabriel, "p'r'aps it's just as well in the long run. Ef ye don't see her, she'll know it ain't your fault. I'll let on that much to her." And having disposed of this unimportant feature of the interview, he continued, "Ye haven't heard nought o' Grace—ye mind Grace? Dumphy!—a purty little girl ez was with me up thar. Ye ain't heerd anything o' her—nor seen her, may be—hev you?"

Of course this question at such a moment was to Mr. Dumphy susceptible of only one meaning. It was that Mrs. Conroy had confessed everything to Gabriel, and that he wished to use Dumphy's complicity in the deceit as a lever in future business transactions. Mr. Dumphy felt he had to deal with two consummate actors—one of whom was a natural hypocrite. For the first time in his life he was impatient of evil. We never admire truth and sincerity so highly as when we find it wanting in an adversary.

"Ran off with some fellow, didn't she? Yes, I remember. You won't see her again. It's just as well for you! I'd call her dead, anyway."

Although Dumphy was convinced that Gabriel's interest in the fate of his sister was hypocritical, he was not above a Christian hope that this might wound a brother's feelings. He turned to go.

"Can't you come back this way and hev a little talk about ol' times?" said Gabriel, warming toward Dumphy under the magic of old associations, and ignoring with provoking unconsciousness the sting of his last speech. "There's Olly ez 'ud jest admire to see ye. Ye mind Olly?—the baby, Grace's little sister, growed a fine likely gal now. See yer," continued Gabriel with sudden energy, putting down his pick and shovel, "I'll jess go over thar with ye now."

"No! no!" said Dumphy quickly. "Busy! Can't! 'Nother time! Good-day; see you again some time. So long!" and he hurriedly departed, retracing his steps until the claim and its possessor were lost in the intervening foliage.

Then he paused, hesitated, and then striking across the summit of the hill, made his way boldly to Gabriel's cottage.

Either Mrs. Conroy was expecting him, or had detected him coming through the woods, for she opened the door to him and took him into her little parlour with a graciousness of demeanour and an elaboration of toilet that would have been dangerous to any other man. But, like most men with a deservedly bad reputation among women, Mr. Dumphy always rigidly separated any weakness of gallantry from his business.

"Here only for a few moments. Sorry can't stay longer. You're looking well!" said Mr. Dumphy.

Mrs. Conroy said she had not expected the pleasure of a personal interview; Mr. Dumphy must be *so* busy always.

"Yes. But I like to bring good news myself. The specimens you sent have been assayed by first-class, reliable men. They'll do. No gold—but eighty per cent. silver. Hey! P'r'aps you expected it."

But Mr. Dumphy could see plainly from Mrs. Conroy's eager face that she had not expected it.

"Silver," she gasped—"eighty per cent!"

He was mystified, but relieved. It was evident that she had not consulted anybody else, and that he was first on the ground. So he said curtly—

"What do you propose?"

"I don't know," began the lady. "I haven't thought"——

"Exactly!" interrupted Humphy. "Haven't got any proposition. Excuse me—but" (taking out his watch) "time's nearly up. Look here. Eighty per cent.'s big thing! But silver mine takes gold mine to run it. All expense first—no profit till you get down. Works, smelting—cost twenty per cent. Here's my proposition. Put whole thing in joint-stock company; 100 shares; five millions capital. You take fifty shares. I'll take twenty-five—dispose of other twenty-five as I can. How's that? Hey? You can't say! Well—think of it!"

But all Mrs. Conroy could think of was two and a half millions! It stared at her, stretching its gigantic ciphers across the room. It blazed in golden letters on cheques, —it rose on glittering piles of silver coin to the ceiling of the parlour. Yet she turned to him with a haggard face, and said—

"But this—this money—is only in prospective."

"Cash your draft for the sum ten minutes after the stock's issued. That's business."

With this certainty Mrs. Conroy recovered herself.

"I will talk—with—my husband," she said.

Mr. Dumphy smiled—palpably, openly, and shamelessly. Mrs. Conroy coloured quickly, but not from the consciousness Mr. Dumphy attributed to her, of detected cunning. She had begun to be ashamed of the position she believed she occupied in this man's eyes, and fearful that he should have discovered her husband's indifference to her.

"I've already seen him," said Mr. Dumphy quietly.

The colour dropped from Mrs. Conroy's cheeks.

"He knows nothing of this," she said faintly.

"Of course," said Dumphy half contemptuously, "he said so; referred to you. That's all right. That's business."

"You did not tell him—you dared not"——she said excitedly.

Mr. Dumphy looked curiously at her for a moment. Then he rose and shut the door.

"Look here," he said, facing Mrs. Conroy in a hard, matter-of-fact way, "do you mean to say that what that man—your husband—said, was true? That he knows nothing of you; of the circumstances under which you came here?"

"He does not—I swear to God he does not," she said passionately.

It was inexplicable, but Mr. Dumphy believed her.

"But how will you explain this to him? You can do nothing without him."

"Why should *he* know more? If he has discovered this mine, it is *his*—free of any gift of mine—as independent of any claim of mine as if we were strangers. The law makes him the owner of the mine that he discovers, no matter on whose land it may be found. In personating his sister, I only claimed a grant to the land. He has made the discovery which gives it its value! Even that sister," she added with a sudden flash in her eyes—"even that sister, were she living, could not take it from him now!"

It was true! This woman, with whose weakness he had played, had outwitted them all, and slipped through their fingers almost without stain or blemish. And in a way so simple! Duped as he had been, he could hardly restrain his admiration, and said quite frankly and heartily—

"Good—that's business!"

And then—ah me! this clever creature—this sharp adventuress, this Anonyma Victrix began to cry, and to beg him not to tell *her husband!*

At this familiar sign of the universal feminine weakness, Dumphy picked up his ears and arts again.

"Where's your proof that your husband is the first discoverer?" he said curtly, but not unkindly. "Won't that paper that Dr. Devarges gave his sister show that the doctor was really the discoverer of this lead?"

"Yes; but Dr. Devarges is dead, and I hold the paper."

"Good!" He took out his watch. "I've five minutes more. Now look here. I'm not going to say that you haven't managed this thing well—you have!—and that you can, if you like, get along without me—you can! See! I'm not going to say that I went into this thing without the prospect of making something out of it myself. I have! That's business. The thing for you to consider now is this: understanding each other as we do, couldn't you push this thing through better with my help—and helping me—than to go elsewhere! Understand me! You could find a dozen men in San Francisco who would make you as good an offer and better! But it wouldn't be to their interest to keep down any unpleasant reminders of the past as it would be mine. You understand?"

Mrs. Conroy replied by extending her hand.

"To keep my secret from every one—from *him*," she said earnestly.

"Certainly—*that's* business."

Then these two artful ones shook hands with a heartfelt and loyal admiration and belief for each other that I fear more honest folks might have profited by, and Mr. Dumphy went off to dine.

As Mrs. Conroy closed the front door, Olly came running in from the back piazza. Mrs. Conroy caught her in her arms and discharged her pent-up feelings, and, let us hope, her penitence, in a joyful and passionate embrace. But Olly struggled to extricate herself. When at last she got her head free, she said angrily—

"Let me go. I want to see him."

"Who—Mr. Dumphy?" asked Mrs. Conroy, still holding the child, with a half-hysterical laugh.

"Yes. Gabe said he was here. Let me go, I say!"

"What do you want with him?" asked her captor with shrill gaiety.

"Gabe says—Gabe says—let me go, will you? Gabe says he knew"——

"Whom?"

"My dear, dear sister Grace! There! I didn't mean to hurt you—but I must go!"

And she did, leaving the prospective possessor of two and a half millions, vexed, suspicious, and alone.

CHAPTER III.

MR. DUMPHY MEETS AN OLD FRIEND.

PETER DUMPHY was true to his client. A few days after he had returned to San Francisco he dispatched a note to Victor, asking an interview. He had reasoned that, although Victor was vanquished and helpless regarding the late discovery at One Horse Gulch, yet his complicity with Mrs. Conroy's earlier deceit might make it advisable that his recollection of that event should be effaced. He was waiting a reply when a card was brought to him by a clerk. Mr. Dumphy glanced at it impatiently, and read the name of "Arthur Poinsett." Autocrat as Dumphy was in his own counting-house and business circle, the name was one of such recognised power in California that he could not ignore its claims to his attention. More than that, it represented a certain respectability and social elevation which Dumphy, with all his scepticism and democratic assertion, could not with characteristic shrewdness afford to undervalue. He said, "Show him in," without lifting his head from the papers that lay upon his desk.

The door opened again to an elegant-looking young man, who lounged carelessly into the awful presence without any of that awe with which the habitual business visitors approached Peter Dumphy. Indeed, it was possible that never before had Mr. Dumphy's door opened to one who was less affected by the great capitalist's reputation. Nevertheless, with the natural ease of good breeding, after depositing his hat on the table, he walked quietly to the fireplace, and stood with his back toward it with courteous, but perhaps too indifferent patience. Mr. Dumphy was at last obliged to look up.

"Busy, I see," yawned Poinsett, with languid politeness.

"Don't let me disturb you. I thought your man said you were disengaged. Must have made a mistake."

Mr. Dumphy was forced to lay aside his pen, and rise, inwardly protesting.

"You don't know me by my card. I have the advantage, I think," continued the young man with a smile, "even in the mere memory of faces. The last time I saw you was—let me see—five years ago. Yes! you were chewing a scrap of buffalo hide to keep yourself from starving."

"Philip Ashley!" said Mr. Dumphy in a low voice, looking hastily around, and drawing nearer the stranger.

"Precisely," returned Poinsett somewhat impatiently, raising his own voice. "That was my *nom de guerre.* But Dumphy seems to have been *your* real name after all."

If Dumphy had conceived any idea of embarrassing Poinsett by the suggestion of an *alias* in his case, he could have dismissed it after this half-contemptuous recognition of his own proper cognomen. But he had no such idea. In spite of his utmost effort he felt himself gradually falling into the same relative position—the same humble subordination he had accepted five years before. It was useless to think of his wealth, of his power, of his surroundings. Here in his own bank parlour he was submissively waiting the will and pleasure of this stranger. He made one more desperate attempt to regain his lost prestige.

"You have some business with me, eh? Poinsett!" He commenced the sentence with a dignity, and ended it with a familiarity equally inefficacious.

"Of course," said Poinsett carelessly, shifting his legs before the fire. "Shouldn't have called otherwise on a man of such affairs at such a time. You are interested, I hear, in a mine recently discovered at One Horse Gulch on the Rancho of the Blessed Innocents. One of my clients holds a grant, not yet confirmed, to the Rancho."

"Who?" said Mr. Dumphy quickly.

"I believe that is not important nor essential for you to know until we make a formal claim," returned Arthur quietly, "but I don't mind satisfying your curiosity. It's Miss Dolores Salvatierra."

Mr. Dumphy felt relieved, and began with gathering courage and brusqueness, "That don't affect"——

"Your mining claim; not in the least," interrupted Arthur quietly. "I am not here to press or urge any rights that we may have. We may not even submit the grant for patent. But my client would like to know something of the present tenants, or, if you will, owners. You represent them, I think? A man and wife. The woman appears first as a spinster, assuming to be a Miss Grace Conroy, to whom an alleged transfer of an alleged grant was given. She next appears as the wife of one Gabriel Conroy, who is, I believe, an alleged brother of the alleged Miss Grace Conroy. You'll admit, I think, it's a pretty mixed business, and would make a pretty bad showing in court. But this adjudicature we are not yet prepared to demand. What we want to know is this—and I came to you, Dumphy, as the man most able to tell us. Is the sister or the brother real—or are they both impostors? Is there a legal marriage? Of course *your* legal interest is not jeopardised in any event."

Mr. Dumphy partly regained his audacity.

"*You* ought to know—*you* ran away with the real Grace Conroy," he said, putting his hands in his pockets.

"Did I? Then this is not she, if I understand you. Thanks! And the brother"——

"Is Gabriel Conroy, if I know the man," said Dumphy shortly, feeling that he had been entrapped into a tacit admission. "But why don't you satisfy yourself?"

"You have been good enough to render it unnecessary," said Arthur, with a smile. "I do not doubt your word.

I am, I trust, too much of a lawyer to doubt the witness I myself have summoned. But who is this woman?"

"The widow of Dr. Devarges."

"The *real* thing?"

"Yes, unless Grace Conroy should lay claim to that title and privilege. The old man seems to have been pretty much divided in his property and affections."

The shaft did not apparently reach Arthur, for whom it was probably intended. He only said,

"Have you legal evidence that she *is* the widow? If it were a fact, and a case of ill-treatment or hardship, why it might abate the claim of my client, who is a rich woman, and whose sympathies are of course in favour of the real brother and real sister. By the way, there is another sister, isn't there?"

"Yes, a mere child."

"That's all. Thank you. I sha'n't trespass further upon your time. Good-day."

He had taken up his hat and was moving toward the door. Mr. Dumphy, who felt that whatever might have been Poinsett's motives in this interview, he, Dumphy, had certainly gained nothing, determined to retrieve himself, if possible, by a stroke of audacity.

"One moment," he said, as Poinsett was carefully settling his hat over his curls. "You know whether this girl is living or not. What has become of her?"

"But I don't," returned Poinsett calmly, "or I shouldn't come to *you*."

There was something about Poinsett's manner that prevented Dumphy from putting him in the category of "all men," that both in his haste and his deliberation Mr. Dumphy was apt to say "were liars."

"When and where did you see her last?" he asked less curtly.

"I left her at a hunter's cabin near the North Fork while I went back for help. I was too late. A relief party from the valley had already discovered the other dead. When I returned for Grace she was gone—possibly with the relief party. I always supposed it was the expedition that succoured you."

There was a pause, in which these two scamps looked at each other. It will be remembered that both had deceived the relief party in reference to their connexions with the unfortunate dead. Neither believed, however, that the other was aware of the fact. But the inferior scamp was afraid to ask another question that might disclose his own falsehood; and the question which might have been an embarrassing one to Arthur, and have changed his attitude toward Dumphy, remained unasked. Not knowing the reason of Dumphy's hesitation, Arthur was satisfied of his ignorance, and was still left the master. He nodded carelessly to Dumphy and withdrew.

As he left the room he brushed against a short, thickset man, who was entering at the same moment. Some instinct of mutual repulsion caused the two men to look at each other. Poinsett beheld a sallow face, that, in spite of its belonging to a square figure, seemed to have a consumptive look; a face whose jaw was narrow and whose lips were always half-parted over white, large, and protruding teeth; a mouth that apparently was always breathless—a mouth that Mr. Poinsett remembered as the distinguishing and unpleasant feature of some one vaguely known to him professionally. As the mouth gasped and parted further in recognition, Poinsett nodded carelessly in return, and attributing his repulsion to that extraordinary feature thought no more about it.

Not so the new-comer. He glanced suspiciously after Arthur and then at Mr. Dumphy. The latter, who had recovered his presence of mind and his old audacity, turned them instantly upon him.

"Well! What have you got to propose?" he said, with his usual curt formula.

"It is you have something to say; you sent for *me*," said his visitor.

"Yes. You left me to find out that there was another grant to that mine. What does all this mean, Ramirez?"

Victor raised his eyes and yellow fringes to the ceiling, and said, with a shrug—

"*Quien sabe?* there are grants and grants!"

"So it seems. But I suppose you know that we have a title now better than any grant—a mineral discovery."

Victor bowed and answered with his teeth, "*We*, eh?"

"Yes, I am getting up a company for her husband."

"Her husband—good!"

Dumphy looked at his accomplice keenly. There was something in Victor's manner that was vaguely suspicious. Dumphy, who was one of those men to whose courage the habit of success in all things was essential, had been a little shaken by his signal defeat in his interview with Poinsett, and now became irritable.

"Yes—her husband. What have you got to propose about it, eh? Nothing? Well, look here, I sent for you to say that as everything now is legal and square, you might as well dry up in regard to her former relations or your first scheme. You sabe?" Dumphy became slangy as he lost his self-control. "You are to know nothing about Miss Grace Conroy."

"And there is no more any sister, eh—only a wife?"

"Exactly."

"So."

"You will of course get something for these preliminary steps of yours, although you understand they have been useless, and that your claim is virtually dead. You are, in fact, in no way connected with her present success. Unless—unless," added Dumphy, with a gratuitous malice that defeat had engendered, "unless you expect something for having been the means of making a match between her and Gabriel."

Victor turned a little more yellow in the thin line over his teeth. "Ha! ha! good—a joke," he laughed. "No, I make no charge to you for that; not even to you. No—ha! ha!" At the same moment had Mr. Dumphy known what was passing in his mind he would have probably moved a little nearer the door of his counting-room.

"There's nothing we can pay you for but silence. We may as well understand each other regarding that. That's your interest; it's ours only so far as Mrs. Conroy's social standing is concerned, for I warn you that exposure might seriously compromise you in a business way, while it would not hurt us. I could get the value of Gabriel's claim to the mine advanced to-morrow, if the whole story were known to-night. If you remember, the only evidence of a previous discovery exists in a paper in our possession. Perhaps we pay you for that. Consider it so, if you like. Consider also that any attempt to get hold of it legally or otherwise would end in its destruction. Well, what do you say? All right. When the stock is issued I'll write you a cheque: or perhaps you'd take a share of stock?"

"I would prefer the money," said Victor, with a peculiar laugh.

Dumphy affected to take no notice of the sarcasm. "Your head is level, Victor," he said, returning to his papers. "Don't meddle with stocks. Good day!"

Victor moved toward the door. "By the way, Victor," said Dumphy, looking up, calmly, "if you know the owner of this lately discovered grant, you might intimate that any litigation wouldn't pay. That's what I told their counsel a moment ago."

"Poinsett?" asked Victor, pausing, with his hand on the door.

"Yes! But as he also happens to be Philip Ashley—the chap who ran off with Grace Conroy, you had better go and see him. Perhaps he can help you better than I. Good day."

And, turning from the petrified Victor, Mr. Dumphy, conscious that he had fully regained his prestige, rang his bell to admit the next visitor.

CHAPTER IV.

MR. JACK HAMLIN TAKES A HOLIDAY.

FOR some weeks Mr. Hamlin had not been well, or, as he more happily expressed it, had been "off colour." The celebrated Dr. Duchesne, an ex-army surgeon, after a careful diagnosis, had made several inquiries of Jack, in a frank way that delighted Mr. Hamlin, and then had said very quietly—

"You are not doing justice to your profession, Jack. Your pulse is 75, and that won't do for a man who habitually deals faro. Been doing pretty well lately, and having a good time, eh? I thought so! You've been running too fast, and under too high pressure. You must take these weights off the safety valve, Jack—better take the blower down altogether. Bank your fires and run on half steam. For the next two months I shall run you. You must live like a Christian." Noticing the horror of Jack's face, he added hastily, "I mean go to bed before midnight, get up before you want to, eat more and drink less, don't play to win, bore yourself thoroughly, and by that time I'll be able to put you back at that table as strong and cool as ever. You used to sing, Jack; sit down at the piano and give me a taste of your quality. * * * There, that'll do; I thought so! You're out of practice and voice. Do that every day, for a week, and it will come easier. I haven't seen you stop and talk to a child for a month. What's become of that little boot-black that you used to bedevil? I've a devilish good mind to send you to a foundling hospital for the good of the babies and yourself. Find out some poor ranchero with a dozen children, and teach 'em singing. Don't mind what you eat, as long as you eat regularly. I'd have more hopes of you, Jack, if I'd dragged you out of Starvation Camp, in the Sierras, as I did a poor fellow six years ago, than finding you here in these luxurious quarters. Come! Do as I say, and I'll stop that weariness, dissipate that giddiness, get rid of that pain, lower that pulse, and put you back where you were. I don't like your looks, Jack, at all. I'd buck against any bank you ran, all night."

From which the intelligent reader will, I hope and trust, perceive that this popular doctor's ideas of propriety resided wholly in his intentions. With the abstract morality of Hamlin's profession as a gambler he did not meddle; with his competency to practise that profession only was he concerned. Indeed, so frank was he in his expression, that a few days later he remarked to a popular clergyman, "I must put you under the same treatment as I did Jack Hamlin—do you know him?—a gambler and a capital fellow; you remind me of him. Same kind of trouble—cured him as I will you." And he did.

The result of which advice was that in two weeks Mr. Jack Hamlin found himself dreadfully bored and *ennuyé*, but loyal to his trust with his physician, wandering in the lower coast counties. At San Luis Rey, he attended a bull-fight, and was sorely tempted to back the bull heavily, and even conceived the idea of introducing a grizzly bear, taking all the odds himself, but remembered his promise, and fled the fascination. And so the next day, in a queer old-fashioned diligence, he crossed the coast range, and drifted into the quiet Mission of San Antonio. Here he was so done up and bored with the journey and the unpromising aspect of the town, that he quietly yielded his usual profane badinage of the landlord to his loyal henchman and negro body-servant, "Pete," and went to bed at the solitary "Fonda," in the usual flea-infested bedroom of the Spanish California inn.

"What does she look like, Pete?" said Jack, languidly.

Pete, who was familiar with his master's peculiarities of speech, knew that the feminine pronoun referred to the town, and responded with great gravity—

"De fac' is, Mahs Jack, dah don't peah to be much show heah foh you. Deys playin' three-card monte in the bah room, but 'taint no squar game. It 'ud do you no good, it might jess rile you. Deys a fass pinto hoss hitched to a poss in de yard—a hoss dat de owner don't seem to understand nohow. If you was right smart agin, I might let you go down thar and get a bet outer some o' dem Greasers. But 'twon't do nohow. Deys a kind o' school—Sunday-school, I reckon—nex doah. Lots o' little children saying prayers, singin' and praisin' de Lord, sah."

"What day is this?" asked Jack, with sudden trepidation.

"Sunday, sah."

Jack uttered a plaintive groan and rolled over.

"Give one of these children a quarter, and tell him there's another quarter waiting for him up here."

"You won't get no child to fool wid dis day, Mahs Jack, shuah. Deys bound to get licked when dey goes. Folks is mighty hard on dem boys, Sunday, sah; and it's de Lord's day, Mahs Jack."

Partly for the sake of horrifying his attendant, who notwithstanding his evil associations was very devout, Jack gave way to violent denunciation of any system of theology that withheld children from romping with him any day he might select.

"Open that window," he groaned, finally, "and shove the bed alongside of it. That'll do. Hand me that novel. You needn't read to me to-day; you can finish that Volney's 'Ruins' another time."

It may be remarked here that it had been Jack's invalid habit to get Pete to read to him. As he had provided himself with such books as were objectionable to Pete, as they were always utterly incomprehensible when filtered through his dialect, and as he always made the reader repeat the more difficult words, he extracted from this diversion a delicious enjoyment, which Pete never suspected.

"You can go now," he said, when Pete had arranged him comfortably. "I shan't want you this afternoon. Take some money. I reckon you won't find any church of your kind here, but if anybody interferes with you, jest lambaste him! If you can't do it, jest spot him, and *I* will!" (Mr. Hamlin never allowed anybody but himself to object to his follower's religious tendencies.) "Have a good time, Pete! Don't tangle yourself up if you can help it. The liquor about here is jest pizen."

With this parting adjuration Mr. Hamlin turned over and tried to devote himself to his book. But after reading a few lines the letters somehow got blurred and indistinct, and he was obliged to put the book down with a much graver recollection of the doctor's warning than he had ever had before. He was obliged to confess to a singular weariness and lassitude that had become habitual, and to admit that he had more pain at times than—as he put it—"a man ought to have." The idea of his becoming blind or paralysed dawned upon him gradually, at first humorously; wondering if he couldn't deal faro as well without the use of his legs, for instance, which were of no account to a man under the table; if there could not be raised cards for the blind as well as raised letters. The idea of feeling a "pair" or a "flush" amused him greatly, and then he remembered more gravely poor Gordon, who, becoming gradually paralysed, blew his brains out. "The best thing he could do," he soliloquised, seriously. The reflection, however, had left such a depressing effect upon his mind that the exaltation of liquor for a moment seemed to be the proper thing for him; but the next moment, remembering his promise to the doctor, he changed his mind, and—with an effort—his reflections.

For relief he turned his paling face to the window. It gave upon a dusty courtyard, the soil of which was pulverised by the pawing of countless hoofs during the long, dry summer; upon a tiled roof that rose above an adobe wall, over which again rose the two square whitewashed towers of the Mission church. Between these towers he caught a glimpse of dark green foliage, and beyond this the shining sea.

It was very hot and dry. Scarcely a wave of air stirred the curtains of the window. That afternoon the trade-winds which usually harried and bullied the little Mission of San Antonio did not blow, and a writhing weeping willow near the window, that whipped itself into trifling hysterics on the slightest pretext, was surprised into a stony silence. Even the sea beyond glittered and was breathless. It reminded Jack of the mouth of the man he met in Sacramento at the hotel, and again had quarrelled with in San Francisco. And there, absolutely, was the man, the very man, gazing up at the hotel from the shadows of the courtyard. Jack was instantly and illogically furious.

Had Pete been there he would at once have sent an insulting message; but, while he was looking at him, a sound rose upon the air which more pleasantly arrested his attention.

It was an organ. Not a very fine instrument, nor skilfully played; but an instrument that Jack was passionately fond of. I forgot to say that he had once occupied the position of organist in the Second Presbyterian Church of Sacramento, until a growing and more healthy public sentiment detected an incongruity between his secular and Sunday occupations, and a prominent deacon, a successful liquor-dealer, demanded his resignation. Although he afterwards changed his attentions to a piano, he never entirely lost his old affections. To become the possessor of a large organ, to introduce it gradually, educating the public taste, as a special feature of a first-class gambling saloon, had always been one of Jack's wildest ambitions. So he raised himself upon his elbow and listened. He could see also that the adjacent building was really a recent addition to the old Mission church, and that what appeared to be a recess in the wall was only a deeply embrasured window. Presently a choir of fresh young voices joined the organ. Mr. Hamlin listened more attentively; it was one of Mozart's masses with which he was familiar.

For a few moments he forgot his pain and lassitude, and lying there hummed in unison. And then, like a true enthusiast, unmindful of his surroundings, he lifted his voice—a very touching tenor, well known among his friends—and joined in, drowning, I fear, the feebler pipe of the little acolytes within. Indeed, it was a fine sight to see this sentimental scamp, lying sick nigh unto dissolution through a dissipated life and infamous profession, down upon his back in the dingy *cuarto* of a cheap Spanish inn, voicing the litanies of the Virgin. Howbeit, once started in he sang it through, and only paused when the antiphonal voices and organ ceased. Then he lifted his head, and, leaning on his elbow, looked across the courtyard. He had hoped for the appearance of some of the little singers, and had all ready a handful of coin to throw to them, and a few of those ingenious epithets and persuasive arguments by which he had always been successful with the young. But he was disappointed.

"I reckon school ain't out yet," he said to himself, and was about to lie down again, when a face suddenly appeared at the grating of the narrow window.

Mr. Hamlin as suddenly became breathless, and the colour rose to his pale face. He was very susceptible to female beauty, and the face that appeared at the grating was that of a very beautiful Indian girl. He thought, and was ready to swear, that he had never seen anything half so lovely. Framed in the recess of the embrasure as a shrine, it might have been a shadowed devotional image, but that the face was not so angelically beautiful as it was femininely fascinating, and that the large deeply fringed eyes had an expression of bright impatience and human curiosity. From his secure vantage behind the curtain Mr. Hamlin knew that he could not be seen, and so lay and absorbed this lovely bronze apparition which his voice seemed to have evoked from the cold bronze adobe wall. And then, as suddenly, she was gone, and the staring sunlight and glittering sea beyond seemed to Mr. Hamlin to have gone too.

When Pete returned at sunset, he was amazed and alarmed to find his master dressed and sitting by the window. There was a certain brightness in his eye and an unwonted colour in his cheek that alarmed him still more.

"You ain't bin and gone done nuffin' agin de doctor's orders, Mahs Jack?" he began.

"You'll find the whisky flask all right, unless you've been dippin' into it, you infernal old hypocrite," responded Jack, cheerfully, accepting the implied suspicion of his servant. "I've dressed myself because I'm goin' to church to-night, to find out where you get your liquor. I'm happy because I'm virtuous. Trot out that Volney's 'Ruins,' and wade in. You're gettin' out o' practice, Pete. Stop. Because you're religious, do you expect me to starve? Go and order supper first! Stop. Where in blank are you going? Here, you've been gone three hours on an errand for me, and if you ain't runnin' off without a word about it."

"Gone on an errand foh you, sah?" gasped the astonished Pete.

"Yes! Didn't I tell you to go round and see what was the kind of religious dispensation here?" continued Jack, with an unmoved face. "Didn't I charge you particularly to observe if the Catholic Church was such as a professing Christian and the former organist of the Second Presbyterian Church of Sacramento could attend? And now I suppose I've got to find out myself. I'd bet ten to one you ain't been there at all!"

In sheer embarrassment Pete began to brush his master's clothes with ostentatious and apologetic diligence, and said—

"I'se no Papist, Mahs Jack, but if I'd thought"——

"Do you suppose I'm going to sit here without my supper while you abuse the Catholic Church—the only church that a gentleman"—— but the frightened Pete was gone.

The Angelus bell had just rung, and it lacked a full half hour yet before vespers, when Mr. Hamlin lounged into the old Mission church. Only a few figures knelt here and there—mere vague, black shadows in the gloom. Aided, perhaps, more by intuition than the light of the dim candles on the high altar, he knew that the figure he looked for was not among them; and seeking the shadow of a column he calmly waited its approach. It seemed a long time. A heavy-looking woman, redolent of garlic, came in and knelt nearly opposite. A yellow vaquero, whom Mr. Hamlin recalled at once as one he had met on the road hither, —a man whose Spanish profanity, incited by unruly cattle, had excited Jack's amused admiration,—dropped on his knees, and with equally characteristic volubility began a supplication to the Virgin. Then two or three men, whom Jack recognised as the monte-players of the "Fonda," began, as it seemed to Jack, to bewail their losses in lachrymose accents. And then Mr. Hamlin, highly excited, with a pulse that would have awakened the greatest concern of his doctor, became nervously and magnetically aware that some one else was apparently waiting and anxious as himself, and had turned *his* head at the entrance of each one of the congregation. It was a figure Jack had at first overlooked. Safe in the shadow of the column, he could watch it without being seen himself. Even in the gloom he could see the teeth and eyes of the man he had observed that afternoon—his old antagonist at Sacramento.

Had it been anywhere else Jack would have indulged his general and abstract detestation of Victor by instantly picking a quarrel with him. As it was, he determined upon following him when he left the church—of venting on him any possible chagrin or disappointment he might then have, as an excitement to mitigate the unsupportable dreariness of the Mission. The passions are not so exclusive as moralists imagine, for Mr. Hamlin was beginning to have his breast filled with wrath against Victor, in proportion as his doubts of the appearance of the beautiful stranger grew stronger in his mind, when two figures momentarily darkened the church porch, and a rustle of silk stole upon his ear. A faint odour of spice penetrated through the incense. Jack looked up, and his heart stopped beating.

It was she. As she reached the stall nearly opposite, she put aside her black veil, and disclosed the same calm, nymph-like face he had seen at the window. It was doubly beautiful now. Even the strange complexion had for Jack a bewildering charm. She looked around, hesitated for a moment, and then knelt between the two monte-players. With an almost instinctive movement Jack started forward, as if to warn her of the contaminating contact. And then he stopped, his own face crimsoned with shame. For the first time he had doubted the morality of his profession.

The organ pealed out; the incense swam; the monotonous voice of the priest rose upon the close, sluggish air, and Mr. Jack Hamlin dreamed a dream. He had dispossessed the cold, mechanical organist, and, seating himself at the instrument, had summoned all the powers of reed and voice to sing the pæans—ah me! I fear not of any abstract Being, but of incarnate flesh and blood. He heard her pure, young voice lifted beside his; even in that cold, passionless commingling there was joy unspeakable, and he knew himself exalted. Yet he was conscious even in his dream, from his own hurried breathing, and something that seemed to swell in his throat, that he could not have sung a note. And then he came back to his senses, and a close examination of the figure before him. He looked at the graceful, shining head, the rich lace veil, the quiet elegance of attire, even to the small satin slipper that stole from beneath her silken robe—all united with a refinement and an air of jealous seclusion, that somehow removed him to an immeasurable distance.

The anthem ceased, the last notes of the organ died away, and the lady rose. Half an hour before, Jack would have gladly stepped forward to have challenged even a passing glance from the beautiful eyes of the stranger; now a timidity and distrust new to the man took possession of him. He even drew back closer in the shadow as she stepped toward the pillar, which supported on its face a font of holy water. She had already slipped off her glove, and now she leaned forward—so near he could almost feel her warm breath—and dipped her long slim fingers into the water. As she crossed herself with the liquid symbol, Jack gave a slight start. One or two drops of holy water thrown from her little fingers had fallen on his face.

CHAPTER V.

VICTOR MAKES A DISCOVERY.

HAPPILY for Mr. Hamlin, the young girl noticed neither the effect of her unconscious baptismal act, nor its object, but moved away slowly to the door. As she did so, Jack stepped from the shadow of the column, and followed her with eyes of respectful awe and yearning. She had barely reached the porch, when she suddenly and swiftly turned and walked hurriedly back, almost brushing against Mr. Hamlin. Her beautiful eyes were startled and embarrassed, her scarlet lips parted and paling rapidly, her whole figure and manner agitated and discomposed. Without noticing him she turned toward the column, and under the pretext of using the holy water, took hold of the font, and leaned against it, as if for support, with her face averted from the light. Jack could see her hands tighten nervously on the stone, and fancied that her whole figure trembled as she stood there.

He hesitated for a moment, and then moved to her side; not audaciously and confident, as was his wont with women, but with a boyish colour in his face, and a timid, half-embarrassed manner.

"Can I do anything for you, Miss?" he said, falteringly. "You don't seem to be well. I mean you look tired. Shan't I bring you a chair? It's the heat of this hole—I mean it's so warm here. Shan't I go for a glass of water, a carriage?"

Here she suddenly lifted her eyes to his, and his voice and presence of mind utterly abandoned him.

"It's nothing," she said, with a dignified calm, as sudden and as alarming to Jack as her previous agitation—"nothing," she added, fixing her clear eyes on his, with a look so frank, so open, and withal, as it seemed to Jack, so cold and indifferent, that his own usually bold glance fell beneath it, "nothing but the heat and closeness; I am better now."

"Shall I"—— began Jack, awkwardly.

"I want nothing, thank you."

Seeming to think that her conduct required some explanation, she added, hastily—

"There was a crowd at the door as I was going out, and in the press I felt giddy. I thought some one—some man—pushed me rudely. I daresay I was mistaken."

She glanced at the porch against which a man was still leaning.

The suggestion of her look and speech—if it were a suggestion—was caught instantly by Jack. Without waiting for her to finish the sentence, he strode to the door. To his wrathful surprise the lounger was Victor. Mr. Hamlin did not stop for explanatory speech. With a single expressive word, and a single dexterous movement of his arm and foot, he tumbled the astonished Victor down the steps at one side, and then turned toward his late companion.

But she had been equally prompt. With a celerity quite inconsistent with her previous faintness, she seized the moment that Victor disappeared to dart by him and gain her carriage, which stood in waiting at the porch. But as it swiftly drove away, Mr. Hamlin caught one grateful glance from those wonderful eyes, one smile from those perfect lips, and was happy. What matters that he had an explanation—possibly a quarrel on his hands? Ah me! I fear this added zest to the rascal's satisfaction.

A hand was laid on his shoulder. He turned and saw the face of the furious Victor, with every tooth at a white heat, and panting with passion. Mr. Hamlin smiled pleasantly.

"Why, I want to know!" he ejaculated, with an affectation of rustic simplicity, "if it ain't you, Johnny. Why, darn my skin! And this is your house? You and St. Anthony in partnership, eh? Well, that gets me! And here I tumbled you off your own stoop, didn't I? I might have known it was you by the way you stood there. Mightn't I, Johnny?"

"My name is not Johnny—*Carámba!*" gasped Victor, almost beside himself with impatient fury.

"Oh, it's that, is it? Any relation to the *Carámbas* of Dutch Flat? It ain't a pretty name. I like Johnny better. And I would'nt make a row here now. Not to-day, Johnny; it's Sunday. I'd go home. I'd go quietly home, and I'd beat some woman or child to keep myself in training. But I'd go home first. I wouldn't draw that knife, neither, for it might cut your fingers, and frighten the folks around town. I'd go home quietly, like a good nice little man. And in the morning I'd come round to the hotel on the next square, and I'd ask for Mr. Hamlin, Mr. Jack Hamlin, Room No. 29; and I'd go right up to his room, and I'd have such a time with him—such a high old time; I'd just make that hotel swim with blood."

Two or three of the monte players had gathered around Victor, and seemed inclined to take the part of their countryman. Victor was not slow to improve this moment of adhesion and support.

"Is it dogs that we are, my compatriots?" he said to them bitterly; "and he—this one—a man infamous!"

Mr. Hamlin, who had a quick ear for abusive and interjaculatory Spanish, overheard him. There was a swift chorus of "*Carámba!*" from the allies, albeit wholesomely restrained by something in Mr. Hamlin's eye which was visible, and probably a suspicion of something in Mr. Hamlin's pocket which was not visible. But the remaining portion of Mr. Hamlin was ironically gracious.

"Friends of yours, I suppose?" he inquired, affably. "'*Carámbas*' all of them, too! Perhaps they'll call with you? Maybe they haven't time and are in a hurry now? If my room isn't large enough, and they can't wait, there's a handy lot o' ground beyond on the next square—*Plaza del Toros*, eh? What did you say? I'm a little deaf in this ear."

Under the pretence of hearing more distinctly, Jack Hamlin approached the nearest man, who, I grieve to say, instantly and somewhat undignifiedly retreated. Mr. Hamlin laughed. But already a crowd of loungers had gathered, and he felt it was time to end this badinage, grateful as it was to his sense of humour. So he lifted his hat gravely to Victor and his friends, replaced it perhaps aggressively tilted a trifle over his straight nose, and lounged slowly back to his hotel, leaving his late adversaries in secure but unsatisfactory and dishonourable possession of the field. Once in his own quarters, he roused the sleeping Pete, and insisted upon opening a religious discussion, in which, to Pete's great horror, he warmly espoused the Catholic Church, averring, with several strong expletives, that it was the only religion fit for a white man, and ending somewhat irreverently by inquiring into the condition of the pistols.

Meanwhile Victor had also taken leave of his friends.

"He has fled—this most infamous!" he said; "he dared not remain and face us! Thou didst observe his fear, Tiburcio? It was thy great heart that did it!"

"Rather he recognised thee, my Victor, and his heart was that of the coyote."

"It was the Mexican nation, ever responsive to the appeal of manhood and liberty, that made his liver as blanched as that of the chicken," returned the gentleman who had retreated from Jack. "Let us then celebrate this triumph with a little glass."

And Victor, who was anxious to get away from his friends, and saw in the prospective *aguardiente* a chance for escape, generously led the way to the first wine-shop.

It chanced to be the principal one of the town. It had the generic quality—that is, was dirty, dingy, ill-smelling, and yellow with cigarette smoke. Its walls were adorned by various prints—one or two French in origin, excellent in art, and defective in moral sentiment, and several of Spanish origin, infamous in art, and admirable in religious feeling. It had a portrait of Santa Anna, and another of the latest successful revolutionary general. It had an allegorical picture representing the Genius of Liberty descending with all the celestial machinery upon the Mexican Confederacy. Moved apparently by the same taste for poetry and personification, the proprietor had added to his artistic collection a highly coloured American handbill representing the Angel of Healing presenting a stricken family with a bottle of somebody's Panacea. At the farther extremity of the low room a dozen players sat at a green-baize table absorbed in monte. Beyond them, leaning against the wall, a harp-player twanged the strings of his instrument, in a lugubrious air, with that singular stickiness of touch and reluctancy of finger peculiar to itinerant performers on that instrument. The card-players were profoundly indifferent to both music and performer.

The face of one of the players attracted Victor's attention. It was that of the odd English translator—the irascible stranger upon whom he had intruded that night of his memorable visit to Don José. Victor had no difficulty in recognising him, although his slovenly and negligent working-dress had been changed to his holiday antique black suit. He did not lift his eyes from the game until he had lost the few silver coins placed in a pile before him, when he rose grimly, and nodding brusquely to the other players, without speaking left the room.

"He has lost five half-dollars—his regular limit—no more, no less," said Victor to his friend. "He will not play again to-night!"

"You know of him?" asked Vincente, in admiration of his companion's superior knowledge.

"Si!" said Victor. "He is a jackal, a dog of the Americanos," he added, vaguely intending to revenge himself on the stranger's former brusqueness by this depreciation. "He affects to know our history—our language. Is it a question of the fine meaning of a word—the shade of a technical expression?—it is him they ask, not us! It is thus they treat us, these heretics! *Carámba!*"

"*Carámba!*" echoed Vincente, with a vague patriotism superinduced by *aguardiente.* But Victor had calculated to unloose Vincente's tongue for his private service.

"It is the world, my friend," he said, sententiously. "These Americanos—come they here often?"

"You know the great American advocate—our friend—Don Arturo Poinsett?"

"Yes," said Victor, impatiently. "Comes he?"

"Eh! does he not?" laughed Vincente. "Always. Ever. Eternally. He has a client—a widow, young, handsome, rich, eh?—one of his own race."

"Ah! you are wise, Vincente!"

Vincente laughed a weak spirituous laugh.

"Ah! it is a transparent fact. Truly—of a verity. Believe me!"

"And this fair client—who is she?"

"Donna Maria Sepulvida!" said Vincente, in a drunken whisper.

"How is this? You said she was of his own race."

"Truly, I did. She is *Americana*. But it is years ago. She was very young. When the Americans first came, she was of the first. She taught the child of the widower Don José Sepulvida, herself almost a child; you understand? It was the old story. She was pretty, and poor, and young; the Don grizzled, and old, and rich. It was fire and tow. Eh? Ha! Ha! The Don meant to be kind, you understand, and made a rich wife of the little *Americana*. He was kinder than he meant, and in two years, *Carámba!* made a richer widow of the Donna."

If Vincente had not been quite thrown by his potations, he would have seen an undue eagerness in Victor's mouth and eyes.

"And she is pretty—tall and slender like the Americans, eh?—large eyes, a sweet mouth?"

"An angel. Ravishing!"

"And Don Arturo—from legal adviser turns a lover!"

"It is said," responded Vincente, with drunken cunning and exceeding archness; "but thou and I, Victor, know better. Love comes not with a brief! Eh? Look, it is an old flame, believe me. It is said it is not two months that he first came here, and she fell in love with him at the first glance. *Absurdo! Disparátado!* Hear me, Victor; it was an old flame; an old quarrel made up. Thou and I have heard the romance before. Two lovers not rich, eh? Good! Separation; despair. The Señorita marries the rich man, eh?"

Victor was too completely carried away by the suggestion of his friend's speech, to conceal his satisfaction. Here was the secret at last. Here was not only a clue, but absolutely the missing Grace Conroy herself. In this young *Americana*—this—widow—this client of her former lover, Philip Ashley, he held the secret of three lives. In his joy he slapped Vincente on the back, and swore roundly that he was the wisest of men.

"I should have seen her—the heroine of this romance—my friend. Possibly, she was at mass?"

"Possibly not. She is Catholic, but Don Arturo is not. She does not often attend when he is here."

"As to-day?"

"As to-day."

"You are wrong, friend Vincente," said Victor, a little impatiently. "I was there; I saw her."

Vincente shrugged his shoulders and shook his head with drunken gravity.

"It is impossible, Señor Victor, believe me."

"I tell you I saw her," said Victor, excitedly. "*Borrachon!* She was there! By the pillar. As she went out she partook of *agua bendita.* I saw her; large eyes, an oval face, a black dress and mantle."

Vincente, who, happily for Victor, had not heard the epithet of his friend, shook his head and laughed a conceited drunken laugh.

"Tell me not this, friend Victor. It was not her thou didst see. Believe me, I am wise. It was the Donna Dolores who partook of *agua bendita*, and alone. For there is none, thou knowest, that has a right to offer it to her. Look you, foolish Victor, she has large eyes, a small mouth, an oval face. And dark—ah, she is dark!"

"'In the dark all are as the devil,'" quoted Victor, impatiently, "how should I know? Who then *is* she?" he demanded almost fiercely, as if struggling with a rising fear. "Who is this Donna Dolores?"

"Thou art a stranger, friend Victor. Hark ye. It is the half-breed daughter of the old commander of San Ysabel. Yet, such is the foolishness of old men, she is his heiress! She is rich, and lately she has come into possession of a great grant, very valuable. Thou dost understand, friend Victor? Well, why dost thou stare? She is a recluse. Marriage is not for her; love, love! the tender, the subduing, the delicious, is not for her. She is of the Church, my Victor. And to think that thou didst mistake this ascetic, this nun, this little brown novice, this Donna Dolores Salvatierra for the little American coquette. Ha! Ha! It is worth the fee of another bottle? Eh? Victor, my friend! Thou dost not listen. Eh? Thou wouldst fly, traitor. Eh? what's that thou sayst? Bobo! Dupe thyself!"

For Victor stood before him, dumb, but for that single epithet. Was he not a dupe? Had he not been cheated again, and this time by a blunder in his own malice? If he had really, as he believed, identified Grace Conroy in this dark-faced devotee whose name he now learned for the first time, by what diabolical mischance had he deliberately put her in possession of the forged grant, and so blindly restored her the missing property? Could Don Pedro have been treacherous? Could he have known, could they all—Arthur Poinsett, Dumphy, and Julie Devarges—have known this fact of which he alone was ignorant? Were they not laughing at him now? The thought was madness.

With a vague impression of being shaken rudely off by a passionate hand, and a drunken vision of a ghastly and passionate face before him uttering words of impotent rage and baffled despair, Vincente, the wise and valiant, came slowly and amazedly to himself, lying over the table. But his late companion was gone.

CHAPTER VI.

AN EXPERT.

A COLD, grey fog hac that night stolen noiselessly in from the sea, and, after possessing the town, had apparently intruded itself in the long, low plain before the *hacienda* of the Rancho of the Holy Trinity, where it sullenly lingered even after the morning sun had driven in its eastern outposts. Viewed from the Mission towers, it broke a cold grey sea against the corral of the *hacienda*, and half hid the white walls of the *hacienda* itself. It was characteristic of the Rancho that, under such conditions, at certain times it seemed to vanish entirely from the sight, or rather to lose and melt itself into the outlines of the low foot-hills, and Mr. Perkins, the English translator, driving a buggy that morning in that direction, was forced once or twice to stop and take his bearings anew, until the grey sea fell, and the *hacienda* again heaved slowly into view.

Although Mr. Perkins' transformations were well known to his intimate associates, it might have been difficult for any stranger to have recognised the slovenly drudge of Pacific Street, in the antique dandy who drove the buggy. Mr. Perkins' hair was brushed, curled, and darkened by dye. A high stock of a remote fashion encompassed his neck, above which his face, whitened by cosmetics to conceal his high complexion, rested stiffly and expressionless as a mask. A light blue coat buttoned tightly over his breast, and a pair of close-fitting trousers strapped over his japanned leather boots, completed his remarkable *ensemble.* It was a figure well known on Montgomery Street after three o'clock—seldom connected with the frousy visitor of the Pacific Street den, and totally unrecognisable on the plains of San Antonio.

It was evident, however, that this figure, eccentric as it was, was expected at the *hacienda,* and recognised as having an importance beyond its antique social distinction. For, when Mr. Perkins drew up in the courtyard, the grave *major domo* at once ushered him into the formal, low-studded drawing-room already described in these pages, and in another instant the Donna Dolores Salvatierra stood before him.

With a refined woman's delicacy of perception, Donna Dolores instantly detected under this bizarre exterior something that atoned for it, which she indicated by the depth of the half-formal curtsey she made it. Mr. Perkins met the salutation with a bow equally formal and respectful. He was evidently agreeably surprised at his reception, and impressed with her manner. But like most men of ill-assured social position, he was a trifle suspicious and on the defensive. With a graceful gesture of her fan, the Donna pointed to a chair, but her guest remained standing.

"*I* am a stranger to you, Señor, but *you* are none to me," she said, with a gracious smile. "Before I ventured upon the boldness of seeking this interview, your intelligence, your experience, your honourable report was already made known to me by your friends. Let me call myself one of these—even before I break the business for which I have summoned you."

The absurd figure bowed again, but even through the pitiable chalk and cosmetics of its complexion, an embarrassed colour showed itself. Donna Dolores noticed it, but delicately turned toward an old-fashioned secretary, and opened it, to give her visitor time to recover himself. She drew from a little drawer a folded, legal-looking document, and then placing two chairs beside the secretary, seated herself in one. Thus practically reminded of his duty, Mr. Perkins could no longer decline the proffered seat.

"I suppose," said Donna Dolores, "that my business, although familiar to you generally—although you are habitually consulted upon just such questions—may seem strange to you, when you frankly learn my motives. Here is a grant purporting to have been made to my—father—the late Don José Salvatierra. Examine it carefully, and answer me a single question to the best of your judgment." She hesitated, and then added—"Let me say, before you answer yes or no, that to me there are no pecuniary interests involved—nothing that should make you hesitate to express an opinion which you might be called upon legally to prove. *That* you will never be required to give. Your answer will be accepted by me in confidence; will not, as far as the world is concerned, alter the money value of this document—will leave you free hereafter to express a different opinion, or even to reverse your judgment publicly if the occasion requires it. You seem astounded, Señor Perkins. But I am a rich woman. I have no need to ask your judgment to increase my wealth."

"Your question is"—— said Mr. Perkins, speaking for the first time without embarrassment.

"Is that document a forgery?"

He took it out of her hand, opened it with a kind of professional carelessness, barely glanced at the signature and seals, and returned it.

"The signatures are genuine," he said, with business-like brevity; then he added, as if in explanation of that brevity, "I have seen it before."

Donna Dolores moved her chair with the least show of uneasiness. The movement attracted Mr. Perkins' attention. It was something novel. Here was a woman who appeared actually annoyed that her claim to a valuable property was valid. He fixed his eyes upon her curiously.

"Then you think it is a genuine grant?" she said, with a slight sigh.

"As genuine as any that receive a patent at Washington," he replied, promptly.

"Ah!" said Donna Dolores, simply. The feminine interjection appeared to put a construction upon Señor Perkins' reply that both annoyed and challenged him. He assumed the defensive.

"Have you any reason to doubt the genuineness of this particular document?"

"Yes. It was only recently discovered among Don José's papers, and there is another in existence."

Señor Perkins again reached out his hand, took the paper, examined it attentively, held it to the light and then laid it down. "It is all right," he said. "Where is the other?"

"I have it not," said Donna Dolores.

Señor Perkins shrugged his shoulders respectfully as to Donna Dolores, but scornfully of an unbusiness-like sex. "How did you expect me to institute a comparison?"

"There is no comparison necessary if that document is genuine," said the Donna, quickly.

Señor Perkins was embarrassed for a moment. "I mean there might be some mistake. Under what circumstances is it held—who holds it? To whom was it given?"

"That is a part of my story. It was given five years

ago to a Dr. Devarges—I beg your pardon, did you speak?"

Señor Perkins had not spoken, but was staring with grim intensity at Donna Dolores. "You—said—Dr. Devarges," he repeated, slowly.

"Yes. Did you know him?" It was Donna Dolores' turn to be embarrassed. She bit her lip and slightly contracted her eyebrows. For a moment they both stood on the defensive.

"I have heard the name before," Mr. Perkins said at last, with a forced laugh.

"Yes, it is the name of a distinguished *savant*," said Donna Dolores, composedly. "Well—*he* is dead. But he gave this grant to a young girl named—named"—Dolores paused as if to recall the name—"named Grace Conroy."

She stopped and raised her eyes quickly to her companion, but his face was unmoved, and his momentary excitement seemed to have passed. He nodded his head for her to proceed.

"Named Grace Conroy," repeated Donna Dolores, more rapidly, and with freer breath. "After the lapse of five years a woman—an impostor—appears to claim the grant under the name of Grace Conroy. But perhaps finding difficulty in carrying out her infamous scheme, by some wicked, wicked art, she gains the affections of the brother of this Grace, and marries him as the next surviving heir." And Donna Dolores paused, a little out of breath, with a glow under her burnished cheek and a slight metallic quality in her voice. It was perhaps no more than the natural indignation of a quickly sympathising nature, but Mr. Perkins did not seem to notice it. In fact, within the last few seconds his whole manner had become absent and preoccupied; the stare which he had fixed a moment before on Donna Dolores was now turned to the wall, and his old face, under its juvenile mask, looked still older.

"Certainly, certainly," he said at last, recalling himself with an effort. "But all this only goes to prove that the grant may be as fraudulent as the owner. Then, you have nothing really to make you suspicious of your own claim but the fact of its recent discovery? Well, that I don't think need trouble you. Remember your grant was given when lands were not valuable, and your late father might have overlooked it as unimportant." He rose with a slight suggestion in his manner that the interview had closed. He appeared anxious to withdraw, and not entirely free from the same painful pre-absorption that he had lately shown. With a slight shade of disappointment in her face Donna Dolores also rose.

In another moment he would have been gone, and the lives of these two people thus brought into natural yet mysterious contact have flowed on unchanged in each monotonous current. But as he reached the door he turned to ask a trivial question. On that question trembled the future of both.

"This real Grace Conroy then I suppose has disappeared. And this—Doctor—Devarges"—he hesitated at the name as something equally fictitious—"you say is dead. How then did this impostor gain the knowledge necessary to set up the claim? Who is *she?*"

"Oh, she is—that is—she married Gabriel Conroy under the name of the widow of Dr. Devarges. Pardon me! I did not hear what you said. Holy Virgin! What is the matter? You are ill. Let me call Sanchez! Sit here!"

He dropped into a chair, but only for an instant. As she turned to call assistance he rose and caught her by the arm.

"I am better," he said. "It is nothing—I am often

taken in this way. Don't look at me. Don't call anybody except to get me a glass of water—there, that will do."

He took the glass she brought him, and instead of drinking it threw back his head and poured it slowly over his forehead and face as he leaned backward in the chair. Then he drew out a large silk handkerchief and wiped his face and hair until they were dry. Then he sat up and faced her. The chalk and paint was off his face, his high stock had become unbuckled, he had unbuttoned his coat and it hung loosely over his gaunt figure; his hair, although still dripping, seemed to have become suddenly bristling and bushy over his red face. But he was perfectly self-possessed, and his voice had completely lost its previous embarrassment.

"Rush of blood to the head," he said, quietly; "felt it coming on all the morning. Gone now. Nothing like cold water and sitting posture. Hope I didn't spoil your carpet. And now to come back to your business." He drew up his chair, without the least trace of his former diffidence, beside Donna Dolores. "Let's take another look at your grant." He took it up, drew a small magnifying glass from his pocket and examined the signature. "Yes, yes! signature all right. Seal of the Custom House. Paper all regular." He rustled it in his fingers. "You're all right—the swindle is with Madame Devarges. There's the forgery—there's this spurious grant."

"I think not," said Donna Dolores, quietly.

"Why?"

"Suppose the grant is exactly like this in everything, paper, signature, seal and all."

"That proves nothing," said Mr. Perkins, quickly. "Look you. When this grant was drawn—in the early days—there were numbers of these grants lying in the

Custom House like waste paper, drawn and signed by the Governor, in blank, only wanting filling in by a clerk to make them a valid document. She !—this impostor—this Madame Devarges, has had access to these blanks, as many have since the American Conquest, and that grant is the result. But she is not wise, no! I know the handwriting of the several copyists and clerks—I was one myself. Put me on the stand, Donna Dolores—put me on the stand, and I'll confront her as I have the others."

"You forget," said Donna Dolores, coldly, "that I have no desire to legally test this document. And if Spanish grants are so easily made, why might not this one of mine be a fabrication? You say you know the handwriting of the copyists—look at this."

Mr. Perkins seized the grant impatiently, and ran his eye quickly over the interlineations between the printed portions. "Strange!" he muttered. "This is not my own nor Sanchez; nor Ruiz; it is a new hand. Ah! what have we here—a correction in the date—in still another hand? And this—surely I have seen something like it in the office. But where?" He stopped, ran his fingers through his hair, but after an effort at recollection abandoned the attempt. "But why?" he said, abruptly, "why should this be forged?"

"Suppose that the other were genuine, and suppose that this woman got possession of it in some wicked way. Suppose that some one, knowing of this, endeavoured by this clever forgery to put difficulties in her way without exposing her."

"But who would do that?"

"Perhaps the brother—her husband! Perhaps some one," continued Donna Dolores, embarrassedly, with the colour struggling through her copper cheek, "some—one

—who—did—not—believe that the real Grace Conroy was dead or missing!"

"Suppose the devil!—I beg your pardon. But people don't forge documents in the interests of humanity and justice. And why should it be given to *you?*"

"I am known to be a rich woman," said Donna Dolores. "I believe," she added, dropping her eyes with a certain proud diffidence that troubled even the preoccupied man before her, "I—believe—that is I am told—that I have a reputation for being liberal, and—and just."

Mr. Perkins looked at her for a moment with undisguised admiration. "But suppose," he said, with a bitterness that seemed to grow out of that very contemplation, "suppose this woman, this adventuress, this impostor, were a creature that made any such theory impossible. Suppose she were one who could poison the very life and soul of any man—to say nothing of the man who was legally bound to her; suppose she were a devil who could deceive the mind and heart, who could make the very man she was betraying most believe her guiltless and sinned against; suppose she were capable of not even the weakness of passion; but that all her acts were shrewd, selfish, pre-calculated even to a smile or a tear—do you think such a woman—whom, thank God! such as *you* cannot even imagine—do you suppose such a woman would not have guarded against even this? No! no!"

"Unless," said Donna Dolores, leaning against the secretary with the glow gone from her dark face and a strange expression trembling over her mouth, "unless it were the revenge of some rival."

Her companion started. "Good! It is so," he muttered to himself. "*I* would have done it. I could have done it! You are right, Donna Dolores." He walked to the window and then came hurriedly back, buttoning his coat as he did so, and rebuckling his stock. "Some one is coming! Leave this matter with me. I will satisfy you and myself concerning this affair. Will you trust this paper with me?" Donna Dolores without a word placed it in his hand. "Thank you," he said, with a slight return of his former embarrassment, that seemed to belong to his ridiculous stock and his buttoned coat rather than any physical or moral quality. "Don't believe me entirely disinterested either," he added, with a strange smile. "*Adios.*"

She would have asked another question, but at that instant the clatter of hoofs and sound of voices arose from the courtyard, and with a hurried bow he was gone. The door opened again almost instantly to the bright laughing face and coquettish figure of Mrs. Sepulvida.

"Well!" said that little lady, as soon as she recovered her breath. "For a religiously inclined young person and a notorious recluse, I must say you certainly have more masculine company than falls to the lot of the worldly. Here I ran across a couple of fellows hanging around the *casa* as I drove up, and come in only to find you closeted with an old exquisite. Who was it—another lawyer, dear? I declare, it's too bad. *I* have only one!"

"And that one is enough, eh?" smiled Donna Dolores, somewhat gravely, as she playfully tapped Mrs. Sepulvida's fair cheek with her fan.

"Oh yes!" she blushed a little coquettishly—"of course! And here I rode over, post haste, to tell you the news. But first, tell me who is that wicked, dashing-looking fellow outside the courtyard? It can't be the lawyer's clerk."

"I don't know who you mean; but it is, I suppose," said Donna Dolores, a little wearily. "But tell me the news. I am all attention."

But Mrs. Sepulvida ran to the deep embrasured window and peeped out. "It isn't the lawyer, for he is driving away in his buggy, as if he were hurrying to get out of the fog, and my gentleman still remains. Dolores!" said Mrs. Sepulvida, suddenly facing her friend with an expression of mock gravity and humour, "this won't do! Who is that cavalier?"

With a terrible feeling that she was about to meet the keen eyes of Victor, Donna Dolores drew near the window from the side where she could look out without being herself seen. Her first glance at the figure of the stranger satisfied her that her fears were unfounded; it was not Victor. Reassured, she drew the curtain more boldly. At that instant the mysterious horseman wheeled, and she met full in her own the black eyes of Mr. Jack Hamlin. Donna Dolores instantly dropped the curtain and turned to her friend.

"I don't know!"

"Truly, Dolores?"

"Truly, Maria."

"Well, I believe you. I suppose then it must be *me!*"

Donna Dolores smiled, and playfully patted Mrs. Sepulvida's joyous face.

"Well, then?" she said invitingly.

"Well, then," responded Mrs. Sepulvida, half in embarrassment and half in satisfaction.

"The news!" said Donna Dolores.

"Oh—well," said Mrs. Sepulvida, ith mock deliberation, "it has come at last!"

"It has?" said Donna Dolores, looking gravely at her friend.

"Yes. He has been there again to-day."

"And he asked you?" said Donna Dolores, opening her .an and turning her face toward the window.

"He asked me."

"And you said"——

Mrs. Sepulvida tripped gaily toward the window and looked out.

"I said"——

"What?"

"NO!"

BOOK V.

THE VEIN.

CHAPTER I.

IN WHICH GABRIEL RECOGNISES THE PROPRIETIES.

AFTER the visit of Mr. Peter Dumphy, One Horse Gulch was not surprised at the news of any stroke of good fortune. It was enough that he, the great capitalist, the successful speculator, had been there! The information that a company had been formed to develop a rich silver mine recently discovered on Conroy's Hill was received as a matter of course. Already the theories of the discovery were perfectly well established. That it was simply a grand speculative *coup* of Dumphy's—that upon a boldly conceived plan this man intended to build up the town of One Horse Gulch—that he had invented "the lead" and backed it by an ostentatious display of capital in mills and smelting works solely for a speculative purpose; that five years before he had selected Gabriel Conroy as a simple-minded tool for this design; that Gabriel's Two and One Half Millions was merely an exaggerated form of expressing the exact wages—One Thousand dollars a year, which was all Dumphy had paid him for the use of his name, and that it was the duty of every man to endeavour to realise quickly on the advance of property before this enormous bubble burst—this was the theory of one-half the people of One Horse Gulch. On the other hand, there was a large party who knew exactly the reverse. That the whole thing was purely accidental; that Mr. Peter Dumphy being called by other business to One Horse Gulch, while walking with Gabriel Conroy one day had picked up a singular piece of rock on Gabriel's claim, and had said, "This looks like silver;" that Gabriel Conroy had laughed at the suggestion, whereat Mr. Peter Dumphy, who never laughed, had turned about curtly and demanded in his usual sharp business way, "Will you take Seventeen Millions for all your right and title to this claim?" That Gabriel—"you know what a blank fool Gabe is!"—had assented, "and this way, sir, actually disposed of a property worth, on the lowest calculation, One Hundred and Fifty Millions." This was the generally accepted theory of the other and more imaginative portion of One Horse Gulch.

Howbeit within the next few weeks following the advent of Mr. Dumphy, the very soil seemed to have quickened through that sunshine, and all over the settlement pieces of plank and scantling—thin blades of new dwellings—started up under that beneficent presence. On the bleak hill sides the more extensive foundations of the Conroy Smelting Works were laid. The modest boarding-house and restaurant of Mrs. Markle was found inadequate to the wants and inconsistent with the greatness of One Horse Gulch, and a new hotel was erected. But here I am anticipating another evidence of progress—namely, the daily newspaper, in which these events were reported with a combination of ease and elegance one may envy yet never attain. Said the *Times*:—

"The Grand Conroy House, now being inaugurated, will be managed by Mrs. Susan Markle, whose talents as a *chef de cuisine* are as well known to One Horse Gulch as her rare social graces and magnificent personal charms. She will be aided by her former accomplished assistant, Miss Sarah Clark. As hash-slinger, Sal can walk over anything of her weight in Plumas."

With these and other evidences of an improvement in public taste, the old baleful title of "One Horse Gulch" was deemed incongruous. It was proposed to change that name to "Silveropolis," there being, in the figurative language of the Gulch, "more than one horse could draw."

Meanwhile, the nominal and responsible position of Superintendent of the new works was filled by Gabriel, although the actual business and executive duty was performed by a sharp, snappy young fellow of about half Gabriel's size, supplied by the Company. This was in accordance with the wishes of Gabriel, who could not bear idleness; and the Company, although distrusting his administrative ability, wisely recognised his great power over the workmen through the popularity of his easy democratic manners, and his disposition always to lend his valuable physical assistance in cases of emergency. Gabriel had become a great favourite with the men ever since they found that prosperity had not altered his simple nature. It was pleasant to them to be able to point out to a stranger this plain, unostentatious, powerful giant, working like themselves, and with themselves, with the added information that he owned half the mine, and was worth Seventeen Millions! Always a shy and rather lonely man, his wealth seemed to have driven him, by its very oppressiveness, to the society of his humble fellows for relief. A certain deprecatoriness of manner whenever his riches were alluded to, strengthened the belief of some in that theory that he was merely the creature of Dumphy's speculation.

Although Gabriel was always assigned a small and insignificant part in the present prosperity of One Horse Gulch, it was somewhat characteristic of the peculiar wrongheadedness of this community that no one ever suspected his wife of any complicity in it. It had been long since settled that her superiority to her husband was chiefly the feminine charm of social grace and physical attraction. That, warmed by the sunshine of affluence, this butterfly would wantonly flit from flower to flower, and eventually quit her husband and One Horse Gulch for some more genial clime, was never doubted. "She'll make them millions fly ef she hez to fly with it," was the tenor of local criticism. A pity, not unmixed with contempt, was felt for Gabriel's apparent indifference to this prophetic outlook; his absolute insensibility to his wife's ambiguous reputation was looked upon as the hopelessness of a thoroughly deceived man. Even Mrs. Markle, whose attempts to mollify Olly had been received coldly by that young woman—even she was a convert to the theory of the complete domination of the Conroy household by this alien and stranger.

But despite this baleful prophecy, Mrs. Conroy did not fly nor show any inclination to leave her husband. A new house was built, with that rapidity of production that belonged to the climate, among the pines of Conroy's Hill, which on the hottest summer day still exuded the fresh sap of its green timbers and exhaled a woodland spicery. Here the good taste of Mrs. Conroy flowered in chintz, and was always fresh and feminine in white muslin curtains and pretty carpets, and here the fraternal love of Gabriel brought a grand piano for the use of Olly, and a teacher. Hither also came the best citizens of the county—even the notabilities of the State, feeling that Mr. Dumphy had, to a certain extent, made One Horse Gulch respectable, soon found out also that Mrs. Conroy was attractive; the Hon. Blank had dined there on the occasion of his last visit to his constituents of the Gulch; the Hon. Judge Beeswinger had told in her parlour several of his most effective stories. Colonel Starbottle's manly breast had dilated over her dish-covers, and he had carried away with him not only a vivid appreciation of her charms capable of future eloquent expression, but an equally vivid idea of his own fascinations, equally incapable of concealment. Gabriel himself rarely occupied the house except for the exigencies of food and nightly shelter. If decoyed there at other times by specious invitations of Olly, he compromised by sitting on the back porch in his shirt sleeves, alleging as a reason his fear of the contaminating influence of his short black pipe.

"Don't ye mind *me*, July," he would say, when his spouse with anxious face and deprecatory manner would waive her native fastidiousness and aver that "she liked it." "Don't ye mind me, I admire to sit out yer. I'm a heap more comfortable outer doors, and allus waz. I reckon the smell might get into them curtings, and then—and then," added Gabriel, quietly ignoring the look of pleased expostulation with which Mrs. Conroy recognised this fancied recognition of her tastes, "and then *Olly's friends and thet teacher*, not being round like you and me allez and used to it, *they* mightn't like it. And I've heerd that the smell of nigger-head terbacker do git inter the strings of a pianner and kinder stops the music. A pianner's a mighty cur'us thing. I've heerd say they're as dilikit and ailin' ez a child. Look in 'em and see them little strings a twistin' and crossin' each other like the reins of a six mule team, and it 'tain't no wonder they gets mixed up often."

It was not Gabriel's way to notice his wife's manner very closely, but if he had at that moment he might have fancied that there were other instruments whose fine chords were as subject to irritation and discordant disturbance. Perhaps only vaguely conscious of some womanish sullenness on his wife's part, Gabriel would at such times disengage himself as being the possible disorganising element, and lounge away. His favourite place of resort was his former cabin, now tenantless and in rapid decay, but which he had refused to dispose of, even after the erection of his two later dwellings rendered it an unnecessary and unsightly encumbrance of his lands. He loved to linger by the deserted hearth and smoke his pipe in solitude, not from any sentiment, conscious or unconscious, but from a force of habit, that was in this lonely man almost as pathetic.

He may have become aware at this time that a certain growing disparity of sentiment and taste which he had before noticed with a vague pain and wonder, rendered his gradual separation from Olly a necessity of her well-doing. He had indeed revealed this to her on several occasions with that frankness which was natural to him. He had apologised with marked politeness to her music teacher, who once invited him to observe Olly's proficiency, by saying in general terms that he "took no stock in chunes. I reckon it's about ez easy, Miss, if ye don't ring me in. Thet chile's got to get on without thinkin' o' me—or my 'pinion—allowin' it was wuth thinkin' on." Once meeting Olly walking with some older and more fashionable school friends whom she had invited from Sacramento, he had delicately avoided them with a sudden and undue consciousness of his great bulk, and his slow moving intellect, painfully sensitive to what seemed to him to be the preternatural quickness of the young people, and turned into a by-path.

On the other hand, it is possible that with the novelty of her new situation, and the increased importance that wealth brought to Olly, she had become more and more oblivious of her brother's feelings, and perhaps less persistent in her endeavours to draw him toward her. She knew that he had attained an equal importance among his fellows from this very wealth, and also a certain evident, palpable, superficial respect which satisfied her. With her restless ambition and the new life that was opening before her, his slower old-fashioned methods, his absolute rusticity—that day by day appeared more strongly in contrast to his surroundings—began to irritate where it had formerly only touched her sensibilities. From this irritation she at last escaped by the unfailing processes of youth and the fascination of newer impressions. And so, day by day and hour by hour, they drifted slowly apart. Until one day Mrs. Conroy was pleasantly startled by an announcement from Gabriel, that he had completed arrangements to send Olly to boarding-school in Sacramento. It was understood, also, that this was only a necessary preliminary to the departure of herself and husband for a long-promised tour of Europe.

As it was impossible for one of Gabriel's simple nature to keep his plans entirely secret, Olly was perfectly aware of his intention, and prepared for the formal announcement, which she knew would come in Gabriel's quaint serious way. In the critical attitude which the child had taken toward him, she was more or less irritated, as an older person might have been, with the grave cautiousness with which Gabriel usually explained that conduct and manner which was perfectly apparent and open from the beginning. It was during a long walk in which the pair had strayed among the evergreen woods, when they came upon the little dismantled cabin. Here Gabriel stopped. Olly glanced around the spot and shrugged her shoulders. Gabriel, more mindful of Olly's manner than he had ever been of any other of her sex, instantly understood it.

"It ain't a purty place, Olly," he began, rubbing his hands, "but we've had high ole times yer—you and me.

Don't ye mind the nights I used to kem up from the gulch and pitch in to mendin' your gownds, Olly, and you asleep? Don't ye mind that—ar dress I copper fastened?" and Gabriel laughed loudly, and yet a little doubtfully.

Olly laughed too, but not quite so heartily as her brother, and cast her eyes down upon her own figure. Gabriel followed the direction of her glance. It was not perhaps easy to re-create in the figure before him the outré little waif who such a short time—such a long time—ago had sat at his feet in that very cabin. It is not alone that Olly was better dressed, and her hair more tastefully arranged, but she seemed in some way to have become more refined and fastidious—a fastidiousness that was plainly an outgrowth of something that she possessed but *he* did not. As he looked at her, another vague hope that he had fostered—a fond belief that as she grew taller she would come to look like Grace, and so revive the missing sister in his memory—this seemed to fade away before him. Yet it was characteristic of the unselfishness of his nature, that he did not attribute this disappointment to her alone, but rather to some latent principle in human nature whereof he had been ignorant. He had even gone so far as to invite criticism on a hypothetical case from the sagacious Johnson. "It's the difference atween human natur and brute natur," that philosopher had answered promptly. "A purp's the same purp allez, even arter it's a grown dorg, but a child ain't—it's the difference atween reason and instink."

But Olly, to whom this scene recalled another circumstance, did not participate in Gabriel's particular reminiscence.

"Don't you remember, Gabe," she said, quickly, "the first night that sister July came here and stood right in that very door? Lord! how flabergasted we was to be sure! And if anybody'd told me, Gabe, that *she* was going to marry *you*—I'd, I'd a knocked 'em down," she blurted out, after hesitating for a suitable climax.

Gabriel, who in his turn did not seem to be particularly touched with Olly's form of reminiscence, rose instantly above all sentiment in a consideration of the proprieties. "Ye shouldn't talk o' knockin' people down, Olly—it ain't decent for a young gal," he said, quickly. "Not that I mind it," he added, with his usual apology, "but allowin' that some of them purty little friends o' yours or teacher now, should hear ye! Sit down for a spell, Olly. I've suthin' to tell ye."

He took her hand in his, and made her sit beside him on the rude stone that served as the old doorstep of the cabin.

"Maybe ye might remember," he went on, lightly lifting her hand in his, and striking it gently across his knee to beget an easy confidential manner, "maybe ye might remember that I allers allowed to do two things ef ever I might make a strike—one was to give you a good schoolin'—the other was to find Grace, if so be as she was above the yearth. They waz many ways o' finding out—many ways o' settin' at it, but they warn't *my* ways. I allus allowed that ef thet child waz in harkenin' distance o' the reach o' my call, she'd hear me. I mout have took other men to help me—men ez was sharp in them things, men ez was in that trade—but I didn't. And why?"

Olly intimated by an impatient shake of her head that she didn't know.

"Because she was that shy and skary with strangers. Ye disremember how shy she was, Olly, in them days, for ye was too young to notice. And then, not bein' shy yourself, but sorter peart, free and promisskiss, ready and able to keep up your end of a conversation with anybody, and allus ez chipper as a jay-bird—why, ye don't kinder allow that fur Gracy as I do. And thar was reasons why that purty chile should be shy—reasons ye don't understand now, Olly, but reasons pow'ful and strong to such a child as thet."

"Ye mean, Gabe," said the shamelessly direct Olly, "that she was bashful, hevin' ran away with her bo."

That perplexity which wiser students of human nature than Gabriel have experienced at the swift perception of childhood in regard to certain things left him speechless. He could only stare hopelessly at the little figure before him.

"Well, wot did *you* do, Gabe? Go on!" said Olly, impatiently.

Gabriel drew a long breath.

"Thar bein' certing reasons why Gracy should be thet shy—reasons consarning propperty o' her deceased parients," boldly invented Gabriel, with a lofty ignoring of Olly's baser suggestion, "I reckoned that she should get the first word from *me* and not from a stranger. I knowed she warn't in Californy, or she'd hev seen them handbills I issued five years ago. What did I do? Thar is a paper wot's printed in New York, called the *Herald.* Thar is a place in that thar paper whar they print notisses to people that is fur, fur away. They is precious words from fathers to their sons, from husbands to their wives, from brothers to sisters, ez can't find each other, from"——

"From sweethearts to thar bo's," said Olly, briskly; "I know."

Gabriel paused in speechless horror.

"Yes," continued Olly. "They calls 'em 'Personals.' Lord! I know all 'bout them. Gals get bo's by them, Gabe!"

Gabriel looked up at the bright, arching vault above him. Yet it did not darken nor split into fragments. And he hesitated. Was it worth while to go on? Was there anything he could tell this terrible child—his own sister—which she did not already know better than he?

"I wrote one o' them Pursonals," he went on to say, doggedly, "in this ways." He paused, and fumbling in his waistcoat pocket, finally drew out a well-worn newspaper slip, and straightening it with some care from its multitudinous enfoldings, read it slowly, and with that peculiar patronising self-consciousness which distinguishes the human animal in the rehearsal of its literary composition.

"Ef G. C. will communicate with sufferin' and anxious friends, she will confer a favour on ole Gabe. I will come and see her, and Olly will rise up and welcome her. Ef G. C. is sick or don't want to come she will write to G. C. G. C. is same as usual, and so is Olly. All is well. Address G. C., One Horse Gulch, Californy—till further notiss."

"Read it over again," said Olly.

Gabriel did so, readily.

"Ain't it kinder mixed up with them G. C.'s?" queried the practical Olly.

"Not for she," responded Gabriel, quickly, "that's just what July said when I showed her the 'Pursonal.' But I sed to her as I sez to you, it taint no puzzle to Gracy. *She* knows ez our letters is the same. And ef it 'pears queer to strangers, wots the odds? Thet's the idee ov a 'pursonal.' Howsomever, it's all right, Olly. Fur," he continued, lowering his voice confidentially, and drawing his sister closer to his side, "*it's bin ansered!*"

"By Grace?" asked Olly.

"No," said Gabriel, in some slight confusion, "not by Grace, exactly—that is—but yer's the anser." He drew from his bosom a small chamois-skin purse, such as miners used for their loose gold, and extracted the more precious slip. "Read it," he said to Olly, turning away his head.

Olly eagerly seized and read the paper.

"G. C.—Look no more for the missing one who will never return. Look at home. Be happy.—P. A."

Olly turned the slip over in her hands. "Is that all?" she asked, in a higher key, with a rising indignation in her pink cheeks.

"That's all," responded Gabriel; "short and shy—that's Gracy, all over."

"Then all I got to say is it's mean!" said Olly, bringing her brown fist down on her knee. "And that's wot I'd say to that thar P. A.—that Philip Ashley—if I met him."

A singular look, quite unlike the habitual placid, good-humoured expression of the man, crossed Gabriel's face as he quietly reached out and took the paper from Olly's hand.

"Thet's why I'm goin' off," he said, simply.

"Goin' off," repeated Olly.

"Goin' off—to the States. To New York," he responded, "July and me. July sez—and she's a peart sort o' woman in her way, ef not o' your kind, Olly," he interpolated, apologetically, "but pow'ful to argyfy and plan, and she allows ez New York 'ud nat'rally be the stampin' ground o' sich a high-toned feller ez him. And that's why I want to talk to ye, Olly. Thar's only two things ez 'ud ever part you and me, dear, and one on 'em ez this very thing—it's my dooty to Gracy, and the other ez my dooty to you. Et ain't to be expected that when you oughter be gettin' your edykation you'd be cavortin' round the world with me. And you'll stop yer at Sacramento in a A-1 first-class school, ontil I come back. Are ye hark'nin', dear?"

"Yes," said Olly, fixing her clear eyes on her brother.

"And ye ain't to worrit about me. And it 'ud be as well, Olly, ez you'd forget all 'bout this yer gulch, and the folks. Fur yer to be a lady, and in bein' thet brother Gabe don't want ennythin' to cross ye. And I want to say to thet feller, Olly, 'Ye ain't to jedge this yer fammerly by me, fur the men o' that fammerly gin'rally speakin' runs to size, and ain't, so to speak, strong up yer,'" continued Gabriel, placing his hands on his sandy curls; "'but thar's a little lady in school in Californy ez is jest what Gracy would hev bin if she'd had the schoolin'. And ef ye wants to converse with her she kin give you pints enny time.' And then I brings you up, and nat'rally I reckon thet you ain't goin' back on brother Gabe—in 'stronomy, grammar, 'rithmetic and them things."

"But wot's the use of huntin' Grace if she says she'll never return?" said Olly, sharply.

"Ye musn't read them 'pursonals' ez ef they was square. They're kinder conundrums, ye know—puzzles. It says G. C. will never return. Well, s'pose G. C. has another name. Don't you see?"

"Married, maybe," said Olly, clapping her hands.

"Surely," said Gabriel, with a slight colour in his cheeks. "Thet's so."

"But s'pose it doesn't mean Grace after all?" persisted Olly.

Gabriel was for a moment staggered.

"But July sez it does," he answered, doubtfully.

Olly looked as if this evidence was not entirely satisfactory.

"But what does 'look at home' mean?" she continued.

"Thet's it," said Gabriel, eagerly. "Thet reads—'Look at little Olly—ain't she there?' And thet's like Gracy—*allus thinkin' o' somebody else.*"

"Well," said Olly, "I'll stop yer, and let you go. But wot are *you* goin' to do without me?"

Gabriel did not reply. The setting sun was so nearly level with his eyes that it dazzled them, and he was fain to hide them among the clustering curls of Olly, as he held the girl's head in both his hands. After a moment he said—

"Do ye want to know why I like this old cabin and this yer chimbly, Olly?"

"Yes," said Olly, whose eyes were also affected by the sun, and who was glad to turn them to the object indicated.

"It ain't because you and me hez sot there many and many a day, fur that's suthin' that we ain't goin' to think about any more. It's because, Olly, the first lick I ever struck with a pick on this hill was just yer. And I raised this yer chimbly with the rock. Folks thinks thet it was over yonder in the slope whar I struck the silver lead, thet I first druv a pick. But it warn't. And I sometimes think, Olly, that I've had as much square comfort outer thet first lick ez I'll ever get outer the lead yonder. But come, Olly, come! July will be wonderin' whar you is, and ther's a stranger yonder comin' up the road, and I reckon I ain't ez fine a lookin' bo ez a young lady ez you ez, orter to co-mand. Never mind, Olly, he needn't know ez you and me is any relashuns. Come!"

In spite of Gabriel's precautionary haste, the stranger, who was approaching by the only trail which led over the rocky hillside, perceived the couple, and turned toward them interrogatively. Gabriel was forced to stop, not, however, without first giving a slight reassuring pressure to Olly's hand.

"Can you tell me the way to the hotel—the Grand Conroy House I think they call it?" the traveller asked politely.

He would have been at any time an awe-inspiring and aggressive object to One Horse Gulch and to Gabriel, and at this particular moment he was particularly discomposing. He was elaborately dressed, buttoned and patent-leather booted in the extreme limit of some bygone fashion, and had the added effrontery of spotless ruffled linen. As he addressed Gabriel he touched a tall black hat, sacred in that locality to clergymen and gamblers. To add to Gabriel's discomfiture, at the mention of the Grand Conroy House he had felt Olly stiffen aggressively under his hand.

"Foller this yer trail to the foot of the hill, and ye'll strike Main Street; that'll fetch ye thar. I'd go with ye a piece, but I'm imployed," said Gabriel, with infinite tact and artfulness, accenting each word with a pinch of Olly's arm, "imployed by this yer young lady's friends to see her home, and bein' a partikler sort o' fammerly, they makes a row when I don't come reg'lar. Axin' your parding, don't they, Miss?" and to stop any possible retort from Olly before she could recover from her astonishment, he had hurried her into the shadows of the evergreen pines of Conroy Hill.

CHAPTER II.

TRANSIENT GUESTS AT THE GRAND CONROY.

THE Grand Conroy Hotel was new, and had the rare virtue of comparative cleanliness. As yet the odours of bygone dinners, and forgotten suppers, and long dismissed breakfasts had not possessed and permeated its halls and passages. There was no distinctive flavour of preceding guests in its freshly clothed and papered rooms. There was a certain virgin coyness about it, and even the active ministration of Mrs. Markle and Sal was delicately veiled from the public by the interposition of a bar-keeper and Irish waiter. Only to a few of the former *habitués* did these ladies appear with their former frankness and informality. There was a public parlour, glittering with gilt framed mirrors and gorgeous with red plush furniture, which usually froze the geniality of One Horse Gulch, and repressed its larger expression, but there was a little sitting-room beyond sacred to the widow and her lieutenant Sal, where visitors were occasionally admitted. Among the favoured few who penetrated this arcana was Lawyer Maxwell. He was a widower, and was supposed to have a cynical distrust of the sex that was at once a challenge to them and a source of danger to himself.

Mrs. Markle was of course fully aware that Mrs. Conroy had been Maxwell's client, and that it was while on a visit to him she had met with the accident that resulted in her meeting with Gabriel. Unfortunately Mrs. Markle was unable to entirely satisfy herself if there had been any previous acquaintance. Maxwell had declared to her that to the best of his knowledge there had been none, and that the meeting was purely accidental. He could do this without violating the confidence of his client, and it is fair to presume that upon all other matters he was loyally uncommunicative. That Madame Devarges had consulted him regarding a claim to some property was the only information he imparted. In doing this, however, he once accidentally stumbled, and spoke of Mrs. Devarges as "Grace Conroy." Mrs. Markle instantly looked up. "I mean Mrs. Conroy," he said hastily.

"Grace—that was his sister who was lost—wasn't it?"

"Yes," replied Maxwell, demurely, "did he ever talk much to you about her?"

"No-o," said Mrs. Markle, with great frankness, "he and

me only talked on gin'ral topics; but from what Olly used to let on, I reckon that sister was the only woman he ever loved."

Lawyer Maxwell, who, with an amused recollection of his extraordinary interview with Gabriel in regard to the woman before him, was watching her mischievously, suddenly became grave. "I guess you'll find, Mrs. Markle, that his present wife amply fills the place of his lost sister," he said, more seriously than he had intended.

"Never," said Mrs. Markle, quickly. "Not she—the designin', crafty hussy!"

"I am afraid you are not doing her justice," said Maxwell, wiping away a smile from his lips, after his characteristic habit; "but then it's not strange that two bright, pretty women are unable to admire each other. What reason have you to charge *her* with being designing?" he asked again, with a sudden return of his former seriousness.

"Why, her marryin' him," responded Mrs. Markle, frankly; "look at that simple, shy, bashful critter, do you suppose he'd marry her—marry any woman—that didn't throw herself at his head, eh?"

Mrs. Markle's pique was so evident that even a philosopher like Maxwell could not content himself with referring it to the usual weakness of the sex. No man cares to have a woman exhibit habitually her weakness for another man, even when he possesses the power of restraining it. He answered somewhat quickly as he raised his hand to his mouth to wipe away the smile that, however, did not come. "But suppose that you—and others—are mistaken in Gabriel's character. Suppose all this simplicity and shyness is a mask. Suppose he is one of the most perfect and successful actors on or off the stage. Suppose he should turn out to have deceived everybody—even his present wife!"—and Lawyer Maxwell stopped in time.

Mrs. Markle instantly fired. "Suppose fiddlesticks and flapjacks! I'd as soon think o' suspectin' thet child," she said, pointing to the unconscious Manty. "You lawyers are allus suspectin' what you can't understand!" She paused as Maxwell wiped his face again. "What do you mean anyway—why don't yer speak out? What do you know of him?"

"Oh, nothing! only it's as fair to say all this of him as of her—on about the same evidence. For instance, here's a simple, ignorant fellow"——

"He ain't ignorant," interrupted Mrs. Markle, sacrificing argument to loyalty.

"Well, this grown-up child! He discovers the biggest lead in One Horse Gulch, and manages to get the shrewdest financier in California to manage it for him, and that too after he has snatched up an heiress and a pretty woman before the rest of 'em got a sight of her. That may be simplicity; but my experience of guilelessness is that, ordinarily, it isn't so lucky."

"They won't do him the least good, depend upon it," said Mrs. Markle, with the air of triumphantly closing the argument.

It is very possible that Mrs. Markle's dislike was sustained and kept alive by Sal's more active animosity, and the strict espionage that young woman kept over the general movements and condition of the Conroys. Gabriel's loneliness, his favourite haunt on the hillside, the number and quality of Mrs. Conroy's visitors, even fragments of conversation held in the family circle, were all known to Sal, and re-delivered to Mrs. Markle with Sal's own colouring. It is possible that most of the gossip concerning Mrs. Conroy already hinted at, had its origin in the views and observations of this admirable young woman, who did not confine her confidences entirely to her mistress. And when one day a stranger and guest, staying at the Grand Conroy House, sought to enliven the solemnity of breakfast by social converse with Sal regarding the Conroys, she told him nearly everything that she had already told Mrs. Markle.

I am aware that it is alleged that some fascinating quality in this stranger's manner and appearance worked upon the susceptible nature and loosened the tongue of this severe virgin, but beyond a certain disposition to minister personally to his wants, to hover around him archly with a greater quantity of dishes than that usually offered the transient guest, and to occasionally expatiate on the excellence of some extra viand, there was really no ground for the report. Certainly, the guest was no ordinary man; was quite unlike the regular *habitués* of the house, and perhaps to some extent justified this favouritism. He was young, sallow-faced, with very white teeth and skin, yellow hands, and a tropical, impulsive manner, which Miss Sarah Clark generally referred to as "Eyetalian." I venture to transcribe something of his outward oral expression.

"I care not greatly for the flapjack, nor yet for the dried apples," said Victor, whom the intelligent reader has at once recognised, "but a single cup of coffee sweetened by those glances and offered by those fair hands—which I kiss!—are to me enough. And you think that the Meestrees Conroy does not live happily with her husband. Ah! you are wise, you are wise, Mees Clark, I would not for much money find myself under these criticism, eh?"

"Well, eyes bein' given to us to see with by the Lord's holy will, and it ain't for weak creeturs like us to misplace our gifts or magnify 'em," said Sal, in shrill, bashful confusion, allowing an underdone fried egg to trickle from the plate on the coat-collar of the unconscious Judge Beeswinger, "I do say when a woman sez to her husband, ez she's sworn to honour and obey, 'This yer's *my* house, and this yer's *my* land, and yer kin git,' thar ain't much show o' happiness thar. Ef it warn't for hearin' this with my own ears, bein' thar accidental like, and in a sogial way, I wouldn't hev believed it. And she allowin' to be a lady, and afeared to be civil to certain folks ez is ez good ez she and far better, and don't find it necessary to git married to git a position—and could hev done it a thousand times over ef so inclined. But folks is various and self praise is open disgrace. Let me recommend them beans. The pork, ez we allus kills ourselves fur the benefit o' transient gests, bein' a speciality."

"It is of your kindness, Mees Clark, I am already full. And of the pork I touch not, it is an impossibility," said Victor, showing every tooth in his head. "It is much painful to hear of this sad, sad affair. It is bad—and yet you say he has riches—this man. Ah! the what is the world. See, the great manner it has treated those! No, I will not more. I am sufficient now. Ah! eh! what have we here?"

He lowered his voice and eyes as a stranger—the antique dandy Gabriel had met on Conroy's hill the evening before—rose from some unnoticed seat at a side table, and unconcernedly moved away. Victor instantly recognised the card player of San Antonio, his former chance acquaintance of Pacific Street, and was filled with a momentary feeling of suspicion and annoyance. But Sal's *sotto voce* reply that the stranger was a witness attending court seemed to be a reasonable explanation, and the fact that the translator did not seem to recognise him promptly relieved his mind. When he had gone Sal returned to her confidences: "Ez to his riches, them ez knows best hez their own say o' that. Thar was a party yer last week—gents ez was free with their money, and not above exchanging the time o' day with working folk, and though it ain't often ez me or

Sue Markle dips into conversation with entire strangers, yet," continued Sal, with parenthetical tact and courtesy, "Eyetalians,—furriners in a strange land bein' an exception —and them gents let on thet thet vein o' silver on Conroy's hill hed been surveyed and it wazent over a foot wide, and would be played out afore a month longer, and thet old Peter Dumphy knowed it, and hed sold out, and thet thet's the reason Gabriel Conroy was goin' off—jest to be out o' the way when the killapse comes."

"Gabriel! going away, Mees Sal? this is not possible!" ejaculated the fascinating guest, breathing very hard, and turning all his teeth in a single broadside upon the susceptible handmaid. At any other moment, it is possible that Sal might have been suspicious of the stranger's excitement, but the fascination of his teeth held and possessed this fluttering virgin.

"Ef thar ever waz a man ez had an angelic smile," she intimated afterwards in confidence to Mrs. Markle, "it waz thet young Eyetalian." She handed him several dishes, some of them empty, in her embarrassment, and rejoined with an affectation of arch indignation, "Thank ye fur sayin' 'I lie,'—and it's my pay fur bein' a gossip and ez good ez I send—but thar's Olympy Conroy packed away to school fur six months, and thar's the new superintendent ez is come up to take Gabriel's situation, and he a sittin' in a grey coat next to ye a minit ago! Eh? And ye won't take nothin' more? Appil or cranbear' pie?—our own make? I'm afeerd ye ain't made out a dinner!" But Victor had already risen hurriedly and departed, leaving Sal in tormenting doubt whether she had not in her coquettish indignation irritated the tropical nature of this sensitive Italian. "I orter allowed fur his bein' a furriner and not bin so free. Pore young man! I thought he did luk tuk back when I jest allowed that he said I lied." And with a fixed intention of indicating her forgiveness and goodwill the next morning by an extra dish, Sal retired somewhat dejectedly to the pantry. She made a point, somewhat later, of dusting the hall in the vicinity of Victor's room, but was possibly disappointed to find the door open, and the tenant absent. Still later, she imparted some of this interview to Mrs. Markle with a certain air of fatigued politeness and a suggestion that, in the interest of the house solely, she had not repressed perhaps as far as maidenly pride and strict propriety demanded, the somewhat extravagant advances of the stranger. "I'm sure," she added, briskly, "why he kept a lookin' and a talkin' at me in that way, mind can't consave, and transients did notiss. And if he did go off mad, why, he kin git over it." Having thus delicately conveyed the impression of an ardent Southern nature checked in its exuberance, she became mysteriously reticent and gloomy.

It is probable that Miss Clark's theory of Gabriel's departure was not original with her, or entirely limited to her own experience. A very decided disapprobation of Gabriel's intended trip was prevalent in the gulches and bar-room. He quickly lost his late and hard-earned popularity; not a few questioned his moral right to leave One Horse Gulch until its property was put beyond a financial doubt in the future. The men who had hitherto ignored the proposition that he was in any way responsible for the late improvement in business, now openly condemned him for abandoning the position they declared he never had. The *Silveropolis Messenger* talked vaguely of the danger of "changing superintendents" at such a moment, and hinted that the stock of the company would suffer. The rival paper—for it was found that the interests of the town required a separate and distinct expression—had an editorial on "absenteeism," and spoke, crushingly, of those men who, having enriched themselves out of the resources of One Horse Gulch, were now seeking to dissipate that wealth in the excesses of foreign travel.

Meanwhile, the humble object of this criticism, oblivious in his humility of any public interest in his movements or intentions, busied himself in preparations for his departure. He had refused the offer of a large rent for his house from the new superintendent, but had retained a trusty servant to keep it with a view to the possible return of Grace. "Ef thar mout ever come a young gal yer lookin' fur me," he said privately to this servant, "yer not to ax any questions, partiklaly ef she looks sorter shy and bashful, but ye'll gin her the best room in the house, and send to me by igspress, and ye needn't say anythin' to Mrs. Conroy about it." Observing the expression of virtuous alarm on the face of the domestic—she was a married woman of some comeliness who was not living with her husband on account of his absurdly jealous disposition—he added hastily, "She's a young woman o' proputty ez hez troubil about it, and wishes to be kep' secret," and, having in this way thoroughly convinced his handmaid of the vileness of his motives and the existence of a dark secret in the Conroy household, he said no more, but paid a flying visit to Olly, secretly, packed away all the remnants of his deceased mother's wardrobe, cut (God knows for what purpose) small patches from the few old dresses that Grace had worn that were still sacredly kept in his wardrobe, and put them in his pocket-book; wandered in his usual lonely way on the hill-side, and spent solitary hours in his deserted cabin; avoided the sharp advances of Mrs. Markle, who once aggressively met him in his long post-prandial walks, as well as the shy propinquity of his wife, who would fain have delayed him in her bower, and so having after the fashion of his sex made the two women who loved him exceedingly uncomfortable, he looked hopefully forward to the time when he should be happy without either.

CHAPTER III.

IN WHICH MR. DUMPHY TAKES A HOLIDAY.

It was a hot day on the California coast. In the memory of the oldest American inhabitant its like had not been experienced, and although the testimony of the Spanish Californian was deemed untrustworthy where the interests of the American people were concerned, the statement that for sixty years there had been no such weather was accepted without question. The additional fact, vouchsafed by Don Pedro Peralta, that the great earthquake which shook down the walls of the Mission of San Juan Bautista had been preceded by a week of such abnormal meteorology, was promptly suppressed as being of a quality calculated to check immigration. Howbeit it was hot. The usual afternoon trade-winds had pretermitted their rapid, panting breath, and the whole coast lay, as it were, in the hush of death. The evening fogs that always had lapped the wind-abraded surfaces of the bleak seaward hills were gone too; the vast Pacific lay still and glassy, glittering, but intolerable. The outlying sand dunes, unmitigated by any breath of air, blistered the feet and faces of chance pedestrians. For once the broad verandahs, piazzas, and balconies of San Francisco cottage architecture were consistent and serviceable. People lingered upon them in shirt-sleeves, with all the exaggeration of a novel experience. French windows, that had always been barred against the fierce afternoon winds, were suddenly thrown open; that brisk, energetic step, with which the average San Franciscan hurried to business or pleasure, was changed to an idle, purposeless lounge. The saloons were crowded with thirsty multitudes, the quays and wharves with a people who had never before appreciated the tonic of salt air; the avenues leading over the burning sand-hills to the ocean all day were thronged with vehicles. The numerous streets and by-ways, abandoned by their great scavenger, the wind, were foul and ill-smelling. For twenty-four hours business was partly forgotten; as the heat continued and the wind withheld its customary tribute, there were some changes in the opinions and beliefs of the people; doubts were even expressed of the efficacy of the climate; a few heresies were uttered regarding business and social creeds, and Mr. Dumphy and certain other financial magnates felt vaguely that if the thermometer continued to advance the rates of interest must fall correspondingly.

Equal to even this emergency, Mr. Dumphy had sat in his office all the morning, resisting with the full strength of his aggressive nature any disposition on the part of his customers to succumb financially to the unusual weather. Mr. Dumphy's shirt-collar was off; with it seemed to have departed some of his respectability, and he was perhaps, on the whole, a trifle less imposing than he had been. Nevertheless, he was still dominant, in the suggestion of his short bull neck, and two visitors who entered, observing the *déshabillé* of this great man, felt that it was the proper thing for them to instantly unbutton their own waistcoats and loosen their cravats.

"It's hot," said Mr. Pilcher, an eminent contractor.

"You bet!" responded Mr. Dumphy. "Must be awful on the Atlantic coast! People dying by hundreds of sunstroke; that's the style out there. Here there's nothing of the kind! A man stands things here that he couldn't there."

Having thus re-established the supremacy of the California climate, Mr. Dumphy came directly to business. "Bad news from One Horse Gulch!" he said, quickly.

As that was the subject his visitors came to speak about —a fact of which Mr. Dumphy was fully aware—he added, sharply, "What do you propose?"

Mr. Pilcher, who was a large stockholder in the Conroy mine, responded, hesitatingly, "We've heard that the lead opens badly."

"D——n bad!" interrupted Dumphy. "What do you propose?"

"I suppose," continued Mr. Pilcher, "the only thing to do is to get out of it before the news becomes known."

"No!" said Dumphy, promptly. The two men stared at each other. "No!" he continued, with a quick, short laugh, which was more like a logical expression than a mirthful emotion. "No, we must hold on, sir! Look yer! there's a dozen men as you and me know, that we could unload to to-morrow. Suppose we did? Well, what happens? They go in on four hundred thousand—that's about the figures we represent. Well. They begin to examine and look around; them men, Pilcher"—(in Mr. Dumphy's more inspired moods he rose above considerations of the English grammar)—"them men want to know what that four hundred thousand's invested in; they ain't goin' to take our word after we've got their money—that's human nature—and in twenty-four hours they find they're sold! That don't look well for me nor you—does it?"

There was not the least assumption of superior honour or integrity—indeed, scarcely any self-consciousness or sentiment of any kind, implied in this speech—yet it instantly affected both of these sharp business men, who might have been suspicious of sentiment, with an impression of being both honourable and manly. Mr. Pilcher's companion, Mr. Wyck, added a slight embarrassment to his reception of these great truths, which Mr. Dumphy noticed.

"No," he went on; "what we must do is this. Increase the capital stock just as much again. That will enable us to keep everything in our hands—news and all—and if it should leak out afterwards, we have half a dozen others with us to keep the secret. Six months hence will be time to talk of selling; just now buying is the thing! You don't believe it?—eh? Well, Wyck, I'll take yours at the figure you paid. What do you say?—quick!"

Mr. Wyck, more confused than appeared necessary, declared his intention of holding on; Mr. Pilcher laughed, Mr. Dumphy barked behind his hand.

"That offer's open for ninety days—will you take it? No! Well, then, that's all!" and Mr. Dumphy turned again to his desk. Mr. Pilcher took the hint, and drew Mr. Wyck away.

"Devilish smart chap, that Dumphy!" said Pilcher, as they passed out of the door.

"An honest man, by——!" responded Wyck.

When they had gone Mr. Dumphy rang his bell. "Ask Mr. Jaynes to come and see me at once. D——n it, go now! You must get there before Wyck does. Run!"

The clerk disappeared. In a few moments Mr. Jaynes, a sharp but very youthful looking broker, entered the office parlour. "Mr. Wyck will want to buy back that stock he put in your hands this morning, Jaynes. I thought I'd tell you, it's worth 50 advance now!"

The precocious youth grinned intelligently and departed. By noon of that day it was whispered that notwithstanding the rumours of unfavourable news from the Conroy mine, one of the heaviest stockholders had actually bought back, at an advance of $50 per share, some stock he had previously sold. More than that, it was believed that Mr.

Dumphy had taken advantage of these reports, and was secretly buying. In spite of the weather, for some few hours there had been the greatest excitement.

Possibly from some complacency arising from this, possibly from some singular relaxing in the atmosphere, Mr. Dumphy at two o'clock shook off the cares of business and abandoned himself to recreation—refusing even to take cognisance of the card of one Colonel Starbottle, which was sent to him with a request for an audience. At half-past two he was behind a pair of fast horses, one of a carriage-load of ladies and gentlemen, rolling over the scorching sandhills towards the Pacific, that lay calm and cool beyond. As the well-appointed equipage rattled up the Bush Street Hill, many an eye was turned with envy and admiration toward it. The spectacle of two pretty women among the passengers was perhaps one reason; the fact that everybody recognised in the showy and brilliant driver the celebrated Mr. Rollingstone, an able financier and rival of Mr. Dumphy's, was perhaps equally potent. For Mr. Rollingstone was noted for his "turnout," as well as for a certain impulsive South Sea extravagance and picturesque hospitality which Dumphy envied and at times badly imitated. Indeed, the present excursion was one of Mr. Rollingstone's famous *fetes champetres*, and the present company was composed of the *élite* of San Francisco, and made self-complacent and appreciative by an enthusiastic Eastern tourist.

Their way lay over shifting sand dunes, now motionless and glittering in the cruel, white glare of a Californian sky, only relieved here and there by glimpses of the blue bay beyond, and odd marine-looking buildings, like shells scattered along the beach, as if they had been cast up and forgotten by some heavy tide. Farther on, their road skirted the base of a huge solitary hill, broken in outline by an outcrop of gravestones, sacred to the memory of worthy pioneers who had sealed their devotion to the "healthiest climate in the world" with their lives. Occasionally these gravestones continued to the foot of the hill, where, struggling with the drifting sand, they suggested a half-exhumed Pompeii to the passing traveller. They were the skeletons at the feast of every San Francisco pleasure-seeker, the *memento mori* of every picnicing party, and were visible even from the broad verandahs of the suburban pavilions, where the gay and thoughtless citizen ate, drank, and was merry. Part of the way the busy avenue was parallel with another, up which, even at such times, occasionally crept the lugubrious procession of hearse and mourning coach to other pavilions, scarcely less crowded, where there were "funeral baked meats," and sorrow and tears. And beyond this again was the grey eternal sea, and at its edge, perched upon a rock, and rising out of the very jaws of the gushing breakers, a stately pleasure dome, decreed by some speculative and enterprising San Francisco landlord—the excuse and terminus of this popular excursion.

Here Rollingstone drew up, and, alighting, led his party into a bright, cheery room, whose windows gave upon the sea. A few other guests, evidently awaiting them, were mitigating their impatience by watching the uncouth gambols of the huge sea-lions, who, on the rocks beyond, offered a contrast to the engaging and comfortable interior that was at once pleasant and exciting. In the centre of the room a table overloaded with overgrown fruits and grossly large roses somewhat ostentatiously proclaimed the coming feast!

"Here we are!" said Mr. Dumphy, bustling into the room with that brisk, business-like manner which his friends fondly believed was frank cheerfulness, "and on time, too!" he added, drawing out his watch. "Inside of thirty minutes—how's that, eh?" He clapped his nearest neighbour on the back, who, pleased with this familiarity from a man worth five or six millions, did not stop to consider the value of this celerity of motion in a pleasure excursion on a hot day.

"Well!" said Rollingstone, looking around him, "you all know each other, I reckon, or will soon. Mr. Dumphy, Mr. Poinsett, Mr. Pilcher, Mr. Dyce, Mr. Wyck, Mrs. Sepulvida and Miss Rosey Ringround, gentlemen; Mr. and Mrs. Raynor, of Boston. There, now, that's through! Dinner's ready. Sit down anywhere and wade in. No formality, gentlemen—this is California."

There was, perhaps, some advantage in this absence of ceremony. The guests almost involuntarily seated themselves according to their preferences, and Arthur Poinsett found himself beside Mrs. Sepulvida, while Mr. Dumphy placed Miss Ringround—a pretty though boyish-looking blonde, slangy in speech and fashionable in attire—on his right hand.

The dinner was lavish and luxurious, lacking nothing but restraint and delicacy. There was game in profusion, fat but flavourless. The fruits were characteristic. The enormous peaches were blowsy in colour and robust in fibre; the pears were prodigious and dropsical, and looked as if they wanted to be tapped; the strawberries were overgrown and yet immature—rather as if they had been arrested on their way to become pine-apples; with the exception of the grapes, which were delicate in colour and texture, the fruit might have been an ironical honouring by nature of Mr. Dumphy's lavish drafts.

It is probable, however, that the irony was lost on the majority of the company, who were inclined to echo the extravagant praise of Mr. Raynor, the tourist. "Wonderful! wonderful!" said that gentleman; "if I had not seen this I wouldn't have believed it. Why, that pear would make four of ours."

"That's the way we do things here," returned Dumphy, with the suggestion of being personally responsible for these abnormal growths. He stopped suddenly, for he caught Arthur Poinsett's eye. Mr. Dumphy ate little in public, but he was at that moment tearing the wing of a grouse with his teeth, and there was something so peculiar and characteristic in the manner that Arthur looked up with a sudden recollection in his glance. Dumphy put down the wing, and Poinsett resumed his conversation with Mrs. Sepulvida. It was not of a quality that interruption seriously impaired; Mrs. Sepulvida was a charming but not an intellectual woman, and Mr. Poinsett took up the lost thread of his discourse quite as readily from her eyes as her tongue.

"To have been consistent, Nature should have left a race of giants here," said Mr. Poinsett, meditatively. "I believe," he added, more pointedly, and in a lower voice, "the late Don José was not a large man."

"Whatever he was, he thought a great deal of me!" pouted Mrs. Sepulvida.

Mr. Poinsett was hastening to say that if "taking thought" like that could add a "cubit to one's stature," he himself was in a fair way to become a son of Anak, when he was interrupted by Miss Rosey—

"What's all that about big men? There are none here. They're like the big trees. They don't hang around the coast much! You must go to the mountains for your Goliahs."

Emboldened quite as much by the evident annoyance of her neighbour as the amused look of Arthur Poinsett, she went on—

"I have seen the pre-historic man!—the original

athletic sharp! He is seven feet high, is as heavy as a sea-lion, and has shoulders like Tom Hyer. He slings an awful left. He's got blue eyes as tender as a seal's. He has hair like Samson before that woman went back on him. He's as brave as a lion and as gentle as a lamb. He blushes like a girl, or as girls used to; I wish I could start up such a colour on even double the provocation!"

Of course everybody laughed—it was the usual tribute of Miss Rosey's speech—the gentlemen frankly and fairly, the ladies perhaps a little doubtfully and fearfully. Mrs. Sepulvida, following the amused eyes of Arthur, asked Miss Rosey patronisingly where she had seen her phenomenon.

"Oh, it's no use, my dear, positively—no use. He's married. These phenomena always get married. No, I didn't see him in a circus, Mr. Dumphy, nor in a menagerie, Mr. Dyce, but in a girls' school!"

Everybody stared; a few laughed as if this were an amusing introduction to some possible joke from Miss Rosey.

"I was visiting an old schoolmate at Madame Eclair's *Pension* at Sacramento; he was taking his little sister to the same school," she went on, coolly, "so he told me. I love my love with a G, for he is Guileless and Gentle. His name is Gabriel, and he lives in a Gulch."

"Our friend the superintendent—I'm blessed," said Dyce, looking at Dumphy.

"Yes; but not so very guileless," said Pilcher, "eh, Dyce?"

The gentlemen laughed; the ladies looked at each other and then at Miss Ringround. That fearless young woman was equal to the occasion.

"What have you got against my giant? Out with it!"

"Oh, nothing," said Mr. Pilcher; "only your guileless, simple friend has played the sharpest game on record in Montgomery Street."

"Go on!" said Miss Rosey.

"Shall I?" asked Pilcher of Dumphy.

Dumphy laughed his short laugh. "Go on."

Thus supported, Mr. Pilcher assumed the ease of a graceful *raconteur.* "Miss Rosey's guileness friend, ladies and gentlemen, is the superintendent and shareholder in a certain valuable silver mine in which Dumphy is largely represented. Being about to leave the country, and anxious to realise on his stock, he contracted for the sale of a hundred shares at $1000 each, with our friend Mr. Dyce, the stocks to be delivered on a certain date—ten days ago. Instead of the stock, that day comes a letter from Conroy—a wonderful piece of art—simple, ill-spelled, and unbusiness-like, saying, that in consequence of recent disappointment in the character and extent of the lead, he shall not hold Dyce to his contract, but will release him. Dyce, who has already sold that identical stock at a pretty profit, rushes off to Dumphy's broker, and finds two hundred shares held at $1200. Dyce smells a large-sized rat, writes that he shall hold Gabriel to the performance of his contract, makes him hand over the stock, delivers it in time, and then loads up again with the broker's 200 at $1200 *for a rise.* That rise don't come—won't come—for that sale was *Gabriel's too*—as Dumphy can tell you. There's guilelessness! There's simplicity! And it cleared a hundred thousand by the operation."

Of the party none laughed more heartily than Arthur Poinsett. Without analysing his feelings he was conscious of being greatly relieved by this positive evidence of Gabriel's shrewdness. And when Mrs. Sepulvida touched his elbow, and asked if this were not the squatter who held the forged grant, Arthur, without being conscious of any special meanness, could not help replying with unnecessary significance that it was.

"I believe the whole dreadful story that Donna Dolores told me," said she, "how he married the woman who personated his sister, and all that—the deceitful wretch."

"I've got that letter here," continued Mr. Pilcher, drawing from his pocket a folded sheet of letter paper. "It's a curiosity. If you'd like to see the documentary evidence of your friend's guilelessness, here it is," he added, turning to Miss Ringround.

Miss Rosey took the paper defiantly, and unfolded it, as the others gathered round her, Mr. Dumphy availing himself of that opportunity to lean familiarly over the arm of her chair. The letter was written with that timid, uncertain ink, peculiar to the illiterate effort, and suggestive of an occasional sucking of the pen in intervals of abstraction or difficult composition. Saving that characteristic, it is reproduced literally below:—

"1, Hoss Gulch, Argus the 10th.

"DEAR SIR,—On acount of thar heving ben bad Luck in the Leed witch has droped, I rite thes few lins hopping you air Well. I have to say we are disapinted in the Leed, it is not wut we thougt it was witch is wy I rite thes few lins. now sir purheps you ixpict me to go on with our contrak, and furniss you with 100 shars at 1 Thousin dolls pur shar. It issint wuth no 1 Thousin dols pur shar, far frummit. No sir, it issint, witch is wy I rite you thes few lins, and it Woddent be Rite nor squar for me to tak it. This is to let you off Mister Dyce, and hopin it ant no trubbil to ye, fur I shuddint sell atal things lookin this bad it not bein rite nor squar, and hevin' tor up the contrak atween you and me. So no more at pressen from yours respectfuly. G. CONROY.

"P. S.—You might mind my sayin to you about my sister witch is loss sens 1849. If you happind to com acrost any Traks of hers, me bein' away, you can send the sam to me in Care of Wels Farko & Co., New York Citty, witch is a grate favor and will be pade sure. G. C."

"I don't care what you say, that's an honest letter," said Miss Rosey, with a certain decision of character new to the experience of her friends, "as honest and simple as ever was written. You can bet your pile on that."

No one spoke, but the smile of patronising superiority and chivalrous toleration was exchanged by all the gentlemen except Poinsett. Mr. Dumphy added to his smile his short characteristic bark. At the reference to the writer's sister, Mrs. Sepulvida shrugged her pretty shoulders and looked doubtingly at Poinsett. But to her great astonishment that gentleman reached across the table, took the letter, and having glanced over it, said positively, "You are right, Miss Rosey, it is genuine."

It was characteristic of Poinsett's inconsistency that this statement was as sincere as his previous assent to the popular suspicion. When he took the letter in his hand, he at once detected the evident sincerity of its writer, and as quickly recognised the quaint honesty and simple nature of the man he had known. It was Gabriel Conroy, all over. More than that, he even recalled an odd memory of Grace in this frank directness and utter unselfishness of the brother who so plainly had never forgotten her. That all this might be even reconcilable with the fact of his marriage to the woman who had personated the sister, Arthur easily comprehended. But that it was his own duty, after he had impugned Gabriel's character, to make any personal effort to clear it, was not so plain. Nevertheless, he did not answer Mrs. Sepulvida's look, but walked gravely to the window, and looked out upon the sea. Mr. Dumphy, who, with the instincts of jealousy, saw in Poinsett's remark only a desire to ingratiate himself with Miss Rosey, was quick to follow his lead.

"It's a clear case of *quien sabe* anyway," he said to the young lady, "and maybe you're right. Joe, pass the champagne."

Dyce and Pilcher looked up inquiringly at their leader, who glanced meaningly towards the open-mouthed Mr. Raynor, whose astonishment at this sudden change in public sentiment was unbounded.

"But look here," said that gentleman, "bless my soul! if this letter is genuine, your friends here—these gentlemen —have lost a hundred thousand dollars! Don't you see? If this news is true, and this man's information is correct, the stock really isn't worth"——

He was interrupted by a laugh from Messrs. Dyce and Pilcher.

"That's so. It would be a devilish good thing on Dyce!" said the latter, good-humouredly. "And as I'm in myself about as much again, I reckon I should take the joke about as well as he."

"But," continued the mystified Mr. Raynor, "do you really mean to say that you have any idea this news is true?"

"Yes," responded Pilcher, coolly.

"Yes," echoed Dyce, with equal serenity.

"You do?"

"We do."

The astonished tourist looked from the one to the other with undisguised wonder and admiration, and then turned to his wife. Had she heard it? Did she fully comprehend that here were men accepting and considering an actual and present loss of nearly a quarter of a million of dollars, as quietly and indifferently as if it were a postage stamp! What superb coolness! What magnificent indifference! What supreme and royal confidence in their own resources. Was this not a country of gods? All of which was delivered in a voice that, although pitched to the key of matrimonial confidence, was still entirely audible to the gods themselves.

"Yes, gentlemen," continued Pilcher; "it's the fortune of war. T'other man's turn to day, ours to-morrow. Can't afford time to be sorry in this climate. A man's born again here every day. Move along and pass the bottle."

What was that?

Nothing, apparently, but a rattling of windows and shaking of the glasses—the effect of a passing carriage or children running on the piazza without. But why had they all risen with a common instinct, and with faces bloodless and eyes fixed in horrible expectancy? These were the questions which Mr. and Mrs. Raynor asked themselves hurriedly, unconscious of danger, yet with a vague sense of alarm at the terror so plainly marked upon the countenances of these strange, self-poised people, who, a moment before, had seemed the incarnation of reckless self-confidence, and inaccessible to the ordinary annoyances of mortals. And why were these other pleasure-seekers rushing by the windows, and was not that a lady fainting in the hall? Arthur was the first to speak and tacitly answer the unasked question.

" It was from east to west," he said, with a coolness that he felt was affected, and a smile that he knew was not mirthful. "It's over now, I think." He turned to Mrs. Sepulvida, who was very white. " You are not frightened? Surely this is nothing new to you? Let me help you to a glass of wine."

Mrs. Sepulvida took it with a hysterical little laugh. Mrs. Raynor, who was now conscious of a slight feeling of nausea, did not object to the same courtesy from Mr. Pilcher, whose hand shook visibly as he lifted the champagne. Mr. Dumphy returned from the doorway, in which, to his own and everybody's surprise, he was found standing, and took his place at Miss Rosey's side. The young woman was first to recover her reckless hilarity.

"It was a judgment on you for slandering Nature's noblest specimen," she said, shaking her finger at the capitalist.

Mr. Rollingstone, who had returned to the head of his table, laughed.

"But *what* was it?" gasped Mr. Raynor, making himself at last heard above the somewhat pronounced gaiety of the party.

"An earthquake," said Arthur, quietly.

CHAPTER IV.

MR. DUMPHY HAS NEWS OF A DOMESTIC CHARACTER.

"AN earthquake!" echoed Mr. Rollingstone, cheerfully, to his guests; "now you've had about everything we have to show. Don't be alarmed, madam," he continued to Mrs. Raynor, who was beginning to show symptoms of hysteria, "nobody ever was hurt by 'em."

"In two hundred years there hasn't been as many persons killed by earthquakes in California as are struck by lightning on your coast in a single summer," said Mr. Dumphy.

"Never have 'em any stronger than this," said Mr. Pilcher, with a comforting suggestion of there being an absolute limitation of Nature's freaks on the Pacific coast.

"Over in a minute, as you see," said Mr. Dumphy, "and —hello! what's that?"

In a moment they were on their feet, pale and breathless again. This time Mr. Raynor and his wife among the number. But it was only a carriage—driving away.

"Let us adjourn to the piazza," said Mr. Dumphy, offering his arm to Mrs. Raynor with the air of having risen solely for that purpose.

Mr. Dumphy led the way, and the party followed with some celerity. Mrs. Sepulvida hung back a moment with Arthur, and whispered—

"Take me back as soon as you can!"

"You are not seriously alarmed?" asked Arthur.

"We are too near the sea here," she replied, looking toward the ocean with a slight shudder. "Don't ask questions now," she added, a little sharply. "Don't you see these Eastern people are frightened to death, and they may overhear."

But Mrs. Sepulvida had not long to wait, for in spite of the pointed asseverations of Messrs. Pilcher, Dyce, and Dumphy, that earthquakes were not only harmless, but absolutely possessed a sanitary quality, the piazzas were found deserted by the usual pleasure-seekers, and even the eloquent advocates themselves betrayed some impatience to be once more on the open road.

A brisk drive of an hour put the party again in the highest spirits, and Mr. and Mrs. Raynor again into the condition of chronic admiration and enthusiasm.

Mrs. Sepulvida and Mr. Poinsett followed in an open buggy behind. When they were fairly upon their way, Arthur asked an explanation of his fair companion's fear of the sea.

"There is an old story," said Donna Maria, "that the Point of Pines—you know where it is, Mr. Poinsett—was once covered by a great wave from the sea that followed an earthquake. But tell me, do you really think that letter of this man Conroy is true?"

"I do," said Arthur, promptly.

"And that—there—is—a—prospect—that—the—stock of this big mine may—de—pre—ciate in value?"

"Well—possibly—yes!"

"And if you knew that I had been foolish enough to put a good deal of money in it, you would still talk to me as you did the other day—down there?"

"I should say," responded Arthur, changing the reins to his left hand that his right might be free for some purpose—goodness knows what!—"I should say that I am more than ever convinced that you ought to have some person to look after you."

What followed this remarkable speech I really do not know how to reconcile with the statement that Mrs. Sepulvida made to the Donna Dolores a few chapters ago, and I therefore discreetly refrain from transcribing it here. Suffice it to say that the buggy did not come up with the *char-à-banc* and the rest of the party until long after they had arrived at Mr. Dumphy's stately mansion on Rincon Hill, where another costly and elaborate collation was prepared. Mr. Dumphy evidently was in spirits, and had so far overcome his usual awe and distrust of Arthur, as well as the slight jealousy he had experienced an hour or so before, as to approach that gentleman with a degree of cheerful familiarity that astonished and amused the self-sustained Arthur—who perhaps at that time had more reason for his usual conceit than before. Arthur, who knew, or thought he knew, that Miss Ringround was only coquetting with Mr. Dumphy for the laudable purpose of making the more ambitious of her sex miserable, and that she did not care for his person or position, was a good deal amused at finding the young lady the subject of Mr. Dumphy's sudden confidences.

"You see, Poinsett, as a man of business I don't go as much into society as you do, but she seems to be a straight up and down girl, eh?" he queried, as they stood together in the vestibule after the ladies had departed. It is hardly necessary to say that Arthur was positive and sincere in his praise of the young woman. Mr. Dumphy by some obscure mental process, taking much of the praise to himself, was highly elated and perhaps tempted to a greater vinous indulgence than was his habit. Howbeit the last bottle of champagne seemed to have obliterated all past suspicion of Arthur, and he shook him warmly by the hand. "I tell ye what now, Poinsett, if there are any points I can give you don't you be afraid to ask for 'em. I can see what's up between you and the widow—honour, you know—all right, my boy—she's in the Conroy lode pretty deep, but I'll help her out and you too! You've got a good thing there—Poinsett—and I want you to realise. We understand each other, eh? You'll find me a square man with my friends, Poinsett. Pitch in—pitch in!—my advice to you is to just pitch in and marry the widow. She's worth it—you can realise on her. You see you and me's—so to speak—ole pards, eh? You rek'leck ole times on Sweetwater, eh? Well—if you mus' go, goo'-bi! I s'pose she's waitin' for ye. Look you, Poinsy, d'ye see this yer posy in my buttonhole? She give it to me. Rosey did! eh? ha! ha! Won't tak' nothin' drink? Lesh open n'or bo'll. No? Goori!" until struggling between disgust, amusement, and self-depreciation, Arthur absolutely tore himself away from the great financier and his degrading confidences.

When Mr. Dumphy staggered back into his drawing-room, a servant met him with a card.

"The gen'lman says it's very important business, and he must see you to-night," he said, hastily, anticipating the oath and indignant protest of his master. "He says it's your business, sir, and not his. He's been waiting here since you came back, sir."

Mr. Dumphy took the card. It bore the inscription in pencil, "Colonel Starbottle, Siskiyou, on important business." Mr. Dumphy reflected a moment. The magical word "business" brought him to himself. "Show him in—in the office," he said savagely, and retired thither.

Anybody less practical than Peter Dumphy would have dignified the large, showy room in which he entered as the library. The rich mahogany shelves were filled with a heterogeneous collection of recent books, very fresh, very new and glaring as to binding and subject; the walls were hung with files of newspapers and stock reports. There was a velvet-lined cabinet containing minerals—all of them gold or silver bearing. There was a map of an island that Mr. Dumphy owned—there was a marine view, with a representation of a steamship also owned by Mr. Dumphy. There was a momentary relief from these facts in a very gorgeous and badly painted picture of a tropical forest and sea-beach, until inquiry revealed the circumstance that the sugar-house in the corner under a palm-tree was "run" by Mr. Dumphy, and that the whole thing could be had for a bargain.

The stranger who entered was large and somewhat inclined to a corpulency that was, however, restrained in expansion by a blue frock coat, tightly buttoned at the waist, which had the apparent effect of lifting his stomach into the higher thoracic regions of moral emotion—a confusion to which its owner lent a certain intellectual assistance. The Colonel's collar was very large, open and impressive; his black silk neckerchief loosely tied around his throat, occupying considerable space over his shirt front, and expanding through the upper part of a gilt-buttoned white waistcoat, lent itself to the general suggestion that the Colonel had burst his sepals and would flower soon. Above this unfolding the Colonel's face, purple, aquiline-nosed, throttle-looking as to the eye, and moist and sloppy-looking as to the mouth, uptilted above his shoulders. The Colonel entered with that tiptoeing celerity of step affected by men who are conscious of increasing corpulency. He carried a cane hooked over his forearm; in one hand a large white handkerchief, and in the other a broad-brimmed hat. He thrust the former gracefully in his breast, laid the latter on the desk where Mr. Dumphy was seated, and taking an unoffered chair himself, coolly rested his elbow on his cane in an attitude of easy expectancy.

"Say you've got important business?" said Dumphy. "Hope it is, sir—hope it is! Then out with it. Can't afford to waste time any more here than at the Bank. Come! What is it?"

Not in the least affected by Mr. Dumphy's manner, whose habitual brusqueness was intensified to rudeness, Colonel Starbottle drew out his handkerchief, blew his nose, carefully returned apparently only about two inches of the cambric to his breast, leaving the rest displayed like a ruffled shirt, and began with an airy gesture of his fat white hand.

"I was here two hours ago, sir, when you were at the—er—festive board. I said to the boy, 'Don't interrupt your master. A gentleman worshipping at the shrine of Venus and Bacchus and attended by the muses and immortals, don't want to be interrupted.' Ged, sir, I knew a man in Louisiana—Hank Pinckney—shot his boy—a little yellow boy worth a thousand dollars—for interrupting him at a poker party—and no ladies present! And the boy only coming in to say that the gin house was in flames. Perhaps you'll say an extreme case. Know a dozen such. So I said, 'Don't interrupt him, but when the ladies have risen, and Beauty, sir, no longer dazzles and—er—gleams, and the table round no longer echoes the—er—light jest, then spot him! And over the deserted board, with—er—social glass between us, your master and I will have our little confab.'"

He rose, and before the astonished Dumphy could interfere, crossed over to a table where a decanter of whisky and a carafe of water stood, and filling a glass half-full of liquor, reseated himself and turned it off with an easy yet dignified inclination towards his host.

For once only Mr. Dumphy regretted the absence of

dignity in his own manner. It was quite evident that his usual brusqueness was utterly ineffective here, and he quickly recognised in the Colonel the representative of a class of men well known in California, from whom any positive rudeness would have provoked a demand for satisfaction. It was not a class of men that Mr. Dumphy had been in the habit of dealing with, and he sat filled with impotent rage, but wise enough to restrain its verbal expression, and thankful that none of his late guests were present to witness his discomfiture. Only one good effect was due to his visitor. Mr. Dumphy through baffled indignation and shame had become sober.

"No, sir," continued Colonel Starbottle, setting his glass upon his knee, and audibly smacking his large lips. "No, sir, I waited in the—er—ante-chamber until I saw you part with your guests—until you bade—er—adieu to a certain fair nymph—Ged, sir, I like your taste, and I call myself a judge of fine women—'Blank it all,' I said to myself, 'Blank it all, Star, you ain't goin' to pop out upon a man just as he's ministering to Beauty and putting a shawl upon a pair of alabaster shoulders like that!' Ha! ha! Ged, sir, I remembered myself that in '43 in Washington at a party at Tom Benton's I was in just such a position, sir. 'Are you never going to get that cloak on, Star?' she says to me—the most beautiful creature, the acknowledged belle of that whole winter—'43, sir—as a gentleman yourself you'll understand why I don't particularise—'If I had my way, madam,' I said, 'I never would!' I did, blank me. But you're not drinking, Mr. Dumphy, eh? A thimbleful, sir, to our better acquaintance."

Not daring to trust himself to speak, Mr. Dumphy shook his head somewhat impatiently, and Colonel Starbottle rose. As he did so it seemed as if his shoulders had suddenly become broader and his chest distended until his handkerchief and white waistcoat protruded through the breast of his buttoned coat like a bursting grain of "pop corn." He advanced slowly and with deliberate dignity to the side of Dumphy.

"If I have intruded upon your privacy, Mr. Dumphy," he said, with a stately wave of his white hand, "if, as I surmise, from your disinclination, sir, to call it by no other name, to exchange the ordinary convivial courtesies common between gentlemen, sir,—you are disposed to resent any reminiscences of mine as reflecting upon the character of the young lady, sir, whom I had the pleasure to see in your company—if such be the case, sir, Ged!—I am ready to retire now, sir, and to give you to-morrow, or at any time, the satisfaction which no gentleman ever refuses another, and which Culpepper Starbottle has never been known to deny. My card, sir, you have already; my address, sir, is St. Charles Hotel, where I and my friend, Mr. Dumphy, will be ready to receive you."

"Look here," said Mr. Dumphy, in surly but sincere alarm, "I don't drink because I've been drinking. No offence, Mr. Starbottle. I was only waiting for you to open what you had on your mind in the way of business, to order up a bottle of *Cliquot* to enable us to better digest it. Take your seat, Colonel. Bring champagne and two glasses." He rose, and under pretence of going to the sideboard, added in a lower tone to the servant who entered, "Stay within call, and in about ten minutes bring me some important message from the Bank—you hear? A glass of wine with you, Colonel. Happy to make your acquaintance! Here we go!"

The Colonel uttered a slight cough as if to clear away his momentary severity, bowed with gracious dignity, touched the glass of his host, drew out his handkerchief, wiped his mouth, and seated himself once more.

"If my object," he began, with a wave of dignified depreciation, "were simply one of ordinary business, I should have sought you, sir, in the busy mart, and not among your Lares and Penates, nor in the blazing lights of the festive hall. I should have sought you at that temple which report and common rumour says that you, sir, as one of the favoured sons of Fortune, have erected to her worship. In my intercourse with the gifted John C. Calhoun I never sought him, sir, in the gladiatorial arena of the Senate, but rather with the social glass in the privacy of his own domicile. Ged, sir, in my profession, we recognise some quality in our relations even when professional with gentlemen that keep us from approaching them like a Yankee pedlar with goods to sell!"

"What's your profession?" asked Mr. Dumphy.

"Until elected by the citizens of Siskiyou to represent them in the legislative councils I practised at the bar. Since then I have been open occasionally to retainers in difficult and delicate cases. In the various intrigues that arise in politics, in the more complicated relations of the two sexes—in, I may say, the two great passions of mankind, Ambition and Love, my services have, I believe, been considered of value. It has been my office, sir, to help the steed of vaulting ambition—er—er—over the fence, and to dry the—er—tearful yet glowing cheek of Beauty. But for the necessity of honour and secrecy in my profession, sir, I could give you the names of some of the most elegant women, and some of the first—the very first men in the land as the clients of Culpepper Starbottle."

"Very sorry," began Mr. Dumphy, "but if you're expecting to put me among your list of clients, I"——

Without taking the least notice of Dumphy's half-returned sneer, Colonel Starbottle interrupted him coolly:

"Ged, sir!—it's out of the question, I'm retained on the other side."

The sneer instantly faded from Dumphy's face, and a look of genuine surprise took its place.

"What do you mean?" he said curtly.

Colonel Starbottle drew his chair beside Dumphy, and leaning familiarly over his desk took Mr. Dumphy's own penholder and persuasively emphasised the points of his speech upon Mr. Dumphy's arm with the blunt end. "Sir, when I say retained by the other side, it doesn't keep me from doing the honourable thing with the defendant—from recognising a gentleman and trying to settle this matter as between gentlemen."

"But what's all this about? Who is your plaintiff?" roared Dumphy, forgetting himself in his rage.

"Ged, sir—it's a woman—of course. Don't think I'm accusing you of any political ambition. Ha! ha! No, sir. You're like me! it's a woman—lovely woman—I saw it at a glance! Gentlemen like you and me don't go through to fifty years without giving some thought to these dear little creatures. Sir, I despise a man who did. It's the weakness of a great man, sir."

Mr. Dumphy pushed his chair back with the grim deliberation of a man who had at last measured the strength of his adversary and was satisfied to risk an encounter.

"Look here, Colonel Starbottle, I don't know or care who your plaintiff is. I don't know or care how she may have been deceived or wronged or disappointed or bamboozled, or what is the particular game that's up now. But you're a man of the world, you say, and as a man of the world and a man of sense, you know that no one in my position ever puts himself in any woman's power. I can't afford it! I don't pretend to be better than other men, but

I ain't a fool. That's the difference between me and your clients!"

"Yes—but, my boy, that *is* the difference! Don't you see? In other cases the woman's a beautiful woman, a charming creature, you know. Ged, sometimes she's as proper and pious as a nun, but then the relations, you see, ain't legal! But hang it all, my boy, this is—YOUR WIFE!"

Mr. Dumphy, with colourless cheeks, tried to laugh a reckless scornful laugh. "My wife is dead!"

"A mistake—Ged, sir!—a most miserable mistake. Understand me. I don't say that she hadn't ought to be! Ged, sir, from the look that that little blue-eyed hussy gave you an hour ago—there ain't much use of another woman around, but the fact is that she *is* living. You thought she was dead, and left her up there in the snow. She goes so far as to say—you know how these women talk, Dumphy; Ged, sir, they'll say anything when they get down on a man—she says it ain't your fault if she wasn't dead! Eh? Sho?"

"A message, sir, business of the Bank, very important," said Dumphy's servant, opening the door.

"Get out!" said Dumphy, with an oath.

"But, sir, they told me, sir"——

"Get out! will you?" roared Dumphy.

The door closed on his astonished face. "It's all—a—mistake," said Dumphy, when he had gone. "They died of starvation—all of them—while I was away hunting help. I've read the accounts."

Colonel Starbottle slowly drew from some vast moral elevation in his breast pocket a well-worn paper. It proved when open to be a faded, blackened, and be-thumbed document in Spanish. "Here is the report of the Commander of the Presidio who sent out the expedition. You read Spanish? Well. The bodies of all the other women were identified except your wife's. Hang it, my boy, don't you see why she was excepted? She wasn't there."

The Colonel darted a fat forefinger at his host and then drew back, and settled his purpled chin and wattled cheeks conclusively in his enormous shirt collar. Mr. Dumphy sank back in his chair at the contact as if the finger of Fate had touched him.

CHAPTER V.

MRS. CONROY HAS AN UNEXPECTED VISITOR

THE hot weather had not been confined to San Francisco. San Pablo Bay had glittered, and the yellow currents of the San Joaquin and Sacramento glowed sullenly with a dull sluggish lava-like flow. No breeze stirred the wild oats that drooped on the western slope of the Contra Costa hills; the smoke of burning woods on the eastern hillsides rose silently and steadily; the great wheat fields of the intermediate valleys clothed themselves humbly in dust and ashes. A column of red dust accompanied the Wingdam and One Horse Gulch stage-coach, a pillar of fire by day as well as by night, and made the fainting passengers look longingly toward the snow-patched Sierras beyond. It was hot in California; few had ever seen the like, and those who had were looked upon as enemies of their race. A rashly scientific man of Murphy's Camp who had a theory of his own, and upon that had prophesied a continuance of the probable recurrence of the earthquake shock, concluded he had better leave the settlement until the principles of meteorology were better recognised and established.

It was hot in One Horse Gulch—in the oven-like Gulch, on the burning sands and scorching bars of the river. It was hot even on Conroy's Hill, among the calm shadows of the dark-green pines—on the deep verandahs of the Conroy *cottage orné*. Perhaps this was the reason why Mrs. Gabriel Conroy, early that morning after the departure of her husband for the mill, had evaded the varnished and white-leaded heats of her own house and sought the more fragrant odours of the sedate pines beyond the hill-top. I fear, however, that something was due to a mysterious note which had reached her clandestinely the evening before, and which, seated on the trunk of a prostrate pine, she was now reperusing.

I should like to sketch her as she sat there. A broad-brimmed straw hat covered her head, that although squared a little too much at the temples for shapeliness, was still made comely by the good taste with which—aided by a crimping-iron—she had treated her fine-spun electrical blonde hair. The heat had brought out a delicate dewy colour in her usually pale face, and had heightened the intense nervous brightness of her vivid grey eyes. From the same cause, probably, her lips were slightly parted, so that the rigidity that usually characterised their finely chiselled outlines was lost. She looked healthier; the long flowing skirts which she affected, after the fashion of most *petite* women, were gathered at a waist scarcely as sylph-like and unsubstantial as that which Gabriel first clasped after the accident in the fateful cañon. She seemed a trifle more languid—more careful of her personal comfort, and spent some time in adjusting herself to the inequalities of her uncouth seat with a certain pouting peevishness of manner that was quite as new to her character as it was certainly feminine and charming. She held the open note in her thin, narrow, white-tipped fingers, and glanced over it again with a slight smile. It read as follows :—

"At ten o'clock I shall wait for you at the hill near the Big Pine! You shall give me an interview if you know yourself well. I say beware! I am strong, for I am injured!—VICTOR."

Mrs. Conroy folded the note again, still smiling, and placed it carefully in her pocket. Then she sat patient, her hands clasped lightly between her knees, the parasol open at her feet—the very picture of a fond, confiding tryst. Then she suddenly drew her feet under her, sideways, with a quick, nervous motion, and examined the ground carefully with sincere distrust of all artful lurking vermin who lie in wait for helpless womanhood. Then she looked at her watch.

It was five minutes past the hour. There was no sound in the dim, slumbrous wood, but the far-off sleepy caw of a rook. A squirrel ran impulsively halfway down the bark of the nearest pine, and catching sight of her tilted parasol, suddenly flattened himself against the bark, with outstretched limbs, a picture of abject terror. A bounding hare came upon it suddenly and had a palpitation of the heart that he thought he really never should get over. And then there was a slow crackling in the underbrush as of a masculine tread, and Mrs. Conroy, picking up her terrible parasol, shaded the cold fires of her grey eyes with it and sat calm and expectant.

A figure came slowly and listlessly up the hill. When within a dozen yards of her, she saw it was *not* Victor. But when it approached nearer she suddenly started to her feet with pallid cheeks and an exclamation upon her lips. It was the Spanish translator of Pacific Street. She would have flown, but on the instant he turned and recognised her with a cry, a start, and a passion equal to her own.

For a moment they stood glaring at each other breathless but silent!

"Devarges!" said Mrs. Conroy, in a voice that was scarcely audible. "Good God!"

The stranger uttered a bitter laugh. "Yes! Devarges! —the man who ran away with you—Devarges the traitor! Devarges the betrayer of your husband. Look at me! You know me—Henry Devarges! Your husband's brother!—your old accomplice—your lover—your dupe!"

"Hush," she said, imploringly glancing around through the dim woods, "for God's sake, hush!"

"And who are you," he went on, without heeding her, "which of the Mesdames Devarges is it now? Or have you taken the name of the young sprig of an officer for whom you deserted me and maybe in turn married? Or did he refuse you even that excuse for your perfidy? Or is it the wife and accomplice of this feeble-minded Conroy? What name shall I call you? Tell me quick! Oh, I have much to say, but I wish to be polite, madame; tell me to whom I am to speak!"

Despite the evident reality of his passion and fury there was something so unreal and grotesque in his appearance—in his antique foppery, in his dyed hair, in his false teeth, in his padded coat, in his thin strapped legs, that this relentless woman cowered before him in very shame, not of her crime but of her accomplice! "Hush," she said, "call me your friend; I am always your friend, Henry. Call me anything, but let me go from here. For God's sake, do you hear? Not so loud! Another time and another place I will listen," and she drew slowly back, until, scarce knowing what he did, she had led him away from the place of rendezvous toward the ruined cabin. Here she felt that she was at least safe from the interruption of Victor. "How came you here? How did you find out what had become of me? Where have you been these long years?" she asked hastily.

Within the last few moments she had regained partially the strange power that she had always exerted over all men except Gabriel Conroy. The stranger hesitated, and then answered in a voice that had more of hopelessness than bitterness in its quality—

"I came here six years ago, a broken, ruined, and disgraced man. I had no ambition but to hide myself from all who had known me, from that brother whose wife I had stolen, and whose home I had broken up—from you—you, Julie! you and your last lover—from the recollection of your double treachery!" He had raised his voice here, but was checked by the unflinching eye and cautionary gesture of the woman before him. "When you abandoned me in St. Louis, I had no choice but death or a second exile. I could not return to Switzerland, I could not live in the sickening shadow of my crime and its bitter punishment. I came here. My education, my knowledge of the language stood me in good stead. I might have been a rich man, I might have been an influential one, but I only used my opportunities for the bare necessaries of life and the means to forget my trouble in dissipation. I became a drudge by day, a gambler by night. I was always a gentleman. Men thought me crazy, an enthusiast, but they learned to respect me. Traitor as I was in a larger trust, no one doubted my honour or dared to question my integrity. But bah! what is this to you? You!"

He would have turned from her again in very bitterness, but in the act he caught her eye, and saw in it if not sympathy, at least a certain critical admiration, that again brought him to her feet. For despicable as this woman was, she was pleased at this pride in the man she had betrayed, was gratified at the sentiment that lifted him above his dyed hair and his pitiable foppery, and felt a certain honourable satisfaction in the fact that, even after the lapse of years, he had proved true to her own intuitions of him.

"I had been growing out of my despair, Julie," he went on, sadly; "I was, or believed I was, forgetting my fault, forgetting even *you*, when there came to me, the news of my brother's death—by starvation. Listen to me, Julie. One day there came to me for translation a document, revealing the dreadful death of him—your husband, my brother—do you hear?—by starvation! Driven from his home by shame, he had desperately sought to hide himself as I had—accepted the hardship of emigration—he, a gentleman and a man of letters—with the boors and rabble of the plains, had shared their low trials and their vulgar pains, and died among them, unknown and unrecorded."

"He died as he had lived," said Mrs. Conroy, passionately, "a traitor and a hypocrite; he died following the fortunes of his paramour, an uneducated, vulgar rustic, to whom, dying, he willed a fortune—this girl—Grace Conroy. Thank God, I have the record! Hush! what's that?"

Whatever it was—a falling bough or the passing of some small animal in the underbush—it was past now. A dead silence enwrapped the two solitary actors; they might have been the first man and the first woman, so encompassed were they by Nature and solitude.

"No," she went on, hurriedly, in a lower tone, "it was the same old story—the story of that girl at Basle—the story of deceit and treachery which brought us first together, which made you, Henry, my friend, which turned our sympathies into a more dangerous passion. You have suffered. Ah, well, so have I. We are equal now."

Henry Devarges looked speechlessly upon his companion. Her voice trembled, there were tears in her eyes, that had replaced the burning light of womanly indignation.

He had come there knowing her to have been doubly treacherous to her husband and himself. She had not denied it. He had come there to tax her with an infamous imposture, but had found himself within the last minute glowing with sympathetic condemnation of his own brother, and ready to accept the yet unoffered and perfectly explicable theory of that imposture. More than that, he began to feel that his own wrongs were slight in comparison with the injuries received by this superior woman. The woman who endeavours to justify herself to her jealous lover, always has a powerful ally in his own self-love, and Devarges was quite willing to believe that even if he had lost her love, he had never at least been deceived. And the answer to the morality of this imposture was before him. Here was she married to the surviving brother of the girl she had personated. Had he—had Dr. Devarges ever exhibited as noble trust, as perfect appreciation of her nature and sufferings? Had they not thrown away the priceless pearl of this woman's love through ignorance and selfishness? You and I, my dear sir, who are not in love with this most reprehensible creature, will be quick to see the imperfect logic of Henry Devarges, but when a man constitutes himself accuser, judge, and jury of the woman he loves, he is very apt to believe he is giving a verdict when he is only entering a *nolle prosequi.* It is probable that Mrs. Conroy had noticed this weakness in her companion, even with her preoccupied fears of the inopportune appearance of Victor, whom she felt she could have accounted for much better in his absence. Victor was an impulsive person, and there are times when this quality, generally adored by a self-restrained sex, is apt to be confounding.

"Why did you come here to see me?" asked Mrs. Conroy, with a dangerous smile. "Only to abuse me?"

"There is another grant in existence for the same land

that you claim as Grace Conroy or Mrs. Conroy," returned Devarges, with masculine bluntness, "a grant given prior to that made to my brother Paul. A suspicion that some imposture has been practised is entertained by the party holding the grant, and I have been requested to get at the facts."

Mrs. Conroy's grey eyes lightened. "And how were these suspicions aroused?"

"By an anonymous letter."

"And you have seen it?"

"Yes; both it and the handwriting in portions of the grant are identical."

"And you know the hand?"

"I do; it is that of a man now here, an old Californian—Victor Ramirez!"

He fixed his eyes upon her; unabashed she turned her own clear glance on his, and asked, with a dazzling smile—

"But does not your client know that, whether this grant is a forgery or not, my husband's title is good?"

"Yes; but the sympathies of my client, as you call *her*, are interested in the orphan girl Grace."

"Ah!" said Mrs. Conroy, with the faintest possible sigh, "your client, for whom you have travelled—how many miles?—is a woman."

Half-pleased, but half-embarrassed, Devarges said "Yes."

"I understand," said Mrs. Conroy slowly. "A young woman, perhaps a good, a *pretty* one! And you have said, 'I will prove this Mrs. Conroy an impostor,' and you are here. Well, I do not blame you. You are a man. It is well perhaps it is so.

"But, Julie, hear me!" interrupted the alarmed Devarges.

"No more!" said Mrs. Conroy, rising, and waving her thin white hand, "I do not blame you. I could expect—I deserve—no more! Go back to your client, sir, tell her that you have seen Julie Devarges, the impostor. Tell her to go and press her claim, and that you will assist her. Finish the work that the anonymous letter-writer has begun, and earn your absolution for your crime and my folly. Get your reward—you deserve it—but tell her to thank God for having raised up to her better friends than Julie Devarges ever possessed in the heyday of her beauty. Go! Farewell! No; let me go, Henry Devarges, I am going to my husband. He at least has known how to forgive and protect a friendless and erring woman."

Before the astonished man could recover his senses, elusive as a sunbeam, she had slipped through his fingers and was gone. For a moment only he followed the flash of her white skirt through the dark aisles of the forest, and then the pillared trees, crowding in upon each other, hid her from view.

Perhaps it was well, for a moment later Victor Ramirez, flushed, wild-eyed, dishevelled, and panting, stumbled blindly upon the trail, and blundered into Devarges' presence. The two men eyed each other in silence.

"A hot day for a walk!" said Devarges, with an ill-concealed sneer.

"Vengeance of God! you are right, it is," returned Victor. "And you?"

"Oh, I have been fighting flies. Good-day!"

CHAPTER VI.

GABRIEL DISCARDS HIS HOME AND WEALTH.

I AM sorry to say that Mrs. Conroy's expression as she fled was not entirely consistent with the grieved and heart-broken manner with which she had just closed the interview with Henry Devarges. Something of a smile lurked about the corners of her thin lips as she tripped up the steps of her house, and stood panting a little with the exertion in the shadow of the porch. But here she suddenly found herself becoming quite faint, and entering the apparently empty house, passed at once to her boudoir, and threw herself exhaustedly on the lounge with a certain peevish discontent at her physical weakness. No one had seen her enter; the Chinese servants were congregated in the distant wash-house. Her housekeeper had taken advantage of her absence to ride to the town. The unusual heat was felt to be an apology for any domestic negligence.

She was very thoughtful. The shock she had felt on first meeting Devarges was past; she was satisfied she still retained an influence over him sufficient to keep him her ally against Ramirez, whom she felt she now had reason to fear. Hitherto his jealousy had only shown itself in vapouring and bravado; she had been willing to believe him capable of offering her physical violence in his insane fury, and had not feared it, but this deliberately planned treachery made her tremble. She would see Devarges again; she would recite the wrongs she had received from the dead brother and husband, and in Henry's weak attempt to still his own conscience with that excuse, she could trust to him to keep Ramirez in check, and withhold the exposure until she and Gabriel could get away. Once out of the country, she could laugh at them both; once away, she could devote herself to win the love of Gabriel, without which she had begun to feel her life and schemes had been in vain. She would hurry their departure at once. Since the report had spread affecting the value of the mine, Gabriel, believing it true, had vaguely felt it his duty to stand by his doubtful claim and accept its fortunes, and had delayed his preparations. She would make him believe that it was Dumphy's wish that he should go at once; she would make Dumphy write him to that effect. She smiled as she thought of the power she had lately achieved over the fears of this financial magnate. She would do all this, but for her physical weakness. She ground her teeth as she thought of it: that at such a time she should be—and yet a moment later a sudden fancy flashed across her mind, and she closed her eyes that she might take in its delusive sweetness more completely. It might be that it wanted only this to touch his heart—some men were so strange—and if it were, O God!—she stopped.

What was that noise? The house had been very quiet, so still that she had heard a woodpecker tapping on its roof. But now she heard distinctly the slow, heavy tread of a man in one of the upper chambers, which had been used as a lumber-room. Mrs. Conroy had none of the nervous apprehension of her sex in regard to probable ghosts or burglars—she had too much of a man's practical pre-occupation for that, yet she listened curiously. It came again. There was no mistaking it now. It was the tread of the man with whom her thoughts had been busy—her husband.

What was he doing here? In the few months of their married life he had never been home before at this hour. The lumber-room contained among other things the *disjecta membra* of his old mining life and experience. He may have wanted something. There was an old bag which she remembered he said contained some of his mother's dresses. Yet it was so odd that he should go there now. Any other time but this. A terrible superstitious dread—a dread that any other time she would have laughed to scorn, began to creep over her. Hark! he was moving. She stopped breathing.

The tread recommenced. It passed into the upper hall, and came slowly down the stairs, each step recording itself in her heart-beats. It reached the lower hall and seemed to hesitate; then it came slowly along toward her door, and again hesitated.

Another moment of suspense, and she felt she would have screamed. And then the door slowly opened, and Gabriel stood before her.

In one swift, intuitive, hopeless look she read her fate. He knew all! And yet his eyes, except that they bore less of the usual perplexity and embarrassment with which they had habitually met hers, though grave and sad, had neither indignation nor anger. He had changed his clothes to a rough miner's blouse and trousers, and carried in one hand a miner's pack, and in the other a pick and shovel. He laid them down slowly and deliberately, and seeing her eyes fixed upon them with a nervous intensity, began apologetically—

"They contains, ma'am, on'y a blanket and a few duds ez I allus used to carry with me. I'll open it ef you say so. But you know me, ma'am, well enough to allow that I'd take nothin' outer this yer house ez I didn't bring inter it."

"You are going away," she said, in a voice that was not audible to herself, but seemed to vaguely echo in her mental consciousness.

"I be. Ef ye don't know why, ma'am, I reckon ez you'll hear it from the same vyce ez I did. It's on'y the squar thing to say afore I go, ez it ain't my fault nor hiz'n. I was on the hill this mornin' in the ole cabin."

It seemed as if he had told her this before, so old and self-evident the fact appeared.

"I was sayin' I woz on the hill, when I heerd vyces, and lookin' out I seed you with a stranger. From wot ye know o' me and my ways, ma'am, it ain't like me to listen to thet wot ain't allowed for me to hear. And ye might hev stood thar ontel now ef I hadn't seed a chap dodgin' round behind the trees, spyin' and list'nin'. When I seed thet man I knowed him to be a pore Mexican, whose legs I'd tended yer in the Gulch mor'n a year ago. I went up to him, and when he seed me he'd hev run. But I laid my hand onto him—and—he stayed!"

There was something so unconsciously large and fine in the slight gesture of this giant's hand as he emphasised his speech, that even through her swiftly rising pride Mrs. Conroy was awed and thrilled by it. But the next moment she found herself saying—whether aloud or not she could not tell—"If he had loved me, he would have killed him then and there."

"Wot thet man sed to me—bein' flustered and savage-like, along o' bein' choked hard to keep him from singin' out and breakin' in upon you and thet entire stranger—ain't fur me to say. Knowin' him longer than I do, I reckon you suspect 'bout wot it was. That it ez the truth I read it in your face now, ma'am, ez I reckon I might hev read it off and on in many ways and vari's styles sens we've been yer together, on'y I waz thet weak and ondecided yer."

He raised his hand to his forehead here, and with his broad palm appeared to wipe away the trouble and perplexity that had overshadowed it. He then drew a paper from his breast.

"I've drawed up a little paper yer ez I'll hand over to Lawyer Maxwell, makin' over back agin all ez I once hed o' you and all ez I ever expect to hev. For I don't agree with that Mexican thet wot was gi'n to Grace belongs to me. I allow ez she kin settle thet herself, ef she ever comes, and ef I know thet chile, ma'am, she ain't goin' tech it with a two-foot pole. We've allus bin simple folks, ma'am—though it ain't the squar thing to take me for a sample—and oneddicated and common, but thar ain't a Conroy ez lived ez was ever pinted for money, or ez ever took more outer the kompany's wages than his grub and his clothes."

It was the first time that he had ever asserted himself in her presence, and even then he did it half apologetically, yet with an unconscious dignity in his manner that became him well. He reached down as he spoke and took up his pick and his bundle, and turned to go.

"There is nothing then that you are leaving behind you?" she asked.

He raised his eyes squarely to hers.

"No," he said, simply, "nothing."

Oh, if she could have only spoken! Oh, had she but dared to tell him that he had left behind that which he could not take away, that which the mere instincts of his manhood would have stirred him to tenderness and mercy, that which would have appealed to him through its very helplessness and youth. But she dared not. That eloquence which an hour before had been ready enough to sway the feelings of the man to whom she had been faithless and did not love, failed her now. In the grasp of her first and only hopeless passion this arch-hypocrite had lost even the tact of the simplest of her sex. She did not even assume an indifference! She said nothing; when she raised her eyes again he was gone.

She was wrong. At the front door he stopped, hesitated a moment, and then returned slowly and diffidently to the room. Her heart beat rapidly, and then was still.

"Ye asked just now," he said, falteringly, "ef thar was anything ez I was leavin' behind. Thar is—ef ye'll overlook my sayin' it. When you and me allowed to leave fur furrin parts, I reckoned to leave thet housekeeper behind, and unbeknowed to ye I gin her some money and a charge. I told her thet if ever thet dear chile—Sister Grace—came here, thet she should take her in and do by her ez I would, and let me know. Et may be a heap to ask, but ef it 'tain't too much—I—I shouldn't—like—yer—to turn—thet innocent insuspectin' chile away from the house thet she might take to be mine. Ye needn't let on anythin' thet's gone—ye needn't tell her what a fool I've been, but jest take her in and send for me. Lawyer Maxwell will gin ye my address."

The sting recalled her benumbed life. She rose with a harsh dissonant laugh and said, "Your wishes shall be fulfilled—if"—she hesitated a moment—"*I* am here."

But he did not hear the last sentence, and was gone.

CHAPTER VII.

WHAT PASSED UNDER THE PINE AND WHAT REMAINED THERE.

RAMIREZ was not as happy in his revenge as he had anticipated. He had, in an instant of impulsive rage, fired his mine prematurely, and, as he feared, impotently. Gabriel had not visibly sickened, faded, nor fallen blighted under the exposure of his wife's deceit. It was even doubtful, as far as Ramirez could judge from his quiet reception of the revelation, whether he would even call that wife to account for it. Again, Ramirez was unpleasantly conscious that this exposure had lost some of its dignity and importance by being wrested from him as a *confession* made under pressure or duress. Worse than all, he had lost the opportunity of previously threatening Mrs. Conroy with the disclosure, and the delicious spectacle of her discomfiture. In point of fact his revenge had been limited to the cautious cowardice of the anonymous letter-writer, who, stabbing in the dark, enjoys neither the contemplation of the agonies of his victim, nor the assertion of his own individual power.

To this torturing reflection a terrible suspicion of the

Spanish translator, Perkins, was superadded. For Gabriel, Ramirez had only that contempt which every lawless lover has for the lawful husband of his mistress, while for Perkins he had that agonising doubt which every lawless lover has for every other man but the husband. In making this exposure had he not precipitated a catastrophe as fatal to himself as to the husband? Might they not both drive this woman into the arms of another man? Ramirez paced the little bedroom of the Grand Conroy Hotel, a prey to that bastard remorse of all natures like his own,—the overwhelming consciousness of opportunities for villany misspent.

Come what might he would see her again, and at once. He would let her know that he suspected her relations with this translator. He would tell her that he had written the letter—that he had forged the grant—that——

A tap at the door recalled him to himself. It opened presently to Sal, coy, bashful, and conscious. The evident agitation of this young forcigner had to Sal's matter-of-fact comprehension only one origin—a hopeless, consuming passion for herself.

"Dinner hez bin done gone an hour ago," said that arch virgin, "but I put suthin' by for ye. Ye was inquirin' last night about them Conroys. I thought I'd tell ye thet Gabril hez bin yer askin' arter Lawyer Maxwell—which he's off to Sacramento—altho' one o' Sue Markle's most intymit friends and steddeyist boarders!"

But Mr. Ramirez had no ear for Gabriel now.

"Tell to me, Mees Clark," he said, suddenly turning all his teeth on her, with gasping civility, "where is this Señor Perkins, eh?"

"Thet shiny chap—ez looks like a old turned alpacker gownd!" said Sal; "thet man ez I can't abear," she continued, with a delicately maidenly suggestion that Ramirez need fear no rivalry from that quarter. "I don't mind—and don't keer to know. He hezn't bin yer since mornin'. I reckon he's up somewhar on Conroy's Hill. All I know ez thet he sent a message yer to git ready his volise to put aboard the Wingdam stage to-night. Are ye goin' with him?"

"No," said Ramirez, curtly.

"Axin' yer parding for the question, but seein' ez he'd got booked for two places, I tho't ez maybe ye'd got tired o' plain mounting folks and mounting ways, and waz goin' with him," and Sal threw an arch yet reproachful glance at Ramirez.

"Booked for two seats," gasped Victor; "ah! for a lady perhaps—eh, Mees Clark? for a lady?"

Sal bridled instantly at what might have seemed a suggestion of impropriety on her part. "A lady—like his imperance—indeed! I'd like to know who would demean theirselves by goin' with the like o' he! But you're not startin' out agin without your dinner, and it waitin' ye in the oven? No? La! Mr. Ramirez, ye must be in luv! I've heerd tell ez it do take away the appetite; not knowin' o' my own experense, though it's little hez passed my lips these two days, and only when tempted."

But before Sal could complete her diagnosis, Mr. Ramirez gasped a few words of hasty excuse, seized his hat and hurried from the room.

Leaving Sal a second time to mourn over the effect of her coquettish playfulness upon the sensitive Italian nature, Victor Ramirez, toiling through the heat and fiery dust shaken from the wheels of incoming teams, once more brushed his way up the long ascent of Conroy's Hill, and did not stop until he reached its summit. Here he paused to collect his scattered thoughts, to decide upon some plan of action, to control the pulse of his beating temples, quickened by excitement and the fatigue of the ascent, and to wipe the perspiration from his streaming face. He must see her at once; but how and where? To go boldly to her house would be to meet her in the presence of Gabriel, and that was no longer an object; besides, if she were with this stranger it would not probably be there. By haunting this nearest umbrage to the house he would probably intercept them on their way to the Gulch, or overhear any other conference. By lingering here he would avoid any interference from Gabriel's cabin on the right, and yet be able to detect the approach of any one from the road. The spot that he had chosen was, singularly enough, in earlier days, Gabriel's favourite haunt for the indulgence of his noontide contemplation and pipe. A great pine, the largest of its fellows, towered in a little opening to the right, as if it had drawn apart for seclusion, and obeying some mysterious attraction, Victor went toward it and seated himself on an abutting root at its base. Here a singular circumstance occurred, which at first filled him with superstitious fear. The handkerchief with which he had wiped his face—nay, his very shirt-front itself—suddenly appeared as if covered with blood. A moment later he saw that the ensanguined hue was only due to the dust through which he had plunged, blending with the perspiration that on the least exertion still started from every pore of his burning skin.

The sun was slowly sinking. The long shadow of Reservoir Ridge fell upon Conroy's Hill, and seemed to cut down the tall pine that a moment before had risen redly in the sunlight. The sounds of human labour slowly died out of the Gulch below, the far-off whistle of teamsters in the Wingdam road began to fail. One by one the red openings on the wooded hillside opposite went out, as if Nature were putting up the shutters for the day. With the gathering twilight Ramirez became more intensely alert and watchful. Treading stealthily around the lone pine tree, with shining eyes and gleaming teeth, he might have been mistaken for some hesitating animal waiting for that boldness which should come with the coming night. Suddenly he stopped, and leaning forward peered into the increasing shadow. Coming up the trail from the town was a woman. Even at that distance and by that uncertain light, Ramirez recognised the flapping hat and ungainly stride. It was Sal—perdition! Might the devil fly away with her! But she turned to the right with the trail that wound toward Gabriel's hut and the cottage beyond, and Victor breathed, or rather panted, more freely. And then a voice at his very side thrilled him to his smallest fibre, and he turned quickly. It was Mrs. Conroy, white, erect, and truculent.

"What are you doing here?" she said, with a sharp, quick utterance.

"Hush!" said Ramirez, trembling with the passion called up by the figure before him. "Hush! There is one who has just come up the trail."

"What do I care who hears me now? You have made caution unnecessary," she responded, sharply. "All the world knows us now! and so I ask you again, what are *you* doing here?"

He would have approached her nearer, but she drew back, twitching her long white skirt behind her with a single quick feminine motion of her hand, as if to save it from contamination.

Victor laughed uneasily. "You have come to keep your appointment; it is not my fault if I am late."

"I have come here because for the last half-hour I have watched you from my verandah, coursing in and out among the trees like a hound as you are! I have come to whip you off my land as I would a hound. But I have first a word or two to say to you as the man you have assumed to be."

Standing there with the sunset glow over her erect, graceful figure, in the pink flush of her cheek, in the cold fires of her eyes, in all the thousand nameless magnetisms of her presence, there was so much of her old power over this slave of passion, that the scorn of her words touched him only to inflame him, and he would have grovelled at her feet could he have touched the thin three fingers that she warningly waved at him.

"You wrong me, Julie, by the God of Heaven! I was wild, mad, this morning—you understand—for when I came to you I found you with another! I had reason, Mother of God! I had reason for my madness, reason enough; but I came in peace, Julie, I came in peace!"

"In peace," returned Mrs. Conroy, scornfully; "your note was a peaceful one, indeed!"

"Ah! but I knew not how else to make you hear me. I had news—news you understand, news that might save you, for I came from the woman who holds the grant. Ah! you will listen, will you not? For one moment only, Julie, hear me, and I am gone."

Mrs. Conroy, with abstracted gaze, leaned against the tree. "Go on," she said coldly.

"Ah! you will listen then!" said Victor, joyfully; "and when you have listened you shall understand! Well. First I have the fact that the lawyer for this woman is the man who deserted the Grace Conroy in the mountains—the man who was called Philip Ashley, but whose real name is Poinsett."

"Who did you say?" said Mrs. Conroy, suddenly stepping from the tree, and fixing a pair of cruel eyes on Ramirez.

"Arthur Poinsett—an ex-soldier, an officer. Ah, you do not believe—I swear to God it is so!"

"What has this to do with me?" she said scornfully, resuming her position beside the pine. "Go on—or is this all?"

"No, but it is much. Look you! he is the affianced of a rich widow in the Southern Country, you understand? No one knows his past. Ah, you begin to comprehend. He does not dare to seek out the real Grace Conroy. He shall not dare to press the claim of his client. Consequently, he does nothing!"

"Is this all your news?"

"All!—ah, no. There is one more, but I dare not speak it here," he said, glancing craftily around through the slowly darkening wood.

"Then it must remain untold," returned Mrs. Conroy, coldly; "for this is our last and only interview."

"But, Julie!"

"Have you done?" she continued, in the same tone.

Whether her indifference was assumed or not, it was effective. Ramirez glanced again quickly around, and then said, sulkily, "Come nearer, and I will tell you. Ah, you doubt—you doubt? Be it so." But seeing that she did not move, he drew toward the tree, and whispered—"Bend here your head—I will whisper it."

Mrs. Conroy, evading his outstretched hand, bent her head. He whispered a few words in her ear that were inaudible a foot from the tree.

"Did you tell this to him—to Gabriel?" she asked, fixing her eyes upon him, yet without change in her frigid demeanour.

"No!—I swear to you, Julie, no! I would not have told him anything, but I was wild, crazy. And he was a brute, a great bear. He held me fast, here, so! I could not move. It was a forced confession. Yes—Mother of God—by force!"

Luckily for Victor the darkness hid the scorn that momentarily flashed in the woman's eyes at this corroboration of her husband's strength and the weakness of the man before her. "And is this all that you have to tell me?" she only said.

"All—I swear to you, Julie—all."

"Then listen, Victor Ramirez," she said, swiftly stepping from the tree into the path before him, and facing him with a white and rigid face. "Whatever was your purpose in coming here, it has been successful! You have done all that you intended, and more! The man whose mind you came to poison—the man you wished to turn against me—has gone!—has left me—left me never to return!—he never loved me! Your exposure of me was to him a godsend, for it gave him an excuse for the insults he has heaped upon me, for the treachery he has always hidden in his bosom!"

Even in the darkness she could see the self-complacent flash of Victor's teeth, could hear the quick, hurried sound of his breath as he bent his head toward her, and knew that he was eagerly reaching out his hand for hers. He would have caught her gesturing hand and covered it with kisses, but that, divining his intention, without flinching from her position, she whipped both her hands behind her.

"Well—you are satisfied! You have had your say and your way. Now I shall have mine. Do you suppose I came here to-night to congratulate you? No I came here to tell you that, insulted, outraged, and spurned as I have been by my husband, Gabriel Conroy—cast off and degraded as I stand here to-night—*I love him!* Love him as I never loved any man before; love him as I never shall love any man again; love him as I hate you! Love him so that I shall follow him wherever he goes, if I have to drag myself after him on my knees. His hatred is more precious to me than your love. Do you hear me, Victor Ramirez? That is what *I* came here to tell you. More than that—listen! The secret you have whispered to me just now, whether true or false, I shall take to him. I will help him to find his sister. I will make him love me yet if I sacrifice you, everybody, my own life, to do it! Do you hear that, Victor Ramirez, you dog!—you Spanish mongrel!—you half-breed. Oh, grit your teeth there in the darkness—I know you—grit your teeth as you did to-day when Gabriel held you squirming under his thumb! It was a fine sight, Victor—worthy of the manly Secretary who stole a dying girl's papers!—worthy of the valiant soldier who abandoned his garrison to a Yankee pedlar and his mule! Oh, I know you, sir, and have known you from the first day I made you my tool—my dupe! Go on, sir, go on—draw your knife, do! I am not afraid, coward! I shall not scream, I promise you! Come on!"

With an insane, articulate gasp of rage and shame, he sprang toward her with an uplifted knife. But at the same instant she saw a hand reach from the darkness and fall swiftly upon his shoulder, saw him turn and with an oath struggle furiously in the arms of Devarges, and without waiting to thank her deliverer, or learn the result of his interference, darted by the struggling pair and fled.

Possessed only by a single idea, she ran swiftly to her home. Here she pencilled a few hurried lines, and called one of her Chinese servants to her side.

"Take this, Ah Fe, and give it to Mr. Conroy. You will find him at Lawyer Maxwell's, or if not there he will tell you where he has gone. But you must find him. If he has left town already, you must follow him. Find him within an hour and I'll double that"—she placed a gold piece in his hand. "Go at once."

However limited might have been Ah Fe's knowledge of the English language, there was an eloquence in the woman's manner that needed no translation. He nodded his head intelligently, said, "Me shabbe you—muchee quick," caused the gold piece and the letter to instantly vanish up his sleeve, and started from the house in a brisk trot. Nor did he allow any incidental diversion to interfere with the business in hand. The noise of struggling in the underbrush on Conroy's Hill and a cry for help only extracted from Ah Fe the response, "You muchee go-to-hellee—no foolee me!" as he trotted unconcernedly by. In half an hour he had reached Lawyer Maxwell's office. But the news was not favourable. Gabriel had left an hour before, they knew not where. Ah Fe hesitated a moment, and then ran quickly down the hill to where a gang of his fellow-countrymen were working in a ditch at the roadside. Ah Fe paused, and uttered in a high recitative a series of the most extraordinary ejaculations, utterly unintelligible to the few Americans who chanced to be working near. But the effect was magical; in an instant pick and shovel were laid aside, and before the astonished miners could comprehend it the entire gang of Chinamen had dispersed, and in another instant were scattered over the several trails leading out of One Horse Gulch, except one.

That one was luckily taken by Ah Fe. In half an hour he came upon the object of his search, settled on a boulder by the wayside, smoking his evening pipe. His pick, shovel, and pack lay by his side. Ah Fe did not waste time in preliminary speech or introduction. He simply handed the missive to his master, and instantly turned his back upon him and departed. In another half hour every Chinaman was back in the ditch, working silently as if nothing had happened.

Gabriel laid aside his pipe and held the letter a moment hesitatingly between his finger and thumb. Then opening it, he at once recognised the small Italian hand with which his wife had kept his accounts and written from his dictation, and something like a faint feeling of regret overcame him as he gazed at it, without taking the meaning of the text. And then, with the hesitation, repetition, and audible utterance of an illiterate person, he slowly read the following:—

"I was wrong. You have left something behind you—a secret that as you value your happiness, you must take with you. If you come to Conroy's Hill within the next two hours you shall know it, for I shall not enter that house again, and leave here to-night for ever. I do not ask you to come for the sake of your wife, but for the sake of the woman she once personated. You will come because you love Grace, not because you care for JULIE."

There was but one fact that Gabriel clearly grasped in this letter. That was, that it referred to some news of Grace. That was enough. He put away his pipe, rose, shouldered his pack and pick, and deliberately retraced his steps. When he reached the town, with the shamefacedness of a man who had just taken leave of it for ever, he avoided the main thoroughfare, but did this so clumsily and incautiously, after his simple fashion, that two or three of the tunnel-men noticed him ascending the hill by an inconvenient and seldom used by-path. He did not stay long, however, for in a short time—some said ten, others said fifteen minutes—he was seen again, descending rapidly and recklessly, and crossing the Gulch disappeared in the bushes, at the base of Bald Mountain.

With the going down of the sun that night, the temperature fell also, and the fierce, dry, desert heat that had filled the land for the past few days, fled away before a fierce wind which rose with the coldly rising moon, that, during the rest of the night, rode calmly over the twisting tops of writhing pines on Conroy's Hill, over the rattling windows of the town, and over the beaten dust of mountain roads. But even with the night the wind passed too, and the sun arose the next morning upon a hushed and silent landscape. It touched, according to its habit, first the tall top of the giant pine on Conroy's Hill, and then slid softly down its shaft until it reached the ground. And there it found Victor Ramirez, with a knife thrust through his heart, lying dead!

BOOK VI.

A DIP.

CHAPTER I.

MR. HAMLIN'S RECREATION CONTINUED.

WHEN Donna Dolores after the departure of Mrs. Sepulvida missed the figure of Mr. Jack Hamlin from the plain before her window, she presumed he had followed that lady and would have been surprised to have known that he was at that moment within her castle, drinking *aguardiente* with no less a personage than the solemn Don Juan Salvatierra. In point of fact, with that easy audacity which distinguished him, Jack had penetrated the courtyard, gained the hospitality of Don Juan without even revealing his name and profession to that usually ceremonious gentleman, and after holding him in delicious fascination for two hours, had actually left him lamentably intoxicated, and utterly oblivious of the character of his guest. Why Jack did not follow up his advantage by seeking an interview with the mysterious *Señora* who had touched him so deeply I cannot say, nor could he himself afterwards determine. A sudden bashfulness and timidity which he had never before experienced in his relations with the sex, tied his own tongue, while Don Juan with the garrulity which inebriety gave to his, poured forth the gossip of the Mission and the household. It is possible also that a certain vague hopelessness, equally novel to Jack, sent him away in lower spirits than he came. It is not remarkable that Donna Dolores knew nothing of the visit of this guest, until three days afterwards, for during that time she was indisposed and did not leave her room, but it *was* remarkable that on learning it she flew into a paroxysm of indignation and rage that alarmed Don Juan and frightened her attendants.

"And why was *I* not told of the presence of this strange *Americano?* Am I a child, holy St. Anthony! that I am to be kept in ignorance of my duty as the hostess of the Blessed Trinity, or are you, Don Juan, my dueña? A brave *caballero*, who, I surmise from your description, is the same that protected me from insult at Mass last Sunday, and he is not to 'kiss my hand?' Mother of God! And his name—you have forgotten?"

In vain Juan protested that the strange *caballero* had not requested an audience, and that a proper maidenly spirit would have prevented the Donna from appearing, unsought.

"Better that I should have been thought forward—and these *Americanos* are of different habitude, my uncle—than that the Blessed Trinity should have been misrepresented by the guzzling of *aguardiente!*"

Howbeit, Mr. Hamlin had not found the climate of San Antonio conducive to that strict repose that his physician had recommended, and left it the next day with an accession of feverish energy that was new to him. He had idled away three days of excessive heat at Sacramento, and on the fourth had flown to the mountains and found himself on the morning of the first cool day at Wingdam.

"Anybody here I know?" he demanded of his faithful henchman, as Pete brought in his clothes, freshly brushed for the morning toilette.

"No, sah!"

"Nor want to, eh?" continued the cynical Jack, leisurely getting out of bed.

Pete reflected. "Dere is two o' dese yar Yeastern tourists—dem folks as is goin' round inspectin' de country—down in de parlour. Jess come over from de Big Trees. I reckon dey's some o' de same party—dem Frisco chaps—Mass Dumphy and de odders haz been unloadin' to. Dey's mighty green, and de boys along de road has been fillin' 'em up. It's jess so much water on de dried apples dat Pete Dumphy's been shovin' into 'em."

Jack smiled grimly. "I reckon you needn't bring up my breakfast, Pete, I'll go down."

The party thus obscurely referred to by Pete, were Mr. and Mrs. Raynor, who had been "doing" the Big Trees, under the intelligent guidance of a San Francisco editor who had been deputised by Mr. Dumphy to represent Californian hospitality. They were exceedingly surprised during breakfast by the entrance of a pale, handsome, languid gentleman, accurately dressed, whose infinite neatness shamed their own bedraggled appearance, and who, accompanied by his own servant, advanced and quietly took a seat opposite the tourists and their guide. Mrs. Raynor at once became conscious of some negligence in her toilette, and after a moment's embarrassment excused herself and withdrew. Mr. Raynor, impressed with the appearance of the stranger, telegraphed his curiosity by elbowing the editor, who, however, for some reason best known to himself, failed to respond. Possibly he recognised the presence of the notorious Mr. Jack Hamlin in the dark-eyed stranger, and may have had ample reasons for refraining from voicing the popular reputation of that gentleman before his face, or possibly he may have been inattentive. Howbeit, after Mr. Hamlin's entrance he pretermitted the hymn of California praise and became reticent and absorbed in his morning paper. Mr. Hamlin waited for the lady to retire, and then, calmly ignoring the presence of any other individual, languidly drew from his pocket a revolver and bowie-knife, and placing them in an easy habitual manner on either side of his plate, glanced carelessly over the table, and then called Pete to his side.

"Tell them," said Jack, quietly, "that I want some *large* potatoes: ask them what they mean by putting those little things on the table. Tell them to be quick. Is your rifle loaded?"

"Yes, sah," said Pete, promptly, without relaxing a muscle of his serious ebony face.

"Well—take it along with you."

But here the curiosity of Mr. Raynor, who had been just commenting on the really enormous size of the potatoes, got the best of his prudence. Failing to make his companion respond to his repeated elbowings, he leaned over the table toward the languid stranger. "Excuse me, sir," he said, politely, "but did I understand you to say that you thought these potatoes *small*—that there are really larger ones to be had?"

"It's the first time," returned Jack gravely, "that I ever was insulted by having a *whole* potato brought to me. I didn't know it was possible before. Perhaps in this part of the country the vegetables are poor. I'm a stranger to this section. I take it you are too. But because I am a stranger I don't see why I should be imposed upon."

"Ah, I see," said the mystified Raynor, "but if I might ask another question—you'll excuse me if I'm impertinent —I noticed that you just now advised your servant to take his gun into the kitchen with him; surely"——

"Pete," interrupted Mr. Hamlin, languidly, "is a good nigger. I shouldn't like to lose him! Perhaps you're right

—maybe I am a little over-cautious. But when a man has lost two servants by gunshot wounds inside of three months, it makes him careful."

The perfect unconcern of the speaker, the reticence of his companion, and the dead silence of the room in which this extraordinary speech was uttered, filled the measure of Mr. Raynor's astonishment.

"Bless my soul! this is most extraordinary. I have seen nothing of this," he said, appealing in dumb show to his companion.

Mr. Hamlin followed the direction of his eyes. "Your friend is a Californian and knows what we think of any man who lies, and how most men resent such an imputation, and I reckon he'll endorse me!"

The editor muttered a hasty assent that seemed to cover Mr. Hamlin's various propositions, and then hurriedly withdrew, abandoning his charge to Mr. Hamlin. What advantage Jack took of this situation, what extravagant accounts he gravely offered of the vegetation in Lower California, of the resources of the country, of the reckless disregard of life and property, do not strictly belong to the record of this veracious chronicle. Nowithstanding all this, Mr. Raynor found Mr. Hamlin an exceedingly fascinating companion, and later, when the editor had rejoined them, and Mr. Hamlin proceeded to beg that gentleman to warn Mr. Raynor against gambling as the one seductive, besetting sin of California, alleging that it had been the ruin of both the editor and himself, the tourist was so struck with the frankness and high moral principle of his new acquaintance as to insist upon his making one of their party, an invitation that Mr. Hamlin might have accepted but for the intervention of a singular occurrence.

During the conversation he had been curiously impressed by the appearance of a stranger who had entered and modestly and diffidently taken a seat near the door. To Mr. Hamlin this modesty and diffidence appeared so curiously at variance with his superb physique, and the exceptional strength and power shown in every muscle of his body, that with his usual audacity he felt inclined to go forward and inquire "what was his little game?" That he was lying in wait to be "picked up"—the reader must really excuse me if I continue to borrow Mr. Hamlin's expressive vernacular—that his diffidence and shyness was a deceit and intended to entrap the unwary, he felt satisfied, and was proportionably thrilled with a sense of admiration for him. That a rational human being who held such a hand should be content with a small *ante*, without "raising the other players,"—but I beg the fastidious reader's forgiveness.

He was dressed in the ordinary miner's garb of the Southern mines, perhaps a little more cleanly than the average miner by reason of his taste, certainly more picturesque by reason of his statuesque shapeliness. He wore a pair of white duck trousers, a jumper or loose blouse of the same material, with a low-folded sailor's collar and sailor-knotted neckerchief, which displayed, with an unconsciousness quite characteristic of the man, the full, muscular column of his sunburnt throat, except where it was hidden by a full, tawny beard. His long, sandy curls fell naturally and equally on either side of the centre of his low, broad forehead. His fair complexion, although greatly tanned by exposure, seemed to have faded lately as by sickness or great mental distress, a theory that had some confirmation in the fact that he ate but little. His eyes were downcast, or, when raised, were so shy as to avoid critical examination. Nevertheless his mere superficial exterior was so striking as to attract the admiration of others besides Mr. Hamlin; to excite the enthusiastic attention of Mr.

Raynor, and to enable the editor to offer him as a fair type of the mining population. Embarrassed at last by a scrutiny that asserted itself even through his habitual unconsciousness and pre-occupation, the subject of this criticism arose and returned to the hotel verandah, where his pack and mining implements were lying. Mr. Hamlin, who for the last few days had been in a rather exceptional mood, for some occult reason which he could not explain, felt like respecting the stranger's reserve, and quietly lounged into the billiard-room to wait for the coming of the stage-coach. As soon as his back was turned the editor took occasion to offer Mr. Raynor his own estimate of Mr. Hamlin's character and reputation, to correct his misstatements regarding Californian resources and social habits, and to restore Mr. Raynor's possibly shaken faith in California as a country especially adapted to the secure investment of capital.

"As to the insecurity of life," said the editor, indignantly, "it is as safe here as in New York or Boston. We admit that in the early days the country was cursed by too many adventurers of the type of this very gambler Hamlin, but I will venture to say that you will require no better refutation of these calumnies than this very miner whom you admired. He, sir, is a type of our mining population; strong, manly, honest, unassuming, and perfectly gentle and retiring. We are proud, sir, we admit, of such men—eh? Oh, that's nothing—only the arrival of the up-stage!"

It certainly was something more. A momentarily increasing crowd of breathless men were gathered on the verandah before the window and were peering anxiously over each other's head toward a central group, among which towered the tall figure of the very miner of whom they had been speaking. More than that, there was a certain undefined, restless terror in the air, as when the intense conscious passion or suffering of one or two men communicates itself vaguely without speech, sometimes even without visible sign to others. And then Yuba Bill, the driver of the Wingdam coach, strode out from the crowd into the bar-room, drawing from his hands with an evident effort his immense buckskin gloves.

"What's the row, Bill?" said half-a-dozen voices.

"Nothin'," said Bill, gruffly; "only the Sheriff of Calaveras ez kem down with us hez nabbed his man jest in his very tracks."

"When, Bill?"

"Right yer—on this very verandy—furst man he seed!"

"What for?" "Who?" "What hed he bin doin'?" "Who is it?" "What's up?" persisted the chorus.

"Killed a man up at One Horse Gulch, last night," said Bill, grasping the decanter which the attentive bar-keeper had, without previous request, placed before him.

"Who did he kill, Bill?"

"A little Mexican from 'Frisco by the name o' Ramirez."

"What's the man's name that killed him—the man that you took?"

The voice was Jack Hamlin's.

Yuba Bill instantly turned, put down his glass, wiped his mouth with his sleeve, and then deliberately held out his great hand with an exhaustive grin. "Dern my skin, ole man, if it ain't you! And how's things, eh? Yer lookin' a little white in the gills, but peart and sassy, ez usual. Heerd you was kinder off colour, down in Sacramento lass week. And it's you, ole fell, and jest in time! Bar-keep—hist that pizen over to Jack. Here to ye agin, ole man! But I'm glad to see ye!"

The crowd hung breathless over the two men—awe-struck and respectful. It was a meeting of the gods—

Jack Hamlin and Yuba Bill. None dare speak. Hamlin broke the silence at last, and put down his glass.

"What," he asked, lazily, yet with a slight colour on his cheek, "did you say was the name of the chap that fetched that little Mexican?"

"Gabriel Conroy," said Bill.

CHAPTER II.

MR. HAMLIN TAKES A HAND.

THE capture had been effected quietly. To the evident astonishment of his captor, Gabriel had offered no resistance, but had yielded himself up with a certain composed willingness, as if it were only the preliminary step to the quicker solution of a problem that was sure to be solved. It was observed, however, that he showed a degree of caution that was new to him—asking to see the warrant, the particulars of the discovery of the body, and utterly withholding that voluble explanation or apology which all who knew his character confidently expected him to give, whether guilty or innocent—a caution which, accepted by them as simply the low cunning of the criminal, told against him. He submitted quietly to a search that, however, disclosed no concealed weapon or anything of import. But when a pair of handcuffs were shown him, he changed colour, and those that were nearest to him saw that he breathed hurriedly, and hesitated in the first words of some protest that rose to his lips. The sheriff, a man of known intrepidity, who had the rapid and clear intuition that comes with courageous self-possession, noticed it also, and quietly put the handcuffs back in his pocket.

"I reckon there's no use for 'em here; ef *you're* willin' to take the risks, *I* am."

The eyes of the two men met, and Gabriel thanked him. In that look he recognised and accepted the fact that on a motion to escape he would be instantly killed.

They were to return with the next stage, and in the interval Gabriel was placed in an upper room, and securely guarded. Here, falling into his old apologetic manner, he asked permission to smoke a pipe, which was at once granted by his good-humoured guard, and then threw himself at full length upon the bed. The rising wind rattled the windows noisily, and entering tossed the smoke-wreaths that rose from his pipe in fitful waves about the room. The guard, who was much more embarrassed than his charge, was relieved of an ineffectual attempt to carry on a conversation suitable to the occasion by Gabriel's simple directness—

"You needn't put yourself out to pass the time o' day with me," he said, gently, "that bein' extry to your reg'lar work. Ef you hev any friends ez you'd like to talk to in your own line, invite 'em in, and don't mind me."

But here the guard's embarrassment was further relieved by the entrance of Joe Hall, the sheriff.

"There's a gentleman here to speak with you," he said to Gabriel, "he can stay until we're ready to go." Turning to the guard, he added, "You can take a chair outside the door in the hall. It's all right, it's the prisoner's counsel."

At the word Gabriel looked up. Following the sheriff, Lawyer Maxwell entered the room. He approached Gabriel, and extended with grave cordiality a hand that had apparently wiped from his mouth the last trace of mirthfulness at the door.

"I did not expect to see you again so soon, Gabriel, but as quickly as the news reached me, and I heard that our friend Hall had a warrant for you, I started after him. I would have got here before him, but my horse gave out." He paused, and looked steadily at Gabriel. "Well!"

Gabriel looked at him in return, but did not speak.

"I supposed you would need professional aid," he went on, with a slight hesitation, "perhaps *mine*—knowing that I was aware of some of the circumstances that preceded this affair."

"Wot circumstances?" asked Gabriel, with the sudden look of cunning that had before prejudiced his captors.

"For Heaven's sake, Gabriel," said Maxwell, rising with a gesture of impatience, "don't let us repeat the blunder of our first interview. *This* is a serious matter; *may be* very serious to you. Think a moment. Yesterday you sought my professional aid to deed to your wife all your property, telling me that you were going away never to return to One Horse Gulch. I do not ask you now *why* you did it. I only want you to reflect that I am just now the only man who knows that circumstance—a circumstance that I can tell you as a lawyer is somewhat important in the light of the crime that you are now charged with."

Maxwell waited for Gabriel to speak, wiping away as he waited the usual smile that lingered around his lips. But Gabriel said nothing.

"Gabriel Conroy," said Lawyer Maxwell, suddenly dropping into the vernacular of One Horse Gulch, "are you a fool?"

"Thet's so," said Gabriel, with the simplicity of a man admitting a self-evident proposition. "Thet's so; I reckon I are."

"I shouldn't wonder," said Maxwell, again swiftly turning upon him, "if you were!" He stopped, as if ashamed of his abruptness, and said more quietly and persuasively, "Come, Gabriel, if you won't confess to *me*, I suppose that I must to *you*. Six months ago I thought you an impostor.

Six months ago the woman who is now your wife charged you with being an impostor; with assuming a name and right that did not belong to you; in plain English, said that you had set yourself up as Gabriel Conroy, and that she, who was Grace Conroy, the sister of the real Gabriel, knew that you lied. She substantiated all this by proofs; hang it," continued Maxwell, appealing in dumb show to the walls, "there isn't a lawyer living as wouldn't have said it was a good case, and been ready to push it in any court. Under these circumstances I sought you, and you remember how. You know the result of that interview. I can tell you now that if there ever was a man who palpably confessed to guilt when he was innocent, *you* were that man. Well, after your conduct there was explained by Olly, without, however, damaging the original evidence against you, or prejudicing her rights, this woman came to me and said that she had discovered that you were the man who had saved her life at the risk of your own, and that for the present she could not, in delicacy, push her claim. When afterwards she told me that this gratitude had—well, ripened into something more serious, and that she had engaged herself to marry you, and so condone your offence, why, it was woman-like and natural, and I suspected nothing. I believed her story—believed she had a case. Yes, sir; the last six months I have looked upon you as the creature of that woman's foolish magnanimity. I could see that she was soft on you, and believed that you had fooled her. I did, hang me! There, if you confess to being a fool, I do to having been an infernal sight bigger one."

He stopped, erased the mirthful past with his hand, and went on—

"I began to suspect something when you came to me yesterday with this story of your going away, and this disposal of your property. When I heard of the murder of this stranger—one of your wife's witnesses to her claim—near your house, your own flight, and the sudden disappearance of your wife, my suspicions were strengthened. And when I read this note from your wife, delivered to you last night by one of her servants, and picked up early this morning near the body, my suspicions were confirmed."

As he finished he took from his pocket a folded paper and handed it to Gabriel. He received it mechanically, and opened it. It was his wife's note of the preceding night. He took out his knife, still holding the letter, and with its blade began stirring the bowl of his pipe. Then after a pause, he asked cautiously—

"And how did *ye* come by this yer?"

"It was found by Sal Clark, brought to Mrs. Markle, and given to me. Its existence is known only to three people, and they are your friends."

There was another pause, in which Gabriel deliberately stirred the contents of his pipe. Mr. Maxwell examined him curiously.

"Well," he said, at last, "what is your defence?"

Gabriel sat up on the bed and rapped the bowl of his pipe against the bedpost to loosen some refractory encrustation.

"Wot," he asked, gravely, "would be *your* idee of a good defence? Axin ye ez a lawyer having experin's in them things, and reck'nin' to pay ez high ez eny man fo' the same, wot would *you* call a good defence?" And he gravely laid himself down again in an attitude of respectful attention.

"We hope to prove," said Maxwell, really smiling, "that when you left your house and came to my office the murdered man was alive and at his hotel; that he went over to the hill long before you did; that *you* did not return until the evening—*after* the murder was committed, as the 'secret' mentioned in your wife's mysterious note evidently shows. That for some reason or other it was her design to place you in a suspicious attitude. That the note shows that she refers to some fact of which she was cognisant and not yourself."

"Suthin' that she knowed, and I didn't get to hear," translated Gabriel, quietly.

"Exactly! Now you see the importance of that note."

Gabriel did not immediately reply, but slowly lifted his huge frame from the bed, walked to the open window, still holding the paper in his hands, deliberately tore it into the minutest shreds before the lawyer could interfere, and then threw it from the window.

"Thet paper don't 'mount ter beans, no how!" he said, quietly but explanatively as he returned to the bed.

It was Lawyer Maxwell's turn to become dumb. In his astonished abstraction he forgot to wipe his mouth, and gazed at Gabriel with his nervous smile as if his client had just perpetrated a practical joke of the first magnitude.

"Ef it's the same to you, I'll just gin ye my idee of a de-fence," said Gabriel, apologetically, relighting his pipe, "allowin' o' course that you knows best, and askin' no deducksshun from your charges for advice. Well, you jess stands up afore the jedge, and you slings 'em a yarn suthin' like this: 'Yer's me, for instans,' you sez, sez you, 'ez gambols—gambols very deep—jess fights the tiger, wharever and whenever found, the same bein' onbeknownst ter folks gin'rally, and spechil te my wife, ez was July. Yer's me been gambolin' desprit with this yer man, Victyor Ramyirez, and gets lifted bad! and we hez, so to speak, a differculty about some pints in the game. I allows one thing, he allows another, and this yer man gives me the lie and I stabs him!' Stop—hole your hosses!" interjected Gabriel, suddenly, "thet looks bad, don't it? he bein' a small man, a little feller 'bout your size. No! Well, this yer's the way we puts it up: 'Seving men—*seving*—friends o' his, comes at me, permiskis like, one down, and nex' comes on, and we hez it mighty lively thar fur an hour, until me, bein' in a tight place, hez to use a knife and cuts this yer man bad!' Thar, that's 'bout the thing! Now ez to my runnin' away, you sez, sez you, ez how I disremembers owin' to the 'citement that I hez a 'pintment in Sacramento the very nex' day, and waltzes down yer to keep it, in a hurry. Ef they want to know whar July ez, you sez she gits wild on my not comin' home, and starts that very night arter me. Thar, thet's 'bout my idee—puttin' it o' course in your own shape, and slingin' in them bits o' po'try and garbage, and kinder sassin' the plaintiff's counsel, ez you know goes down afore a jedge and jury."

Maxwell rose hopelessly,—"Then, if I understand you, you intend to admit"——

"Thet I done it? In course!" replied Gabriel; "but," he added, with a cunning twinkle in his eye, "justifybly—justifyble homyside, ye mind!—bein' in fear o' my life from seving men. In course," he added, hurriedly, "I can't identify them seving strangers in the dark, so thar's no harm or suspicion goin' to be done enny o' the boys in the Gulch."

Maxwell walked gravely to the window, and stood looking out without speaking. Suddenly he turned upon Gabriel with a brighter face and more earnest manner. "Where's Olly?"

Gabriel's face fell. He hesitated a moment. "I was on my way to the school in Sacramento whar she iz."

"You must send for her—I must see her at once!"

Gabriel laid his powerful hand on the lawyer's shoulder. "She izn't—that chile—to knows anythin' o' this. You hear?" he said, in a voice that began in tones of deprecation, and ended in a note of stern warning.

"How are you to keep it from her?" said Maxwell, as determinedly. "In less than twenty-four hours every newspaper in the state will have it—with their own version and comments. No; you must see her. She must hear it first from your own lips."

"But—I—can't—see—her just now," said Gabriel, with a voice that for the first time during their interview faltered in its accents.

"Nor need you," responded the lawyer, quickly. "Trust that to me. *I* will see her, and you shall afterwards. You need not fear I will prejudice your case. Give me the address! Quick!" he added, as the sound of footsteps and voices approaching the room, came from the hall. Gabriel did as he requested. "Now one word," he continued hurriedly, as the footsteps halted at the door.

"Yes," said Gabriel.

"As you value your life and Olly's happiness, hold your tongue."

Gabriel nodded with cunning comprehension. The door opened to Mr. Jack Hamlin, diabolically mischievous, self-confident, and audacious! With a familiar nod to Maxwell he stepped quickly before Gabriel and extended his hand. Simply, yet conscious of obeying some vague magnetic influence, Gabriel reached out his own hand and took Jack's white, nervous fingers in his own calm, massive grasp.

"Glad to see you, pard!" said that gentleman, showing his white teeth and reaching up to clap his disengaged hand on Gabriel's shoulder. "Glad to see you, old boy,—even if you have cut in and taken a job out of my hands that I was rather lyin' by to do myself. Sooner or later I'd have fetched that Mexican—if you hadn't dropped into my seat and taken up my hand. Oh, it's all right, Mack!" he said, intercepting the quick look of caution that Maxwell darted at his client, "don't do that. We're all friends here.

If you want me to testify, I'll take my oath that there hasn't been a day this six months that that infernal hound, Ramirez, wasn't jest pantin' to be planted in his tracks! I can hardly believe I ain't done it myself." He stopped, partly to enjoy the palpable uneasiness of Maxwell, and perhaps in some admiration of Gabriel's physique.

Maxwell quickly seized this point of vantage. "You can do your friend here a very great service," he said to Jack, lowering his voice as he spoke.

Jack laughed. "No, Mack, it won't do! They wouldn't believe me! There ain't judge or jury you could play that on!"

"You don't understand me," said Maxwell, laughing a little awkwardly. "I didn't mean that, Jack. This man was going to Sacramento to see his little sister"——

"Go on," said Jack, with much gravity; "of course he was. I know that. 'Dear brother, dear brother, come home with me now!' Certainly. So'm I. Goin' to see an innocent little thing 'bout seventeen years old, blue eyes and curly hair! Always go there once a week. Says he must come! Says she'll"—— he stopped in the full tide of his irony, for, looking up, he caught a glimpse of Gabriel's simple, troubled face and sadly reproachful eyes. "Look here," said Jack, turning savagely on Maxwell, "what are you talking about anyway?"

"I mean what I say," returned Maxwell, quickly. "He was going to see his sister—a mere child. Of course he can't go now. But he must see her—if she can be brought to him. Can you—*will* you do it?"

Jack cast another swift glance at Gabriel. "Count me in," he said, promptly; "when shall I go?"

"Now—at once."

"All right. Where shall I fetch her to?"

"One Horse Gulch."

"The game's made," said Jack, sententiously. "She'll be there by sundown to-morrow." He was off like a flash, but as swiftly returned, and called Maxwell to the door. "Look here," he said, in a whisper, "p'r'aps it would be as well if the sheriff didn't know I was *his* friend," he went on, indicating Gabriel with a toss of his head and a wink of his black eye, "because, you see, Joe Hall and I ain't friends. We had a little difficulty, and some shootin' and foolishness down at Marysville last year. Joe's a good, square man, but he ain't above prejudice, and it might go against our man."

Maxwell nodded, and Jack once more darted off.

But his colour was so high, and his exaltation so excessive, that when he reached his room his faithful Pete looked at him in undisguised alarm. "Bress us—it tain't no whisky, Mars Jack, arter all de doctors tole you?" he said, clasping his hands in dismay.

The bare suggestion was enough for Jack in his present hilarious humour. He instantly hiccuped, lapsed wildly over against Pete with artfully simulated alcoholic weakness, tumbled him on the floor, and grasping his white, woolly head, waved over it a boot-jack, and frantically demanded "another bottle." Then he laughed; as suddenly got up with the greatest gravity and a complete change in his demeanour, and wanted to know, severely, what he, Pete, meant by lying there on the floor in a state of beastly intoxication?

"Bress me! Mars Jack, but ye *did* frighten me. I jiss allowed dem tourists downstairs had been gettin' ye tight."

"You did—you degraded old ruffian! If you'd been reading Volney's 'Ruins,' or reflectin' on some of those moral maxims that I'm just wastin' my time and health unloading to you, instead of making me the subject of your inebriated reveries, you wouldn't get picked up so often. Pack my valise, and chuck it into some horse and buggy—no matter whose. Be quick."

"Is we gwine to Sacramento, Mars Jack?"

"*We?* No, sir. *I'm* going—alone! What I'm doing now, sir, is only the result of calm reflection—of lying awake nights taking points and jest spottin' the whole situation. And I'm convinced, Peter, that I can stay with you no longer. You've been hackin' the keen edge of my finer feelin's; playin' it very low down on my moral and religious nature, generally ringin' in a cold deck on my spiritual condition for the last five years. You've jest cut up thet rough with my higher emotions thet there ain't enough left to chip in on a ten-cent ante. Five years ago," continued Jack, coolly, brushing his curls before the glass, "I fell into your hands a guileless, simple youth, in the first flush of manhood, knowin' no points, easily picked up on my sensibilities, and travellin', so to speak, on my shape! And where am I now? Echo answers 'where?' and passes for a euchre! No, Peter, I leave you to-night. Wretched misleader of youth, gummy old man with the strawberry eyebrows, farewell!"

Evidently this style of exordium was no novelty to Pete, for without apparently paying the least attention to it, he went on surlily packing his master's valise. When he had finished he looked up at Mr. Hamlin, who was humming, in a heart-broken way, "*Yes, we must part,*" varied by occasional glances of exaggerated reproach at Pete, and said, as he shouldered the valise—

"Dis yer ain't no woman foolishness, Mars Jack, like down at dat yar Mission?"

"Your suggestion, Peter," returned Jack, with dignity, "emanates from a moral sentiment debased by Love Feasts and Camp Meetings, and an intellect weakened by Rum and Gum and the contact of Lager Beer Jerkers. It is worthy of a short-card sharp and a keno flopper, which I have, I regret to say, long suspected you to be. Farewell! You will stay here until I come back. If I don't come back by the day after to-morrow, come to One Horse Gulch. Pay the bill, and don't knock down for yourself more than seventy-five per cent. Remember I am getting old and feeble. You are yet young, with a brilliant future before you. Git."

He tossed a handful of gold on the bed, adjusted his hat carefully over his curls, and strode from the room. In the lower hall he stopped long enough to take aside Mr. Raynor, and with an appearance of the greatest conscientiousness, to correct an error of two feet in the measurements he had given him that morning of an enormous pine tree in whose prostrate trunk he, Mr. Hamlin, had once found a peaceful, happy tribe of one hundred Indians living. Then lifting his hat with marked politeness to Mrs. Raynor, and totally ignoring the presence of Mr. Raynor's mentor and companion, he leaped lightly into the buggy and drove away.

"An entertaining fellow," said Mr. Raynor, glancing after the cloud of dust that flew from the untarrying wheels of Mr. Hamlin's chariot.

"And so gentlemanly," smiled Mrs. Raynor.

But the journalistic conservator of the public morals of California, in and for the city and county of San Francisco, looked grave, and deprecated even that feeble praise of the departed. "His class are a curse to the country. They hold the law in contempt; they retard by the example of their extravagance the virtues of economy and thrift; they are consumers and not producers; they bring the fair fame of this land into question by those who foolishly take them for a type of the people."

"But, dear me," said Mrs. Raynor, pouting, "where

your gamblers and bad men are so fascinating, and your honest miners are so dreadfully murderous, and kill people, and then sit down to breakfast with you as if nothing had happened, what are you going to do?"

The journalist did not immediately reply. In the course of some eloquent remarks, as unexceptionable in morality as in diction, which I regret I have not space to reproduce here, he, however, intimated that there was still an Unfettered Press, which "scintillated" and "shone" and "lashed" and "stung" and "exposed" and "tore away the veil," and became at various times a Palladium and a Watchtower, and did and was a great many other remarkable things peculiar to an Unfettered Press in a pioneer community, when untrammelled by the enervating conditions of an effete civilisation.

"And what have they done with the murderer?" asked Mr. Raynor, repressing a slight yawn.

"Taken him back to One Horse Gulch half an hour ago. I reckon he'd as lief stayed here," said a bystander. "From the way things are pintin', it looks as if it might be putty lively for him up thar!"

"What do you mean?" asked Raynor, curiously.

"Well, two or three of them old Vigilantes from Angel's passed yer a minit ago with their rifles, goin' up that way," returned the man, lazily. "Mayn't be nothing in it, but it looks mighty like"——

"Like what?" asked Mr. Raynor, a little nervously.

"Lynchin'!" said the man.

CHAPTER III.

IN WHICH MR. DUMPHY TAKES POINSETT INTO HIS CONFIDENCE.

THE cool weather of the morning following Mr. Dumphy's momentous interview with Colonel Starbottle, contributed somewhat to restore the former gentleman's tranquillity, which had been considerably disturbed. He had, moreover, a vague recollection of having invited Colonel Starbottle to visit him socially, and a nervous dread of meeting this man, whose audacity was equal to his own, in the company of others. Braced, however, by the tonic of the clear exhilarating air, and sustained by the presence of his clerks and the respectful homage of his business associates, he despatched a note to Arthur Poinsett requesting an interview. Punctually at the hour named that gentleman presented himself, and was languidly surprised when Mr. Dumphy called his clerk and gave positive orders that their interview was not to be disturbed and to refuse admittance to all other visitors. And then Mr. Dumphy, in a peremptory, practical statement which his business habits and temperament had brought to a perfection that Arthur could not help admiring, presented the details of his interview with Colonel Starbottle. "Now, I want you to help me. I have sent to you for that business purpose. You understand, this is not a matter for the Bank's regular counsel. Now what do you propose?"

"First, let me ask you, do you believe your wife is living?"

"No," said Dumphy, promptly, "but of course I don't know."

"Then let me relieve your mind at once, and tell you that she is not."

"You know this to be a fact?" asked Dumphy.

"I do. The body supposed to be Grace Conroy's and so identified, was your wife's. I recognised it at once, knowing Grace Conroy to have been absent at the culmination of the tragedy."

"And why did you not correct the mistake?"

"That is *my* business," said Arthur, haughtily, "and I believe I have been invited here to attend to *yours*. Your wife is dead."

"Then," said Mr. Dumphy, rising with a brisk business air, "if you are willing to testify to that fact, I reckon there is nothing more to be done."

Arthur did not rise, but sat watching Mr. Dumphy with an unmoved face. After a moment Mr. Dumphy sat down again, and looked aggressively but nervously at Arthur. "Well," he said, at last.

"Is that all?" asked Arthur, quietly; "are you willing to go on and establish the fact?"

"Don't know what you mean!" said Dumphy, with an attempted frankness which failed signally.

"One moment, Mr. Dumphy. You are a shrewd business man. Now do you suppose the person—whoever he or she may be, who has sent Colonel Starbottle to you, relies alone upon your inability to legally prove your wife's death? May they not calculate somewhat on your *indisposition* to prove it legally; on the theory that you'd rather not open the case, for instance?"

Mr. Dumphy hesitated a moment and bit his lip. "Of course," he said, shortly, "there'd be some talk among my enemies about my deserting my wife"——

"And child," suggested Arthur.

"And child," repeated Dumphy, savagely, "and not

coming back again—there'd be suthin' in the papers about it, unless I paid 'em, but what's that!—deserting one's wife isn't such a new thing in California."

"That is so," said Arthur, with a sarcasm that was none the less sincere because he felt its applicability to himself.

"But we're not getting on," said Mr. Dumphy, impatiently. "What's to be done? That's what I've sent to you for."

"Now that we know it is not your *wife*—we must find out *who* it is that stands back of Colonel Starbottle. It is evidently some one who knows, at least, as much as we do of the facts; we are lucky if they know no more. Can you think of any one? Who are the survivors? Let's see: you, myself, possibly Grace"——

"It couldn't be Grace Conroy, really alive!" interrupted Dumphy, hastily.

"No," said Arthur, quietly, "you remember *she* was not present at the time."

"Gabriel?"

"I hardly think so. Besides, he is a friend of yours."

"It couldn't be"—Dumphy stopped in his speech, with a certain savage alarm in his looks. Arthur noticed it—and quietly went on.

"Who 'couldn't' it be?"

"Nothing—nobody. I was only thinking if Gabriel or somebody could have told the story to some designing rascal."

"Hardly—in sufficient detail."

"Well," said Dumphy, with his coarse bark-like laugh, "if I've got to pay to see Mrs. Dumphy decently buried, I suppose I can rely upon you to see that it's done without a chance of resurrection. Find out who Starbottle's friend is and how much he or she expects. If I've got to pay for this thing I'll do it now, and get the benefit of absolute silence.

So I'll leave it in your hands," and he again rose as if dismissing the subject and his visitor, after his habitual business manner.

"Dumphy," said Arthur, still keeping his own seat, and ignoring the significance of Dumphy's manner. "There are two professions that suffer from a want of frankness in the men who seek their services. Those professions are Medicine and the Law. I can understand why a man seeks to deceive his physician, because he is humbugging himself; but I can't see why he is not frank to his lawyer! You are no exception to the rule. You are now concealing from *me*, whose aid you have sought, some very important reason why you wish to have this whole affair hidden beneath the snow of Starvation Camp."

"Don't know what you're driving at," said Dumphy. But he sat down again.

"Well, listen to me, and perhaps I can make my meaning clearer. My acquaintance with the late Dr. Devarges began some months before we saw you. During our intimacy he often spoke to me of his scientific discoveries, in which I took some interest, and I remember seeing among his papers frequent records and descriptions of localities in the oot-hills, which he thought bore the indications of great mineral wealth. At that time the Doctor's theories and speculations appeared to me to be visionary, and the records of no value. Nevertheless, when we were shut up in Starvation Camp, and it seemed doubtful if the Doctor would survive his discoveries, at his request I deposited his papers and specimens in a cairn at Monument Point. After the catastrophe, on my return with the relief party to camp, we found that the cairn had been opened by some one and the papers and specimens scattered on the snow. We supposed this to have been the work of Mrs. Brackett, who, in search of food, had broken the cairn, taken out the specimens, and died from the effects of the poison with which they had been preserved."

He paused and looked at Dumphy, who did not speak.

"Now," continued Arthur, "like all Californians I have followed your various successes with interest and wonder. I have noticed, with the gratification that all your friends experience, the singular good fortune which has distinguished your mining enterprises, and the claims you have located. But I have been cognisant of a fact, unknown I think to any other of your friends, that nearly all of the localities of your successful claims, by a singular coincidence, agree with the memorandums of Dr. Devarges!"

Dumphy sprang to his feet with a savage, brutal laugh. "So," he shouted, coarsely, "that's the game, is it! So it seems I'm lucky in coming to you—no trouble in finding this *woman* now, hey? Well, go on, this is getting interesting; let's hear the rest! What are your propositions, what if I refuse, hey?"

"My first proposition," said Arthur, rising to his feet with a cold wicked light in his grey eyes, "is that you shall instantly take that speech back and beg my pardon! If you refuse, by the living God, I'll throttle you where you stand!"

For one wild moment all the savage animal in Dumphy rose, and he instinctively made a step in the direction of Poinsett. Arthur did not move. Then Mr. Dumphy's practical caution asserted itself. A physical personal struggle with Arthur would bring in witnesses—witnesses perhaps of something more than that personal struggle. If he were victorious, Arthur, unless killed outright, would revenge himself by an exposure. He sank back in his chair again. Had Arthur known the low estimate placed upon his honour by Mr. Dumphy he would have been less complacent in his victory.

"I didn't mean to suspect *you*," said Dumphy at last, with a forced smile, "I hope you'll excuse me. I know you're my friend. But you're all wrong about these papers; you are, Poinsett, I swear. I know if the fact were known to outsiders it would look queer if not explained. But whose business is it, anyway, legally, I mean?"

"No one's, unless Devarges has friends or heirs."

"He hadn't any."

"There's that wife!"

"Bah!—she was divorced!"

"Indeed! You told me on our last interview that she really was the widow of Devarges."

"Never mind that now," said Dumphy, impatiently. "Look here! You know as well as I do that no matter how many discoveries Devarges made, they weren't worth a d—n if he hadn't done some work on them—improved or opened them."

"But that is not the point at issue just now," said Arthur. "Nobody is going to contest your claim or sue you for damages. But they might try to convict you of a crime. They might say that breaking into the cairn was burglary, and the taking of the papers theft."

"But how are they going to prove that?"

"No matter. Listen to me, and don't let us drift away from the main point. The question that concerns you is this. An impostor sets up a claim to be your wife; you and I know she is an impostor, and can prove it. She knows that, but knows also that in attempting to prove it you lay yourself open to some grave charges which she doubtless stands ready to make."

"Well, then, the first thing to do is to find out *who* she is, what she knows, and what she wants, eh?" said Dumphy.

"No," said Arthur, quietly, "the first thing to do is to prove that your wife is really dead, and to do that you must show that Grace Conroy was alive when the body purporting to be hers, but which was really your wife's, was discovered. Once establish *that* fact and you destroy the credibility of the Spanish reports, and you need not fear any revelation from that source regarding the missing papers. And that is the only source from which evidence against you can be procured. But when you destroy the validity of that report, you of course destroy the credibility of all concerned in making it. And as I was concerned in making it, of course it won't do for you to put *me* on the stand."

Notwithstanding Dumphy's disappointment, he could not help yielding to a sudden respect for the superior rascal who thus cleverly slipped out of responsibility. "But," added Arthur, coolly, "you'll have no difficulty in establishing the fact of Grace's survival by others."

Dumphy thought at once of Ramirez. Here was a man who had seen and conversed with Grace when she had, in the face of the Spanish Commander, indignantly asserted her identity and the falsity of the report. No witness could be more satisfactory and convincing. But to make use of him he must first take Arthur into his confidence; must first expose the conspiracy of Madame Devarges to personate Grace, and his own complicity with the transaction. He hesitated. Nevertheless, he had been lately tortured by a suspicion that the late Madame Devarges was in some way connected with the later conspiracy against himself, and he longed to avail himself of Arthur's superior sagacity, and after a second reflection he concluded to do it. With the same practical conciseness of statement that he had used in relating Colonel Starbottle's interview with himself, he told the story of Madame

Devarges' brief personation of Grace Conroy, and its speedy and felicitous ending in Mrs. Conroy. Arthur listened with unmistakable interest and a slowly brightening colour. When Dumphy had concluded he sat for a moment apparently lost in thought.

"Well?" at last said Dumphy, interrogatively and impatiently.

Arthur started. "Well," he said, rising, and replacing his hat with the air of a man who had thoroughly exhausted his subject, "your frankness has saved me a world of trouble."

"How?" said Dumphy.

"There is no necessity for looking any further for your alleged wife. She exists at present as Mrs. Conroy, *alias* Madame Devarges, *alias* Grace Conroy. Ramirez is your witness. You couldn't have a more willing one."

"Then my suspicions are correct."

"I don't know on what you based them. But here is a woman who has unlimited power over men, particularly over one man, Gabriel!—who alone, of all men but ourselves, knows the facts regarding your desertion of your wife in Starvation Camp, her death, and the placing of Dr. Devarges' private papers by me in the cairn. He knows, too, of your knowledge of the existence of the cairn, its locality, and contents. He knows this because he was in the cabin that night when the Doctor gave me his dying injunctions regarding his property—the night that you—excuse me, Dumphy, but nothing but frankness will save us now—the night that you stood listening at the door and frightened Grace with your wolfish face. Don't speak! she told me all about it! Your presence there that night gained you the information that you have used so profitably; it was your presence that fixed her wavering resolves and sent her away with me."

Both men had become very pale and earnest. Arthur moved toward the door. "I will see you to-morrow, when I will have matured some plan of defence," he said, abstractedly. "We have"—he used the plural of advocacy with a peculiar significance—"*We* have a clever woman to fight who may be more than our match. Meantime, remember that Ramirez is our defence; he is our man, Dumphy, hold fast to him as you would to your life. Good-day."

In another moment he was gone. As the door closed upon him a clerk entered hastily from the outer office. "You said not to disturb you, sir, and here is an important despatch waiting for you from Wingdam."

Mr. Dumphy took it mechanically, opened it, read the first line, and then said hurriedly, "Run after that man, quick!—Stop! Wait a moment. You need not go! There, that will do!"

The clerk hurriedly withdrew into the outer office. Mr. Dumphy went back to his desk again, and once more devoured the following lines:—

"WINGDAM, 7th, 6 A.M.—Victor Ramirez murdered last night on Conroy's Hill. Gabriel Conroy arrested. Mrs. Conroy missing. Great excitement here; strong feeling against Gabriel. Wait instructions.—FITCH."

At first Mr. Dumphy only heard as an echo beating in his brain, the parting words of Arthur Poinsett, "Ramirez is our defence; hold fast to him as you would your life." And now he was dead—gone; their only witness; killed by Gabriel the plotter! What more was wanted to justify his worst suspicions? What should they do? He must send after Poinsett again; the plan of defence must be changed at once; to-morrow might be too late. Stop!

One of his accusers in prison charged with a capital crime! The other—the real murderer—for Dumphy made no doubt that Mrs. Conroy was responsible for the deed—a fugitive from justice! What need of any witness now? The blow that crippled these three conspirators had liberated him! For a moment Mr. Dumphy was actually conscious of a paroxysm of gratitude toward some indefinitely Supreme Being—a God of special providence—special to himself! More than this, there was that vague sentiment, common, I fear, to common humanity in such crises, that this Providence was a tacit endorsement of himself. It was the triumph of Virtue (Dumphy) over Vice (Conroy *et al.*).

But there would be a trial, publicity, and the possible exposure of certain things by a man whom danger might make reckless. And could he count upon Mrs. Conroy's absence or neutrality? He was conscious that her feeling for her husband was stronger than he had supposed, and she might dare everything to save him. What had a woman of that kind to do with such weakness? Why hadn't she managed it so as to kill Gabriel too? There was an evident want of practical completeness in this special Providence that, as a business man, Mr. Dumphy felt he could have regulated. And then he was seized with an idea—a damnable inspiration!—and set himself briskly to write. I regret to say that despite the popular belief in the dramatic character of all villany, Mr. Dumphy at this moment presented only the commonplace spectacle of an absorbed man of business; no lurid light gleamed from his pale blue eyes; no Satanic smile played around the corners of his smoothly shaven mouth; no feverish exclamation stirred his moist, cool lips. He wrote methodically and briskly, without deliberation or undue haste. When he had written half-a-dozen letters he folded and sealed them, and without summoning his clerk, took them himself into the outer office and thence into the large counting-room. The news of the murder had evidently got abroad;

the clerks were congregated together, and the sound of eager, interested voices ceased as the great man entered and stood among them.

"Fitch, you and Judson will take the quickest route to One Horse Gulch to-night. Don't waste any time on the road or spare any expense. When you get there deliver these letters, and take your orders from my correspondents. Pick up all the details you can about this affair and let me know. What's your balance at the Gulch, Mr. Peebles? never mind the exact figures!"

"Larger than usual, sir, some heavy deposits!"

"Increase your balance then if there should be any d—d fools who connect the Bank with this matter."

"I suppose," said Mr. Fitch, respectfully, "we're to look after your foreman, Mr. Conroy, sir?"

"You are to take your orders from my correspondent, Mr. Fitch, and not to interfere in any way with public sentiment. We have nothing to do with the private acts of anybody. Justice will probably be done to Conroy. It is time that these outrages upon the reputation of the California miner should be stopped. When the fame of a whole community is prejudiced and business injured by the rowdyism of a single ruffian," said Mr. Dumphy, raising his voice slightly as he discovered the interested and absorbed presence of some of his most respectable customers, "it is time that prompt action should be taken." In fact, he would have left behind him a strong Roman flavour and a general suggestion of Brutus, had he not unfortunately effected an anti-climax by adding, "that's business, sir," as he retired to his private office.

CHAPTER IV.

MR. HAMLIN IS OFF WITH AN OLD LOVE.

MR. JACK HAMLIN did not lose much time on the road from Wingdam to Sacramento. His rapid driving, his dust bespattered vehicle, and the exhausted condition of his horse on arrival, excited but little comment from those who knew his habits, and for other criticism he had a supreme indifference. He was prudent enough, however, to leave his horse at a stable on the outskirts, and having reconstructed his toilet at a neighbouring hotel, he walked briskly toward the address given him by Maxwell. When he reached the corner of the street and was within a few paces of the massive shining door plate of Madame Eclair's *Pensionnat*, he stopped with a sudden ejaculation, and after a moment's hesitation, turned on his heel deliberately and began to retrace his steps.

To explain Mr. Hamlin's singular conduct I shall be obliged to disclose a secret of his, which I would fain keep from the fair reader. On receiving Olly's address from Maxwell, Mr. Hamlin had only cursorily glanced at it, and it was only on arriving before the house that he recognised to his horror that it was a boarding-school, with one of whose impulsive inmates he had whiled away his idleness a few months before in a heart-breaking but innocent flirtation, and a soul-subduing but clandestine correspondence, much to the distaste of the correct Principal. To have presented himself there in his proper person would be to have been refused admittance or subjected to a suspicion that would have kept Olly from his hands. For once, Mr. Hamlin severely regretted his infelix reputation among the sex. But he did not turn his back on his enterprise. He retraced his steps only to the main street, visited a barber's shop and a jeweller's, and reappeared on the street again with a pair of enormous green goggles and all traces of his long distinguishing silken black moustache shaven from his lip. When it is remembered that this rascal was somewhat vain of his personal appearance, the reader will appreciate his earnestness and the extent of his sacrifice.

Nevertheless, he was a little nervous as he was ushered into the formal reception-room of the *Pensionnat*, and waited until his credentials, countersigned by Maxwell, were submitted to Madame Eclair. Mr. Hamlin had no fear of being detected by his real name; in the brief halcyon days of his romance he had been known as Clarence Spifflington,—an ingenious combination of the sentimental and humorous which suited his fancy, and to some extent he felt expressed the character of his affection. Fate was propitious; the servant returned saying that Miss Conroy would be down in a moment, and Mr. Hamlin looked at his watch. Every moment was precious; he was beginning to get impatient when the door opened again and Olly slipped into the room.

She was a pretty child, with a peculiar boyish frankness of glance and manner, and a refinement of feature that fascinated Mr. Hamlin, who, fond as he was of all childhood, had certain masculine preferences for good looks. She seemed to be struggling with a desire to laugh when she entered, and when Jack turned towards her with extended hands she held up her own warningly, and closing the door behind her cautiously, said, in a demure whisper—

"She'll come down as soon as she can slip past Madame's door."

"Who?" asked Jack.

"Sophy."

"Who's Sophy?" asked Jack, seriously. He had never known the name of his Dulcinea. In the dim epistolatory region of sentiment she had existed only as "The Blue Moselle," so called from the cerulean hue of her favourite raiment, and occasionally, in moments of familiar endearment, as "Mosey."

"Come, now, pretend you don't know, will you?" said Olly, evading the kiss which Jack always had ready for childhood. "If I was her, I wouldn't have anything to say to you after that!" she added, with that ostentatious chivalry of the sex towards each other, in the presence of their common enemy. "Why, she saw you from the window when you first came this morning, when you went back again and shaved off your moustache; she knew you. And you don't know her! It's mean, ain't it?—they'll grow again, won't they?"—Miss Olly referred to the mustachios and not the affections!

Jack was astonished and alarmed. In his anxiety to evade or placate the duenna, he had never thought of her charge—his sweetheart. Here was a dilemma! "Oh yes!" said Jack hastily, with a well simulated expression of arch affection, "Sophy—of course—that's my little game! But I've got a note for you too, my dear," and he handed Olly the few lines that Gabriel had hastily scrawled. He watched her keenly, almost breathlessly, as she read them. To his utter bewilderment she laid the note down indifferently and said, "That's like Gabe—the old simpleton!"

"But you're goin' to do what he says," asked Mr. Hamlin, "ain't you?"

"No," said Olly, promptly, "I ain't! Why, Lord! Mr. Hamlin, you don't know that man; why, he does this sort o' thing every week!" Perceiving Jack stare, she went on, "Why, only last week, didn't he send to me to meet him out on the corner of the street, and he my own brother, instead o' comin' here, ez he hez a right to do. Go to him at Wingdam? No! ketch me!"

"But suppose he can't come," continued Mr. Hamlin.

"Why can't he come? I tell you, it's just foolishness and the meanest kind o' bashfulness. Jes because there happened to be a young lady here from San Francisco, Rosey Ringround, who was a little took with the old fool. If he could come to Wingdam, why couldn't he come here,—that's what I want to know?"

"Will you let me see that note?" asked Hamlin.

Olly handed him the note, with the remark, "He don't spell well—and he won't let me teach him—the old Muggins!"

Hamlin took it and read as follows:—

"DEAR OLLY,—If it don't run a fowl uv yer lessings and the Maddam's willin' and the young laddies, Brother Gab's waitin' fer ye at Wingdam, so no more from your affeshtunate brother, GAB."

Mr. Hamlin was in a quandary. It never had been part of his plan to let Olly know the importance of her journey. Mr. Maxwell's injunctions to bring her "quietly," his own fears of an outburst that might bring a questioning and sympathetic school about his ears, and lastly, and not the least potently, his own desire to enjoy Olly's company in the long ride to One Horse Gulch without the preoccupation of grief, with his own comfortable conviction that he could eventually bring Gabriel out of this "fix" without Olly knowing anything about it, all this forbade his telling her the truth. But here was a coil he had not thought of. Howbeit, Mr. Hamlin was quick at expedients.

"Then you think Sophy can see me," he added, with a sudden interest.

"Of course she will!" said Olly, archly. "It was right smart in you to get acquainted with Gabe and set him up to writing that, though it's just like him. He's that soft that anybody could get round him. But there she is now,

Mr. Hamlin; that's her step on the stairs. And I don't suppose you two hez any need of me now."

And she slipped out of the room, as demurely as she had entered, at the same moment that a tall, slim, and somewhat sensational young lady in blue came flying in.

I can, in justice to Mr. Hamlin, whose secrets have been perhaps needlessly violated in the progress of this story, do no less than pass over as sacred, and perhaps wholly irrelevant to the issue, the interview that took place between himself and Miss Sophy. That he succeeded in convincing that young woman of his unaltered loyalty, that he explained his long silence as the result of a torturing doubt of the permanence of her own affection, that his presence at that moment was the successful culmination of a long-matured and desperate plan to see her once more and learn the truth from her own lips, I am sure that no member of my own disgraceful sex will question, and I trust no member of a too fond and confiding sex will doubt. That some bitterness was felt by Mr. Hamlin, who was conscious of certain irregularities during this long interval, and some tears shed by Miss Sophy, who was equally conscious of more or less aberration of her own magnetic instincts during his absence, I think will be self-evident to the largely comprehending reader. Howbeit, at the end of ten tender yet tranquillising minutes Mr. Hamlin remarked, in low thrilling tones—

"By the aid of a few confiding friends, and playin' it rather low on them, I got that note to the Conroy girl, but the game's up, and we might as well pass in our checks now, if she goes back on us, and passes out, which I reckon's her little game. If what you say is true, Sophy, and you do sometimes look back to the past, and things is generally on the square, you'll go for that Olly and fetch her, for if I go back without that child, and throw up my hand, it's just tampering with the holiest affections and playing it mighty rough on as white a man as ever you saw, Sophy, to say nothing of your reputation, and everybody ready to buck agin us who has ten cents to chip in on. You must make her go back with me and put things on a specie basis."

In spite of the mixed character of Mr. Hamlin's metaphor, his eloquence was so convincing and effective that Miss Sophy at once proceeded with considerable indignation to insist upon Olly's withdrawing her refusal.

"If this is the way you are going to act, you horrid little thing! after all that me and him's trusted you, I'd like to see the girl in school that will ever tell *you* anything again, that's all!" a threat so appalling that Olly, who did not stop to consider that this confidence was very recent and had been forced upon her, assented without further delay, exhibited Gabriel's letter to Madame Eclair, and having received that lady's gracious permission to visit her brother, was in half an hour in company with Mr. Hamlin on the road.

CHAPTER V.

THE THREE VOICES.

ONCE free from the trammelling fascinations of Sophy and the more dangerous espionage of Madame Eclair, and with the object of his mission accomplished, Mr. Hamlin recovered his natural spirits, and became so hilarious that Olly, who attributed this exaltation to his interview with Sophy, felt constrained to make some disparaging remarks about that young lady, partly by way of getting even with her for her recent interference, and partly in obedience to some well known but unexplained law of the sex. To her great surprise, however, Mr. Hamlin's spirits were in no way damped, nor did he make any attempt to defend his Lalage. Nevertheless, he listened attentively, and when she had concluded he looked suddenly down upon her chip hat and thick yellow tresses, and said—

"Ever been in the Southern country, Olly?"

"No," returned the child.

"Never down about San Antonio, visiting friends or relations?"

"No," said Olly, decidedly.

Mr. Hamlin was silent for some time, giving his exclusive attention to his horse, who was evincing a disposition to "break" into a gallop. When he had brought the animal back into a trot again he continued—

"*There's* a woman! Olly."

"Down in San Antonio?" asked Olly.

Mr. Hamlin nodded.

"Purty?" continued the child.

"It ain't the word," responded Mr. Hamlin, seriously. "Purty ain't the word."

"As purty as Sophy?" continued Olly, a little mischievously.

"Sophy be hanged!" Mr. Hamlin here quickly pulled up himself and horse, both being inclined to an exuberance startling to the youth and sex of the third party. "That is—I mean something in a different suit entirely."

Here he again hesitated, doubtful of his slang.

"I see," quoth Olly; "diamonds—Sophy's in spades."

The gambler (in sudden and awful admiration), "Diamonds—you've just struck it! but what do *you* know 'bout cards?"

Olly, *pomposaménte*, "Everything! Tell our fortunes by 'em—we girls! I'm in hearts—Sophy's in spades—you're in clubs! Do you know," in a thrilling whisper, "only last night I had a letter, a journey, a death, and a gentleman in clubs, dark complected—that's you."

Mr. Hamlin—a good deal more at ease through this revelation of the universal power of the four suits—"Speakin' of women, I suppose down there (indicating the school) you occasionally hear of angels. What's their general complexion?"

Olly, dubiously, "In the pictures?"

Hamlin, "Yes;" with a leading question, "sorter dark complected sometimes, hey?"

Olly, positively, "Never! always white."

Jack, "Always white?"

Olly, "Yes, and flabby!"

They rode along for some time silently. Presently Mr. Hamlin broke into a song, a popular song, one verse of which Olly supplied with such deftness of execution and melodiousness of pipe that Mr. Hamlin instantly suggested a duet, and so over the dead and barren wastes of the Sacramento plains they fell to singing, often barbarously, sometimes melodiously, but never self-consciously, wherein, I take it, they approximated to the birds and better class of poets, so that rough teamsters, rude packers, and weary wayfarers were often touched, as with the birds and poets aforesaid, to admiration and tenderness; and when they stopped for supper at a wayside station, and Jack Hamlin displayed that readiness of resource, audacity of manner and address, and perfect and natural obliviousness to the criticism of propriety or the limitations of precedent, and when, moreover, the results of all this was a much better supper than perhaps a more reputable companion could have procured, she thought she had never known a more engaging person than this Knave of Clubs.

When they were fairly on the road again, Olly began to

exhibit some curiosity regarding her brother, and asked some few questions about Gabriel's family, which disclosed the fact that Jack's acquaintance with Gabriel was comparatively recent.

"Then you never saw July at all?" asked Olly.

"July," queried Jack, reflectively; "what's she like?"

"I don't know whether she's a heart or a spade," said Olly, as thoughtfully.

Jack was silent for some moments, and then after a pause, to Olly's intense astonishment, proceeded to sketch, in a few vigorous phrases, the external characteristics of Mrs. Conroy.

"Why, you said you never saw her!" ejaculated Olly.

"No more I did," responded the gambler, with a quick laugh; "this is only a little bluff."

It had grown cold with the brief twilight and the coming on of night. For some time the black, unchanging outlines of the distant Coast Range were sharply *silhouetted* against a pale, ashen sky, that at last faded utterly, leaving a few stars behind as emblems of the burnt-out sunset. The red road presently lost its calm and even outline in the swiftly gathering shadows, or to Olly's fancy was stopped by shapeless masses of rock or giant-like trunks of trees that in turn seemed to give way before the skilful hand and persistent will of her driver. At times a chill exhalation from a roadside ditch came to Olly like the damp breath of an open grave, and the child shivered even beneath the thick travelling shawl of Mr. Hamlin, with which she was enwrapped. Whereat Jack at once produced a flask and prevailed upon Olly to drink something that set her coughing, but which that astute and experienced child at once recognised as whisky. Mr. Hamlin, to her surprise, however, did not himself partake, a fact which she at once pointed out to him.

"At an early age, Olly," said Mr. Hamlin, with infinite gravity, "I promised an infirm and aged relative never to indulge in spirituous liquors, except on a physician's prescription. I carry this flask subject to the doctor's orders. Never having ordered me to drink any, I don't."

As it was too dark for the child to observe Mr. Hamlin's eyes, which, after the fashion of her sex, she consulted much oftener than his speech for his real meaning, and was as often deceived, she said nothing, and Mr. Hamlin relapsed into silence. At the end of five minutes he said—

"*She* was a woman, Olly—you bet!"

Olly, with great tact and discernment, instantly referring back to Mr. Hamlin's discourse of an hour before, queried, "That girl in the Southern country?"

"Yes," said Mr. Hamlin.

"Tell me all about her," said Olly—"all you know."

"That ain't much," mused Hamlin, with a slight sigh. "Ah, Olly, *she* could sing!"

"With the piano?" said Olly, a little superciliously.

"With the organ," said Hamlin.

Olly, whose sole idea of this instrument was of the itinerant barrel variety, yawned slightly, and with a very perceptible lack of interest said that she hoped she would see her some time when she came up that way and was "going 'round."

Mr. Hamlin did not laugh, but after a few minutes' rapid driving, began to explain to Olly with great earnestness the character of a church organ.

"I used to play once, Olly, in a church. They did say that I used sometimes to fetch that congregation, jest snatch 'em bald-headed, Olly, but it's a long time ago! There was one hymn in particular that I used to run on consid'rable—one o' them Masses o' Mozart—one that I heard *her* sing, Olly; it went something like this;" and

Jack proceeded to lift his voice in the praise of Our Lady of Sorrows, with a serene unconsciousness to his surround ings, and utter absorption in his theme that would have become the most enthusiastic acolyte. The springs creaked, the wheels rattled, the mare broke, plunged, and recovered herself, the slight vehicle swayed from side to side, Olly's hat bruised and flattened itself against his shoulder, and still Mr. Hamlin sang. When he had finished he looked down at Olly. She was asleep!

Jack was an artist and an enthusiast, but not unreasonable nor unforgiving. "It's the whisky," he murmured to himself, in an apologetic recitation to the air he had just been singing. He changed the reins to his other hand with infinite caution and gentleness, slowly passed his disengaged arm round the swaying little figure, until he had drawn the chip hat and the golden tresses down upon his breast and shoulder. In this attitude, scarcely moving a muscle lest he should waken the sleeping child, at midnight he came upon the twinkling lights of Fiddletown. Here he procured a fresh horse, dispensing with an ostler and harnessing the animal himself, with such noiseless skill and quickness that Olly, propped up in the buggy with pillows and blankets borrowed from the Fiddletown hostelry, slept through it all, nor wakened even after they were again upon the road, and had begun the long ascent of the Wingdam turnpike.

It wanted but an hour of daybreak when he reached the summit, and even then he only slackened his pace when his wheels sank to their hubs in the beaten dust of the stage road. The darkness of that early hour was intensified by the gloom of the heavy pine woods through which the red road threaded its difficult and devious way. It was very still. Hamlin could hardly hear the dead, muffled plunge of his own horse in the dusty track before him, and yet once or twice he stopped to listen. His quick ear detected the sound of voices and the jingle of Mexican spurs, apparently approaching behind him. Mr. Hamlin knew that he had not passed any horseman and was for a moment puzzled. But then he recalled the fact that a few hundred yards beyond, the road was intersected by the "cut-off" to One Horse Gulch, which, after running parallel with the Wingdam turnpike for half a mile, crossed it in the forest. The voices were on that road going the same way. Mr. Hamlin pushed on his horse to the crossing, and hidden by the darkness and the trunks of the giant pines, pulled up to let the strangers precede him. In a few moments the voices were abreast of him and stationary. The horsemen had apparently halted.

"Here seems to be a road," said a voice quite audibly.

"All right, then," returned another, "it's the 'cut-off. We'll save an hour, sure."

A third voice here struck in potentially, "Keep the stage road. If Joe Hall get's wind of what's up, he'll run his man down to Sacramento for safe keeping. If he does he'll take this road—it's the only one—sabe?—we can't miss him!"

Jack Hamlin leaned forward breathlessly in his seat.

"But it's an hour longer this way," growled the second voice. "The boys will wait," responded the previous speaker. There was a laugh, a jingling of spurs, and the invisible procession moved slowly forward in the darkness.

Mr. Hamlin did not stir a muscle until the voices failed before him in the distance. Then he cast a quick glance at the child; she still slept quietly, undisturbed by the halt or those ominous voices which had brought so sudden a colour into her companion's cheek and so baleful a light in his dark eyes. Yet for a moment Mr. Hamlin hesitated. To go forward to Wingdam now would necessitate his following cautiously in the rear of the Lynchers, and so prevent his giving a timely alarm. To strike across to One Horse Gulch by the "cut-off" would lose him the chance of meeting the Sheriff and his prisoner, had they been forewarned and were escaping in time. But for the impediment of the unconscious little figure beside him, he would have risked a dash through the party ahead of him. But that was not to be thought of now. He must follow them to Wingdam, leave the child, and trust to luck to reach One Horse Gulch before them. If they delayed a moment at Wingdam it could be done. A feeling of yearning tenderness and pity succeeded the slight impatience with which he had a moment before regarded his encumbering charge. He held her in his arms, scarcely daring to breathe lest he should waken her—hoping that she might sleep until they reached Wingdam, and that leaving her with his faithful henchman "Pete," he might get away before she was aroused to embarrassing inquiry. Mr. Hamlin had a man's dread of scenes with even so small a specimen of the sex, and for once in his life he felt doubtful of his own readiness, and feared lest in his excitement he might reveal the imminent danger of her brother. Perhaps he was never before so conscious of that danger; perhaps he was never before so interested in the life of any one. He began to see things with Olly's eyes—to look upon events with reference to *her* feelings rather than his own; if she had sobbed and cried this sympathetic rascal really believed that he would have cried too. Such was the unconscious and sincere flattery of admiration. He was relieved, when with the first streaks of dawn, his mare wearily clattered over the scattered river pebbles and "tailings" that paved the outskirts of Wingdam. He was still more relieved when the Three Voices of the Night, now faintly visible as three armed horsemen, drew up before the verandah of the Wingdam Hotel, dismounted, and passed into the bar-room. And he was perfectly content, when a moment later he lifted the still sleeping Olly in his arms and bore her swiftly yet cautiously to his room. To awaken the sleeping Pete on the floor above, and drag him half-dressed and bewildered into the presence of the unconscious child, as she lay on Jack Hamlin's own bed, half buried in a heap of shawls and rugs, was only the work of another moment.

"Why, Mars Jack! Bress de Lord—it's a chile!" said Pete, recoiling in sacred awe and astonishment.

"Hold your jaw!" said Jack, in a fierce whisper, "you'll waken her! Listen to me, you chattering idiot. Don't waken her, if you want to keep the bones in your creaking old skeleton whole enough for the doctors to buy. Let her sleep as long as she can. If she wakes up and asks after me, tell her I'm gone for her brother. Do you hear? Give her anything she asks for—except—the truth! What are you doing, you old fool?"

Pete was carefully removing the mountain of shawls and blankets that Jack had piled upon Olly. "'Fore God, Mars Jack—you's smuddering dat chile!" was his only response. Nevertheless Jack was satisfied with a certain vague tenderness in his manipulation, and said curtly, "Get me a horse!"

"It ain't to be did, Mars Jack; de stables is all gone—cleaned! Dey's a rush over to One Horse Gulch, all day!"

"There are three horses at the door," said Jack, with wicked significance.

"For de love of God, Mars Jack, don't ye do dat!" ejaculated Pete, in unfeigned and tremulous alarm. "Dey don't take dem kind o' jokes yer worth a cent—dey'd be doin' somefin' awful to ye, sah—shuah's yer born!"

But Jack, with the child lying there peaceably in his own bed, and the Three Voices growing husky in the bar-room below, regained all his old audacity. "I haven't made up my mind," continued Jack, coolly, "which of the three I'll take, but you'll find out from the owner when I do! Tell him that Mr. Jack Hamlin left his compliments and a mare and buggy for him. You can say that if he keeps the mare from breaking and gives her her head down hill, she can do her mile inside of 2.45. Hush! not a word! Bye-bye." He turned, lifted the shawl from the fresh cheek of the sleeping Olly, kissed her, and shaking his fist at Pete, vanished.

For a few moments the negro listened breathlessly. And then there came the sharp, quick clatter of hoofs from the rocky road below, and he sank dejectedly at the foot of the bed. "He's gone—done it! Lord save us! but it's a hangin' matter yer!" And even as he spoke Mr. Jack Hamlin, mounted on the fleet mustang that had been ridden by the Potential Voice, with his audacious face against the red sunrise and his right shoulder squarely advanced, was butting away the morning mists that rolled slowly along the river road to One Horse Gulch.

CHAPTER VI.

MR. DUMPHY IS PERPLEXED BY A MOVEMENT IN REAL ESTATE.

MR. DUMPHY'S confidence in himself was so greatly restored that several business enterprises of great pith and moment, whose currents for the past few days had been turned awry, and so "lost the name of action," were taken up by him with great vigour and corresponding joy to the humbler business associates who had asked him just to lend his name to that project, and make "a big thing of it." He had just given his royal sanction and a cheque to an Association for the Encouragement of Immigration, by the distribution through the sister States of one million seductive pamphlets, setting forth the various resources and advantages of California for the farmer, and proving that one hundred and fifty dollars spent for a passage thither was equal to the price of a farm; he had also assisted in sending the eloquent Mr. Blowhard and the persuasive Mr. Windygust to present these facts orally to the benighted dwellers of the East, and had secured the services of two eminent Californian statisticians to demonstrate the fact, that more people were killed by lightning and frozen to death in the streets of New York in a single year than were ever killed by railroad accidents or human violence in California during the past three centuries; he had that day conceived the "truly magnificent plan" of bringing the waters of Lake Tahoe to San Francisco by ditches, thereby enabling the citizens to keep the turf in their door-yards green through the summer. He had started two banks, a stage line, and a watering place, whose climate and springs were declared healthful by edict, and were aggressively advertised; and he had just projected a small suburban town that should bear his name. He had returned from this place in high spirits with a company of friends in the morning after this interview with Poinsett. There was certainly no trace of the depression of that day in his manner.

It was a foggy morning, following a clear, still night—an atmospheric condition not unusual at that season of the year to attract Mr. Dumphy's attention, yet he was conscious on reaching his office of an undue oppressiveness in the air that indisposed him to exertion, and caused him to remove his coat and cravat. Then he fell to work upon his morning's mail, and speedily forgot the weather. There was a letter from Mrs. Sepulvida, disclosing the fact that, owing to the sudden and unaccountable drying up of the springs on the lower plains, large numbers of her cattle had died of thirst and were still perishing. This was of serious import to Mr. Dumphy, who had advanced money on this perishable stock, and he instantly made a memorandum to check this sudden freak of Nature, which he at once attributed to feminine carelessness of management. Further on Mrs. Sepulvida inquired particularly as to the condition of the Conroy mine, and displayed a disposition characteristic of her sex, to realise at once on her investment. Her letter ended thus : " But I shall probably see you in San Francisco. Pepe says that this morning the markings on the beach showed the rise of a tide or wave during the night higher than any ever known since one thousand eight hundred. I do not feel safe so near the beach, and shall rebuild in the spring. Mr. Dumphy smiled grimly to himself. He had at one time envied Poinsett. But here was the woman he was engaged to marry, careless, improvident, with a vast estate, and on the eve of financial disaster through her carelessness, and yet actually about to take a journey of two hundred miles because of some foolish, womanish whim or superstition. It would be a fine thing if this man, to whom good fortune fell without any effort on his part—this easy, elegant, supercilious Arthur Poinsett, who was even indifferent to that good fortune, should find himself tricked and deceived ! should have to apply to him, Dumphy, for advice and assistance ! And this, too, after his own advice and assistance regarding the claims of Colonel Starbottle's client had been futile. The revenge would be complete. Mr. Dumphy rubbed his hands in prospective satisfaction.

When, a few moments later, Colonel Starbottle's card was

put into his hand Mr. Dumphy's satisfaction was complete. This was the day that the gallant Colonel was to call for an answer; it was evident that Arthur had not seen him, nor had he made the discovery of Starbottle's unknown client. The opportunity of vanquishing this man without the aid or even knowledge of Poinsett was now before him. By way of preparing himself for the encounter, as well as punishing the Colonel, he purposely delayed the interview, and for full five minutes kept his visitor cooling his heels in the outer office.

He was seated at his desk, ostentatiously preoccupied, when Colonel Starbottle was at last admitted. He did not raise his head when the door opened, nor in fact until the Colonel, stepping lightly forward, walked to Dumphy's side, and deliberately unhooking his cane from its accustomed rest on his arm, laid it, pronouncedly, on the desk before him. The Colonel's face was empurpled, the Colonel's chest was efflorescent and bursting, the Colonel had the general effect of being about to boil over the top button of his coat, but his manner was jauntily and daintily precise.

"One moment!—a single moment, sir!" he said, with husky politeness. "Before proceeding to business—er—we will devote a single moment to the necessary explanations of—er—er—a gentleman. The kyard now lying before you, sir, was handed ten minutes ago to one of your subordinates. I wish to inquire, sir, if it was then delivered to you?"

"Yes," said Mr. Dumphy, impatiently.

Colonel Starbottle leaned over Mr. Dumphy's desk and coolly rung his bell. Mr. Dumphy's clerk instantly appeared at the door. "I wish—" said the Colonel, addressing himself to the astounded employé as he stood loftily over Mr. Dumphy's chair—"I have—er—in fact sent for you, to withdraw the offensive epithets I addressed to you, and the threats—of er—of er—personal violence! The offence—is not, yours—but—er—rests with your employer, for whose apology I am—er—now waiting. Nevertheless I am ready, sir, to hold myself at your service—that is—er—of course—after my responsibility—er—with your master—er—ceases!"

Mr. Dumphy, who in the presence of Colonel Starbottle felt his former awkwardness return, signed with a forced smile to his embarrassed clerk to withdraw, and said hastily, but with an assumption of easy familiarity, "Sorry, Colonel, sorry, but I was very busy, and am now. No offence. All a mistake, you know! business man and business hours," and Mr. Dumphy leaned back in his chair, and emitted his rare cachinnatory bark.

"Glad to hear it, sir, I accept your apology," said the Colonel, recovering his good humour and his profanity together, "hang me, if I didn't think it was another affair like that I had with old Maje Tolliver, of Georgia. Called on him in Washington in '48 during session. Boy took up my kyard. Waited ten minutes, no reply! Then sent friend, poor Jeff Boomerang, dead now, killed in New Orleans by Ben Pastor—with challenge. Hang me, sir, after the second shot, Maje sends for me, lying thar with hole in both lungs, gasping for breath. 'It's all a blunder, Star,' he says, 'boy never brought kyard. Horsewhip the nigger for me, Star, for I reckon I won't live to do it,' and died like a gentleman, blank me!"

"What have you got to propose?" said Mr. Dumphy, hastily, seeing an opportunity to stop the flow of the Colonel's recollections.

"According to my memory, at our last interview over the social glass in your own house, I think something was said of a proposition coming from you. That is—er," continued the Colonel, loftily, "I hold myself responsible for the mistake, if any."

It had been Mr. Dumphy's first intention to assume the roughly offensive; to curtly inform Colonel Starbottle of the flight of his confederate, and dare him to do his worst. But for certain vague reasons he changed his plan of tactics. He drew his chair closer to the Colonel, and clapping his hand familiarly on his shoulder, began—

"You're a man of the world, Starbottle, so am I. *Sabe?* You're a gentleman—so am I," he continued, hastily. "But I'm a business man, and you're not. *Sabe?* Let's understand each other. No offence, you know, but in the way of business. This woman, claiming to be my wife, don't exist—it's all right, you know, I understand. I don't blame *you*, but you've been deceived, and all that sort of thing. I've got the proofs. Now as a man of the world and a gentleman and a business man, when I say the game's up! you'll understand me. Look at that—there!" He thrust into Starbottle's hand the telegram of the preceding day, "There! the man's hung by this time—lynched! The woman's gone!"

Colonel Starbottle read the telegram without any perceptible dismay or astonishment.

"Conroy! Conroy!—don't know the man. There was a McConroy, of St. Jo, but I don't think it's the same. No, sir! This ain't like him, sir! Don't seem to be a duel, unless he'd posted the man to kill on sight—murder's an ugly word to use to gentlemen. D—n me, sir, I don't know but he could hold the man responsible who sent that despatch. It's offensive, sir—very!"

"And you don't know Mrs. Conroy?" continued Mr. Dumphy, fixing his eyes on Colonel Starbottle's face.

"Mrs. Conroy! The wife of the superintendent—one of the most beautiful women! Good Ged, sir, I do! And I'm dev'lish sorry for her. But what's this got to do with our affair? Oh! I see, Ged!"—the Colonel suddenly chuckled, drew out his handkerchief, and waved it in the air with deprecatory gallantry, "gossip, sir, all gossip. People will talk! A fine woman! Blank me, if she was inclined to show some attention to Colonel Starbottle—Ged, sir, it was no more than other women have. You comprehend, Dumphy? Ged, sir, so the story's got round, eh?—husband's jealous—killed wrong man! Folks think she's run off with Colonel Starbottle, ha! ha! No, sir," he continued, suddenly dropping into an attitude of dignified severity. "You can say that Colonel Starbottle branded the story as a lie, sir! That whatever might have been the foolish indiscretion of a susceptible sex, Colonel Starbottle will defend the reputation of that lady, sir, with his life—with his life!"

Absurd and ridiculous as this sudden diversion of Colonel Starbottle from the point at issue had become, Dumphy could not doubt his sincerity, nor the now self-evident fact that Mrs. Conroy was *not* his visitor's mysterious client! Mr. Dumphy felt that his suddenly built up theory was demolished and his hope with it. He was still at the mercy of this conceited braggart and the invisible power behind him—whoever or whatever it might be. Mr. Dumphy was not inclined to superstition, but he began to experience a strange awe of his unknown persecutor, and resolved at any risk to discover who it was. Could it be really his wife?—had not the supercilious Poinsett been himself tricked—or was he not now trying to trick him, Dumphy? Couldn't Starbottle be bribed to expose at least the name of his client? He would try it.

"I said just now you had been deceived in this woman who represents herself to be my wife. I find I have been mistaken in the person, who I believe imposed upon you, and it is possible that I may be otherwise wrong. My wife may be alive. I am willing to admit it. Bring her here to-morrow and I will accept it as a fact."

"You forget that she refuses to see you again," said Colonel Starbottle, "until she has established her claim by process of law."

"That's so! that's all right, old fellow; *we* understand each other. Now, suppose that we business men—as a business maxim, you know—always prefer to deal with principals. Now suppose we even go so far as to do that and yet pay an agent's commission, perhaps—you understand me—even a *bonus*. Good! That's business! You understand that as a gentleman and a man of the world. Now, I say, bring me your principal—fetch along that woman, and I'll make it all right with *you*. Stop! I know what you're going to say; you're bound by honour and all that—I understand your position as a gentleman, and respect it. Then let me know where I can find her! Understand—you sha'n't be compromised as bringing about the interview in any way. I'll see that you're protected in your commissions from your client; and for my part—if a cheque for five thousand dollars will satisfy you of my desire to do the right thing in this matter, it's at your service."

The Colonel rose to his feet and applied himself apparently to the single and silent inflation of his chest, for the space of a minute. When the upper buttons of his coat seemed to be on the point of flying off with a report, he suddenly extended his hand and grasped Dumphy's with fervour. "Permit me," he said, in a voice husky with emotion, "to congratulate myself on dealing with a gentleman and a man of honour. Your sentiments, sir, I don't care if I do say it, do you credit! I am proud, sir," continued the Colonel, warmly, "to have made your acquaintance! But I regret to say, sir, that I cannot give you the information you require. I do not myself know the name or address of my client."

The look of half-contemptuous satisfaction which had irradiated Dumphy's face at the beginning of this speech, changed to one of angry suspicion at its close. "That's a d——d queer oversight of yours," he ejaculated, with an expression as nearly insulting as he dared to make it. Colonel Starbottle did not apparently notice the manner of his speech, but drawing his chair close beside Dumphy, he laid his hand upon his arm.

"Your confidence as a man of honour and a gentleman," he began, "demands equal confidence and frankness on my part, and Culp. Starbottle of Virginia is not the man to withhold it! When I state that I do *not* know the name and address of my client, I believe, sir, there is no one now living, who will—er—er—require or—er—deem it necessary for me to repeat the assertion! Certainly not, sir," added the Colonel, lightly waving his hand, "the gentleman who has just honoured me with his confidence and invited mine—I thank you, sir," he continued, as Mr. Dumphy made a hasty motion of assent, "and will go on.

"It is not necessary for me to name the party who first put me in possession of the facts. You will take my word as a gentleman—er—that it is some one unknown to you, of unimportant position, though of strict respectability, and one who acted only as the agent of my real client. When the case was handed over to me there was also put into my possession a sealed envelope containing the name of my client and principal witness. My injunctions were not to open it until all negotiations had failed and it was necessary to institute legal proceedings. That envelope I have here. You perceive it is unopened!"

Mr. Dumphy unconsciously reached out his hand. With a gesture of polite deprecation Colonel Starbottle evaded it, and placing the letter on the table before him, continued, "It is unnecessary to say that—er—there being in my judgment no immediate necessity for the beginning of a suit—the injunctions still restrain me, and I shall not open the letter. If, however, I accidentally mislay it on this table and it is returned to me to-morrow, sealed as before, I believe, sir, as a gentleman and a man of honour I violate no pledge."

"I see," said Mr. Dumphy, with a short laugh.

"Excuse me, if I venture to require another condition, merely as a form among men of honour. Write as I dictate." Mr. Dumphy took up a pen. Colonel Starbottle placed one hand on his honourable breast and began slowly and meditatively to pace the length of the room with the air of a second measuring the distance for his principal. "Are you ready?"

"Go on," said Dumphy, impatiently.

"I hereby pledge myself—er—er—that in the event of any disclosure by me—er—of confidential communications from Colonel Starbottle to me, I shall hold myself ready to afford him the usual honourable satisfaction—er—common among gentlemen, at such times or places, and with such weapons as he may choose, without further formality of challenge, and that—er—er—failing in that I do thereby proclaim myself, without posting, a liar, poltroon, and dastard."

In the full pre-occupation of his dignified composition, and possibly from an inability to look down over the increased exaggeration of his swelling breast, Colonel Starbottle did not observe the contemptuous smile which curled the lip of his amanuensis. Howbeit Mr. Dumphy signed the document and handed it to him. Colonel Starbottle put it in his pocket. Nevertheless he lingered by Mr. Dumphy's side.

"The—er—er—cheque," said the Colonel, with a slight cough, "had better be to your order, endorsed by you—to spare any criticism hereafter."

Mr. Dumphy hesitated a moment. He would have preferred as a matter of business to have first known the contents of the envelope, but with a slight smile he dashed off the cheque and handed it to the Colonel. "If—er—it would not be too much trouble," said the Colonel, jauntily, "for the same reason just mentioned, would you give that—er—piece of paper to one of your clerks to draw the money for me?"

Mr. Dumphy impatiently, with his eyes on the envelope, rang his bell and handed the cheque to the clerk, while Colonel Starbottle, with an air of abstraction, walked discreetly to the window.

For the rest of Colonel Starbottle's life he never ceased to deplore this last act of caution, and regret that he had not put the cheque in his pocket. For as he walked to the window the floor suddenly appeared to rise beneath his feet and as suddenly sank again, and he was thrown violently against the mantelpiece. He felt sick and giddy. With a terrible apprehension of apoplexy in his whirling brain, he turned toward his companion, who had risen from his seat and was supporting himself by his swinging desk with a panic-stricken face and a pallor equal to his own. In another moment a bookcase toppled with a crash to the floor, a loud outcry arose from the outer offices, and amidst the sounds of rushing feet, the breaking of glass, and the creaking of timber, the two men dashed with a common instinct to the door. It opened two inches and remained fixed. With the howl of a caged wild beast Dumphy threw himself against the rattling glass of the window that opened on the level of the street. In another instant Colonel Starbottle was beside him on the sidewalk, and the next they were separated, unconsciously, uncaringly, as if they had been the merest strangers in contact in a crowd. The business that had brought them together, the unfinished, incomplete, absorbing interests of a moment ago were forgotten—were buried in the oblivion of another existence, which had no sympathy with this, whose only instinct was to fly—where, they knew not!

The middle of the broad street was filled with a crowd of breathless, pallid, death-stricken men who had lost all sense but the common instinct of animals. There were hysterical men, who laughed loudly without a cause, and talked incessantly of what they knew not. There were dumb, paralysed men, who stood helplessly and hopelessly beneath cornices and chimneys that toppled over and crushed them. There were automatic men, who flying, carried with them the work on which they were engaged—one whose hands were full of bills and papers, another who held his ledger under his arm. There were men who had forgotten the ordinary instincts of decency—some half-dressed. There were men who rushed from the fear of death into its presence; two were picked up, one who had jumped through a skylight, another who had blindly leaped from a fourth-story window. There were brave men who trembled like children; there was one whose life had been spent in scenes of daring and danger, who cowered paralysed in the corner of the room from which a few inches of plastering had fallen. There were hopeful men who believed that the danger was over, and having passed, would, by some mysterious law, never recur; there were others who shook their heads and said that the next shock would be fatal. There were crowds around the dust that arose from fallen chimneys and cornices, around runaway horses that had dashed as madly as their drivers against lamp-posts, around telegraph and newspaper offices eager to know the extent of the disaster. Along the remoter avenues and cross-streets dwellings were deserted, people sat upon their doorsteps or in chairs upon the sidewalks, fearful of the houses they had built with their own hands, and doubtful even of this blue arch above them that smiled so deceitfully; of those far-reaching fields beyond, which they had cut into lots and bartered and sold, and which now seemed to suddenly rise against them, or slip and wither away from their very feet. It seemed so outrageous that this dull, patient earth, whose homeliness they had adorned and improved, and which, whatever their other fortune or vicissitudes, at least had been their sure inheritance, should have become so faithless. Small wonder that the owner of a little house, which had sunk on the reclaimed water front, stooped in the speechless and solemn absurdity of his wrath to shake his clenched fist in the face of the Great Mother.

The real damage to life and property had been so slight and in such pronounced contrast to the prevailing terror, that half an hour later only a sense of the ludicrous remained with the greater masses of the people. Mr. Dumphy, like all practical, unimaginative men, was among the first to recover his presence of mind with the passing of the immediate danger. People took confidence when this great man, who had so much to lose, after sharply remanding his clerks and everybody else back to business, re-entered his office. He strode at once to his desk. But the envelope was gone! He looked hurriedly among his papers—on the floor—by the broken window—but in vain.

Mr. Dumphy instantly rang his bell. The clerk appeared.

"Was that draft paid?"

"No, sir; we were counting the money when"——

"Stop it!—return the draft to me."

The young man was confiding to his confrères his suspicions of a probable "run" on the bank as indicated by Mr. Dumphy's caution, when he was again summoned by Mr. Dumphy.

"Go to Mr. Poinsett's office and ask him to come here at once."

In a few moments the clerk returned out of breath.

"Mr. Poinsett left a quarter of an hour ago, sir, for San Antonio."

"San Antonio?"

"Yes, sir—they say there's bad news from the Mission."

CHAPTER VII.

IN WHICH BOTH JUSTICE AND THE HEAVENS FALL.

THE day following the discovery of the murder of Victor Ramirez was one of the intensest excitement in One Horse Gulch. It was not that killing was rare in that pastoral community—foul murder had been done there upon the bodies of various citizens of more or less respectability, and the victim in the present instance was a stranger and a man who awakened no personal sympathy; but the suspicion that swiftly and instantly attached to two such important people as Mr. and Mrs. Conroy, already objects of severe criticism, was sufficient to exalt this particular crime above all others in thrilling interest. For two days business was practically suspended.

The discovery of the murder was made by Sal, who stumbled upon the body of the unfortunate Victor early the next morning during a walk on Conroy's Hill, manifestly in search of the missing man, who had not returned to the hotel that night. A few flippant souls, misunderstanding Miss Clark's interest in the stranger, asserted that he had committed suicide to escape her attentions, but all jocular hypothesis ceased when it became known that Gabriel and his wife had fled. Then came the report that Gabriel had been seen by a passing miner early in the day "shoving" the stranger along the trail, with his hand on his collar, and exchanging severe words. Then the willing testimony of Miss Clark that she had seen Mrs. Conroy in secret converse with Victor before the murder; then the unwilling evidence of the Chinaman who had overtaken Gabriel with the letter, but who heard the sounds of quarrelling and cries for help in the bushes after his departure; but this evidence was excluded from the inquest, by virtue of the famous Californian law that a Pagan was of necessity a liar, and that truth only resided in the breast of the Christian Caucasian, and was excluded from the general public for its incompatibility with Gabriel's subsequent flight, and the fact that the Chinaman, being a fool, was probably mistaken in the hour. Then there was the testimony of the tunnel-men to Gabriel's appearance on the hill that night. There was only one important proof not submitted to the public or the authorities—Mrs. Conroy's note—picked up by Sal, handed to Mrs. Markle, and given by her to Lawyer Maxwell. The knowledge of this document was restricted to the few already known to the reader.

A dozen or more theories of the motive of the deed at different hours of the day occupied and disturbed the public mind. That Gabriel had come upon a lover of his wife in the act of eloping with her, and had slain him out of hand, was the first. That Gabriel had decoyed the man to an interview by simulating his wife's handwriting, and then worked his revenge on his body, was accepted later as showing the necessary deliberation to constitute murder. That Gabriel and his wife had conjointly taken this method to rid themselves of a former lover who threatened exposure, was a still later theory. Towards evening, when One Horse Gulch had really leisure to put its heads together, it was generally understood that Gabriel and Mrs. Conroy had put out of their way a dangerous and necessarily rightful claimant to that mine which Gabriel had pretended to discover. This opinion was for some time—say two hours—the favourite one, agreeing as it did with the popular opinion of Gabriel's inability to discover a mine himself, and was only modified by another theory that Victor was not the real claimant, but a dangerous witness that the Conroys had found it necessary to dispose of. And when, possibly from some unguarded expression of Lawyer Maxwell, it was reported that Gabriel Conroy was an impostor under an assumed name, all further speculation was deemed unnecessary. The coroner's jury brought in a verdict against "John Doe, alias Gabriel Conroy," and One Horse Gulch added this injury of false pretence to other grievances complained of. One or two cases of horse-stealing and sluice-robbing in the neighbourhood were indefinitely but strongly connected with this discovery. If I am thus particular in citing these evidences of the various gradations of belief in the guilt of the accused, it is because they were peculiar to One Horse Gulch, and of course never obtained in more civilised communities.

It is scarcely necessary to say that one person in One Horse Gulch never wavered in her opinion of Gabriel's innocence, nor that that person was Mrs. Markle. That he was the victim of a vile conspiracy—that Mrs. Conroy was the real culprit, and had diabolically contrived to fasten the guilt upon her husband, Mrs. Markle not only believed herself, but absolutely contrived to make Lawyer Maxwell and Sal believe also. More than that, it had undoubtedly great power in restraining Sal's evidence before the inquest, which that impulsive and sympathetic young woman persisted in delivering behind a black veil and in a suit of the deepest mourning that could be hastily improvised in One Horse Gulch.

"Miss Clark's evidence," said the *Silveropolis Messenger*, "although broken by sobs and occasional expressions of indignation against the murderer, strongly impressed the jury as the natural eloquence of one connected with the tenderest ties to the unfortunate victim. It is said that she was an old acquaintance of Ramirez, who was visiting her in the hope of inducing her to consent to a happy termination of a life-long courtship, when the dastard hand of the murderer changed the bridal wreath to the veil of mourning. From expressions that dropped from the witness's lips, although restrained by natural modesty, it would not be strange if jealousy were shown to be one of the impelling causes. It is said that previous to his marriage the alleged Gabriel Conroy was a frequent visitor at the house of Miss Clark."

I venture to quote this extract not so much for its suggestion of a still later theory in the last sentence, as for its poetical elegance, and as an offset to the ruder record of the *One Horse Gulch Banner*, which, I grieve to say, was as follows :—

"Sal was no slouch of a witness. Rigged out in ten yards of Briggs' best black glazed muslin, and with a lot of black mosquito netting round her head, she pranced round the stand like a skittish hearse horse in fly-time. If Sal calculates to go into mourning for every man she has to sling hash to, we'd recommend her to buy up Briggs' stock and take one of Pat Hoolan's carriages for the season. There is a strong feeling among men whose heads are level, that this Minstrel Variety Performance is a bluff of the *Messenger* to keep from the public the real motives of the murder, which it is pretty generally believed concerns some folks a little higher-toned than Sal. We mention no names, but we would like to know what the Editor of the *Messenger* was doing in the counting-room of one of Pete Dumphy's emissaries at ten o'clock last evening. Looking up his bank account, eh? What's the size of the figures to-day? You hear us!"

At one o'clock that morning the Editor of the *Messenger* fired at the Editor of the *Banner* and missed him. At half-past one two men were wounded by pistol shots in a difficulty at Briggs' warehouse—cause not stated. At nine o'clock half a dozen men lounged down the main street and ascended the upper loft of Briggs' warehouse. In ten or fifteen minutes a dozen more from different saloons in the town lounged as indifferently in the direction of Briggs', until at half-past nine the assemblage in the loft numbered fifty men. During this interval a smaller party had gathered, apparently as accidentally and indefinitely as to purpose, on the steps of the little two-story brick Court House in which the prisoner was confined. At ten o'clock a horse was furiously ridden into town, and dropped exhausted at the outskirts. A few moments later a man hurriedly crossed the plaza toward the Court House. It was Mr. Jack Hamlin. But the Three Voices had preceded him, and from the steps of the Court House were already uttering the popular mandate.

It was addressed to a single man. A man who, deserted by his *posse*, and abandoned by his friends, had for the last twelve hours sat beside his charge, tireless, watchful, defiant, and resolute—Joe Hall, the Sheriff of Calaveras! He had been waiting for this summons, behind barricaded doors, with pistols in his belt, and no hope in his heart; a man of limited ideas and restricted resources, constant only to one intent—that of dying behind those bars, in defence of that legal trust, which his office and an extra fifty votes at the election only two months before had put into his hands. It had perplexed him for a moment that he heard the voices of some of these voters below him clamouring against him, but above their feebler pipe always rose another mandatory sentence, "We command you to take and safely keep the body of Gabriel Conroy," and being a simple man the recollection of the quaint phraseology strengthened him and cleared his mind. Ah me, I fear he had none of the external marks of a hero; as I remember him he was small, indistinctive, and fidgety, without the repose of strength; a man who at that extreme moment chewed tobacco and spat vigorously on the floor; who tweaked the ends of his scanty beard, paced the floor, and tried the locks of his pistols. Presently he stopped before Gabriel and said almost fiercely—

"You hear that—they are coming!"

Gabriel nodded. Two hours before, when the contemplated attack of the Vigilance Committee had been revealed to him, he had written a few lines to Lawyer Maxwell, which he entrusted to the sheriff. He had then relapsed into his usual tranquillity—serious, simple, and when he had occasion to speak, diffident and apologetic.

"Are you going to help me?" continued Hall.

"In course," said Gabriel, in quiet surprise, "ef *you* say so. But don't ye do nowt ez would be gettin' yourself into troubil along o' me. I ain't worth it. Maybe it 'ud be jest as square ef ye handed me over to them chaps out yer—allowin' I was a heep o' troubil to you—and reckonin' you'd about hed *your sheer* o' the keer o' me, and kinder passin' me round. But ef you *do* feel obligated to take keer o' me, ez hevin' promised the jedges and jury" (it is almost impossible to convey the gentle deprecatoriness of Gabriel's voice and accent at this juncture), "why," he added, "I'm with ye. I'm thar! You understand me!"

He rose slowly, and with quiet but powerfully significant deliberation placed the chair he had been sitting on back against the wall. The tone and act satisfied the sheriff. The seventy-four gunship, Gabriel Conroy, was clearing the decks for action.

There was an ominous lull in the outcries below, and then the solitary lifting up of a single voice, the Potential Voice of the night before! The sheriff walked to a window in the hall and opened it. The besieger and besieged measured each other with a look. Then came the Homeric chaff:—

"Git out o' that, Joe Hall, and run home to your mother. She's getting oneasy about ye!"

"The h—ll you say!" responded Hall, promptly, "and the old woman in such a hurry she had to borry Al. Barker's hat and breeches to come here! Run home, old gal, and don't parse yourself off for a man agin!"

"This ain't no bluff, Joe Hall! Why don't ye call? Yer's fifty men; the returns are agin ye, and two precincts yet to hear from." (This was a double thrust, at Hall's former career as a gambler, and the closeness of his late election vote.)

"All right! send 'em up by express—mark 'em C. O. D." (The previous speaker was the expressman.)

"Blank you! Git!"

"Blank you! Come on!"

Here there was a rush at the door, the accidental discharge of a pistol, and the window was slammed down. Words ceased, deeds began.

A few hours before, Hall had removed his prisoner from the uncertain tenure and accessible position of the cells below to the open court-room of the second floor, inaccessible by windows, and lit by a skylight in the roof, above the reach of the crowd, whose massive doors were barricaded by benches and desks. A smaller door at the side, easily secured, was left open for reconnoitring. The approach to the court-room was by a narrow stairway, halfway down whose length Gabriel had thrust the long court-room table as a barricade to the besiegers. The lower outer door, secured by the sheriff after the desertion of his underlings, soon began to show signs of weakening under the vigorous battery from without. From the landing the two men watched it eagerly. As it slowly yielded, the sheriff drew back toward the side door and beckoned Gabriel to follow; but with a hasty sign Gabriel suddenly sprang forward and dropped beneath the table as the door with a crash fell inward, beaten from its hinges. There was a rush of trampling feet to the stairway, a cry of baffled rage over the impeding table, a sudden scramble up and upon it, and then, as if on its own volition, the long table suddenly reared itself on end, and staggering a moment toppled backward with its clinging human burden on the heads of the thronging mass below. There was a cry, a sudden stampede of the Philistines to the street, and Samson, rising to his feet, slowly walked to the side door, and re-entered the court-room. But at the same instant an agile besieger who, unnoticed, had crossed the Rubicon, darted from his concealment, and dashed by Gabriel into the room. There was a shout from the sheriff, the door was closed hastily, a shot, and the intruder fell. But the next moment he staggered to his knees, with outstretched hands, "Hold up! I'm yer to help ye!"

It was Jack Hamlin! haggard, dusty, grimy; his gay feathers bedraggled, his tall hat battered, his spotless shirt torn open at the throat, his eyes and cheeks burning with fever, the blood dripping from the bullet wound in his leg, but still Jack Hamlin, strong and audacious. By a common instinct both men dropped their weapons, ran and lifted him in their arms.

"There—shove that chair under me! that'll do," said Hamlin, coolly, "We're even now, Joe Hall; that shot wiped out old scores, even if it has crippled me, and lost ye my valuable aid. Dry up! and listen to me, and then leave me here! there's but one way of escape. It's up there!" (he pointed to the skylight) "the rear wall hangs over the Wingdam ditch and gully. Once on the roof you can drop over with this rope, which you must unwind from my body, for I'm d—d if I can do it myself. Can you reach the skylight?"

"There's a step-ladder from the gallery," said the sheriff, joyously, "but won't they see us, and be prepared?"

"Before they can reach the gully by going round, you'll be half a mile away in the woods. But what in blank are you waiting for? Go! You can hold on here for ten minutes more if they attack the same point; but if they think of the skylight, and fetch ladders, you're gone in! Go!"

There was another rush on the staircase without; the surging of an immense wave against the heavy folding doors, the blows of pick and crowbar, the gradual yielding of the barricade a few inches, and the splintering of benches by a few pistol shots fired through the springing crevices of the doors. And yet the sheriff hesitated. Suddenly Gabriel stooped down, lifted the wounded man to his shoulder as if he had been an infant, and beckoning to the sheriff started for the gallery. But he had not taken two steps before he staggered and lapsed heavily against Hall, who, in his turn, stopped and clutched the railing. At the same moment the thunder of the besiegers seemed to increase; not only the door, but the windows rattled, the heavy chandelier fell with a crash, carrying a part of the plaster and the elaborate cornice with it, a shower of bricks fell through the skylight, and a cry, quite distinct from anything heard before, rose from without. There was a pause in the hall, and then the sudden rush of feet down the staircase, and all was still again. The three men gazed in each other's whitened faces.

"An earthquake," said the sheriff.

"So much the better," said Jack. "It gives us time—forward!"

They reached the gallery and the little step-ladder that led to a door that opened upon the roof, Gabriel preceding with his burden. There was another rush up the staircase without the court room, but this time there was no yielding in the door; the earthquake that had shaken the foundations and settled the walls had sealed it firmly.

Gabriel was first to step out on the roof, carrying Jack Hamlin. But as he did so another thrill ran through the building and he dropped on his knees to save himself from falling, while the door closed smartly behind him. In another moment the shock had passed, and Gabriel, putting down his burden, turned to open the door for the sheriff. But to his alarm it did not yield to his pressure; the earthquake had sealed it as it had the door below, and Joe Hall was left a prisoner.

It was Gabriel's turn to hesitate and look at his companion. But Jack was gazing into the street below. Then he looked up and said, "We must go on now, Gabriel,—for—for *they've got a ladder!*"

Gabriel rose again to his feet and lifted the wounded man. The curve of the domed roof was slight; in the centre, on a rough cupola or base, the figure of Justice, fifteen feet high, rudely carved in wood, towered above them with drawn sword and dangling scales. Gabriel reached the cupola and crouched behind it, as a shout rose from the street below that told he was discovered. A few shots were fired, one bullet imbedded itself in the naked blade of the Goddess, and another with cruel irony, shattered the equanimity of her balance. "Unwind the cord from me," said Hamlin. Gabriel did so. "Fasten one end to the chimney or the statue." But the chimney was levelled by the earthquake, and even the statue was trembling on its pedestal. Gabriel secured the rope to an iron girder of the skylight, and crawling on the roof dropped it cautiously over the gable. But it was several feet too short—too far for a cripple to drop! Gabriel crawled back to Hamlin. "You must go first," he said, quietly, "I will hold the rope over the gable. You can trust me."

Without waiting for Hamlin's reply he fastened the rope under his arms and half-lifted, half-dragged him to the gable. Then pressing his hand silently, he laid himself down and lowered the wounded man safely to the ground. He had recovered the rope again, and crawling to the cupola, was about to fasten the line to the iron girder when something slowly rose above the level of the roof beyond him. The uprights of a ladder!

The Three Voices had got tired of waiting a reply to their oft-reiterated question, and had mounted the ladder by way of forcing an answer at the muzzles of their revolvers. They reached the level of the roof, one after another, and again propounded their inquiry. And then as it seemed to their awe-stricken fancy, the only figure there—the statue of Justice—awoke to their appeal. Awoke! leaned towards them; advanced its awful sword and shook its broken balance, and then toppling forward with one mighty impulse, came down upon them, swept them from the ladder, and silenced the Voices for ever! And from behind its pedestal Gabriel arose, panting, pale, but triumphant.

CHAPTER VIII.

IN TENEBRIS SERVARE FIDEM.

ALTHOUGH a large man, Gabriel was lithe and active, and dropped the intervening distance where the rope was scant, lightly, and without injury. Happily the falling of the statue was looked upon as the result of another earthquake shock, and its disastrous effect upon the storming party for awhile checked the attack. Gabriel lifted his half-fainting ally in his arms, and gaining the friendly shelter of the ditch, in ten minutes was beyond the confines of One Horse Gulch, and in the shadow of the pines of Conroy's Hill. There were several tunnel openings only known to him. Luckily the first was partly screened by a fall of rock loosened by the earthquake from the hill above, and satisfied that it would be unrecognised by any eye less keen than his own, Gabriel turned into it with his fainting burden. And it was high time. For the hæmorrhage from Jack Hamlin's wound was so great that that gentleman, after a faint attempt to wave his battered hat above his dishevelled curls, suddenly succumbed, and lay as cold and senseless and beautiful as a carven Apollo.

Then Gabriel stripped him, and found an ugly hole in his thigh that had narrowly escaped traversing the femoral artery, and set himself about that rude surgery which he had acquired by experience, and that more delicate nursing which was instinctive with him. He was shocked at the revelation of a degree of emaciation in the figure of this young fellow that he had not before suspected. Gabriel had nursed many sick men, and here was one who clearly ought to be under the doctor's hands, economising his vitality as a sedentary invalid, who had shown himself to him hitherto only as a man of superabundant activity and animal spirits. Whence came the power that had animated this fragile shell? Gabriel was perplexed; he looked down upon his own huge frame with a new and sudden sense of apology and depreciation, as if it were an offence to this spare and bloodless Adonis.

And then with an infinite gentleness, as of a young mother over her newborn babe, he stanched the blood and bound up the wounds of his new friend, so skilfully that he never winced, and with a peculiar purring accompaniment that lulled him to repose. Once only, as he held him in his arms, did he change his expression, and that was when a shadow and a tread—perhaps of a passing hare or squirrel—crossed the mouth of his cave, when he suddenly caught the body to his breast with the fierceness of a lioness interrupted with her cubs. In his own rough experience he was much awed by the purple and fine linen of this fine gentleman's underclothing—not knowing the prevailing habits of his class—and when he had occasion to open his bosom to listen to the faint beatings of his heart, he put aside with great delicacy and instinctive honour a fine gold chain from which depended some few relics and keepsakes which this scamp wore. But one was a photograph, set in an open locket, that he could not fail to see, and that at once held him breathless above it. It was the exact outline and features of his sister Grace, but with a strange shadow over that complexion which he remembered well as beautiful, that struck him with superstitious awe. He scanned it again eagerly. "Maybe it was a dark day when she sot!" he murmured softly to himself; "maybe it's the light in this yer tunnel; maybe the heat o' this poor chap's buzzum hez kinder turned it. It ain't measles, fur she hed 'em along o' Olly." He paused and looked at the unconscious man before him, as if trying to connect him with the past. "No," he said simply, with a resigned sigh, "it's agin reason! She never knowed him! It's only my foolishness, and my thinkin' and thinkin' o' her so much! It's another gal, and none o' your business, Gabe, and you a' prying inter another man's secrets, and takin' advantage of him when he's down." He hurriedly replaced it in his companion's bosom, and closed the collar of his shirt, as Jack's lips moved. "Pete!" he called, feebly.

"It's his pardner, maybe, he's callin' on," said Gabriel to himself; then aloud, with the usual, comforting professional assent, "In course, Pete, surely! He's coming, right off—he'll be yer afore you know it."

"Pete," continued Jack, forcibly, "take the mare off my leg, she's breaking it! Don't you see? She's stumbled! D—n it, quick! I'll be late. They'll string him up before I get there!"

In a moment Gabriel's stout heart sank. If fever should set in—if he should become delirious, they would be lost. Providentially, however, Jack's aberration was only for a moment; he presently opened his black eyes and stared at Gabriel. Gabriel smiled assuringly. "Am I dead and buried," said Jack, gravely, looking around the dark vault, "or have I got 'em again?"

"Ye wuz took bad fur a minit—that's all," said Gabriel, reassuringly, much relieved himself, "yer all right now!"

Hamlin tried to rise but could not. "That's a lie," he said, cheerfully. "What's to be done?"

"Ef you'd let me hev my say, without gettin' riled," said Gabriel, apologetically, "I'd tell ye. Look yer," he continued, persuasively, "ye ought to hev a doctor afore thet wound gets inflamed; and ye ain't goin' to get one, bein' packed round by me. Now don't ye flare up, but harkin! Allowin' I goes out to them chaps ez is huntin' us, and sez, 'look yer, you kin take me, provided ye don't bear no malice agin my friend, and you sends a doctor to fetch him outer the tunnel.' Don't yer see, they can't prove anythin' agin ye, anyway," continued Gabriel, with a look of the intensest cunning, "I'll swear I took you pris'ner, and Joe won't go back on his shot."

In spite of his pain and danger this proposition afforded Jack Hamlin apparently the largest enjoyment. "Thank ye," he said, with a smile, "but as there's a warrant, by this time, out against me for horse-stealing, I reckon I won't put myself in the way of their nursing. They might forgive you for killing a Mexican of no great market value, but they ain't goin' to extend the right hand of fellowship to me after running off with their ringleader's mustang! Particularly when that animal's foundered and knee-sprung. No, sir!"

Gabriel stared at his companion without speaking.

"I was late coming back with Olly to Wingdam. I had to swap the horse and buggy for the mare without having time to arrange particulars with the owner. I don't wonder you're shocked," continued Jack, mischievously, affecting to misunderstand Gabriel's silence, "but thet's me. Thet's the kind of company you've got into. Procrastination and want of punctuality has brought me to this. Never procrastinate, Gabriel. Always make it a point to make it a rule, never to be late at the Sabbath school!"

"Ef I hed owt to give ye," said Gabriel, ruefully, "a drop o' whisky, or suthin' to keep up your stren'th!"

"I never touch intoxicating liquors without the consent of my physician," said Jack, gravely, "they're too exciting! I must be kept free from all excitement. Something soothing, or sedentary like this," he added, striking his leg. But even through his mischievous smile his face paled, and a spasm of pain crossed it.

"I reckon we'll hev to stick yer ontil dark," said Gabriel, "and then strike acrost the gully to the woods on Conroy's

Hill. Ye'll be easier thar, and we're safe ontil sun-up, when we kin hunt another tunnel. Thar ain't no choice," added Gabriel, apologetically.

Jack made a grimace, and cast a glance around the walls of the tunnel. The luxurious scamp missed his usual comfortable surroundings. "Well," he assented, with a sigh, "I suppose the game's made anyway! and we've got to stick here like snails on a rock for an hour yet. Well," he continued, impatiently, as Gabriel, after improvising a rude couch for him with some withered pine tassels gathered at the mouth of the tunnel, sat down beside him, "are you goin' to bore me to death, now that you've got me here—sittin' there like an owl? Why don't you say something?"

"Say what?" asked Gabriel, simply.

"Anything! Lie if you want to; only talk!"

"I'd like to put a question to ye, Mr. Hamlin," said Gabriel, with great gentleness,—"allowin' in course, ye'll answer or no jest ez as is agree'ble to ye—reckonin' it's no business o' mine nor pryin' into secrets, ony jess to pass away the time ontil sundown. When you was tuk bad a spell ago, unloosin' yer shirt thar, I got to see a pictur that ye hev around yer neck. I ain't askin' who nor which it is—but ony this—ez thet—thet—thet young woman dark complected ez that picter allows her to be?"

Jack's face had recovered its colour by the time that Gabriel had finished, and he answered promptly, "A d—d sight more so! Why, that picture's fair alongside of her!"

Gabriel looked a little disappointed. Hamlin was instantly up in arms. "Yes, sir—and when I say that," he returned, "I mean, by thunder, that the whitest faced woman in the world don't begin to be as handsome. Thar ain't an angel that she couldn't give points to and beat! That's *her* style! It don't," continued Mr. Hamlin, taking the picture from his breast, and wiping its face with his handkerchief—

"it don t begin to do her justice. What," he asked suddenly and aggressively, "have *you* got to say about it, anyway?"

"I reckoned it kinder favoured my sister Grace," said Gabriel, submissively. "Ye didn't know her, Mr. Hamlin? She was lost sence '49—thet's all!"

Mr. Hamlin measured Gabriel with a contempt that was delicious in its sublime audacity and unconsciousness. "Your sister?" he repeated, "that's a healthy lookin' *sister* of such a man as you—ain't it? Why, look at it," roared Jack, thrusting the picture under Gabriel's nose. "Why, it's—it's a *lady!*"

"Ye musn't jedge Gracey by me, nor even Olly," interposed Gabriel, gently, evading Mr. Hamlin's contempt.

But Jack was not to be appeased. "Does your sister sing like an angel, and talk Spanish like Governor Alvarado: is she connected with one of the oldest Spanish families in the state; does she run a rancho and thirty square leagues of land, and is Dolores Salvatierra her nickname? Is her complexion like the young bark of the madroño—the most beautiful thing ever seen—did every other woman look chalky beside her, eh?"

"No!" said Gabriel, with a sigh—"it was just my foolishness, Mr. Hamlin. But seein' that picter, kinder"——

"I stole it," interrupted Jack, with the same frankness. "I saw it in her parlour, on the table, and I froze to it when no one was looking. Lord, *she* wouldn't have given it to *me.* I reckon those relatives of hers would have made it very lively for me if they'd suspected it. Hoss stealing ain't a circumstance to this, Gabriel," said Jack, with a reckless laugh. Then with equal frankness, and a picturesque freedom of description, he related his first and only interview with Donna Dolores. I am glad to say that this scamp exaggerated, if anything, the hopelessness of his case, dwelt but slightly on his own services, and concealed the fact that Donna Dolores had even thanked him. "You can reckon from this the extent of my affection for that Johnny Ramirez, and why I just froze to you when I heard you'd dropped him. But come now, it's your deal; tell us all about it. The boys put it up that he was hangin' round your wife,—and you went for him for all he was worth. Go on—I'm waiting—and," added Jack, as a spasm of pain passed across his face, "and aching to that degree that I'll yell if you don't take my mind off it."

But Gabriel's face was grave and his lips silent as he bent over Mr. Hamlin to adjust the bandages. "Go on," said Jack, darkly, "or I'll tear off these rags and bleed to death before your eyes. What are you afraid of? I know all about your wife—you can't tell me anything about her. Didn't I spot her in Sacramento—before she married you—when she had this same Chilino, Ramirez, on a string. Why, she's fooled him as she has you. You ain't such a blasted fool as to be stuck after her still, are you?" and Jack raised himself on his elbow the more intently to regard this possible transcendent idiot.

"You was speakin' o' this Mexican, Ramirez," said Gabriel, after a pause, fixing his now clear and untroubled eyes on his interlocutor.

"Of course," roared out Jack, impatiently, "did you think I was talking of ——?" Here Mr. Hamlin offered a name that suggested the most complete and perfect antithesis known to modern reason.

"I didn't kill him!" said Gabriel, quietly.

"Of course not," said Jack, promptly. "He sorter stumbled and fell over on your bowie-knife as you were pickin' your teeth with it. But go on—how did you do it? Where did you spot him? Did he make any fight? Has he got any sand in him?"

"I tell ye I didn't kill him!"

"Who did, then?" screamed Jack, furious with pain and impatience.

"I don't know—I reckon—that is——" and Gabriel stopped short with a wistful perplexed look at his companion.

"Perhaps, Mr. Gabriel Conroy," said Jack, with sudden coolness and deliberation of speech, and a baleful light in his dark eyes, "perhaps you'll be good enough to tell me what this means—what *is* your little game? Perhaps you'll kindly inform me what I'm lying here crippled for? What you were doing up in the Court House, when you were driving those people crazy with excitement? What you're hiding here in this blank family vault for? And maybe, if you've got time, you'll tell me what was the reason I made that pleasant little trip to Sacramento? I know I required the exercise, and then there was the honour of being introduced to your little sister—but perhaps you'll tell me WHAT IT WAS FOR!"

"Jack," said Gabriel, leaning forward, with a sudden return of his old trouble and perplexity, "I thought *she* did it! and thinkin' that—when they asked me—I took it upon *myself!* I didn't allow to ring *you* into this, Jack! I thought—I thought—thet—it 'ud all be one—thet they'd hang me up afore this—I did, Jack, honest!"

"And you didn't kill Ramirez?"

"No."

"And you reckoned your wife did?"

"Yes."

"And you took the thing on yourself?"

"I did."

"*You* did!"

"I did!"

"You DID?"

"I did!"

Mr. Hamlin rolled over on his back, and began to whistle "When the spring time comes, gentle Annie!" as the only way of expressing his inordinate contempt for the whole proceeding.

Gabriel slowly slid his hand under Mr. Hamlin's helpless back, and under pretext of arranging his bandages, lifted him in his arms like a truculent babe. "Jack," he said, softly, "ef thet picter of yours—that coloured woman"——

"Which?" said Jack, fiercely.

"I mean—thet purty creature—ef she and you hed been married, and you'd found out accidental like that she'd fooled ye—more belike, Jack," he added, hastily, "o' your own foolishness—than her little game—and"——

"*That* woman was a lady," interrupted Jack, savagely, "and your wife's a"—— But he paused, looking into Gabriel's face, and then added, "Oh git! will you! Leave me alone! 'I want to be an angel and with the angels stand.'"

"And thet woman hez a secret," continued Gabriel, unmindful of the interruption, "and bein' hounded by the man az knows it, up and kills him, ye wouldn't let thet woman—that poor pooty creeture—suffer for it! No, Jack! Ye would rather pint your own toes up to the sky than do it. It ain't in ye, Jack, and it ain't in me, so help me, God!"

"This is all very touching, Mr. Conroy, and does credit, sir, to your head and heart, and I kin feel it drawing Hall's ball out of my leg while you're talkin'," said Jack, with his black eyes evading Gabriel's and wandering to the entrance of the tunnel. "What time is it, you d—d old fool, ain't it dark enough yet to git outer this hole?" He groaned, and after a pause added fiercely, "How do you know your wife did it?"

Gabriel swiftly, and for him even concisely, related the

events of the day from his meeting with Ramirez in the morning, to the time that he had stumbled upon the body of Victor Ramirez on his return to keep the appointment at his wife's written request.

Jack only interrupted him once to inquire why, after discovering the murder, he had not gone on to keep his appointment.

"I thought it wa'n't of no use," said Gabriel, simply; "I didn't want to let her see I knowed it."

Hamlin groaned, "If you had you would have found her in the company of the man who *did* do it, you daddering old idiot!"

"What man?" asked Gabriel.

"The first man you saw your wife with that morning; the man I ought to be helping now, instead of lyin' here."

"You don't mean to allow, Jack, ez you reckon she *didn't* do it?" asked Gabriel, in alarm.

"I do," said Hamlin, coolly.

"Then what did she reckon to let on by that note?" said Gabriel, with a sudden look of cunning.

"Don't know," returned Jack, "like as not, being a d—d fool, you didn't read it right! hand it over and let me see it."

Gabriel (hesitatingly): "I can't."

Hamlin: "You can't?"

Gabriel (apologetically): "I tore it up!"

Hamlin (with frightful deliberation): "You DID?"

"I did."

Jack (after a long crushing silence): "Were you ever under medical treatment for these spells?"

Gabriel (with great simplicity and submission): "They allers used to allow I waz queer."

Hamlin (after another pause): "Has Pete Dumphy got anything agin you?"

Gabriel (surprisedly): "No."

Hamlin (languidly): "It was his right hand man, his agent at Wingdam that started up the Vigilantes! I heard him, and saw him in the crowd hounding 'em on."

Gabriel (simply): "I reckon you're out thar, Jack, Dumphy's my friend. It was him that first gin me the money to open this yer mine. And I'm his superintendent!"

Jack: "Oh!" (after another pause). "Is there any first-class Lunatic Asylum in this county where they would take in two men, one an incurable, and the other sufferin' from a gunshot wound brought on by playin' with fire-arms?"

Gabriel (with a deep sigh): "Ye mus'n't talk, Jack, ye must be quiet till dark."

Jack, dragged down by pain, and exhausted in the intervals of each paroxysm was quiescent.

Gradually, the faint light that had filtered through the brush and débris before the tunnel faded quite away, and a damp charnel-house chill struck through the limbs of the two refugees, and made them shiver; the flow of water from the dripping walls seemed to have increased; Gabriel's experienced eye had already noted that the earthquake had apparently opened seams in the gully and closed up one of the leads. He carefully laid his burden down again, and crept to the opening. The distant hum of voices and occupation had ceased, the sun was setting; in a few moments, calculating on the brief twilight of the Mountain region, it would be dark, and they might with safety leave their hiding-place. As he was returning, he noticed a slant beam of light, hitherto unobserved, crossing the tunnel from an old drift. Examining it more closely, Gabriel was amazed to find that during the earthquake a "cave" had taken place in the drift, possibly precipitated by the shock, disclosing the more surprising fact that there had been a previous slight but positive excavation on the hill side, above the tunnel, that antedated any record of One Horse Gulch known to Gabriel. He was perfectly familiar with every foot of the hill side, and the existence of this ancient prospecting "hole" had never been even suspected by him. While he was still gazing at the opening, his foot struck against some glittering metallic substance. He stooped and picked up a small tin can, not larger than a sardine box, hermetically sealed and soldered, in which some inscription had been traced, but which the darkness of the tunnel prevented his deciphering. In the faint hope that it might contain something of benefit to his companion, Gabriel returned to the opening, and even ventured to step beyond its shadow. But all attempts to read the inscription were in vain. He opened the box with a sharp stone; it contained, to his great disappointment, only a memorandum book and some papers. He swept them into the pocket of his blouse, and re-entered the tunnel. He had not been absent altogether more than five minutes, but when he reached the place where he had left Jack, he was gone!

CHAPTER IX.

IN WHICH HECTOR ARISES FROM THE DITCH.

He stood for a moment breathless and paralysed with surprise; then he began slowly and deliberately to examine the tunnel step by step. When he had proceeded a hundred feet from the spot, to his great relief he came upon Jack Hamlin, sitting upright in a side drift. His manner was feverish and excited, and his declaration that he had not moved from the place where Gabriel had left him at once was accepted by the latter as the aberration of incipient inflammation and fever. When Gabriel stated that it was time to go, he replied, "Yes," and added with such significance that his business with the murderer of Victor Ramirez was now over, and that he was ready to enter the Lunatic Asylum at once, that Gabriel with great precipitation lifted him in his arms and carried him without delay from the tunnel. Once more in the open air the energies of both men seemed to rally; Jack became as a mere feather in Gabriel's powerful arms, and even forgot his querulous opposition to being treated as a helpless child, while Gabriel trod the familiar banks of the ditch, climbed the long ascent and threaded the aisles of the pillared pines of Reservoir Hill with the free experienced feet of the mountaineer. Here Gabriel knew he was safe until daybreak, and gathered together some withered pine boughs and its fragrant tassels for a couch for his helpless companion. And here, as he feared, fever set in; the respiration of the wounded man grew quick and hurried; he began to talk rapidly and incoherently, of Olly, of Ramirez, of the beautiful girl whose picture hung upon his breast, of Gabriel himself, and finally of a stranger who was, as it seemed to him, his sole auditor, the gratuitous coinage of his excited fancy. Once or twice he raised his voice to a shout, and then to Gabriel's great alarm suddenly he began to sing, and before Gabriel could place his hand upon his mouth he had trolled out the verse of a popular ballad. The rushing river below them gurgled, beat its bars, and sang an accompaniment, the swaying pine sighed and creaked in unison, the patient stars above them stared and bent breathlessly, and then to Gabriel's exalted consciousness an echo of the wounded man's song arose from the gulch below! For a moment he held his breath with an awful mingling of joy and fear. Was he going mad too?

or was it really the voice of little Olly? The delirious man beside him answered his query with another verse; the antiphonal response rose again from the valley. Gabriel hesitated no longer, but with feverish hands gathered a few dried twigs and pine cones into a pile, and touched a match to them. At the next moment they flashed a beacon to the sky, in another there was a crackling of the under-brush and the hurried onset of two figures, and before the slow Gabriel could recover from his astonishment, Olly flew, panting, to his arms, while her companion, the faithful Pete, sank breathlessly beside his wounded and insensible master.

Olly was first to find her speech. That speech, after the unfailing instincts of her sex in moments of excitement, was the instant arraignment of somebody else as the cause of that excitement, and at once put the whole universe on the defensive.

"Why didn't you send word where you was?" she said, impatiently, "and wot did you have it so dark for, and up a steep hill, and leavin' me alone at Wingdam, and why didn't you call without singin'?"

And then Gabriel, after the fashion of *his* sex, ignored all but the present, and holding Olly in his arms, said—

"It's my little girl, ain't it? Come to her own brother Gabe! bless her!"

Whereat Mr. Hamlin, after the fashion of lunatics of any sex, must needs be consistent, and break out again into song.

"He's looney, Olly, what with fever along o' bein' shot in the leg a' savin' me, ez izn't worth savin'," explained Gabriel, apologetically. "It was him ez did the singin'."

Then Olly, still following the feminine instinct, at once deserted conscious rectitude for indefensible error, and flew to Mr. Hamlin's side.

"Oh, where is he hurt, Pete? is he going to die?"

And Pete, suspicious of any medication but his own, replied doubtfully, "He looks bad, Miss Olly, dat's a fac—but now bein' in my han's, bress de Lord A'mighty, and we able to minister to him, we hopes fur de bess. Your brudder meant well, is a fair meanin' man, miss—a toll'able nuss, but he ain't got the peerfeshn'l knowledge dat Mars Jack in de habit o' gettin'." Here Pete unslung from his shoulders a wallet, and proceeded to extract therefrom a small medicine case, with the resigned air of the family physician, who has been called full late to remedy the practice of rustic empiricism.

"How did ye come yer?" asked Gabriel of Olly, when he had submissively transferred his wounded charge to Pete. "What made ye allow I was hidin' yer? How did ye reckon to find me? but ye was allus peart and onhanded, Olly," he suggested, gazing admiringly at his sister.

"When I woke up at Wingdam, after Jack went away, who should I find, Gabe, but Lawyer Maxwell standin' thar, and askin' me a heap o' questions. I supposed you'd been makin' a fool o' yourself agin, Gabe, and afore I let on thet I knowed a word, I jist made him tell me everythin' about you, Gabe, and it was orful! and you bein' arrested fur murder, ez wouldn't harm a fly, let alone that Mexican ez I never liked, Gabe, and all this comes of tendin' his legs instead o' lookin' arter me. And all them questions waz about July, and whether she wasn't your enemy, and if they ever waz a woman, Gabe, ez waz sweet on you, you know it was July! And all thet kind o' foolishness! And then when he couldn't get ennythin' out o' me agin July, he allowed to Pete that he must take me right to you, fur he said ther was talk o' the Vigilantes gettin' hold o' ye afore the trial, and he was goin' to get an order to take you outer the county, and he reckoned they wouldn't dare to tech ye if I waz with ye, Gabe—and I'd like to see 'em try it! and he allowed to Pete that he must take me right to you! And Pete—and thar ain't a whiter nigger livin' than that ole man—said he would—reckonin' you know to find Jack, as he allowed to me they'd hev to kill afore they got you—and he came down yer with me. And when we got yer—you was off—and the sheriff gone—and the Vigilantes—what with bein' killed, the biggest o' them, by the earthquake—what was orful, Gabe, but we bein' on the road didn't get to feel!—jest scared outer their butes! And then a Chinyman gins us your note"——

"My note?" interrupted Gabriel, "I didn't send ye any note."

"Then *his* note," said Olly, impatiently, pointing to Hamlin, "sayin' 'You'll find your friends on Conroy's Hill!'—don't you see, Gabe?" continued Olly, stamping her foot in fury at her brother's slowness of comprehension, "and so we came and heard Jack singin', and a mighty foolish thing it was to do, and yer we are!"

"But he didn't send any note, Olly," persisted Gabriel.

"Well, you awful old Gabe, what difference does it make *who* sent it?" continued the practical Olly; "here we are, along o' thet note, and," she added, feeling in her pocket, "there's the note!"

She handed Gabriel a small slip of paper with the pencilled words, "You'll find your friends waiting for you to-night on Conroy's Hill."

The handwriting was unfamiliar, but even if it were Jack's, how did *he* manage to send it without his knowledge? He had not lost sight of Jack except during the few moments he had reconnoitred the mouth of the tunnel, since they had escaped from the Court House. Gabriel was perplexed; in the presence of this anonymous note he was confused and speechless, and could only pass his hand helplessly across his forehead. "But it's all right now, Gabe," continued Olly, reassuringly, "the Vigilantes hev run away—what was left of them; the sheriff ain't to be found nowhar! This yer earthquake hez frightened everybody outer the idea of huntin' ye—nobody talks of ennything but the earthquake; they even say, Gabe—I forgot to tell ye—that our claim on Conroy Hill has busted, too, and the mine ain't worth shucks now! But there's no one to interfere with us now, Gabe! And we're goin' to get into a waggin that Pete hez bespoke for us at the head of Reservoir Gulch to-morrow mornin' at sun-up! And then Pete sez we kin git down to Stockton and 'Frisco and out to a place called San Antonio, that the devil himself wouldn't think o' goin' to, and thar we kin stay, me and you and Jack, until this whole thing has blown over and Jack gits well agin and July comes back."

Gabriel, still holding the hand of his sister, dared not tell her of the suspicions of Lawyer Maxwell, regarding her sister-in-law's complicity in this murder, nor Jack's conviction of her infidelity, and he hesitated. But after a pause, he suggested with a consciousness of great discretion and artfulness, "Suppose thet July doesn't come back?"

"Look yer, Gabe," said Olly, suddenly, "ef yer goin' to be thet foolish and ridiklus agin, I'll jess quit. Ez if thet woman would ever leave ye." (Gabriel groaned inwardly.) "Why, when she hears o' this, wild hosses couldn't keep her from ye. Don't be a mule, Gabe, don't!" And Gabriel was dumb.

Meantime, under the influence of some anodyne which Pete had found in his medicine chest, Mr. Hamlin became quiet and pretermitted his vocal obligato. Gabriel, whose superb physical adjustment no mental excitement could possibly overthrow, and whose regular habits were never broken by anxiety, nodded, even while holding Olly's hand, and in due time slept, and I regret to say—writing of a hero—snored. After a while Olly herself succumbed to the drowsy coolness of the night, and wrapped in Mr. Hamlin's shawl, pillowed her head upon her brother's broad breast and slept too. Only Pete remained to keep the watch, he being comparatively fresh and strong, and declaring that the condition of Mr. Hamlin required his constant attention.

It was after midnight that Olly dreamed a troubled dream. She thought that she was riding with Mr. Hamlin to seek her brother, when she suddenly came upon a crowd of excited men who were bearing Gabriel to the gallows. She thought that she turned to Mr. Hamlin frantically for assistance, when she saw to her horror that his face had changed—that it was no longer he who sat beside her, but a strange, wild-looking, haggard man—a man whose face was old and pinched, but whose grey hair was discoloured by a faded dye that had worn away, leaving the original colour in patches, and the antique foppery of whose dress was deranged by violent exertion, and grimy with the dust of travel—a dandy whose strapped trousers of a bygone fashion were ridiculously loosened in one leg, whose high stock was unbuckled and awry! She awoke with a start. Even then her dream was so vivid that it seemed to her this face was actually bending over her with such a pathetic earnestness and inquiry that she called aloud. It was some minutes before Pete came to her, but as he averred, albeit somewhat incoherently and rubbing his eyes to show that he had not closed them, that he had never slept a wink, and that it was impossible for any stranger to have come upon them without his knowledge, Olly was obliged to accept it all as a dream! But she did not sleep again. She watched the moon slowly sink behind the serrated pines of Conroy's Hill; she listened to the crackling tread of strange animals in the underbrush, to the far-off rattle of wheels on the Wingdam turnpike, until the dark outline of the tree trunks returned, and with the cold fires of the mountain sunrise the chilly tree-tops awoke to winged life, and the twitter of birds, while the faint mists of the river lingered with the paling moon like tired sentinels for the relief of the coming day. And then Olly awoke her companions. They struggled back into consciousness with characteristic expression, Gabriel slowly and apologetically, as of one who had overslept himself; Jack Hamlin violently and aggressively, as if some unfair advantage had been taken of his human weakness that it was necessary to combat at once. I am sorry to say that his recognition of Pete was accompanied by a degree of profanity and irreverence that was dangerous to his own physical weakness. "And you had to trapse down yer, sniffin' about my tracks, you black and tan idiot," continued Mr. Hamlin, raising himself on his arm, "and after I'd left everything all straight at Wingdam—and jest as I was beginning to reform and lead a new life! How do, Olly? You'll excuse my not rising. Come and kiss me! If that nigger of mine has let you want for anything, jest tell me and I'll discharge him. Well! hang it all! what are you waitin' for? Here it's daybreak and we've got to get down to the head of Reservoir Gulch. Come, little children, the picnic is over!"

Thus adjured, Gabriel rose, and lifting Mr. Hamlin in his arms with infinite care and tenderness, headed the quaint procession. Mr. Hamlin, perhaps recognising some absurdity in the situation, forbore exercising his querulous profanity on the man who held him helpless as an infant, and Olly and Pete followed slowly behind.

Their way led down Reservoir Cañon, beautiful, hopeful,

and bracing in the early morning air. A few birds, awakened by the passing tread, started into song a moment, and then were still. With a cautious gentleness, habitual to the man, Gabriel forbore, as he strode along, to step upon the few woodland blossoms yet left to the dry summer woods. There was a strange fragrance in the air, the light odours liberated from a thousand nameless herbs, the faint melancholy spicing of dead leaves. There was, moreover, that sense of novelty which Nature always brings with the dawn in deep forests; a fancy that during the night the earth had been created anew, and was fresh from the Maker's hand, as yet untried by burden or tribulation, and guiltless of a Past. And so it seemed to the little caravan —albeit fleeing from danger and death—that yesterday and its fears were far away, or had, in some unaccountable way, shrunk behind them in the west with the swiftly dwindling night. Olly once or twice strayed from the trail to pick an opening flower or lingering berry; Pete hummed to himself the fragment of an old camp-meeting song.

And so they walked on, keeping the rosy dawn and its promise before them. From time to time the sound of far-off voices came to them faintly. Slowly the light quickened; morning stole down the hills upon them stealthily, and at last the entrance of the cañon became dimly outlined. Olly uttered a shout and pointed to a black object moving backward and forward before the opening. It was the waggon and team awaiting them. Olly's shout was answered by a whistle from the driver, and they quickened their pace joyfully; in another moment they would be beyond the reach of danger.

Suddenly a voice that seemed to start from the ground before them called on Gabriel to stop! He did so unconsciously, drawing Hamlin closer to him with one hand, and with the other making a broad protecting sweep toward

Olly. And then a figure rose slowly from the ditch at the roadside and barred their passage.

It was only a single man! A small man bespattered with the slime of the ditch and torn with brambles; a man exhausted with fatigue and tremulous with nervous excitement, but still erect and threatening. A man whom Gabriel and Hamlin instantly recognised, even through his rags and exhaustion! It was Joe Hall—the sheriff of Calaveras! He held a pistol in his right hand, even while his left exhaustedly sought the support of a tree! By a common instinct both men saw that while the hand was feeble the muzzle of the weapon covered them.

"Gabriel Conroy, I want you," said the apparition.

"He's got us lined! Drop me," whispered Hamlin, hastily, "drop me! I'll spoil his aim."

But Gabriel, by a swift, dexterous movement that seemed incompatible with his usual deliberation, instantly transferred Hamlin to his other arm, and with his burden completely shielded, presented his own right shoulder squarely to the muzzle of Hall's revolver.

"Gabriel Conroy, you are my prisoner," repeated the voice.

Gabriel did not move. But over his shoulder as a rest, dropped the long shining barrel of Jack's own favourite duelling pistol, and over it glanced the bright eye of its crippled owner. The issue was joined!

There was a deathlike silence.

"Go on!" said Jack, quietly. "Keep cool, Joe. For if *you* miss him, you're gone in; and hit or miss *I've* got *you* sure!"

The barrel of Hall's pistol wavered a moment, from physical weakness but not from fear. The great heart behind it, though broken, was undaunted.

"It's all right," said the voice fatefully. "It's all right,

Jack! Ye'll kill me, I know! But ye can't help sayin' arter all that I did my duty to Calaveras as the sheriff, and 'specially to them twenty-five men ez elected me over Boggs! I ain't goin' to let ye pass. I've been on this yer hunt, up and down this cañon all night. Hevin' no possy I reckon I've got to die yer in my tracks. All right! But ye'll git into thet waggon over my dead body, Jack—over my dead body, sure."

Even as he spoke these words he straightened himself to his full height—which was not much, I fear—and steadied himself by the tree, his weapon still advanced and pointing at Gabriel, but with such an evident and hopeless contrast between his determination and his evident inability to execute it, that his attitude impressed his audience less with its heroism than its half-pathetic absurdity.

Mr. Hamlin laughed. But even then he suddenly felt the grasp of Gabriel relax, found himself slipping to his companion's feet, and the next moment was deposited carefully but ignominiously on the ground by Gabriel, who strode quietly and composedly up to the muzzle of the sheriff's pistol.

"I am ready to go with ye, Mr. Hall," he said, gently, putting the pistol aside with a certain large indifferent wave of the hand, "ready to go with ye—now—at onct! But I've one little favour to ax ye. This yer pore young man, ez yur wounded, unbeknownst," he said, pointing to Hamlin, who was writhing and gritting his teeth in helpless rage and fury, "ez not to be tuk with me, nor for me! Thar ain't nothin' to be done to him. He hez been dragged inter this fight. But I'm ready to go with ye now, Mr. Hall, and am sorry you got into the troubil along o' me."

BOOK VII.

THE BED ROCK.

CHAPTER I.

IN THE TRACK OF A STORM.

A QUARTER of an hour before the messenger of Peter Dumphy had reached Poinsett's office, Mr. Poinsett had received a more urgent message. A telegraph despatched from San Antonio had been put into his hands. Its few curt words, more significant to an imaginative man than rhetorical expression, ran as follows:—

"Mission Church destroyed. Father Felipe safe. Blessed Trinity in ruins and Dolores missing. My house spared. Come at once.—MARIA SEPULVIDA."

The following afternoon at four o'clock Arthur Poinsett reached San Geronimo, within fifteen miles of his destination. Here the despatch was confirmed with some slight local exaggeration.

"Saints and devils! There is no longer a St. Anthony! The *temblor* has swallowed him!" said the innkeeper, sententiously. "It is the end of all! Such is the world. Thou wilt find stones on stones instead of houses, Don Arturo. Wherefore another glass of the brandy of France, or the whisky of the American, as thou dost prefer. But of San Antonio—nothing!—Absolutely—perfectly—truly nothing!"

In spite of this cheering prophecy, Mr. Poinsett did not wait for the slow diligence, but mounting a fleet mustang dashed off in quest of the missing Mission. He was somewhat relieved at the end of an hour by the far-off flash of the sea, the rising of the dark green fringe of the Mission orchard and *Encinal*, and above it the white dome of one of the Mission towers. But at the next moment Arthur checked his horse and rubbed his eyes in wonder. Where was the other tower? He put spurs to his horse again and dashed off at another angle, and again stopped and gazed. *There was but one tower remaining.* The Mission Church must have been destroyed!

Perhaps it was this discovery, perhaps it was some instinct stronger than this; but when Arthur had satisfied himself of this fact he left the direct road, which would have brought him to the Mission, and diverged upon the open plain towards the Rancho of the Blessed Trinity. A fierce wind from the sea swept the broad *llano* and seemed to oppose him, step by step—a wind so persistent and gratuitous that it appeared to Arthur to possess a moral quality, and as such was to be resisted and overcome by his superior will. Here, at least, all was unchanged; here was the dead, flat monotony of land and sky. Here was the brittle, harsh stubble of the summer fields, sun-baked and wind-dried; here were the long stretches of silence, from which even the harrying wind made no opposition nor complaint; here were the formless specks of slowly-moving cattle, even as he remembered them before. A momentary chill came over him as he recalled his own perilous experience on these plains, a momentary glow suffused his cheek as he thought of his rescue by the lovely but cold recluse. Again he heard the name of "Philip" softly whispered in his ears, again he felt the flood of old memories sweep over him as he rode, even as he had felt them when he lay that day panting upon the earth. And yet Arthur had long since convinced his mind that he was mistaken in supposing that Donna Dolores had addressed him at that extreme moment as "Philip;" he had long since believed it was a trick of his disordered and exhausted brain; the conduct of Dolores towards himself, habitually restrained by grave courtesy, never justified him in directly asking the question, nor suggested any familiarity that might have made it probable. She had never alluded to it again—but had apparently forgotten it. Not so Arthur! He had often gone over that memorable scene, with a strange, tormenting pleasure that was almost a pain. It was the one incident of his life, for whose poetry he was not immediately responsible—the one genuine heart-thrill whose sincerity he had not afterwards stopped to question in his critical fashion, the one enjoyment that had not afterwards appeared mean and delusive. And now the heroine of this episode was missing, and he might never perhaps see her again! And yet when he first heard the news he was conscious of a strange sense of relief—rather let me say of an awakening from a dream, that though delicious, had become dangerous and might unfit him for the practical duties of his life. Donna Dolores had never affected him as a real personage—at least the interest he felt in her was, he had always considered, due to her relations to some romantic condition of his mind, and her final disappearance from the plane of his mental vision was only the exit of an actress from the mimic stage. It seemed only natural that she should disappear as mysteriously as she came. There was no shock even to the instincts of his ordinary humanity—it was no catastrophe involving loss of life or even suffering to the subject or spectator.

Such at least was Mr. Poinsett's analysis of his own

mental condition on the receipt of Donna Maria's telegram. It was the cool self-examination of a man who believed himself cold-blooded and selfish, superior to the weakness of ordinary humanity, and yet was conscious of neither pride nor disgrace in the belief. Yet when he diverged from his direct road to the Mission, and turned his horse's head toward the home of Donna Dolores, he was conscious of a new impulse and anxiety that was stronger than his reason. Unable as he was to resist it, he still took some satisfaction in believing that it was nearly akin to that feeling which years before had driven him back to Starvation Camp in quest of the survivors. Suddenly his horse recoiled with a bound that would have unseated a less skilful rider. Directly across his path stretched a chasm in the level plain—thirty feet broad and as many feet in depth, and at its bottom in undistinguishable confusion lay the wreck of the corral of the Blessed Trinity!

Except for the enormous size and depth of this fissure Arthur might have mistaken it for the characteristic cracks in the sun-burnt plain, which the long dry summer had wrought upon its surface, some of which were so broad as to task the agility of his horse. But a second glance convinced him of the different character of the phenomenon. The earth had not cracked asunder nor separated, but had sunk. The width of the chasm below was nearly equal to the width above; the floor of this valley in miniature was carpeted by the same dry, brittle herbs and grasses which grew upon the plain around him.

In the pre-occupation of the last hour he had forgotten the distance he had traversed. He had evidently ridden faster than he had imagined. But if this was really the corral, the walls of the Rancho should now be in sight at the base of the mountain! He turned in that direction. Nothing was to be seen! Only the monotonous plain stretched before him, vast and unbroken. Between the chasm where he stood and the *falda* of the first low foothills neither roof nor wall nor ruin rose above the dull, dead level!

An ominous chill ran through his veins, and for an instant the reins slipped through his relaxed fingers. Good God! Could this have been what Donna Maria meant, or had there been a later convulsion of Nature? He looked around him. The vast, far-stretching plain, desolate and trackless as the shining ocean beyond, took upon itself an awful likeness to that element! Standing on the brink of the revealed treachery of that yawning chasm, Arthur Poinsett read the fate of the Rancho. In the storm that had stirred the depths of this motionless level, the Rancho and its miserable inmates had *foundered* and gone down!

Arthur's first impulse was to push on towards the scene of the disaster, in the vague hope of rendering some service. But the chasm before him was impassable, and seemed to continue to the sea beyond. Then he reflected that the catastrophe briefly told in Donna Maria's despatch had happened twenty-four hours before, and help was perhaps useless now. He cursed the insane impulse that had brought him here, aimlessly and without guidance, and left him powerless even to reach the object of his quest. If he had only gone first to the Mission, asked the advice and assistance of Father Felipe, or learned at least the full details of the disaster! He uttered an oath, rare to his usual calm expression, and wheeling his horse, galloped fiercely back towards the Mission.

Night had deepened over the plain. With the going down of the sun a fog that had been stealthily encompassing the coast-line stole with soft step across the shining beach, dulled its lustre, and then moved slowly and solemnly upon the plain, blotting out the Point of Pines, at first salient with its sparkling Lighthouse, but now undistinguishable from the grey sea above and below, until it reached the galloping horse and its rider, and then, as it seemed to Arthur, isolated them from the rest of the world —from even the pencilled outlines of the distant foot-hills, that it at last sponged from the blue-grey slate before him. At times the far-off tolling of a fog-bell came faintly to his ear, but all sound seemed to be blotted out by the fog; even the rapid fall of his horse's hoofs was muffled and indistinct. By degrees the impression that he was riding in a dream overcame him, and was accepted by him without questioning or deliberation.

It seemed to be a consistent part of the dream or vision when he rode—or rather as it seemed to him, was borne by the fog—into the outlying fields and lanes of the Mission. A few lights, with a nimbus of fog around them, made the narrow street of the town appear still more ghostly and unreal as he plunged through its obscurity towards the plaza and church. Even by the dim grey light he could see that one of the towers had fallen, and that the eastern wing and Refectory were a mass of shapeless ruin. And what would at another time have excited his surprise now only struck him as a natural part of his dream,—the church a blaze of light and filled with thronging worshippers! Still possessed by his strange fancy, Arthur Poinsett dismounted, led his horse beneath the shed beside the remaining tower, and entered the building. The body and nave of the church were intact; the outlandish paintings still hung from the walls; the waxen effigies of the Blessed Virgin and the saints still leaned from their niches, yellow and lank, and at the high altar Father Felipe was officiating. As he entered a dirge broke from the choir; he saw that the altar and its offerings were draped in black, and in the first words uttered by the priest Arthur recognised the mass for the dead! The feverish impatience that had filled his breast and heightened the colour of his cheeks for the last hour was gone. He sunk upon a bench beside one of the worshippers and buried his face in his hands. The voice of the organ rose again faintly; the quaint-voiced choir awoke, the fumes of incense filled the church, and the monotonous accents of the priest fell soothingly upon his ear, and Arthur seemed to sleep. I say seemed to sleep, for ten minutes later he came to himself with a start as if awakening from a troubled dream, with the voice of Padre Felipe in his ear, and the soft, caressing touch of Padre Felipe on his shoulder. The worshippers had dispersed, the church was dark save a few candles still burning on the high altar, and for an instant he could not recall himself.

"I knew you would come, son," said Padre Felipe; "but where is she? Did you bring her with you?"

"Who?" asked Arthur, striving to recall his scattered senses.

"Who? Saints preserve us, Don Arturo! She who sent for you—Donna Maria! Did you not get her message?"

Arthur replied that he had only just arrived, and had at once hastened to the Mission. For some reason that he was ashamed to confess he did not say that he had tried to reach the Rancho of the Blessed Trinity, nor did he admit that he had forgotten for the last two hours even the existence of Donna Maria. "You were having a mass for the dead, Father Felipe?—you have then suffered here?"

He paused anxiously, for in his then confused state of mind he doubted how much of his late consciousness had been real or visionary.

"Mother of God," said Father Felipe, eyeing Arthur curiously. "You know not then for whom was this mass?

You know not that a saint has gone—that Donna Dolores has at last met her reward?"

"I have heard—that is, Donna Maria's despatch said—that she was missing," stammered Arthur, feeling, with a new and unsupportable disbelief in himself, that his face was very pale and his voice uncertain.

"Missing!" echoed Father Felipe, with the least trace of impatience in his voice. "Missing! She will be found when the Rancho of the Blessed Trinity is restored—when the ruins of the *casa*, sunk fifty feet below the surface, are brought again to the level of the plain. Missing, Don Arturo!—ah!—missing indeed!—for ever! always, entirely!"

Moved perhaps by something in Arthur's face, Padre Felipe sketched in a few graphic pictures the details of the catastrophe already forecast by Arthur. It was a repetition of the story of the sunken corral. The earthquake had not only levelled the walls of the Rancho of the Blessed Trinity, but had opened a grave-like chasm fifty feet below it, and none had escaped to tell the tale. The faithful *vaqueros* had rushed from the trembling and undulating plain to the Rancho, only to see it topple into a yawning abyss that opened to receive it. Don Juan, Donna Dolores, the faithful Manuela, and Alejandro, the *major domo*, with a dozen peons and retainers, went down with the crumbling walls. No one had escaped. Was it not possible to dig in the ruins for the bodies? Mother of God! had not Don Arturo been told that the earth at the second shock had closed over the sunken ruins, burying beyond mortal resurrection all that the Rancho contained? They were digging, but hopelessly—a dozen men. They might—weeks hence—discover the bodies—but who knows?

The meek, fatalistic way that Father Felipe accepted the final doom of Donna Dolores exasperated Arthur beyond bounds. In San Francisco a hundred men would have been digging night and day in the mere chance of recovering the buried family. Here—but Arthur remembered the sluggish, helpless retainers of Salvatierra, the dreadful fatalism which affected them on the occurrence of this mysterious catastrophe, even as shown in the man before him, their accepted guide and leader—and shuddered. Could anything be done? Could he not, with Dumphy's assistance, procure a gang of men from San Francisco? And then came the instinct of caution, always powerful with a nature like Arthur's. If these people, most concerned in the loss of their friends, their relations, accepted it so hopelessly, what right had he—a mere stranger—to interfere?

"But come, my son," said Padre Felipe, laying his large soft hand, parentally, on Arthur's shoulder. "Come, come with me to my rooms. Thanks to the Blessed Virgin I have still shelter and a roof to offer you. Ah!" he added, stroking Arthur's riding-coat, and examining critically as if he had been a large child, "what have we—what is this, eh? You are wet with this heretic fog—eh? Your hands are cold, and your cheeks hot. You have fatigue! Possibly—most possibly, hunger! No! No! It is so. Come with me, come!" and drawing Arthur's passive arm through his own, he opened the vestry door, and led him across the little garden, choked with débris and plaster of the fallen tower, to a small adobe building that had been the Mission schoolroom. It was now hastily fitted up as Padre Felipe's own private apartment and meditative cell. A bright fire burned in the low, oven-like hearth. Around the walls hung various texts illustrating the achievement of youthful penmanship with profound religious instruction. At the extremity of the room there was a small organ. Midway and opposite the hearth was a deep embrasured window—the window at which two weeks before. Mr. Jack Hamlin had beheld the Donna Dolores. "She spent much of her time here, dear child, in the instruction of the young," said Father Felipe, taking a huge pinch of snuff, and applying a large red bandana handkerchief to his eyes and nose. "It is her best monument! Thanks to her largess—and she was ever free-handed, Don Arturo, to the Church—the foundation of the Convent of our Lady of Sorrows, her own patron saint, thou seest here. Thou knowest, possibly—most possibly as her legal adviser—that long ago, by her will, the whole of the Salvatierra Estate is a benefactiòn to the Holy Church, eh?"

"No, I don't!" said Arthur, suddenly, awakening with a glow of Protestant and heretical objection that was new to him, and eyeing Padre Felipe with the first glance of suspicion he had ever cast upon that venerable ecclesiastic. "No, sir, I never heard any intimation or suggestion of the kind from the late Donna Dolores. On the contrary, I was engaged"——

"Pardon—pardon me, my son," interrupted Father Felipe, taking another large pinch of snuff. "It is not now, scarce twenty-four hours since the dear child was translated—not in her masses and while her virgin strewments are not yet faded—that we will talk of this" (he blew his nose violently). "No! All in good time—thou shalt see! But I have something here," he continued, turning over some letters and papers in his desk. "Something for you—possibly, most possibly, more urgent. It is a telegraphic despatch for you, to my care."

He handed a yellow envelope to Arthur. But Poinsett's eyes were suddenly fixed upon a card which lay upon Padre Felipe's table, and which the Padre's search for the despatch had disclosed. Written across its face was the name of Colonel Culpepper Starbottle of Siskiyou! "Do you know that man?" asked Poinsett, holding the despatch unopened in his hand, and pointing to the card.

Father Felipe took another pinch of snuff. "Possibly—most possibly! A lawyer, I think—I think! Some business of the Church property! I have forgotten. But your despatch, Don Arturo. What says it? It does not take you from us? And you—only an hour here?"

Father Felipe paused, and looking up innocently, found the eyes of Arthur regarding him gravely. The two men examined each other intently. Arthur's eyes, at last, withdrew from the clear, unshrinking glance of Padre Felipe, unabashed but unsatisfied. A sudden recollection of the thousand and one scandals against the Church, and wild stories of its far-reaching influence—a swift remembrance of the specious craft and cunning charged upon the religious order of which Padre Felipe was a member—scandals that he had hitherto laughed at as idle—flashed through his mind. Conscious that he was now putting himself in a guarded attitude before the man with whom he had always been free and outspoken, Arthur, after a moment's embarrassment that was new to him, turned for relief to the despatch and opened it. In an instant it drove all other thoughts from his mind. Its few words were from Dumphy and ran, characteristically, as follows: "Gabriel Conroy arrested for murder of Victor Ramirez. What do you propose? Answer."

Arthur rose to his feet. "When does the up-stage pass through San Geronimo?" he asked, hurriedly.

"At midnight!" returned Padre Felipe. "Surely, my son, you do not intend"——

"And it is now nine o'clock," continued Arthur, consulting his watch. "Can you procure me a fresh horse? It is of the greatest importance, Father," he added, recovering his usual frankness.

"Ah! it is urgent!—it is a matter"—— suggested the Padre, gently.

"Of life and death!" responded Arthur gravely.

Father Felipe rang a bell and gave some directions to a servant, while Arthur, seating himself at the table, wrote an answer to the despatch. "I can trust you to send it as soon as possible to the telegraph office," he said, handing it to Father Felipe.

The Padre took it in his hand, but glanced anxiously at Arthur. "And Donna Maria?" he said, hesitatingly; "you have not seen her yet! Surely you will stop at the Blessed Fisherman, if only for a moment, eh?"

Arthur drew his riding-coat and cape over his shoulders with a mischievous smile. "I am afraid not, Father; I shall trust to you to explain that I was recalled suddenly, and that I had not time to call; knowing the fascinations of your society, Father, she will not begrudge the few moments I have spent with you."

Before Father Felipe could reply the servant entered with the announcement that the horse was ready.

"Good-night, Father Felipe," said Arthur, pressing the priest's hands warmly, with every trace of his former suspiciousness gone. "Good night. A thousand thanks for the horse. In speeding the parting guest," he added, gravely, "you have perhaps done more for the health of my soul than you imagine—good-night. *Adios!*"

With a light laugh in his ears, the vision of a graceful, erect figure, waving a salute from a phantom steed, an inward rush of the cold grey fog, and muffled clatter of hoofs over the mouldy and mossy marbles in the churchyard, Father Felipe parted from his guest. He uttered a characteristic adjuration, took a pinch of snuff, and closing the door, picked up the card of the gallant Colonel Starbottle and tossed it into the fire.

But the perplexities of the holy Father ceased not with the night. At an early hour in the morning, Donna Maria Sepulvida appeared before him at breakfast, suspicious, indignant, and irate.

"Tell me, Father Felipe," she said, hastily, "did the Don Arturo pass the night here?"

"Truly no, my daughter," answered the Padre, cautiously. "He was here but for a little"——

"And he went away when?" interrupted Donna Maria.

"At nine."

"And where?" continued Donna Maria, with a rising colour.

"To San Francisco, my child; it was business of great importance—but sit down, sit, little one! This impatience is of the devil, daughter, you must calm yourself."

"And do you know, Father Felipe, that he went away without coming *near me?*" continued Donna Maria, in a higher key, scarcely heeding her ghostly confessor.

"Possibly, most possibly! But he received a despatch—it was of the greatest importance."

"A despatch!" repeated Donna Maria, scornfully. "Truly—from whom?"

"I know not, my child," said Father Felipe, gazing at the pink cheeks, indignant eyes, and slightly swollen eyelids of his visitor; "this impatience—this anger is most unseemly."

"Was it from Mr. Dumphy?" reiterated Donna Maria, stamping her little foot.

Father Felipe drew back his chair. Through what unhallowed spell had this woman—once the meekest and humblest of wives—become the shrillest and most shrewest of widows? Was she about to revenge herself on Arthur for her long suffering with the late Don José? Father Felipe pitied Arthur now and prospectively.

"Are you going to tell me?" said Donna Maria, tremulously, with alarming symptoms of hysteria.

"I believe it was from Mr. Dumphy," stammered Padre Felipe. "At least the answer Don Arturo gave me to send in reply—only these words, 'I will return at once'—was addressed to Mr. Dumphy. But I know not what was the message *he* received."

"You don't!" said Donna Maria, rising to her feet, with white in her cheek, fire in her eyes, and a stridulous pitch in her voice. "You don't! Well! I will tell you! It was the same news that *this* brought." She took a telegraphic despatch from her pocket and shook it in the face of Father Felipe. "There! read it! That was the news sent to him! That was the reason why he turned and ran away like a coward as he is! That was the reason why he never came near me, like a perjured traitor as he is! That is the reason why he came to you with his fastidious airs and his supercilious smile—and his—his—Oh, how I HATE HIM! That is why!—read it! read it! Why don't you read it?" (She had been gesticulating with it, waving it in the air wildly, and evading every attempt of Father Felipe to take it from her.) "Read it! Read it and see why! Read and see that I am ruined!—a beggar!—a cajoled and tricked and deceived woman—between these two villains, Dumphy and Mis—ter—Arthur—Poin—sett! Ah! Read it—or are you a traitor too? You and Dolores and all"——

She crumpled the paper in her hands, threw it on the floor, whitened suddenly round the lips, and then followed the paper as suddenly, at full length, in a nervous spasm at Father Felipe's feet. Father Felipe gazed, first at the paper and then at the rigid form of his friend. He was a man, an old one—with some experience of the sex, and I regret to say he picked up the *paper* first, and straightened *it* out. It was a telegraphic despatch in the following words:—

"Sorry to say telegram just received that earthquake has dropped out lead of Conroy Mine! Everything gone up! Can't make further advances or sell stock.—DUMPHY."

Father Felipe bent over Donna Maria and raised her in his arms. "Poor little one!" he said. "But I don't think Arthur knew it."

CHAPTER II.

THE YELLOW ENVELOPE

FOR once, by a cruel irony, the adverse reports regarding the stability of the Conroy mine were true. A few stockholders still clung to the belief that it was a fabrication to depress the stock, but the fact as stated in Mr. Dumphy's despatch to Donna Maria was in possession of the public. The stock fell to $35, to $30, to $10—to nothing! An hour after the earthquake it was known in One Horse Gulch that the "lead" had "dropped" suddenly, and that a veil of granite of incalculable thickness had been upheaved between the seekers and the treasure, now lost in the mysterious depths below. The vein was gone! Where?—no one could tell. There were various theories, more or less learned: there was one party who believed in the "subsidence" of the vein, another who believed in the "interposition" of the granite, but all tending to the same conclusion—the inaccessibility of the treasure. Science pointed with stony finger to the evidence of previous phenomena of the same character visible throughout the Gulch. But the grim "I told you so" of Nature was, I fear, no more satisfactory to the dwellers of One Horse Gulch than the ordinary prophetic distrust of common humanity.

The news spread quickly and far. It overtook several wandering Californians in Europe, and sent them to their bankers with anxious faces; it paled the cheeks of one or two guardians of orphan children, frightened several widows, drove a confidential clerk into shameful exile, and struck Mr. Raynor in Boston with such consternation, that people for the first time suspected that he had backed his opinion of the resources of California with capital. Throughout the length and breadth of the Pacific slope it produced a movement of aggression which the earthquake had hitherto failed to cover. The probabilities of danger to life and limb by a recurrence of the shock had been dismissed from the public consideration, but this actual loss of characteristic property awakened the gravest anxiety. If Nature claimed the privilege of at any time withdrawing from that implied contract under which so many of California's best citizens had occupied and improved the country, it was high time that something should be done. Thus spake an intelligent and unfettered press. A few old residents talked of returning to the East.

During this excitement Mr. Dumphy bore himself toward the world generally with perfect self-confidence, and, if anything, an increased aggressiveness. His customers dared not talk of their losses before him, or exhibit a stoicism unequal to his own.

"It's a bad business," he would say; "what do you propose?" And as the one latent proposition in each human breast was the return of the money invested, and as no one dared to make that proposition, Mr. Dumphy was, as usual, triumphant. In this frame of mind Mr. Poinsett found him on his return from the Mission of San Antonio, the next morning.

"Bad news, I suppose, down there," said Mr. Dumphy, briskly; "and I reckon the widow, though she has been luckier than her neighbours, don't feel particularly lively, eh? I'm devilish sorry for you, Poinsett, though, as a man, you can see that the investment was a good one. But you can't make a woman understand business. Eh? Well, the Rancho's worth double the mortgage, I reckon. Eh? Ugly, ain't she—of course! Said she'd been swindled? That's like a woman! You and me know 'em! eh, Poinsett?" Mr. Dumphy emitted his characteristic bark, and winked at his visitor.

Arthur looked up in unaffected surprise. "If you mean Mrs. Sepulvida," he said, coldly, "I haven't seen her. I was on my way there when your telegram recalled me. I had some business with Padre Felipe."

"You don't know then that the Conroy mine has gone up with the earthquake, eh? Lead dropped out—eh? and the widow's fifty-six thousand?"—here Mr. Dumphy snapped his finger and thumb, to illustrate the lame and impotent conclusion of Donna Maria's investment—"don't you know that?"

"No," said Arthur, with perfect indifference and a languid abstraction that awed Mr. Dumphy more than anxiety; "no, I don't. But I imagine that isn't the reason you telegraphed me."

"No," returned Dumphy, still eyeing Poinsett keenly for a possible clue to this singular and unheard-of apathy to the condition of the fortune of the woman his visitor was about to marry. "No—of course!"

"Well!" said Arthur, with that dangerous quiet which was the only outward sign of interest and determination in his nature. "I'm going up to One Horse Gulch to offer my services as counsel to Gabriel Conroy. Now for the details of this murder, which, by the way, I don't believe Gabriel committed, unless he's another man than the one I knew! After that you can tell me *your* business with me, for I don't suppose you telegraphed to me on his account solely. Of course, at first you felt it was to your interest to get him and his wife out of the way, now that Ramirez is gone. But now, if you please, let me know what *you* know about this murder."

Mr. Dumphy thus commanded, and completely under the influence of Arthur's quiet will, briefly recounted the particulars already known to the reader, of which he had been kept informed by telegraph.

"He's been recaptured," added Dumphy, "I learn by a later despatch; and I don't reckon there'll be another attempt to lynch him. I've managed *that,*" he continued, with a return of his old self-assertion. "I've got some influence there!"

For the first time during the interview Arthur awoke from his pre-occupation, and glanced keenly at Dumphy. "Of course," he returned, coolly, "I don't suppose you such a fool as to allow the only witness you have of your wife's death to be sacrificed—even if you believed that the impostor who was personating your wife had been charged with complicity in a capital crime and had fled from justice. You're not such a fool as to believe that this Mrs. Conroy won't try to help her husband, that she evidently loves, by every means in her power—that she won't make use of any secret she may have that concerns you to save him and herself. No, Mr. Peter Dumphy," said Arthur significantly; "no, you're too much of a business man not to see that." As he spoke he noted the alternate flushing and paling of Mr. Dumphy's face, and read—I fear with the triumphant and instinctive consciousness of a superior intellect—that Mr. Dumphy *had* been precisely such a fool, and had failed!

"I reckon nobody will put much reliance on the evidence of a woman charged with a capital crime," said Mr. Dumphy, with a show of confidence he was far from feeling.

"Suppose that she and Gabriel both swear that *she* knows your abandoned wife, for instance; suppose that they both swear that she and you connived to personate Grace Conroy for the sake of getting the title to this mine; suppose that she alleges that she repented and married Gabriel, as she did, and suppose that they both admit the killing of this Ramirez—and assert that you were persecuting them through him, and still are; suppose that they show that he forged a second grant to the mine—through *your* instigation?"

"It's a lie," interrupted Dumphy, starting to his feet; "he did it from jealousy."

"Can you *prove* his motives?" said Arthur.

"But the grant was not in my favour—it was to some old Californian down in the Mission of San Antonio. I can prove that," said Dumphy, excitedly.

"Suppose you can? Nobody imagines you so indiscreet as to have had another grant conveyed to *you directly*, while you were negotiating with Gabriel for *his*. Don't be foolish! *I* know you had nothing to do with the forged grant. I am only suggesting how you have laid yourself open to the charges of a woman of whom you are likely to make an enemy, and might have made an ally. If you calculate to revenge Ramirez, consider first if you care to have it proved that he was a confidential agent of yours—as they will, if you don't help *them*. Never mind whether they committed the murder. You are not their judge or accuser. You must help them for your own sake. No!" continued Arthur, after a pause, "congratulate yourself that the Vigilance Committee did not hang Gabriel Conroy, and that you have not to add revenge to the other motives of a desperate and scheming woman."

"But are you satisfied that Mrs. Conroy *is* really the person who stands behind Colonel Starbottle and personates my wife?"

"I am," replied Arthur, positively.

Dumphy hesitated a moment. Should he tell Arthur of Colonel Starbottle's interview with him, and the delivery and subsequent loss of the mysterious envelope?" Arthur read his embarrassment plainly, and precipitated his decision with a single question.

"Have you had any further interview with Colonel Starbottle?"

Thus directly adjured, Dumphy hesitated no longer, but at once repeated the details of his late conversation with Starbottle, his successful bribery of the Colonel, the delivery of the sealed envelope under certain conditions, and its mysterious disappearance. Arthur heard him through with quiet interest, but when Mr. Dumphy spoke of the loss of the envelope, he fixed his eyes on Mr. Dumphy's with a significance that was unmistakable.

"You say you lost this envelope trusted to your honour!" said Arthur, with slow and insulting deliberation. "Lost it, without having opened it or learned its contents? That was very unfortunate, Mr. Dumphy, ve-ry un-for-tu-nate!"

The indignation of an honourable man at the imputation of some meanness foreign to his nature is weak compared with the anger of a rascal accused of an offence which he might have committed, but didn't. Mr. Dumphy turned almost purple! It was so evident that he had not been guilty of concealing the envelope, and did not know its contents, that Arthur was satisfied.

"He denied any personal knowledge of Mrs. Conroy in this affair?" queried Arthur.

"Entirely! He gave me to understand that his instructions were received from another party unknown to me," said Dumphy. "Look yer, Poinsett—you're wrong! I don't believe it is that woman."

Arthur shook his head. "No one else possesses the information necessary to blackmail you. No one else has a motive in doing it."

The door opened to a clerk bearing a card. Mr. Dumphy took it impatiently and read aloud, "Colonel Starbottle of Siskiyou!" He then turned an anxious face to Poinsett.

"Good," said that gentleman, quietly; "admit him." As the clerk disappeared, Arthur turned to Dumphy, "I suppose it was to meet this man you sent for me?"

"Yes," returned Dumphy, with a return of his old brusqueness.

"Then hold your tongue, and leave everything to me."

The door opened as he spoke to Colonel Starbottle's frilled shirt and expanding bosom, followed at a respectful interval by the gallant Colonel himself. He was evidently surprised by the appearance of Mr. Dumphy's guest, but by no means dashed in his usual chivalrous port and bearing. "My legal adviser, Mr. Poinsett," said Dumphy, introducing Arthur briefly.

The gallant Colonel bowed stiffly, while Arthur, with a smile of fascinating courtesy and deference that astonished Dumphy in proportion as it evidently flattered and gratified Colonel Starbottle, stepped forward and extended his hand. "As a younger member of the profession I can hardly claim the attention of one so experienced as Colonel Starbottle, but as the friend of poor Henry Beeswinger, I can venture to take the hand of the man who so gallantly stood by him as his second, two years ago."

"Ged, sir," said Colonel Starbottle, absolutely empurpling with pleasure, and exploding his handkerchief from his sweltering breast. "Ged! you—er—er—do me proud! I am—er—gratified, sir, to meet any friend of—er—er—gentleman like Hank Beeswinger! I remember the whole affair, sir, as if it was yesterday. I do!" with an oath.

"Gratifying, Mr. Poinsett, to every gentleman concerned. Your friend, sir,—I'm proud to meet you—I am,—— me!—killed, sir, second fire! Dropped like a gentleman, ——me! No fuss; no reporters; no arrests. Friends considerate. Blank me, sir, one of the finest, d—— me, I may say, sir, one of the very finest—er—meetings in which I have—er—participated. Glad to know you, sir. You call to mind, sir, one of the—er—highest illustrations of a code of honour—that—er—er—under the present—er—degrading state of public sentiment is—er—er—passing away. We are drifting, sir, drifting—drifting to er—er—political and social condition, where the Voice of Honour, sir, is drowned by the Yankee watchword of Produce and Trade. Trade, sir, blank me!" Colonel Starbottle paused with a rhetorical full stop, blew his nose, and gazed at the ceiling with a plaintive suggestion that the days of chivalry had indeed passed, and that American institutions were indeed retrograding; Mr. Dumphy leaned back in his chair in helpless irritability; Mr. Arthur Poinsett alone retained an expression of courteous and sympathising attention.

"I am the more gratified at meeting Colonel Starbottle," said Arthur, gravely, "from the fact that my friend and client here, Mr. Dumphy, is at present in a condition where he most needs the consideration and understanding of a gentleman and a man of honour. A paper, which has been entrusted to his safe keeping and custody as a gentleman, has disappeared since the earthquake, and it is believed that during the excitement of that moment it was lost! The paper is supposed to be intact, as it was in an envelope that *had never been opened, and whose seals were unbroken.* It is a delicate matter, but I am rejoiced that the gentleman who left the paper in trust is the honourable Colonel Starbottle, whom I know by reputation, and the gentleman who suffered the misfortune of losing it is my personal friend Mr. Dumphy. It enables me at once to proffer my services as mediator, or as Mr. Dumphy's legal adviser and friend, to undertake *all* responsibility in the matter."

The tone and manner were so like Colonel Starbottle's own, that Dumphy looked from Arthur to Colonel Starbottle in hopeless amazement. The latter gentleman dropped his chin and fixed a pair of astonished and staring eyes upon Arthur. "Do I understand—that—er—this gentleman, Mr. Dumphy, has placed you in possession of any confidential statement—that—er "——

"Pardon me, Colonel Starbottle," interrupted Arthur, rising with dignity, "the facts I have just stated are sufficient for the responsibility I assume in this case. I learn from my client that a sealed paper placed in his hands is missing. I have from him the statement that I am bound to believe, that it passed from his hands unopened; where, he knows not. This is a matter, between gentlemen, serious enough without further complication!"

"And the paper and envelope are lost?" continued Colonel Starbottle, still gazing at Arthur.

"Are lost," returned Arthur, quietly. "I have advised my friend, Mr. Dumphy, that as a man of honour, and a business man, he is by no means freed through this unfortunate accident from any promise or contract that he may have entered into with you concerning it. Any deposit as a collateral for its safe delivery which he might have made, *or has promised to make*, is clearly forfeited. This he has been waiting only for your appearance to hand to you." Arthur crossed to Mr. Dumphy's side and laid his hand lightly upon his shoulder, but with a certain significance of grip palpable to Mr. Dumphy, who, after looking into his eyes, took out his cheque book. When he had filled in a duplicate of the cheque he had given Colonel Starbottle two days before, Arthur took it from his hand and touched the bell. "As we will not burden Colonel Starbottle unnecessarily, your cashier's acceptance of this paper will enable him to use it henceforth at his pleasure, and as I expect to have the pleasure of the Colonel's company to my office, will you kindly have this done at once?"

The clerk appeared, and at Mr. Poinsett's direction, took the cheque from the almost passive fingers of Mr. Dumphy.

"Allow me to express my perfect satisfaction with—er—er your explanation!" said Colonel Starbottle, extending one hand to Arthur, while at the same moment he gracefully readjusted his shirt-bosom with the other. "Trouble yourself no further—regarding the—er—er—paper. I trust it will—er—yet be found; if not, sir, I shall—er—er—" added the Colonel, with honourable resignation, "hold myself *personally responsible* to my client, blank me!"

"Was there no mark upon the envelope by which it might be known without explaining its contents?" suggested Arthur.

"None, sir, a plain yellow envelope. Stop!" said the Colonel, striking his forehead with his hand. "Ged, sir! I do remember now that during our conversation I made a memorandum, —— me, a memorandum upon the face of it, across it, a name, Ged, sir, the very name of the party you were speaking of—Gabriel Conroy!"

"You wrote the name of Gabriel Conroy upon it! Good! That may lead to its identification without exposing its contents," returned Arthur. "Well, sir?"

The last two words were addressed to Mr. Dumphy's clerk, who had entered during the Colonel's speech and stood staring alternately at him and his employer, holding the accepted cheque in his hand.

"Give it to the gentleman," said Dumphy, curtly.

The man obeyed. Colonel Starbottle took the cheque, folded it, and placed it somewhere in the moral recesses of his breast-pocket. That done, he turned to Mr. Dumphy. "I need not say—er—that—er—as far as my personal counsel and advice to my client can prevail, it will be my effort to prevent litigation in this—er—delicate affair. Should the envelope—er—er—turn up! you will of course—er—send it to me, who am—er—personally responsible for it. Ged, sir," continued the Colonel, "I should be proud to conclude this affair, conducted as it has been on your side with the strictest honour, over the—er—festive-board—but—er—business prevents me! I leave here in one hour for One Horse Gulch!"

Both Mr. Dumphy and Poinsett involuntarily started.

"One Horse Gulch?" repeated Arthur.

"—— me! yes! Ged, sir, I'm retained in a murder case there; the case of this man Gabriel Conroy."

Arthur cast a swift precautionary look at Dumphy. "Then perhaps we may be travelling companions?" he said to Starbottle, smiling pleasantly. "I am going there too. Perhaps my good fortune may bring us in friendly counsel. You are engaged"——

"For the prosecution," interrupted Starbottle, slightly expanding his chest. "At the request of relatives of the murdered man—a Spanish gentleman of—er—er—large and influential family connections, I shall assist the District Attorney, my old friend, Nelse Buckthorne!"

The excitement kindled in Arthur's eyes luckily did not appear in his voice. It was still pleasant to Colonel Starbottle's ear, as, after a single threatening glance of warning at the utterly mystified and half exploding Dumphy, he turned gracefully toward him. "And if, by the fortunes of war, we should be again on opposite sides, my dear

Colonel, I trust that our relations may be as gratifying as they have been to-day. One moment! I am going your way. Let me beg you to take my arm a few blocks and a glass of wine afterwards as a stirrup-cup on our journey." And with a significant glance at Dumphy, Arthur Poinsett slipped Colonel Starbottle's arm deftly under his own, and actually marched off with that doughty warrior, a blushing, expanding, but not unwilling captive.

When the door closed Mr. Dumphy resumed his speech and action in a single expletive. What more he might have said is not known, for at the same moment he caught sight of his clerk, who had entered hastily at the exit of the others, but who now stood awed and abashed by Mr. Dumphy's passion. "Dash it all! what in dash are you dashingly doing here, dash you?"

"Sorry, sir," said the unlucky clerk; "but overhearing that gentleman say there was writing on the letter that you lost by which it might be identified, sir—we think we've found it—that is, we know where it is!"

"How?" said Dumphy, starting up eagerly.

"When the shock came that afternoon," continued the clerk, "the express bag for Sacramento and Marysville had just been taken out by the expressman, and was lying on top of the waggon. The horses started to run at the second shock, and the bag fell and was jammed against a lamp-post in front of our window, bursting open as it did so and spilling some letters and papers on the side-walk. One of our night watchmen helped the expressman pick up the scattered letters, and picked up among them a plain yellow envelope with no address but the name of Gabriel Conroy written in pencil across the end. Supposing it had dropped from some package in the express bag, he put it back again in the bag. When you asked about a blank envelope missing from your desk, he did not connect it with the one he had picked up, for *that* had writing on it. We sent to the express office just now, and found that they had stamped it, and forwarded it to Conroy at One Horse Gulch, just as they had always done with his letters sent to our care. That's the way of it. Daresay it's there by this time, in his hands, sir, all right!"

CHAPTER III.

GABRIEL MEETS HIS LAWYER.

GABRIEL'S petition on behalf of Mr. Hamlin was promptly granted by the sheriff. The waggon was at once put into requisition to convey the wounded man—albeit screaming and protesting—to the Grand Conroy Hotel, where, in company with his faithful henchman, he was left, to all intents a free man, and a half an hour later a demented one, tossing in a burning fever.

Owing to the insecure condition of the county jail at One Horse Gulch, and possibly some belief in the equal untrustworthiness of the people, the sheriff conducted his prisoner, accompanied by Olly, to Wingdam. Nevertheless, Olly's statement of the changed condition of public sentiment, or rather its pre-occupation with a calamity of more absorbing interest, was in the main correct. The news of the recapture of Gabriel by his legal guardian awoke no excitement nor comment. More than this, there was a favourable feeling toward the prisoner. The action of the Vigilance Committee had been unsuccessful, and had terminated disastrously to the principal movers therein. It is possible that the morality of their action was involved in their success. Somehow the whole affair had not resulted to the business interests of the Gulch. The three most prominent lynchers were dead—and clearly in error! The prisoner, who was still living, was possibly in the right. The *Silverpolis Messenger*, which ten days before had alluded to the "noble spectacle of a free people outraged in their holiest instincts, appealing to the first principles of Justice and Order, and rallying as a single man to their support," now quietly buried the victims and their motives from the public eye beneath the calm statement that they met their fate "while examining the roof of the Court House with a view to estimate the damage caused by the first shock of the earthquake." The *Banner* favoured the same idea a little less elegantly, and suggested ironically that hereafter "none but experts should be allowed to go foolin' round the statue of Justice." I trust that the intelligent reader will not accuse me of endeavouring to cast ridicule upon the general accuracy of spontaneous public emotion, nor the infallibility of the true democratic impulse, which (I beg to quote from the *Messenger*), "in the earliest ages of our history enabled us to resist legalised aggression, and take the reins of government into our own hands," or (I now refer to the glowing language of the *Banner*), "gave us the right to run the machine ourselves and boss the job." And I trust that the reader will observe in this passing recognition of certain inconsistencies in the expression and action of these people, only the fidelity of a faithful chronicler, and no intent of churlish criticism nor moral or political admonition, which I here discreetly deprecate and disclaim.

Nor was there any opposition when Gabriel, upon the motion of Lawyer Maxwell, was admitted to bail pending the action of the Grand Jury, nor any surprise when Mr. Dumphy's agent and banker came forward as his bondsman for the sum of fifty thousand dollars. By one of those strange vicissitudes in the fortunes of mining speculation, this act by Mr. Dumphy was looked upon as an evidence of his trust in the future of the unfortunate mine of which

Gabriel had been original locator and superintendent, and under that belief the stock rallied slightly. "It was a mighty sharp move of Pete Dumphy's bailin' thet Gabe, right in face of that there 'dropped lead' in his busted-up mine! Oh, you've got to set up all night to get any points to show *him!*" And, to their mutual surprise, Mr. Dumphy found himself more awe-inspiring than ever at One Horse Gulch, and Gabriel found himself a free man, with a slight popular flavour of martyrdom about him.

As he still persistently refused to enter again upon the premises which he had deeded to his wife on the day of the murder, temporary lodgings were found for him and Olly at the Grand Conroy Hotel. And here Mrs. Markle, although exhibiting to Lawyer Maxwell the greatest concern in Gabriel's trouble, by one of those inconsistencies of the sex which I shall not attempt to explain, treated the unfortunate accused with a degree of cold reserve that was as grateful, I fear, to Gabriel, as it was unexpected. Indeed, I imagine that if the kind-hearted widow had known the real comfort and assurance that the exasperating Gabriel extracted from her first cold and constrained greeting, she would have spent less of her time in consultation with Maxwell regarding his defence. But perhaps I am doing a large-hearted and unselfish sex a deep injustice. So I shall content myself with transcribing part of a dialogue which took place between them at the Grand Conroy.

Mrs. Markle (loftily, and regarding the ceiling with cold abstraction): "We can't gin ye here, Mister Conroy, the French style and attention ye're kinder habitooal to in your own house on the Hill, bein' plain folks and mounting ways. But we know our place, and don't reckon to promise the comforts of a home! Wot with lookin' arter forty reg'lar and twenty-five transient—ef I don't happen to see ye much myself, Mr. Conroy, ye'll understand. Ef ye ring thet there bell one o' the help will be always on hand. Yer lookin' well, Mr. Conroy. And bizness, I reckon" (the reader will here observe a ladylike ignoring of Gabriel's special trouble), "ez about what it allers waz, though judging from remarks of transients, it's dull!"

Gabriel (endeavouring to conceal a large satisfaction under the thin glossing of conventional sentiment): "Don't let me nor Olly put ye out a cent, Mrs. Markle—a change bein' ordered by Olly's physicians—and variety bein', so to speak, the spice o' life! And ye're lookin' well, Mrs. Markle; that ez" (with a sudden alarm at the danger of compliment), "so to speak, ez peart and strong-handed ez ever! And how's thet little Manty o' yours gettin' on? Jist how it was thet me and Olly didn't get to see ye before ez mighty queer! Times and times ag'in" (with shameless mendacity) "hez me and thet child bin on the p'int o' coming, and suthin' hez jest chipped in and interfered!"

Mrs. Markle (with freezing politeness): "You do me proud! I jest dropped in ez a matter o' not bein' able allers to trust to help. Good night, Mister Conroy. I hope I see you well! Ye kin jest" (retiring with matronly dignity), "ye kin jest touch onto that bell thar, if ye're wantin' anything, and help'll come to ye! Good-night!"

Olly (appearing a moment later at the door of Gabriel's room, truculent and suspicious): "Afore I'd stand thar—chirpin' with thet crockidill—and you in troubil, and not knowin' wot's gone o' July—I'd pizen myself!"

Gabriel (blushing to the roots of his hair, and conscience-stricken to his inmost soul): "It's jest passin' the time o' day, Olly, with old friends—kinder influencin' the public sentyment and the jury. Thet's all. It's the advice o' Lawyer Maxwell, ez ye didn't get to hear, I reckon,—thet's all!"

But Gabriel's experience in the Grand Conroy Hotel was

not, I fear, always as pleasant. A dark-faced, large-featured woman, manifestly in mourning, and as manifestly an avenging friend of the luckless deceased, in whose taking off Gabriel was supposed to be so largely instrumental, presently appeared at the Grand Conroy Hotel, waiting the action of the Grand Jury. She was accompanied by a dark-faced elderly gentleman, our old friend Don Pedro—she being none other than the unstable-waisted Manuela of Pacific Street—and was, I believe, in the opinion of One Horse Gulch, supposed to be charged with convincing and mysterious evidence against Gabriel Conroy. The sallow-faced pair had a way of meeting in the corridors of the hotel and conversing in mysterious whispers in a tongue foreign to One Horse Gulch and to Olly, strongly suggestive of revenge and concealed *stilettos*, that was darkly significant! Happily, however, for Gabriel, he was presently relieved from their gloomy espionage by the interposition of a third party—Sal Clark. That individual, herself in the deepest mourning, and representing the deceased in his holiest affections, it is scarcely necessary to say at once resented the presence of the strangers. The two women glared at each other at the public table, and in a chance meeting in the corridor of the hotel.

"In the name of God, what have we here in this imbecile and forward creature, and why is this so and after this fashion?" asked Manuela of Don Pedro.

"Of a verity, I know not," replied Don Pedro, "it is most possibly a person visited of God!—a helpless being of brains. Peradventure, a person filled with *aguardiente* or the whisky of the Americans. Have a care, little one, thou smallest Manuela" (she weighed at least three hundred pounds), "that she does thee no harm!"

Meanwhile Miss Sarah Clark relieved herself to Mrs. Markle in quite as positive language. "Ef that black mulattar and that dried-up old furriner reckons they're going to monopolise public sentyment in this yer way they're mighty mistaken. Ef thar ever was a shameless piece et's thet old woman—and, goodness knows, the man's a poor critter enyway! Ef anybody's goin' to take the word of that woman under oath, et's mor'n Sal Clark would do—that's all! Who ez she—enyway? I never heard her name mentioned afore!"

And ridiculous as it may seem to the unprejudiced reader, this positive expression and conviction of Miss Clark, like all positive convictions, was not without its influence on the larger unimpanelled Grand Jury of One Horse Gulch, and, by reflection, at last on the impanelled jury itself.

"When you come to consider, gentlemen," said one of those dangerous characters—a sagacious, far-seeing juror—"when you come to consider that the principal witness o' the prosecution and the people at the inquest don't know this yer Greaser woman, and kinder throws off her testimony, and the prosecution don't seem to agree, it looks mighty queer. And I put it to you as far-minded men, if it ain't mighty queer? And this yer Sal Clark one of our own people."

An impression at once inimical to the new mistress and stranger, and favourable to the accused Gabriel, instantly took possession of One Horse Gulch.

Meanwhile the man who was largely responsible for this excitement and these conflicting opinions maintained a gravity and silence as indomitable and impassive as his alleged victim, then slumbering peacefully in the little cemetery on Round Hill. He conversed but little even with his counsel and friend, Lawyer Maxwell, and received with his usual submissiveness and gentle deprecatoriness the statement of that gentleman that Mr. Dumphy had already bespoken the services of one of the most prominent lawyers of San Francisco—Mr. Arthur Poinsett—to assist in the defence. When Maxwell added that Mr. Poinsett had expressed a wish to hold his first consultation with Gabriel privately, the latter replied with his usual simplicity, "I reckon I've nowt to say to him ez I hain't said to ye, but it's all right!"

"Then I'll expect you over to my office at eleven to-morrow?" asked Maxwell.

"Thet's so," responded Gabriel, "though I reckon thet anything you and him might fix up to be dumped onto thet jury would be pleasin' and satisfactory to me."

At a few minutes of eleven the next morning Mr. Maxwell, in accordance with a previous understanding with Mr. Poinsett, put on his hat and left his office in the charge of that gentleman that he might receive and entertain Gabriel in complete privacy and confidence. As Arthur sat there alone, fine gentleman as he was and famous in his profession, he was conscious of a certain degree of nervousness that galled his pride greatly. He was about to meet the man whose cherished sister six years ago he had stolen! Such, at least, Arthur felt was Gabriel's opinion. *He* had no remorse nor consciousness of guilt or wrong-doing in that act. But in looking at the fact in his professional habit of viewing both sides of a question, he made this allowance for the sentiment of the prosecution, and putting himself, in his old fashion, in the position of his opponent, he judged that Gabriel might consistently exhibit some degree of indignation at their first meeting. That there was, however, really any *moral* question involved, he did not believe. The girl, Grace Conroy, had gone with him readily, after a careful and honourable statement of the facts of her situation, and Gabriel's authority or concern in any subsequent sentimental complication he utterly denied. That he, Arthur, had acted in a most honourable, high-minded, and even weakly generous fashion towards Grace, that he had obeyed her frivolous whims as well as her most reasonable demands, that he had gone back to Starvation Camp on a hopeless quest just to satisfy her, that everything had happened exactly as he had predicted, and that when he had returned to her he found that *she* had deserted *him*—these—these were the facts that were incontrovertible! Arthur was satisfied that he had been honourable and even generous—he was quite convinced that this very nervousness that he now experienced, was solely the condition of a mind too sympathetic even with the feelings of an opponent in affliction. "I must *not* give way to this absurd Quixotic sense of honour," said this young gentleman to himself, severely.

Nevertheless, at exactly eleven o'clock, when the staircase creaked with the strong steady tread of the giant Gabriel, Arthur felt a sudden start to his pulse. There was a hesitating rap at the door—a rap that was so absurdly inconsistent with the previous tread on the staircase—as inconsistent as were all the mental and physical acts of Gabriel—that Arthur was amused and reassured. "Come in," he said, with a return of his old confidence, and the door opened to Gabriel, diffident and embarrassed.

"I was told by Lawyer Maxwell," said Gabriel slowly, without raising his eyes, and only dimly cognisant of the slight, strong, elegant figure before him—"I was told that Mr. Arthur Poinsett reckoned to see me to-day at eleven o'clock—so I came. Be you Mr. Poinsett?" (Gabriel here raised his eyes)—"be you, eh?—GOD A'MIGHTY! why, it's—eh?—why—I want to know!—it can't be!—yes, it is!" He stopped—the recognition was complete!

Arthur did not move. If he had expected an outburst from the injured man before him he was disappointed. Gabriel passed his hard palm vaguely and confusedly across his forehead and through his hair, and lifted and put back behind his ears two tangled locks. And then, without heeding Arthur's proffered hand, yet without precipitation, anger, or indignation, he strode toward him, and asked calmly and quietly, as Arthur himself might have done, "Where is Grace?"

"I don't know," said Arthur, bluntly. "I have not known for years. I have never known her whereabouts, living or dead, since the day I left her at a logger's house to return to Starvation Camp to bring help to *you.*" (Arthur could not resist italicising the pronoun, nor despising himself for doing it when he saw that the full significance of his emphasis touched the man before him.) "She was gone when I returned; where, no one knew! I traced her to the Presidio, but there she had disappeared."

Gabriel raised his eyes to Arthur's. The impression of nonchalant truthfulness which Arthur's speech always conveyed to his hearer, an impression that he did not prevaricate because he was not concerned sufficiently in his subject, was further sustained by his calm, clear eyes. But Gabriel did not speak, and Arthur went on—

"She left the logger's camp voluntarily, of her own free will, and doubtless for some reason that seemed sufficient to her. She abandoned me—if I may so express myself—left my care, relieved me of the responsibility I held towards her relatives"—he continued, with the first suggestion of personal apology in his tones—"without a word of previous intimation. Possibly she might have got tired of waiting for me. I was absent two weeks. It was the tenth day after my departure that she left the logger's hut."

Gabriel put his hand in his pocket and deliberately drew out the precious newspaper slip he had once shown to Olly. "Then thet thar 'Personal' wozent writ by you, and thet P. A. don't stand fur Philip Ashley?" asked Gabriel, with a hopeless dejection in his tone.

Arthur glanced quickly over the paper, and smiled. "I never saw this before," he said. "What made you think *I* did it?" he asked curiously.

"Because July—my wife that was—said that P. A. meant you," said Gabriel, simply.

"Oh! *she* said so, did she?" said Arthur, still smiling.

"She did. And ef it wasn't you, who was it?"

"I really don't know," returned Arthur, carelessly; "possibly it might have been herself. From what I have heard of your wife, I think this might be one, and perhaps the most innocent, of her various impostures."

Gabriel cast down his eyes and for a moment was gravely silent. Then the look of stronger inquiry and intelligence that he had worn during the interview faded utterly from his face, and he began again in his old tone of apology. "For answerin' all my questions, I'm obliged to ye, Mr. Ashley, and it's right good in ye to remember ol' times, and ef I hev often thought hard on ye, ye'll kinder pass that by ez the nat'rel allowin's of a man ez was worried about a sister ez hasn't been heerd from sens she left with ye. And ye mustn't think this yer meetin' was o' my seekin'. I kinder dropped in yer," he added wearily, "to see a man o' the name o' Poinsett. He allowed to be yer at eleving o'clock—mebbee it's airly yet—mebbee I've kinder got wrong o' the place!" and he glanced apologetically around the room.

"*My* name is Poinsett," said Arthur, smiling, "the name of Philip Ashley, by which you knew me, was merely the one I assumed when I undertook the long overland trip." He said this in no tone of apology or even explanation, but left the impression on Gabriel's mind that a change of name, like a change of dress, was part of the outfit of a gentleman emigrant. And looking at the elegant young figure before him, it seemed exceedingly plausible. "It was as Arthur Poinsett, the San Francisco lawyer, that I made this appointment with you, and it is now as your old friend Philip Ashley that I invite your confidence, and ask you to tell me frankly the whole of this miserable business. I have come to help you, Gabriel, for your own—for your sister's sake. And I think I can do it!" He held out his hand again, and this time not in vain; with a sudden frank gesture it was taken in both of Gabriel's, and Arthur felt that the greatest difficulty he had anticipated in his advocacy of Gabriel's cause had been surmounted.

"He has told me the whole story, I think," said Arthur, two hours later, when Maxwell returned and found his associate thoughtfully sitting beside the window alone. "And I believe it. He is as innocent of this crime as you or I. Of that I have always been confident. How far he is accessory *after* the fact—I know he is not accessory *before*—is another question. But his story, that to me is perfectly convincing, I am afraid won't do before a jury and the world generally. It involves too much that is incredible, and damning to him secondarily if believed. We must try something else. As far as I can see, really, it seems that his own suggestion of a defence, as you told it to me, has more significance in it than the absurdity you only saw. We must admit the killing, and confine ourselves to showing excessive provocation. I know something of the public sentiment here, and the sympathies of the average jury, and if Gabriel should tell them the story he has just told me, they would hang him at once! Unfortunately for him, the facts show a complication of property interests and impostures on the part of his wife, of which he is perfectly innocent, and which are not really the motive of the murder, but which the jury would instantly accept as a sufficient motive. We must fight, understand, this very story from the outset; you will find it to be the theory of the prosecution; but if we can keep him silent it cannot be proved except by him. The facts are such that if he had really committed the murder he could have defied prosecution, but through his very stupidity and blind anxiety to shield his wife, he has absolutely fixed the guilt upon himself."

"Then you don't think that Mrs. Conroy is the culprit?" asked Maxwell.

"No," said Arthur; "she is capable, but not culpable. The real murderer has never been suspected nor his presence known to One Horse Gulch. But I must see him again, and Olly, and you must hunt up a Chinaman—one Ah Fe—whom Gabriel tells me brought him the note, and who is singularly enough missing, now that he is wanted."

"But you can't use a Chinaman's evidence before a jury?" interrupted Maxwell.

"Not directly; but I can find Christian Caucasians who would be willing to swear to the facts he supplied them with. I shall get at the facts in a few days—and then, my dear fellow," continued Arthur, laying his hand familiarly and patronisingly on the shoulder of his senior, "and then you and I will go to work to see how we can get rid of them."

When Gabriel recounted the events of the day to Olly, and described his interview with Poinsett, she became furiously indignant. "And did that man mean to say he don't know whether Gracey is livin' or dead? And he pertendin' to hev bin her bo?"

"In coorse," explained Gabriel; "ye disremember, Olly, that Gracey never hez let on to *me*, her own brother, whar she ez, and she wouldn't be going to tell a stranger. Thar's them personals as she never answered!"

"Mebbe she didn't want to speak to him ag'in," said Olly,

fiercely, with a toss of her curls. "I'd like to know what he'd bin' sayin' to her—like his impudence. Enny how he ought to hev found her out, and she his sweetheart! Why didn't he go right off to the Presidio? What did he come back for? Not find her, indeed! Why, Gabe, do you suppose as July won't find *you* out soon—why, I bet anythin' she knows jest whar you are" (Gabriel trembled and felt an inward sinking), "and is on'y waitin' to come forward to the trial. And yer you are taken in ag'in and fooled by these yer lawyers!—you old Gabe, you. Let me git at thet Philip—Ashley Poinsett—thet's all!"

CHAPTER IV.

WHAT AH FE DOES NOT KNOW.

THUS admonished by the practical-minded Olly, Gabriel retired precipitately to the secure fastnesses of Conroy's Hill, where, over a consolatory pipe in his deserted cabin, he gave himself up to reflections upon the uncertainty of the sex and the general vagaries of womanhood. At such times he would occasionally extend his wanderings to the gigantic pine tree which still towered pre-eminently above its fellows in ominous loneliness, and seated upon one of its outlying roots, would gently philosophise to himself regarding his condition, the vicissitudes of fortune, the awful prescience of Olly, and the beneficence of a Creator who permitted such awkward triviality and uselessness as was incarnate in himself to exist at all! Sometimes, following the impulse of habit, he would encroach abstractedly upon the limits of his own domain, and find himself under the shadow of his own fine house on the hill, from which, since that eventful parting with his wife, he had always rigidly withheld his foot. As soon as he would make this alarming discovery, he would turn back in honourable delicacy and a slight sense of superstitious awe. Retreating from one of these involuntary incursions one day, in passing through an opening in a little thicket of "buckeye" near his house, he stumbled over a small workbasket lying in the withered grass, apparently mislaid or forgotten. Gabriel instantly recognised it as the property of his wife, and as quickly recalled the locality as one of her favourite resorts during the excessive mid-day heats. He hesitated and then passed on, and then stopped and returned again awkwardly and bashfully. To have touched any property of his wife's, after their separation, was something distasteful and impossible to Gabriel's sense of honour; to leave it there the spoil of any passing Chinaman, or the prey of the elements, was equally inconsistent with a certain respect which Gabriel had for his wife's weaknesses. He compromised by picking it up with the intention of sending it to Lawyer Maxwell, as his wife's trustee. But in doing this, to Gabriel's great alarm (for he would as soon have sacrificed the hand that held this treasure as to have exposed its contents in curiosity or suspicion), part of that multitudinous contents overflowed and fell on the ground, and he was obliged to pick them up and replace them. One of them was a baby's shirt—so small it filled the great hand that grasped it. In Gabriel's emigrant experience, as the frequent custodian and nurse of the incomplete human animal, he was somewhat familiar with those sacred, mummy-like enwrappings usually unknown to childless men, and he recognised it at once.

He did not replace it in the basket, but, with a suffused cheek and an increased sense of his usual awkwardness, stuffed it into the pocket of his blouse. Nor did he send the basket to Lawyer Maxwell, as he had intended, and in fact omitted any allusion to it in his usual account to Olly of his daily experience. For the next two days he was peculiarly silent and thoughtful, and was sharply reprimanded by Olly for general idiocy and an especial evasion of some practical duties.

"Yer's them lawyers hez been huntin' ye to come over and examine that there Chinaman, Ah Fe, ez is jest turned up ag'in, and you ain't no whar to be found; and Lawyer Maxwell sez it's a most important witness. And whar 'bouts was ye found? Down in the Gulch, chirpin' and gossipin' with that Arkansas family, and totin' round Mrs. Welch's baby. And you a growed man, with a fammerly of yer own to look after. I wonder ye ain't got more *sabe!*—prancin' round in this yer shiftless way, and you on trial, and accused o' killin' folks. Yer a high ole Gabe—rentin' yerself out fur a dry nuss for nothin'!"

Gabriel (colouring and hastily endeavouring to awaken Olly's feminine sympathies): "It waz the powerfullest, smallest baby—ye oughter get to see it, Olly! 'Tain't bigger nor a squirrel—on'y two weeks old yesterday!"

Olly (outwardly scornful, but inwardly resolving to visit the phenomenon next week): "Don't stand yawpin' here, but waltz down to Lawyer Maxwell and see that Chinaman."

Gabriel reached the office of Lawyer Maxwell just as that gentleman and Arthur Poinsett were rising from a long, hopeless, and unsatisfactory examination of Ah Fe. The lawyers had hoped to be able to establish the fact of Gabriel's remoteness from the scene of the murder by some corroborating incident or individual that Ah Fe could furnish in support of the detailed narrative he had already given. But it did not appear that any Caucasian had been encountered or met by Ah Fe at the time of his errand. And Ah Fe's memory of the details he had already described was apparently beginning to be defective; it was evident nothing was to be gained from him even if he had been constituted a legal witness. And then, more than all, he was becoming sullen!

"We are afraid that we haven't made much out of your friend, Ah Fe," said Arthur, taking Gabriel's hand. "You might try if *you* can revive his memory, but it looks doubtful."

Gabriel gazed at Ah Fe intently—possibly because he was the last person who had spoken to his missing wife. Ah Fe returned the gaze, discharging all expression from his countenance, except a slight suggestion of the habitual vague astonishment always seen in the face of a newborn infant. Perhaps this peculiar expression, reminding Gabriel as it did of the phenomenon in the Welch family, interested him. But the few vague wandering questions he put were met by equally vague answers. Arthur rose in some impatience; Lawyer Maxwell wiped away the smile that had been lingering around his mouth. The interview was ended.

Arthur and Maxwell passed down the narrow stairway arm in arm. Gabriel would have followed them with Ah Fe, but turning toward that Mongolian, he was alarmed by a swift spasm of expression that suddenly convulsed Ah Fe's face. He winked both his eyes with the velocity of sheet-lightning, nodded his head with frightful rapidity, and snapped and apparently dislocated every finger on his right hand. Gabriel gazed at him in open-mouthed wonder.

"All litee!" said Ah Fe, looking intently at Gabriel.

"Which?" asked Gabriel.

"All litee! You shabbee 'all litee!' *She* say 'all litee."

"Who's *she?*" asked Gabriel, in sudden alarm.

"You lifee!--shabbee?—Missee Conloy! She likee you—shabbee? Me likee you!—shabbee? Miss Conloy she say 'all litee!' You shabbee shelliff?"

"Which?" said Gabriel.

"Shelliff! Man plenty chokee bad man!"

"Sheriff, I reckon," suggested Gabriel, with great gravity.

"Um! Shelliff. Mebbe you shabbee him bimeby. He chokee bad man. Much chokee. Chokee like hellee! *He no chokee you.* No. Shabbee? She say 'shelliff no chokee you.' Shabbee?"

"I see," said Gabriel, significantly.

"She say," continued Ah Fe, with gasping swiftness, "she say you talkee too much. She say me talkee too much. She say Maxwellee talkee too much. All talkee too much. She say 'no talkee!' Shabbee? She say 'ash up!' Shabbee? She say 'dly up!' Shabbee? She say 'bimeby plenty talkee—bimeby all litee!' Shabbee?"

"But whar ez she—whar kin I git to see her?" asked Gabriel.

Ah Fe's face instantly discharged itself of all expression. A wet sponge could not have more completely obliterated all pencilled outline of character or thought from his blank slate-coloured physiognomy than did Gabriel's simple question. He returned his questioner's glance with ineffable calmness and vacancy, patiently drew the long sleeves of his blouse still further over his varnished fingers, crossed them submissively and Orientally before him, and waited apparently for Gabriel to become again intelligible.

"Look yer," said Gabriel, with gentle persuasiveness, "ef it's the same to ye, you'd be doin' me a heap o' good ef you'd let on whar thet July—thet Mrs. Conroy ez. Bein' a man ez in his blindness bows down to wood and stun, ye ain't supposed to allow fur a Christian's feelings. But I put to ye ez a far-minded brethren—a true man and a man whatsoever his colour—that it's a square thing fur ye to allow to me whar thet woman ez ez my relation by marriage ez hidin'! Allowin' it's one o' my idols—I axes you as a brother Pagan—whar ez she?"

A faint, flickering smile of pathetic abstraction and simplicity, as of one listening to far-off but incomprehensible music stole over Ah Fe's face. Then he said kindly, gently, but somewhat vaguely and unsatisfactorily—

"Me no shabbee Melican man. Me washee shirtee *l* dollah and hap dozen!"

CHAPTER V.

THE PEOPLE *v.* JOHN DOE *alias* GABRIEL CONROY, AND JANE ROE *alias* JULIE CONROY. BEFORE BOOMPOINTER, J.

THE day of the trial was one of exacting and absorbing interest to One Horse Gulch. Long before ten o'clock the Court-room, and even the halls and corridors of the lately rehabilitated Court House, were thronged with spectators. It is only fair to say that by this time the main points at issue were forgotten. It was only remembered that some of the first notabilities of the State had come up from Sacramento to attend the trial; that one of the most eminent lawyers in San Francisco had been engaged for the prisoner at a fee variously estimated from fifty to one hundred thousand dollars, and that the celebrated Colonel Starbottle of Siskiyou was to assist in the prosecution; that a brisk duel of words, and it was confidently hoped, a later one of pistols, would grow out of this forensic encounter; that certain disclosures affecting men and women of high social standing were to be expected; and, finally, that in some mysterious way a great political and sectional principle (Colonel Starbottle was from the South and Mr. Poinsett from the North) was to be evolved and upheld during the trial—these were the absorbing fascinations to One Horse Gulch.

At ten o'clock Gabriel, accompanied by his counsel, entered the Court-room, followed by Colonel Starbottle. Judge Boompointer, entering at the same moment, bowed distantly to Arthur, and familiarly to Colonel Starbottle. In his *otium* off the bench, he had been chaffed by the District Attorney, and had lost large sums at play with Colonel Starbottle. Nevertheless he was a trifle uneasy under the calmly critical eyes of the famous young advocate from San Francisco. Arthur was too wise to exhibit his fastidiousness before the Court; nevertheless, Judge Boompointer was dimly conscious that he would on that occasion have preferred that the Clerk who sat below him had put on a cleaner shirt, and himself refrained from taking off his cravat and collar, as was his judicial habit on the Wingdam circuit. There was some slight prejudice on the part of the panel to this well-dressed young lawyer, which they were pleased to specify and define more particularly as his general "airiness." Seeing which, Justice, on the bench, became more dignified, and gazed severely at the panel and at Arthur.

In the selection of the jury there was some difficulty; it was confidently supposed that the prisoner's counsel would challenge the array on the ground of the recent Vigilance excitement, but public opinion was disappointed when the examination of the defence was confined to trivial and apparently purposeless inquiry into the nativity of the several jurors. A majority of those accepted by the defence were men of Southern birth and education. Colonel Starbottle, who, as a representative of the peculiar chivalry of the South, had always adopted this plan himself, in cases where his client was accused of assault and battery, or even homicide, could not in respect to his favourite traditions object to it. But when it was found that there were only two men of Northern extraction on the jury, and that not a few of them had been his own clients, Colonel Starbottle thought he had penetrated the theory of the defence.

I regret that Colonel Starbottle's effort, admirably characterised by the *Banner* as "one of the most scathing and Junius-like gems of legal rhetoric ever known to the Californian Bar," has not been handed down to me *in extenso.* Substantially, however, it appeared that Colonel Starbottle had never before found himself in "so peculiar, so momentous, so—er—delicate a position. A position, sir—er—er—gentlemen, fraught with the deepest social, professional—er—er—he should not hesitate to say, upon his own personal responsibility, a position of the deepest political significance! Colonel Starbottle was aware that this statement might be deprecated—nay, even *assailed* by some. But he did not retract that statement. Certainly not in the presence of that jury, in whose intelligent faces he saw—er—er—er—justice—inflexible justice!—er—er—mingled and—er—mixed with—with chivalrous instinct, and suffused with the characteristic—er—er—glow of—er—er—!" (I regret to add that at this supreme moment, as the Colonel was lightly waving away with his fat right hand the difficulties of rhetoric, a sepulchral voice audible behind the jury suggested "Robinson County whisky" as the origin of the phenomena the Colonel hesitated to describe. The judge smiled blandly and directed the deputy sheriff to preserve order. The deputy obeyed the mandate by looking over into the crowd behind the jury, and saying, in an audible tone, "You'd better dry up thar, Joe White, or git out o' that!" and the Colonel, undismayed, proceeded.) "He well understood the confidence placed by the defence in these gentlemen. He had reason to believe that an attempt would be made to show that this homicide was committed in accordance with certain—er—er—principles held by honourable men—that the act was retributive, and in defence of an invasion of domestic rights and the sanctity of wedlock. But he should show them its fallacy. He should show them that only a base pecuniary motive influenced the prisoner. He should show them—er—er—that the accused had placed himself, firstly, by his antecedent acts, and, secondly, by the manner of the later act, beyond the sympathies of honourable men. He should show them a previous knowledge of certain—er—er—indiscretions on the part of the prisoner's wife, and a condonation by the prisoner of those indiscretions, that effectually debarred the prisoner from the provisions of the code; he should show an inartistic, he must say, even on his own personal responsibility, a certain ungentlemanliness, in the manner of the crime that refused to clothe it with the—er—er—generous mantle of chivalry. The crime of which the prisoner was accused might have—er—er—been committed by a Chinaman or a nigger. Colonel Starbottle did not wish to be misunderstood. It was not in the presence of—er—Beauty—" (the Colonel paused, drew out his handkerchief, and gracefully waved it in the direction of the dusky Manuela and the truculent Sal—both ladies acknowledging the courtesy as an especial and isolated tribute, and exchanging glances of the bitterest hatred)—"it is not, gentlemen, in the presence of an all-sufficient and enthralling sex that I would seek to disparage their influence with man. But I shall prove that this absorbing—er—er—passion, this—er—er—delicious—er—er—fatal weakness, that rules the warlike camp, the—er—er—stately palace, as well as the—er—er—cabin of the base-born churl, never touched the calculating soul of Gabriel Conroy! Look at him, gentlemen! Look at him, and say upon your oaths, upon your experience as men of gallantry, if he is a man to sacrifice himself for a woman. Look at him, and say truly, as men personally responsible for their opinions, if he is a man to place himself in a position of peril through the blandishments of—er—er—Beauty, or sacrifice himself upon the—er—er—altar of Venus !"

Every eye was turned upon Gabriel. And certainly at that moment he did not bear any striking resemblance to a sighing Amintor or a passionate Othello. His puzzled, serious face, which had worn a look of apologetic sadness, was suffused at this direct reference of the prosecution; and the long, heavy lower limbs, which he had diffidently tucked away under his chair to reduce the elevation of his massive knees above the ordinary level of one of the court-room chairs, retired still further. Finding himself, during the Colonel's rhetorical pause, still the centre of local observation, he slowly drew from his pocket a small comb, and began awkwardly to comb his hair, with an ineffective simulation of pre-occupation and indifference.

"Yes, sir," continued the Colonel, with that lofty forensic severity so captivating to the spectator, "you may comb yer hair" (hyar was the Colonel's pronunciation), "but yer can't comb it so as to make this intelligent jury believe that it is fresh from the hands of—er—er—Delilah."

The Colonel then proceeded to draw an exceedingly poetical picture of the murdered Ramirez—"a native, appealing to the sympathies of every Southern man, a native of the tropics, impulsive, warm, and peculiarly susceptible, as we all are, gentlemen, to the weaknesses of the heart." The Colonel "would not dwell further upon this characteristic of the deceased. There were within the sound of his voice, visible to the sympathising eyes of the jury, two beings who had divided his heart's holiest affections—their presence was more eloquent than words. This man," continued the Colonel, "a representative of one of our oldest Spanish families—a family that recalled the days of—er—er—the Cid and Don John—this man had been the victim at once of the arts of Mrs. Conroy and the dastardly fears of Gabriel Conroy; of the wiles of the woman and the stealthy steel of the man."

"Colonel Starbottle would show that personating the character and taking the name of Grace Conroy, an absent sister of the accused, Mrs. Conroy, then really Madame Devarges, sought the professional aid of the impulsive and generous Ramirez to establish her right to a claim then held by the accused—in fact, wrongfully withheld from his own sister, Grace Conroy. That Ramirez, believing implicitly in the story of Madame Devarges with the sympathy of an overflowing nature, gave her that aid until her marriage with Gabriel exposed the deceit. Colonel Starbottle would not characterise the motives of such a marriage. It was apparent to the jury. They were intelligent men, and would detect the unhallowed combination of two confederates, under the sacrament of a holy institution, to deceive the trustful Ramirez. It was a nuptial feast at which—er—er—Mercury presided, and not—er—er—Hymen. Its only issue was fraud and murder. Having obtained possession of the property in a common interest, it was necessary to remove the only witness of the fraud, Ramirez. The wife found a willing instrument in the husband. And how was the deed committed? Openly and in the presence of witnesses? Did Gabriel even assume a virtue, and under the pretext of an injured husband challenge the victim to the field of honour? No! No, gentlemen. Look at the murderer, and contrast his enormous bulk with the—er—slight, graceful, youthful figure of the victim, and you will have an idea of the—er—er—enormity of the crime."

After this exordium came the *testimony—i.e.*, facts coloured more or less unconsciously, according to the honest prejudices of the observer, his capacity to comprehend the fact he had observed, and his disposition to give his theory regarding that fact rather than the fact itself. And when the blind had testified to what they saw, and the halt had stated where they walked and ran, the prosecution rested with a flush of triumph.

They had established severally: that the deceased had died from the effects of a knife-wound; that Gabriel had previously quarrelled with him and was seen on the hill within a few hours of the murder; that he had absconded immediately after, and that his wife was still a fugitive, and that there was ample motive for the deed in the circumstances surrounding the prisoner.

Much of this was shaken on cross-examination. The surgeon who made the autopsy was unable to say whether the deceased, being consumptive, might not have died from consumption that very night. The witness who saw Gabriel pushing the deceased along the road, could not swear positively whether the deceased were not pulling Gabriel instead, and the evidence of Mrs. Conroy's imposture was hearsay only. Nevertheless bets were offered in favour of Starbottle against Poinsett—that being the form in which the interest of One Horse Gulch crystallised itself.

When the prosecution rested, Mr. Poinsett, as counsel for defence, moved for the discharge of the prisoner, no evidence having been shown of his having had any relations with or knowledge of the deceased until the day of the murder, and none whatever of his complicity with the murderess, against whom the evidence of the prosecution and the arguments of the learned prosecuting attorney were chiefly directed.

Motion overruled. A sigh of relief went up from the spectators and the jury. That any absurd technical objection should estop them from that fun which as law-abiding citizens they had a right to expect, seemed oppressive and scandalous; and when Arthur rose to open for the defence, it was with an instinctive consciousness that his audience were eyeing him as a man who had endeavoured to withdraw from a race.

Ridiculous as it seemed in reason, it was enough to excite Arthur's flagging interest and stimulate his combativeness. With ready tact he fathomed the expectation of the audience, and at once squarely joined issue with the Colonel.

Mr. Poinsett differed from his learned friend in believing this case was at all momentous or peculiar. It was a quite common one—he was sorry to say a *very* common one—in the somewhat hasty administration of the law in California. He was willing to admit a peculiarity in his eloquent brother's occupying the line of attack, when his place was as clearly at his, Mr. Poinsett's side. He should overlook some irregularities in the prosecution from this fact, and from the natural confusion of a man possessing Colonel Starbottle's quick sympathies, who found himself arrayed against his principles. He should, however, relieve them from that confusion, by stating that there really was no principle involved beyond the common one of self-preservation. He was willing to admit the counsel's ingenious theory that Mrs. Conroy—who was not mentioned in the indictment, or indeed any other person not specified—had committed the deed for which his client was charged. But as they were here to try Gabriel Conroy only, he could not see the relevancy of the testimony to that fact. He should content himself with the weakness of the accusation. He should not occupy their time, but should call at once to the stand the prisoner; the man who, the jury would remember, was now, against all legal precedent, actually, if not legally, placed again in peril of his life, in the very building which but a few days before had seen his danger and his escape.

He should call Gabriel Conroy !

There was a momentary sensation in the court. Gabriel uplifted his huge frame slowly, and walked quietly toward the witness-box. His face slightly flushed under the half-critical, half-amused gaze of the spectators, and those by whom he brushed as he made his way through the crowd noticed that his breathing was hurried. But when he reached the box, his face grew more composed, and his troubled eyes presently concentrated their light fixedly upon Colonel Starbottle. Then the clerk mumbled the oath, and he took his seat.

"What is your name?" asked Arthur.

"I reckon ye mean my real name?" queried Gabriel, with a touch of his usual apology.

"Yes, certainly, your real name, sir," replied Arthur, a little impatiently.

Colonel Starbottle pricked up his ears, and lifting his eyes, met Gabriel's dull, concentrated fires full in his own.

Gabriel then raised his eyes indifferently to the ceiling. "My real name—my genooine name—is Johnny Dumbledee, J-o-n-n-y, Johnny, D-u-m-b-i-l-d-e, Johnny Dumbledee!"

There was a sudden thrill, and then a stony silence. Arthur and Maxwell rose to their feet at the same moment. "What?" said both those gentlemen, sharply, in one breath.

"Johnny Dumbledee," repeated Gabriel, slowly and with infinite deliberation; "Johnny Dumbledee ez my real name. I hev frequent," he added, turning around in easy confidence to the astonished Judge Boompointer, "I hev frequent allowed I was Gabriel Conroy—the same not being the truth. And the woman ez I married—*her* name was Grace Conroy, and the heap o' lies ez thet old liar over thar" (he indicated the gallant Colonel Starbottle with his finger) "hez told passes my pile! Thet woman, my wife ez was and ez —waz Grace Conroy." (To the Colonel, gravely:) "You hear me! And the only imposture, please your Honour and this yer Court, and you gentl'men, was ME!"

CHAPTER VI.

IN REBUTTAL.

THE utter and complete astonishment created by Gabriel's reply was so generally diffused that the equal participation of Gabriel's own counsel in this surprise was unobserved. Maxwell would have risen again hurriedly, but Arthur laid his hand on his shoulder.

"The man has gone clean mad!—this is suicide," whispered Maxwell, excitedly. "We must get him off the stand. You must explain!"

"Hush!" said Arthur, quietly. "Not a word! Show any surprise and we're lost!"

In another instant all eyes were fixed upon Arthur, who had remained standing, outwardly calm. There was but one idea dominant in the audience. What revelation would the next question bring? The silence became almost painful as Arthur quietly and self-containedly glanced around the Court-room and at the jury, as if coolly measuring the effect of a carefully-planned dramatic sensation. Then, when every neck was bent forward and every ear alert, Arthur turned nonchalantly yet gracefully to the bench.

"We have no further questions to ask, your Honour," he said, quietly, and sat down.

The effect of this simple, natural, and perfectly consistent action was tremendous! In the various triumphs of Arthur's successful career, he felt that he had never achieved as universal and instantaneous popularity. Gabriel was forgotten; the man who had worked up this sensation—a sensation whose darkly mysterious bearing upon the case no one could fathom, or even cared to fathom, but a sensation that each man confidently believed held the whole secret of the crime—this man was the hero! Had it been suggested, the jury would have instantly given a verdict for this hero's client without leaving their seats. The betting was two to one on Arthur. I beg to observe that I am writing of men, impulsive, natural, and unfettered in expression and action by any tradition of logic or artificial law—a class of beings much idealised by poets, and occasionally, I believe, exalted by latter-day philosophers.

Judge Boompointer looked at Colonel Starbottle. That gentleman, completely stunned and mystified by the conduct of the defence, fumbled his papers, coughed, expanded his chest, rose, and began the cross-examination.

"You have said your name was—er—er—Johnny—er—er"—(the Colonel was here obliged to consult his papers)—"er—John Dumbledee. What was your idea, Mr. Dumbledee, in—er—assuming the name of—er—er—Gabriel Conroy?"

Objected to by counsel for defence. Argument:—Firstly, motives, like beliefs, not admissible; case cited, Higginbottom *v.* Smithers. Secondly, not called out on Direct Ex.; see Swinke *v.* Swanke, opinion of Muggins, J., 2 Cal. Rep. Thirdly, witness not obliged to answer questions tending to self-crimination. Objection overruled by the Court. Precedent not cited; real motive, Curiosity. Boompointer, J. Question repeated:—

"What was your idea or motive in assuming the name of Gabriel Conroy?"

Gabriel (cunningly, and leaning confidentially over the arm of his chair): "Wot would be *your* idee of a motif?"

The witness, amidst much laughter, was here severely instructed by the Court that the asking of questions was not the function of a witness. The witness must answer.

Gabriel: "Well, Gabriel Conroy was a purty name—the name of a man ez I onst knew ez died in Starvation Camp. It kinder came easy, ez a sort o' interduckshun, don't ye see, Jedge, toe his sister Grace, ez was my wife. I kinder reckon, between you and me, ez thet name sorter helped the courtin' along—she bein' a shy critter, outer her own fammerly."

Question: "In your early acquaintance with the deceased, were you not known to him as Gabriel Conroy always, and not as—er—er—Johnny Dumbledee?"

Arthur Poinsett here begged to call the attention of the Court to the fact that it had not yet been shown that Gabriel—that is, Johnny Dumbledee—had ever had any *early* acquaintance with the deceased. The Court would not fail to observe that counsel on the direct examination had restricted themselves to a simple question—the name of the prisoner.

Objection sustained by Judge Boompointer, who was beginning to be anxious to get at the facts. Whereat Colonel Starbottle excepted, had no more questions to ask, and Gabriel was commanded to stand aside.

Betting now five to one on Arthur Poinsett; Gabriel's hand, on leaving the witness box, shaken cordially by a number of hitherto disinterested people. Hurried consultation between defendant's counsel. A note handed to Colonel Starbottle. Intense curiosity manifested by Manuela and Sal regarding a closely veiled female, who enters a moment later, and is conducted with an excess of courtesy to a seat by the gallant Colonel. General impatience of audience and jury.

The defence resumed. Michael O'Flaherty called; nativity, County Kerry, Ireland. Business, miner. On the night of the murder, while going home from work, met deceased on Conroy's Hill, dodging in among the trees, for all the wurreld like a thafe. A few minutes later overtook Gabriel Conroy half a mile farther on, on the same road, going in same direction as witness, and walked with him to Lawyer Maxwell's office. Cross examined: Is naturalised. Always voted the Dimmycratic ticket. Was always opposed to the Government—bad cess to it—in the ould counthry, and isn't thet mane to go back on his principles here. Doesn't know that a Chinaman has affirmed to the same fact of Gabriel's *alibi.* Doesn't know what an *alibi* is; thinks he would if he saw it. Believes a Chinaman is worse nor a nigger. Has noticed that Gabriel was left-handed.

Amadee Michet, sworn for defence; nativity, France. Business, foreman of *La Parfait Union.* Frequently walks to himself in the beautiful grove on Conroy's Hill. Comes to him on the night of the 15th, Gabriel Conroy departing from his house. It is then seven hours, possibly more, not less. The night is fine. This Gabriel salutes him in the American fashion, and is gone. Eastward. Ever to the east. Watches M. Conroy because he wears a *triste* look, as if there were great sadness *here* (in the breast of the witness' blouse). Sees him vanish in the gulch. Returns to the hill and there overhears voices, a man's and a woman's. The woman's voice is that of Madame Conroy. The man's voice is to him strange and not familiar. Will swear positively it was not Gabriel's. Remains on the hill about an hour. Did not see Gabriel again. Saw a man and woman leave the hill and pass by the Wingdam road as he was going home. To the best of his belief the woman was Mrs. Conroy. Do not know the man. Is positive it was not Gabriel Conroy. Why? Eh! Mon Dieu, is it possible that one should mistake a giant?

Cross examined. Is a patriot—do not know what is this Democrat you call. Is a hater of aristocrats. Do not know if the deceased was an aristocrat. Was not enraged with Madame Conroy. Never made love to her. Was not jilted by her. This is all what you call too theen, eh? Has noticed that the prisoner was left-handed.

Helling Dittmann; nativity, Germany. Does not know the deceased; does know Gabriel. Met him the night of the 15th on the road from Wingdam; thinks it was after eight o'clock. He was talking to a Chinaman.

Cross examined. Has not been told that these are the facts stated by the Chinaman. Believes a Chinaman as good as any other man. Don't know what you mean. How comes dese dings? Has noticed the prisoner used his left hand efery dime.

Dr. Pressnitz recalled. Viewed the body at nine o'clock on the 16th. The blood-stains on the linen and the body had been slightly obliterated and diluted with water, as if they had been subjected to a watery application. There was an unusually heavy dew at seven o'clock that evening, not later. Has kept a meteorological record for the last three years. Is of the opinion that this saturation might be caused by dew falling on a clot of coagulated blood. The same effect would not be noticeable on a freshly bleeding wound. The hygrometer showed no indication of a later fall of dew. The night was windy and boisterous after eight o'clock, with no humidity. Is of the opinion that the body, as seen by him, first assumed its position before eight o'clock. Would not swear positively that the deceased expired before that time. Would swear positively that the wounds were not received after eight o'clock. From the position of the wound, should say it was received while the deceased was in an upright position, and the arm raised as if in struggling. From the course of the wound should say it could not have been dealt from the left hand of an opponent. On the cross examination, Dr. Pressnitz admitted that many so-called "left-handed men" were really ambidexterous. Was of the opinion that perspiration would *not* have caused the saturation of the dead man's linen. The saturation was evidently after death—the blood had clotted. Dr. Pressnitz was quite certain that a dead man did not perspire.

The defence rested amid a profound sensation. Colonel Starbottle, who had recovered his jaunty spirits, apparently influenced by his animated and gallant conversation with the veiled female, rose upon his short stubby feet, and withdrawing his handkerchief from his breast, laid it upon the table before him. Then carefully placing the ends of two white pudgy fingers upon it, Colonel Starbottle gracefully threw his whole weight upon their tips, and leaning elegantly toward the veiled figure, called "Grace Conroy."

The figure arose, slight, graceful, elegant; hesitated a moment, and then slipped a lissom shadow through the crowd, as a trout glides through a shallow, and before the swaying, moving mass had settled to astonished rest, stood upon the witness-stand. Then with a quick dexterous movement she put aside the veil, that after the Spanish fashion was both bonnet and veil, and revealed a face so exquisitely beautiful and gracious, that even Manuela and Sal were awed into speechless admiration. She took the oath with downcast lids, whose sweeping fringes were so perfect that this very act of modesty seemed to the two female critics as the most artistic coquetry, and then raised her dark eyes and fixed them upon Gabriel.

Colonel Starbottle waved his hand with infinite gallantry.

"What is—er—your name?"

"Grace Conroy."

"Have you a brother by the name of Gabriel Conroy?"

"I have."

"Look around the Court and see if you can recognise him."

The witness with her eyes still fixed on Gabriel pointed him out with her gloved finger. "I do. He is there!"

"The prisoner at the bar?"

"Yes."

"He is Gabriel Conroy?"

"He is."

"How long is it since you have seen him?"

"Six years."

"Where did you see him last, and under what circumstances?"

"At Starvation Camp, in the Sierras. I left there to get help for him and my sister."

"And you have never seen him since?"

"Never!"

"Are you aware that among the—er—er—unfortunates who perished, a body that was alleged to be yours was identified?"

"Yes."

"Can you explain that circumstance?"

"Yes. When I left I wore a suit of boy's clothes. I left my own garments for Mrs. Peter Dumphy, one of our party. It was her body, clothed in my garments, that was identified as myself."

"Have you any proof of that fact other than your statement?"

"Yes. Mr. Peter Dumphy, the husband of Mrs. Dumphy, my brother Gabriel Conroy, and"——

"May it please the Court" (the voice was Arthur

Poinsett's, cool, quiet, and languidly patient), " may it please the Court, we of the defence—to save your Honour and the jury some time and trouble—are willing to admit this identification of our client as Gabriel Conroy, and the witness, without further corroboration than her own word, as his sister. Your Honour and the gentlemen of the jury will not fail to recognise in the evidence of our client as to his own name and origin, a rash, foolish, and, on behalf of myself and my colleague, I must add, unadvised attempt to save the reputation of the wife he deeply loves from the equally unadvised and extraneous evidence brought forward by the prosecution. But we must insist, your Honour, that all this is impertinent to the real issue, the killing of Victor Ramirez by John Doe, *alias* Gabriel Conroy. Admitting the facts just testified to by the witness, Grace Conroy, we have no cross examination to make."

The face of the witness, which had been pale and self-possessed, flushed suddenly as she turned her eyes upon Arthur Poinsett. But that self-contained scamp retained an unmoved countenance as, at Judge Boompointer's unusually gracious instruction that the witness might retire, Grace Conroy left the stand. To a question from the Court, Colonel Starbottle intimated that he should offer no further evidence in rebuttal.

" May it please the Court," said Arthur, quietly, " if we accept the impeachment by a sister of a brother on trial for his life, without comment or cross examination, it is because we are confident—legally confident—of showing the innocence of that brother by other means. Recognising the fact that this trial is not for the identification of the prisoner under any name or *alias*, but simply upon the issue of the fact whether he did or did not commit murder upon the body of Victor Ramirez, as specified in the indictment, we now, waiving all other issues, prepare to prove his innocence by a single witness. That this witness was not produced earlier, was unavoidable; that his testimony was not outlined in the opening, was due to the fact that only within the last half-hour had he been within the reach of the mandate of this Court. He would call Henry Perkins!"

There was a slight stir among the spectators by the door as they made way to a quaint figure that, clad in garments of a bygone fashion, with a pale, wrinkled, yellow face, and grey hair, from which the dye had faded, stepped upon the stand.

Is a translator of Spanish and searcher of deeds to the Land Commission. Is called an expert. Recognises the prisoner at the bar. Saw him only once, two days before the murder, in passing over Conroy's Hill. He was sitting on the door-step of a deserted cabin with a little girl by his side. Saw the deceased twice. Once when he came to Don Pedro's house in San Francisco to arrange for the forgery of a grant that should invalidate one already held by the prisoner's wife. Saw the deceased again, after the forgery, on Conroy's Hill, engaged in conversation with the prisoner's wife. Deceased appeared to be greatly excited, and suddenly drew a knife and made an attack upon the prisoner's wife. Witness reached forward and interposed in defence of the woman, when the deceased turned upon him in a paroxysm of insane rage, and a struggle took place between them for the possession of the knife, witness calling for help. Witness did not succeed in wresting the knife from the hands of deceased; it required all his strength to keep himself from bodily harm. In the midst of the struggle witness heard steps approaching, and again called for help.

The witness' call was responded to by a voice in broken English, unintelligible to witness, apparently the voice of a Chinaman. At the sound of the voice and the approach of footsteps, the deceased broke from witness, and running backward a few steps, plunged the knife into his own breast and fell. Witness ran to his side and again called for help. Deceased turned upon him with a ghastly smile and said, "Bring any one here and I'll accuse you before them of my murder!" Deceased did not speak again, but fell into a state of insensibility. Witness became alarmed, reflecting upon the threat of the deceased, and did not go for help. While standing irresolutely by the body, Mrs. Conroy, the prisoner's wife, came upon him. Confessed to her the details just described, and the threat of the deceased. She advised the instant flight of the witness, and offered to go with him herself. Witness procured a horse and buggy from a livery stable, and at half-past nine at night took Mrs. Conroy from the hillside near the road, where she was waiting. Drove to Markleville that night, where he left her under an assumed name, and came alone to San Francisco and the Mission of San Antonio. Here he learned from the last witness, the prisoner's sister, Grace Conroy, of the arrest of her brother for murder. Witness at once returned to One Horse Gulch, only to find the administration of justice in the hands of a Vigilance Committee. Feeling that his own life might be sacrificed without saving the prisoner's, he took refuge in a tunnel on Conroy's Hill. It chanced to be the same tunnel which Gabriel Conroy and his friend afterwards sought in escaping from the Vigilance Committee after the earthquake. Witness, during the absence of Gabriel, made himself known to Mr. Jack Hamlin, Gabriel's friend and comrade in flight, and assured him of the witness's intention to come forward whenever a fair trial could be accorded to Gabriel. After the re-arrest and bailing of Gabriel, witness returned to San Francisco to procure evidence regarding the forged grant, and proofs of Ramirez's persecution of Mrs. Conroy. Had brought with him the knife, and had found the cutler who sold it to deceased eight months before, when deceased first meditated an assault on Mrs. Conroy. Objected to, and objection overruled by a deeply interested and excited Court.

"That is all," said Arthur.

Colonel Starbottle, seated beside Grace Conroy, did not, for a moment, respond to the impatient eyes of the audience in the hush that followed. It was not until Grace Conroy whispered a few words in his ear, that the gallant Colonel lifted his dilated breast and self-complacent face above the level of the seated counsel.

"What—er—er—was the reason—why did the—er—er—deeply anxious wife, who fled with you, and thus precipitated the arrest of her husband—why did not she return with you to clear him from suspicion? Why does she remain absent?"

"She was taken ill—dangerously ill at Markleville. The excitement and fatigue of the journey had brought on premature confinement. A child was born"——

There was a sudden stir among the group beside the prisoner's chair. Colonel Starbottle, with a hurried glance at Grace Conroy, waved his hand toward the witness and sat down. Arthur Poinsett rose. "We ask a moment's delay, your Honour. The prisoner has fallen in a fit."

CHAPTER VII.

A FAMILY GREETING.

When Gabriel opened his eyes to consciousness, he was lying on the floor of the jury room, his head supported by Olly, and a slight, graceful, womanly figure, that had been apparently bending over him, in the act of slowly withdrawing from his awakening gaze. It was his sister Grace.

"Thar, you're better now," said Olly, taking her brother's hand, and quietly ignoring her sister, on whom Gabriel's eyes were still fixed. "Try and raise yourself inter this chair. Thar—thar now—that's a good old Gabe—thar! I reckon you're more comfortable!"

"It's Gracey!" whispered Gabriel, hoarsely, with his eyes still fixed upon the slight, elegantly dressed woman, who now, leaning against the doorway, stood coldly regarding him. "It's Gracey—your sister, Olly!"

"Ef you mean the woman who hez been tryin' her best to swar away your life, and kem here allowin' to do it—she ain't no sister o' mine—not," added Olly, with a withering glance at the simple elegance of her sister's attire, "not even ef she does trapse in yer in frills and tuckers—more shame for her!"

"If you mean," said Grace, coldly, "the girl whose birthright you took away by marrying the woman who stole it, if you mean the girl who rightfully bears the name that you denied, under oath, in the very shadow of the gallows, she claims nothing of you but her name."

"Thet's so," said Gabriel, simply. He dropped his head between his great hands, and a sudden tremor shook his huge frame.

"Ye ain't goin' to be driv inter histeriks agin along o' that crokodill," said Olly, bending over her brother in alarm. "Don't ye—don't ye cry, Gabe!" whimpered Olly, as a few drops oozed between Gabriel's fingers; "don't ye take on, darling, *afore her!*"

The two sisters glared at each other over the helpless man between them. Then another woman entered who looked sympathetically at Gabriel and then glared at them both. It was Mrs Markle. At which, happily for Gabriel, the family bickering ceased.

"It's all over, Gabriel! you're clar!" said Mrs. Markle, ignoring the sympathies as well as the presence of the two other ladies. "Here's Mr. Poinsett."

He entered quickly, but stopped and flushed slightly under the cold eyes of Grace Conroy. But only for a moment. Coming to Gabriel's side, he said, kindly, "Gabriel, I congratulate you. The acting District Attorney has entered a *nolle prosequi*, and you are discharged."

"Ye mean I kin go?" said Gabriel, suddenly lifting his face.

"Yes. You are as free as air."

"And ez to *her?*" asked Gabriel, quickly.

"Who do you mean?" replied Arthur, involuntarily glancing in the direction of Grace, whose eyes dropped scornfully before him.

"My wife—July—is *she* clar too?"

"As far as this trial is concerned, yes," returned Arthur, with a trifle less interest in his voice, which Gabriel was quick to discern.

"Then I'll go," said Gabriel, rising to his feet. He made a few steps to the door and then hesitated, stopped, and turned toward Grace. As he did so his old apologetic, troubled, diffident manner returned.

"Ye'll exkoos me, miss," he said, looking with troubled eyes upon his newly-found sister, "ye'll exkoos me, ef I haven't the time now to do the agreeable and show ye over yer property on Conroy's Hill. But it's thar! It's all thar, ez Lawyer Maxwell kin testify. It's all thar and the house is open, ez it always was to ye, ez the young woman who keeps the house kin tell ye. I'd go thar with ye ef I hed time, but I'm startin' out now, to-night, to see July. To see my wife, Miss Conroy, to see July ez is expectin'! And I reckon thar'll be a baby—a pore little, helpless newborn baby—ony *so* long!" added Gabriel, exhibiting his fore-finger as a degree of mensuration; "and ez a fammerly man, being ladies, I reckon you reckon I oughter be thar." (I grieve to state that at this moment the ladies appealed to exchanged a glance of supreme contempt, and am proud to record that Lawyer Maxwell and Mr. Poinsett exhibited the only expression of sympathy with the speaker that was noticeable in the group.)

Arthur detected it and said, I fear none the less readily for that knowledge—

"Don't let us keep you, Gabriel; we understand your feelings. Go at once."

"Take me along, Gabe," said Olly, flashing her eyes at her sister, and then turning to Gabriel with a quivering upper lip.

Gabriel turned, swooped his tremendous arm around Olly, lifted her bodily off her feet, and saying, "You're my own little girl," vanished through the doorway.

This movement reduced the group to Mrs. Markle and Grace Conroy, confronted by Mr. Poinsett and Maxwell. Mrs. Markle relieved an embarrassing silence by stepping forward and taking the arm of Lawyer Maxwell and leading him away. Arthur and Grace were left alone.

For the first time in his life Arthur lost his readiness and self-command. He glanced awkwardly at the woman before him, and felt that neither conventional courtesy nor vague sentimental recollection would be effective here.

"I am waiting for my maid," said Grace, coldly; "if, as you return to the Court-room, you will send her here, you will oblige me."

Arthur bowed confusedly.

"Your maid"——

"Yes; you know her, I think, Mr. Poinsett," continued Grace, lifting her arched brows with cold surprise. "Manuela!"

Arthur turned pale and red. He was conscious of being not only awkward but ridiculous.

"Pardon me—perhaps I am troubling you—I will go myself," said Grace, contemptuously.

"One moment, Miss Conroy," said Arthur, instinctively stepping before her as she moved as if to pass him, "one moment, I beg." He paused, and then said, with less deliberation and more impulsively than had been his habit for the last six years, "You will, perhaps, be more forgiving to your brother if you know that I, who have had the pleasure of meeting you since—you were lost to us all—I, who have not had his pre-occupation of interest in another—even I, have been as blind, as foolish, as seemingly heartless as he. You will remember this, Miss Conroy—I hope quite as much for its implied compliment to your complete disguise, and an evidence of the success of your own endeavours to obliterate your identity, as for its being an excuse for your brother's conduct, if not for my own. *I* did not know you."

Grace Conroy paused and raised her dark eyes to his.

"You spoke of my brother's pre-occupation with—with the woman for whom he would have sacrificed anything—*me*—his very life! I can—I am a woman—I can understand *that!* You have forgotten, Don Arturo, you have forgotten—pardon me—I am not finding fault—it is not for me to find fault—but you have forgotten—Donna Maria Sepulvida!"

She swept by him with a rustle of silk and lace, and was gone. His heart gave a sudden bound; he was about to follow her, when he was met at the door by the expanding bosom of Colonel Starbottle.

"Permit me, sir, as a gentleman, as a man of—er—er—er—honour! to congratulate you, sir! When we—er—er—parted in San Francisco I did not think that I would have the—er—er—pleasure—a rare pleasure to Colonel Starbottle, sir, in his private as well as his—er—er—public capacity, of—er—er—a PUBLIC APOLOGY. Ged, sir! I have made it! Ged, sir! when I entered that *nolle pros.*, I said to myself, 'Star., this is an apology—an apology, sir! But you are responsible, sir, you are responsible, Star.! personally responsible!'"

"I thank you," said Arthur, abstractedly, still straining his eyes after the retreating figure of Grace Conroy, and trying to combat a sudden instinctive jealousy of the man before him, "I thank you, Colonel, on behalf of my client and myself."

"Ged, sir," said Colonel Starbottle, blocking up the way, with a general expansiveness of demeanour, "Ged, sir, this is not all. You will remember that our recent interview in San Francisco was regarding another and a different issue. That, sir, I am proud to say, the developments of evidence in this trial have honourably and—er—er—as a lawyer, I may say, have legally settled. With the—er—er—identification and legal—er—er—rehabilitation of Grace Conroy, that claim of my client falls to the ground. You may state to your client, Mr. Poinsett, that—er—er—upon my own personal responsibility I abandon the claim."

Arthur Poinsett stopped and looked fixedly at the gallant Colonel. Even in his sentimental pre-occupation the professional habit triumphed.

"You withdraw Mrs. Dumphy's claim upon Mr. Dumphy?" he said, slowly.

Colonel Starbottle did not verbally reply, but that gallant warrior allowed the facial muscles on the left side of his face to relax so that one eye was partially closed.

"Yes, sir,—there is a matter of a few thousand dollars that—er—er—you understand, I am—er—er—personally responsible for."

"That will never be claimed, Colonel Starbottle," said Arthur, smiling, "and I am only echoing, I am sure, the sentiments of the man most concerned, who is approaching us—Mr. Dumphy."

CHAPTER VIII.

IN WHICH THE FOOTPRINTS RETURN.

Mr. Jack Hamlin was in very bad case. When Dr. Duchesne, who had been summoned from Sacramento, arrived, that eminent surgeon had instantly assumed such light-heartedness and levity toward his patient, such captiousness toward Pete, with an occasional seriousness of demeanour when he was alone, that, to those who knew him, it was equal to an unfavourable prognosis. Indeed, he evaded the direct questioning of Olly, who had lately constituted herself a wondrously light-footed, soft-handed assistant of Pete, until one day, when they were alone, he asked more seriously than was his wont if Mr. Hamlin had ever spoken of his relations, or if she knew of any of his friends who were accessible.

Olly had already turned this subject over in her womanly mind, and had thought once or twice of writing to the Blue Moselle, but on the direct questioning of the doctor, and its peculiar significance, she recalled Jack's confidences on their midnight ride, and the Spanish beauty he had outlined; and so one evening, when she was alone with her patient, and the fever was low, and Jack lay ominously patient and submissive, she began—what the doctor had only lately abandoned—probing a half-healed wound.

"I reckon you'd hev been a heap more comfortable ef this thing hed happened to ye down thar in San Antonio," said Olly.

Jack rolled his dark eyes wonderingly upon his fair persecutor.

"You know you'd hev had thet thar sweetheart o' yours—thet Mexican woman—sittin' by ye, instead o' me—and Pete," suggested the artful Olympia.

Jack nearly leaped from the bed.

"Do you reckon I'd hev rung myself in as a wandering cripple—a tramp thet hed got peppered—on a lady like *her?* Look yer, Olly," continued Mr. Hamlin, raising himself on his elbow, "if you've got the idea thet thet woman is one of them hospital sharps—one of them angels who waltz round a sick man with a bottle of camphor in one hand and a tract in the other—you had better disabuse your mind of it at once, Miss Conroy; take a back seat and wait for a new deal. And don't you go to talkin' of thet lady as my sweetheart—it's—it's—sacrilegious—and the meanest kind of a bluff."

As the day of the trial drew near, Mr. Hamlin had expressed but little interest in it, and had evidently only withheld his general disgust of Gabriel's weakness from consideration of his sister. Once Mr. Hamlin condescended to explain his apparent coldness.

"There's a witness coming, Olly, that'll clear your brother—more shame for him—the man ez *did* kill Ramirez. I'm keeping my sympathies for that chap. Don't you be alarmed. If that man don't come up to the scratch I will. So—don't you go whining round. And ef you'll take my advice, you'll keep clear o' that Court, and let them lawyers fight it out. It will be time enough for you to go when they send for *me.*"

"But you can't move—you ain't strong enough," said Olly.

"I reckon Pete will get me there some way, if he has to pack me on his back. I ain't a heavy weight now," said Jack, looking sadly at his thin white hands; "I've reckoned on that, and even if I should pass in my checks, there's an affidavit already sworn to in Maxwell's hands."

Nevertheless, on the day of the trial, Olly, still doubtful of Gabriel, and still mindful of his capacity to develop

"God-forsaken mulishness," was nervous and uneasy, until a messenger arrived from Maxwell with a note to Hamlin, carrying the tidings of the appearance of Perkins in Court, and closing with a request for Olly's presence.

"Who's Perkins?" asked Olly, as she reached for her hat in nervous excitement.

"He's no slouch," said Jack, sententiously. "Don't ask questions. It's all right with Gabriel now," he added, assuringly. "He's as good as clear. Run away, Miss Conroy. Hold up a minit! There, kiss me! Look here, Olly, say!—do you take any stock in that lost sister of yours that your fool of a brother is always gabbing about? You do? Well, you are as big a fool as he. There! There!—never mind now—she's turned up at last! Much good may it do you. One! two!—go!" and as Olly's pink ribbons flashed through the doorway, Mr. Hamlin lay down again with a twinkle in his eye.

He was alone. The house was very quiet and still; most of the guests, and the hostess and her assistant, were at the all-absorbing trial; even the faithful Pete, unconscious of any possible defection of his assistant, Olly, had taken the opportunity to steal away to hear the arguments of counsel. As the retreating footsteps of Olly echoed along the vacant corridor, he felt that he possessed the house completely.

This consciousness to a naturally active man, bored by illness and the continuous presence of attendants, however kind and devoted, was at first a relief. Mr. Hamlin experienced an instant desire to get up and dress himself, to do various things which were forbidden—but which now an overruling Providence had apparently placed within his reach. He rose with great difficulty, and a physical weakness that seemed altogether inconsistent with the excitement he was then feeling, and partially dressed himself.

Then he was suddenly overtaken with great faintness and vertigo, and struggling to the open window, fell in a chair beside it. The cool breeze revived him for a moment, and he tried to rise, but found it impossible. Then the faintness and vertigo returned, and he seemed to be slipping away somewhere—not altogether unpleasantly, nor against his volition—somewhere where there was darkness and stillness and rest. And then he slipped back, almost instantly as it seemed to him, to a room full of excited and anxious people, all extravagantly, and as he thought, ridiculously concerned about himself. He tried to assure them that he was all right, and not feeling any worse for his exertion, but was unable to make them understand him. Then followed Night, replete with pain, and filled with familiar voices that spoke unintelligibly, and then Day, devoted to the monotonous repetition of the last word or phrase that the doctor, or Pete, or Olly had used, or the endless procession of Olly's pink ribbons, and the tremulousness of a window curtain, or the black, sphinx-like riddle of a pattern on the bed-quilt or the wall-paper. Then there was sleep that was turbulent and conscious, and wakefulness that was lethargic and dim, and then infinite weariness, and then lapses of utter vacuity—the occasional ominous impinging of the shadow of death.

But through this chaos there was always a dominant central figure—a figure partly a memory, and, as such, surrounded by consistent associations; partly a reality and incongruous with its surroundings—the figure of Donna Dolores! But whether this figure came back to Mr. Hamlin out of the dusky arches of the Mission Church in a cloud of incense, besprinkling him with holy water, or whether it bent over him, touching his feverish lips with cool drinks, or smoothing his pillow, a fact utterly unreal and preposterous seen against the pattern of the wall-paper, or sitting on the familiar chair by his bedside—it was always there. And when, one day, the figure stayed longer, and the interval of complete consciousness seemed more protracted, Mr. Hamlin, with one mighty effort, moved his lips, and said feebly—

"Donna Dolores!"

The figure started, leaned its beautiful face, blushing a celestial rosy red, above his own, put its finger to its perfect lips, and said in plain English—

"Hush! I am Gabriel Conroy's sister."

CHAPTER IX.

IN WHICH MR. HAMLIN PASSES.

WITH his lips sealed by the positive mandate of the lovely spectre, Mr. Hamlin resigned himself again to weakness and sleep. When he awoke, Olly was sitting by his bedside; the dusky figure of Pete, spectacled and reading a good book, was dimly outlined against the window—but that was all. The vision—if vision it was—had fled.

"Olly," said Mr. Hamlin, faintly.

"Yes!" said Olly, opening her eyes in expectant sympathy.

"How long have I been dr—I mean how long has this—spell lasted?"

"Three days," said Olly.

"The —— you say!" (A humane and possibly weak consideration for Mr. Hamlin in his new weakness and suffering restricts me to a mere outline of his extravagance of speech.)

"But you're better now," supplemented Olly.

Mr. Hamlin began to wonder faintly if his painful experience of the last twenty-four hours were a part of his convalescence. He was silent for a few moments and then suddenly turned his face toward Olly.

"Didn't you say something about—about—your sister, the other day?"

"Yes—she's got back," said Olly, curtly.

"Here?"

"Here."

"Well?" said Mr. Hamlin, a little impatiently.

"Well," returned Olly, with a slight toss of her curls, "she's got back, and I reckon it's about time she did."

Strange to say, Olly's evident lack of appreciation of her sister seemed to please Mr. Hamlin—possibly because it agreed with his own idea of Grace's superiority and his inability to recognise or accept her as the sister of Gabriel.

"Where has she been all this while?" asked Jack, rolling his large hollow eyes over Olly.

"Goodness knows! Says she's bin livin' in some fammerly down in the South—Spanish, I reckon; thet's whar she gits those airs and graces."

"Has she ever been here—in this room?" asked Mr. Hamlin.

"Of course she has," said Olly. "When I left you to go with Gabe to see his wife at Wingdam, she volunteered to take my place. Thet waz while you waz flighty, Mr. Hamlin. But I reckon she admired to stay here on account of seein' her bo!"

"Her what?" asked Mr. Hamlin, feeling the blood fast rushing to his colourless face.

"Her bo," repeated Olly, "thet thar Ashley, or Poinsett—or whatever he calls hisself now!"

Mr. Hamlin here looked so singular, and his hand tightened so strongly around Olly's, that she hurriedly repeated to him the story of Grace's early wanderings, and her absorbing passion for their former associate, Arthur Poinsett.

The statement was, in Olly's present state of mind, not favourable to Grace. "And she just came up yer only to see Arthur agin. Thet's all. And she nearly swearin' her brother's life away—and pretendin' it was only done to save the fammerly name. Jest ez if it hed been any more comfortable fur Gabriel to have been hung in his own name. And then goin' and accusin' thet innocent ole lamb, Gabe, of conspiring with July to take her name away. Purty goin's on, I reckon. And thet man Poinsett, by her own showin' —never lettin' on to see her nor us—nor anybody. And she sassin' *me* for givin' my opinion of him—and excusin' him by sayin' she didn't want him to know *whar* she was. And she refusin' to see July at all—and pore July lyin' thar at Wingdam, sick with a new baby. Don't talk to me about her!"

"But your sister didn't run away with—with—this chap. She went away to bring you help," interrupted Jack, hastily dragging Olly back to earlier history.

"Did she? Couldn't she trust her bo to go and get help and then come back fur her?—reckonin' he cared for her at all. No, she waz thet crazy after him she couldn't trust him outer her sight—and she left the camp and Gabe and ME for him. And then the idee of *her* talking to Gabriel about bein' disgraced by July. Ez ef she had never done anythin' to spile her own name, and puttin' on such airs and"——

"Dry up!" shouted Mr. Hamlin, turning with sudden savageness upon his pillow. "Dry up!—don't you see you're driving me half-crazy with your infernal buzzing?" He paused, as Olly stopped in mingled mortification and alarm, and then added in milder tones, "There, that'll do. I am not feeling well to-day. Send Dr. Duchesne to me if he's here. Stop one moment—there! good-bye, go!"

Olly had risen promptly. There was always something

in Mr. Hamlin's positive tones that commanded an obedience that she would have refused to any other. Thoroughly convinced of some important change in Mr. Hamlin's symptoms, she sought the doctor at once. Perhaps she brought with her some of her alarm and anxiety, for a moment later that distinguished physician entered with less deliberation than was his habit. He walked to the bedside of his patient, and would have taken his hand, but Jack slipped his tell-tale pulse under the covers, and looking fixedly at the doctor, said—

"Can I be moved from here?"

"You can, but I should hardly advise"——

"I didn't ask that. This is a lone hand I'm playin', doctor, and if I'm euchred, tain't your fault. How soon?"

"I should say," said Dr. Duchesne, with professional caution, "that if no bad symptoms supervene" (he made here a half habitual but wholly ineffectual dive for Jack's pulse), "you might go in a week."

"I must go *now!*"

Dr. Duchesne bent over his patient. He was a quick as well as a patiently observing man, and he saw something in Jack's face that no one else had detected. Seeing this he said, "You can go now, at a great risk—the risk of your life."

"I'll take it!" said Mr. Hamlin, promptly. "I've been playin' agin odds," he added, with a faint but audacious smile, "for the last six months, and it's no time to draw out now. Go on, tell Pete to pack up and get me ready."

"Where are you going?" asked the doctor, quietly, still gazing at his patient.

"To !—blank!" said Mr. Hamlin, impulsively. Then recognising the fact that in view of his having travelling companions, some more definite and practicable locality was necessary, he paused a moment, and said, "To the Mission of San Antonio."

"Very well," said the doctor, gravely.

Strange to say, whether from the doctor's medication, or from the stimulus of some reserved vitality hitherto unsuspected, Mr. Hamlin from that moment rallied. The preparations for his departure were quickly made, and in a few hours he was ready for the road.

"I don't want to have anybody cacklin' around me," he said, in deprecation of any leave-taking. "I leave the board, they can go on with the game."

Notwithstanding which, at the last moment, Gabriel hung awkwardly and heavily around the carriage in which the invalid was seated.

"I'd foller arter ye, Mr. Hamlin, in a buggy," he interpolated, in gentle deprecation of his unwieldy and difficult bulk, "but I'm sorter kept yer with my wife—who is powerful weak along of a pore small baby—about so long—the same not bein' a fammerly man yourself, you don't kinder get the hang of. I thought it might please ye to know that I got bail yesterday for thet Mr. Perkins—ez didn't kill that thar Ramirez—the same havin' killed hisself—ez waz fetched out on the trial, which I reckon ye didn't get to hear. I admire to see ye lookin' so well, Mr. Hamlin, and I'm glad Olly's goin' with ye. I reckon Grace would hev gone too, but she's sorter skary about strangers, hevin' bin engaged these seving years to a young man by the name o' Poinsett ez waz one o' my counsel, and hevin' lately had a row with the same—one o' them lovers' fights—which bein' a young man yourself, ye kin kindly allow for."

"Drive on!" imprecated Mr. Hamlin furiously to the driver; "what are you waiting for?" and with the whirling wheels Gabriel dropped off apologetically in a cloud of dust, and Mr. Hamlin sank back exhaustedly on the cushions.

Notwithstanding, as he increased his distance from One Horse Gulch, his spirits seemed to rise, and by the time they had reached San Antonio he had recovered his old audacity and dash of manner, and raised the highest hopes in the breast of everybody but—his doctor. Yet that gentleman, after a careful examination of his patient one night, said privately to Pete, "I think this exaltation will last about three days longer. I am going to San Francisco. At the end of that time I shall return—unless you telegraph to me before that." He parted gaily from his patient, and seriously from everybody else. Before he left he sought out Padre Felipe. "I have a patient here, in a critical condition," said the doctor; "the hotel is no place for him. Is there any family here—any house that will receive him under your advice for a week? At the end of that time he will be better, or beyond *our* ministration. He is not a Protestant—he is nothing. You have had experience with the heathen, Father Felipe."

Father Felipe looked at Dr. Duchesne. The doctor's well-earned professional fame had penetrated even San Antonio; the doctor's insight and intelligence were visible in his manner, and touched the Jesuit instantly. "It is a strange case, my son; a sad case," he said, thoughtfully. "I will see."

He did. The next day, under the directions of Father Felipe, Mr. Hamlin was removed to the Rancho of the Blessed Fisherman, and notwithstanding the fact that its hostess was absent, was fairly installed as its guest. When Mrs. Sepulvida returned from her visit to San Francisco, she was at first astonished, then excited, and then, I fear, gratified.

For she at once recognised in this guest of Father Felipe the mysterious stranger whom she had, some weeks ago, detected on the plains of the Blessed Trinity. And Jack, despite his illness, was still handsome, and had, moreover, the melancholy graces of invalidism, which go far with an habitually ailing sex. And so she coddled Mr. Hamlin, and gave him her sacred hammock by day over the porch, and her best bedroom at night. And then, at the close of a pleasant day, she said, archly—

"I think I have seen you before, Mr. Hamlin—at the Rancho of the Blessed Trinity. You remember—the house of Donna Dolores?"

Mr. Hamlin was too observant of the sex to be impertinently mindful of another woman than his interlocutor, and assented with easy indifference.

Donna Maria (now thoroughly convinced that Mr. Hamlin's attentions on that eventful occasion were intended for herself, and even delightfully suspicious of some prearranged plan in his present situation): "Poor Donna Dolores! You know we have lost her for ever."

Mr. Hamlin asked, "When?"

"That dreadful earthquake on the 8th."

Mr. Hamlin, reflecting that the appearance of Grace Conroy was on the 10th, assented again abstractedly.

"Ah, yes! so sad! And yet, perhaps, for the best. You know the poor girl had a hopeless passion for her legal adviser—the famous Arthur Poinsett! Ah! you did not? Well, perhaps it was only merciful that she died before she knew how insincere that man's attentions were. You are a believer in special Providences, Mr. Hamlin?"

Mr. Hamlin (doubtfully): "You mean a run of luck?"

Donna Maria (rapidly, ignoring Mr. Hamlin's illustration): "Well, perhaps *I* have reason to say so. Poor Donna Dolores was my friend. Yet, would you believe there were people—you know how ridiculous is the gossip of a town like this—there are people who believed that he was paying attention to ME!"

Mrs. Sepulvida hung her head archly. There was a long pause. Then Mr. Hamlin called faintly—

"Pete!"

"Yes, Mars Jack."

"Ain't it time to take that medicine?"

When Dr. Duchesne returned he ignored all this little byplay, and even the anxious inquiries of Olly, and said to Mr. Hamlin—

"Have you any objection to my sending for Dr. Mackintosh—a devilish clever fellow?"

And Mr. Hamlin had none. And so, after a private telegram, Dr. Mackintosh arrived, and for three or four hours the two doctors talked in an apparently unintelligible language, chiefly about a person whom Mr. Hamlin was satisfied did not exist. And when Dr. Mackintosh left, Dr. Duchesne, after a very earnest conversation with him on their way to the stage office, drew a chair beside Mr. Hamlin's bed.

"Jack!"

"Yes, sir."

"Have you got everything fixed—all right?"

"Yes, sir."

"Jack!"

"Yes, sir."

"You've made Pete very happy this morning."

Jack looked up at Dr. Duchesne's critical face, and the doctor went on gravely—

"Confessing religion to him—saying you believed as he did!"

A faint laugh glimmered in the dark hollows of Jack's eyes.

"The old man," he said, explanatory, "has been preachin'

mighty heavy at me ever since t'other doctor came, and I reckoned it might please him to allow that everything he said was so. You see the old man's bin right soft on me, and between us, doctor, I ain't much to give him in exchange. It's no square game!"

"Then you believe you're going to die?" said the doctor, gravely.

"I reckon."

"And you have no directions to give me?"

"There's a black hound at Sacramento—Jim Briggs, who borrowed and never gave back my silver-mounted Derringers, that I reckoned to give to you! Tell him he'd better give them up or I'll"——

"Jack," interrupted Dr. Duchesne, with infinite gentleness, laying his hand on the invalid's arm, "you must not think of me."

Jack pressed his friend's hand.

"There's my diamond pin up the spout at Wingdam, and the money gone to Lawyer Maxwell to pay witnesses for that old fool Gabriel. And then when Gabriel and me was escaping I happened to strike the very man, Perkins, who was Gabriel's principal witness, and he was dead broke, and I had to give him my solitaire ring to help him get away and be on hand for Gabriel. And Olly's got my gold specimen to be made into a mug for that cub of that old she tiger—Gabriel's woman—that Madame Devarges. And my watch—who *has* got my watch?" said Mr. Hamlin, reflectively.

"Never mind those things, Jack. Have you any word to send—to—anybody?"

"No."

There was a long pause. In the stillness the ticking of a clock on the mantel became audible. Then there was a laugh in the ante-room, where a professional brother of

Jack's had been waiting, slightly under the influence of grief and liquor.

"Scotty ought to know better than to kick up a row in a decent woman's house," whispered Jack, faintly. "Tell him to dry up, or I'll "——

But his voice was failing him, and the sentence remained incomplete.

"Doc——" (after a long effort).

"Jack."

"Don't—let—on—to Pete—I fooled—him."

"No, Jack."

They were both still for several minutes. And then Dr. Duchesne softly released his hand and laid that of his patient, white and thin, upon the coverlid before him. Then he rose gently and opened the door of the ante-room. Two or three eager faces confronted him. "Pete," he said, gravely, "I want Pete—no one else."

The old negro entered with a trembling step. And then catching sight of the white face on the pillow, he uttered one cry—a cry replete with all the hysterical pathos of his race, and ran and dropped on his knees beside—it! And then the black and the white face were near together, and both were wet with tears.

Dr. Duchesne stepped forward and would have laid his hand gently upon the old servant's shoulder. But he stopped, for suddenly both of the black hands were lifted wildly in the air, and the black face with rapt eyeballs turned toward the ceiling, as if they had caught sight of the steadfast blue beyond. Perhaps they had.

"O de Lord God! whose prechiss blood washes de brack sheep and de white sheep all de one colour! O de Lamb ob God! Sabe, sabe dis por', dis por' boy. O Lord God, for MY sake. O de Lord God, dow knowst fo' twenty years Pete, ole Pete, has walked in dy ways—has found de Lord and Him crucified!—and has been dy servant. O de Lord God—O de bressed Lord, ef it's all de same to you, let all dat go fo' nowt. Let ole Pete go! and send down dy mercy and forgiveness fo' *him!*"

CHAPTER X.

IN THE OLD CABIN AGAIN.

THERE was little difficulty in establishing the validity of Grace Conroy's claim to the Conroy grant under the bequest of Dr. Devarges. Her identity was confirmed by Mr. Dumphy—none the less readily that it relieved him of a distressing doubt about the late Mrs. Dumphy, and did not affect his claim to the mineral discovery which he had purchased from Gabriel and his wife. It was true that since the dropping of the lead the mine had been virtually abandoned, and was comparatively of little market value. But Mr. Dumphy still clung to the hope that the missing lead would be discovered.

He was right. It was some weeks after the death of Mr. Hamlin that Gabriel and Olly stood again beneath the dismantled roof-tree and bare walls of his old cabin on Conroy Hill. But the visit this time was not one of confidential disclosure nor lonely contemplation, but with a practical view of determining whether this first home of the brother and sister could be repaired and made habitable, for Gabriel had steadily refused the solicitations of Grace that he should occupy his more recent mansion. Mrs. Conroy and infant were at the hotel.

"Thar, Olly," said Gabriel, "I reckon that a cartload o' boards and a few days' work with willin' hands, will put that thar shanty back ag'in ez it used to be when you and me waz childun."

"Yes," said Olly, abstractedly.

"We've had good times yer, Olly, you and me!"

"Yes," said Olly, with eyes still afar.

Gabriel looked down—a great way—on his sister, and then suddenly took her hand and sat down upon the doorstep, drawing her between his knees after the old fashion.

"Ye ain't hearkenin' to me, Olly dear!"

Whereat Miss Olympia instantly and illogically burst into tears, and threw her small arms about Gabriel's huge bulk. She had been capricious and fretful since Mr. Hamlin's death, and it may be that she embraced the dead man again in her brother's arms. But her outward expression was, "Gracey! I was thinking o' poor Gracey, Gabe!"

"Then," said Gabriel, with intense archness and cunning, "you was thinkin' o' present kempany, for ef I ain't blind, that's them coming up the hill."

There were two figures slowly coming up the hill outlined against the rosy sunset. A man and woman—Arthur Poinsett and Grace Conroy. Olly lifted her head and rose to her feet. They approached nearer. No one spoke. The next instant—impulsively I admit, inconsistently I protest—the sisters were in each other's arms. The two men looked at each other, awkward, reticent, superior.

Then the women having made quick work of it, the two men were treated to an equally illogical, inconsistent embrace. When Grace at last, crying and laughing, released Gabriel's neck from her sweet arms, Mr. Poinsett assumed the masculine attitude of pure reason.

"Now that you have found your sister, permit me to introduce you to my wife," he said to Gabriel, taking Grace's hand in his own.

Whereat Olly flew into Poinsett's arms, and gave him a fraternal and conciliatory kiss. Tableau.

"You don't look like a bride," said the practical Olly to

Mrs. Poinsett, under her breath; "you ain't got no veil, no orange blossoms—and that black dress"——

"We've been married seven years, Olly," said the quick-eared and ready-witted Arthur.

And then these people began to chatter as if they had always been in the closest confidence and communion.

"You know," said Grace to her brother, "Arthur and I are going East, to the States, to-morrow, and really, Gabe, he says he will not leave here until you consent to take back your house—your wife's house, Gabe. You know WE" (there was a tremendous significance in this newly-found personal plural), "WE have deeded it all to you."

"I hev a dooty to per-form to Gracey," said Gabriel Conroy, with astute deliberation, looking at Mr. Poinsett, "a dooty to thet gal, thet must be done afore any trans-fer of this yer proputty is made. I hev to make restitution of certain papers ez hez fallen casooally into my hands. This yer paper," he added, drawing a soiled yellow envelope from his pocket, "kem to me a week ago, the same hevin' lied in the Express Office sens the trial. It belongs to Gracey, I reckon, and I hands it to her."

Grace tore open the envelope, glanced at its contents hurriedly, uttered a slight cry of astonishment, blushed, and put the paper into her pocket.

"This yer paper," continued Gabriel, gravely, drawing another from his blouse, "was found by me in the Empire Tunnel the night I was runnin' from the lynchers. It likewise b'longs to Gracey—and the world gin'rally. It's the record of Dr. Devarges' fust discovery of the silver lead on this yer hill, and," continued Gabriel, with infinite gravity, "wipes out, so to speak, this yer mineral right o' me and Mr. Dumphy and the stockholders gin'rally."

It was Mr. Poinsett's turn to take the paper from Gabriel's hands. He examined it attentively by the fading light. "That is so," he said, earnestly; "it is quite legal and valid."

"And thar ez one paper more," continued Gabriel, this time putting his hand in his bosom and drawing out a buckskin purse, from which he extracted a many-folded paper. "It's the grant that Dr. Devarges gave Gracey, thet thet pore Mexican Ramirez ez—maybe ye may remember—waz killed, handed to my wife, and July, my wife"—said Gabriel, with a prodigious blush—"hez been sorter keepin' IN TRUST for Gracey!"

He gave the paper to Arthur, who received it, but still retained a warm grasp of Gabriel's massive hand.

"And now," added Gabriel, "et's gettin' late, and I reckon et's about the square thing ef we'd ad-journ this yer meeting to the hotel, and ez you're goin' away, maybe ye'd make a partin' visit with yer wife, forgettin' and forgivin' like, to Mrs. Conroy and the baby—a pore little thing—that ye wouldn't believe it, Mr. Poinsett, looks like me!"

But Olly and Grace had drawn aside, and were in the midst of an animated conversation. And Grace was saying—

"So I took the stone from the fire, just as I take this" (she picked up a fragment of the crumbling chimney before her); "it looked black and burnt just like this; and I rubbed it hard on the blanket so, and it shone, just like silver, and Dr. Devarges said"——

"We are going, Grace," interrupted her husband, "we are going to see Gabriel's wife." Grace hesitated a moment, but as her husband took her arm he slightly pressed it with a certain matrimonial caution, whereupon with a quick impulsive gesture, Grace held out her hand to Olly, and the three gaily followed the bowed figure of Gabriel, as he strode through the darkening woods.

CHAPTER XI.

THE RETURN OF A FOOTPRINT.

I REGRET that no detailed account of the reconciliatory visit to Mrs. Conroy has been handed down, and I only gather a hint of it from after comments of the actors themselves. When the last words of parting had been said, and Grace and Arthur had taken their seats in the Wingdam coach, Gabriel bent over his wife's bedside,—

"It kinder seemed ez ef you and Mr. Poinsett recognised each other at first, July," said Gabriel.

"I *have* seen him before—not here! I don't think he'll ever trouble us much, Gabriel," said Mrs. Conroy, with a certain triumphant lighting of the cold fires of her grey eyes. "But look at the baby. He's laughing! He knows you, I declare!" And in Gabriel's rapt astonishment at this unprecedented display of intelligence in one so young, the subject was dropped.

"Why, where did you ever see Mrs. Conroy before?" asked Grace of her husband, when they had reached Wingdam that night.

"I never saw *Mrs. Conroy* before," returned Arthur, with legal precision. "I met a lady in St. Louis years ago under another name, who, I dare say, is now your brother's wife. But—I think, Grace—the less we see of her—the better."

"Why?"

"By the way, darling, what was that paper that Gabriel gave you?" asked Arthur, lightly, avoiding the previous question.

Grace drew the paper from her pocket, blushed slightly, kissed her husband, and then putting her arms around his neck, laid her face in his breast, while he read aloud, in Spanish, the following:—

"This is to give trustworthy statement that on the 18th of May 1848, a young girl, calling herself Grace Conroy, sought shelter and aid at the Presidio of San Geronimo. Being friendless—but of the B. V. M. and the Saints—I adopted her as my daughter, with the name of Dolores Salvatierra. Six months after her arrival, on the 12th November 1848, she was delivered of a dead child, the son of her affianced husband, one Philip Ashley. Wishing to keep her secret from the world and to prevent recognition by the members of her own race and family, by the assistance and advice of an Indian *peon*, Manuela, she consented that her face and hands should be daily washed by the juice of the *Yokoto*—whose effect is to change the skin to the colour of bronze. With this metamorphosis she became known, by my advice and consent, as the daughter of the Indian Princess Nicata and myself. And as such I have recognised in due form her legal right in the apportionment of my estate.

"Given at the Presidio of San Geronimo, this 1st day of December 1848.

"JUAN HERMENIZILDO SALVATIERRA."

"But how did Gabriel get this?" asked Arthur.

"I—don't—know!" said Grace.

"To whom did *you* give it?"

"To—Padre Felipe."

"Oh, I see!" said Arthur. "Then *you* are Mr. Dumphy's long-lost wife?"

"I don't know what Father Felipe did," said Grace, tossing her head slightly. "I put the matter in his hands."

"The whole story?"

"I said nothing about you—you great goose!"

Arthur kissed her by way of acknowledging the justice of the epithet.

"But I ought to have told Mrs. Sepulvida the whole story when she said you proposed to her. You're sure you didn't?" continued Grace, looking into her husband's eyes.

"Never," said that admirable young man, promptly.

CHAPTER XII.

FRAGMENT OF A LETTER FROM OLYMPIA CONROY TO GRACE POINSETT.

"—— the baby is doing well. And only think—Gabe has struck it again! And you was the cause, dear—and he says it all belongs to you—like the old mule that he is. Don't you remember when you was telling me about Doctor Divergers giving you that rock and how you rubed it untill the silver shone, well, you took up a rock from our old chimbly and rubed it, while you was telling it. And thet rock Gabe came across next morning, all shining where you had rubed it. And shure enuff it was sollid silver. And then Gabe says, says he, 'We've struck it agin, fur the chimbly rock was taken from the first hole I dug on the hill only a hundred feet from here.' And shure enuff, yesterday he purspected the hole and found the leed agin. And we are all very ritch agin and comin' to see you next yeer, only that Gabe is such a fool! Your loving Sister,

"OLYMPIA CONROY."

END OF VOL. IV.

STANDARD AND POPULAR

Library Books

SELECTED FROM THE CATALOGUE OF

HOUGHTON, MIFFLIN AND CO.

CONSIDER what you have in the smallest chosen library. A company of the wisest and wittiest men that could be picked out of all civil countries, in a thousand years, have set in best order the results of their learning and wisdom. The men themselves were hid and inaccessible, solitary, impatient of interruptions, fenced by etiquette; but the thought which they did not uncover to their bosom friend is here written out in transparent words to us, the strangers of another age. — Ralph Waldo Emerson.

American Statesmen.

Edited by John T. Morse, Jr.

(*In Preparation.*)

John Quincy Adams. By John T. Morse, Jr.
Alexander Hamilton. By Henry Cabot Lodge.
Andrew Jackson. By Prof. W. G. Sumner.
John C. Calhoun. By Dr. H. Von Holst.
John Randolph. By Henry Adams.
James Madison. By Sidney Howard Gay.
James Monroe. By Pres. D. C. Gilman.
Albert Gallatin. By John Austin Stevens.
Patrick Henry. By Prof. Moses Coit Tyler.
Henry Clay. By Hon. Carl Schurz.

Lives of Jefferson and Webster are expected, and others, to be announced later.

Hans Christian Andersen.

Complete Works. 8vo.

1. The Improvisatore; or, Life in Italy.
2. The Two Baronesses.
3. O. T.; or, Life in Denmark.
4. Only a Fiddler.
5. In Spain and Portugal.
6. A Poet's Bazaar.
7. Pictures of Travel.
8. The Story of my Life. With Portrait.
9. Wonder Stories told for Children. Ninety-two illustrations.
10. Stories and Tales. Illustrated.

Cloth, per volume, $1.50; price of sets in cloth, $15.00.

Francis Bacon.

Works. Collected and edited by Spedding, Ellis, and Heath. With Portraits and Index. In fifteen volumes, crown 8vo, cloth, $33.75.

The same. *Popular Edition.* In two volumes, crown 8vo, with Portraits and Index. Cloth, $5.00.

Bacon's Life.

Life and Times of Bacon. Abridged. By James Spedding. 2 vols. crown 8vo, $5.00.

Björnstjerne Björnson.

Norwegian Novels. 16mo, each $1.00.

Synnöve Solbakken.
Arne.
A Happy Boy.
The Fisher Maiden.

British Poets.

Riverside Edition. In 68 volumes, crown 8vo, cloth, gilt top, per vol. $1.75; the set complete, 68 volumes, cloth, $100.00.

Akenside and Beattie, 1 vol.
Ballads, 4 vols.
Burns, 1 vol.
Butler, 1 vol.
Byron, 5 vols.
Campbell and Falconer, 1 vol.
Chatterton, 1 vol.
Chaucer, 3 vols.
Churchill, Parnell, and Tickell, 2 vols.
Coleridge and Keats, 2 vols.
Cowper, 2 vols.
Dryden, 2 vols.
Gay, 1 vol.
Goldsmith and Gray, 1 vol.
Herbert and Vaughan, 1 vol.
Herrick, 1 vol.
Hood, 2 vols.
Milton and Marvell, 2 vols.
Montgomery, 2 vols.
Moore, 3 vols.
Pope and Collins, 2 vols.
Prior, 1 vol.
Scott, 5 vols.
Shakespeare and Jonson, 1 vol.
Shelley, 2 vols.
Skelton and Donne, 2 vols.
Southey, 5 vols.
Spenser, 3 vols.
Swift, 2 vols.
Thomson, 1 vol.
Watts and White, 1 vol.
Wordsworth, 3 vols.
Wyatt and Surrey, 1 vol.
Young, 1 vol.

John Brown, M. D.

Spare Hours. 2 vols. 16mo, each $1.50.

Robert Browning.

Poems and Dramas, etc. 13 vols. $19.50.

Wm. C. Bryant.

Translation of Homer. The Iliad. 2 vols. royal 8vo, $9.00. Crown 8vo, $4.50. 1 vol. 12mo, $3.00.

The Odyssey. 2 vols. royal 8vo, $9.00. Crown 8vo, $4.50. 1 vol. 12mo, $3.00.

John Burroughs.

Wake-Robin. Illustrated. 16mo, $1.50.
Winter Sunshine. 16mo, $1.50.
Birds and Poets. 16mo, $1.50.
Locusts and Wild Honey. 16mo, $1.50.
Pepacton, and Other Sketches. 16mo, $1.50.

Thomas Carlyle.

Essays. With Portrait and Index. Four volumes, crown 8vo, $7.50. *Popular Edition.* Two volumes, $3.50.

Alice and Phœbe Cary.

Poetical Works, including Memorial by Mary Clemmer. 1 vol. 8vo, $3.50.
Ballads for Little Folk. Illustrated. $1.50.

L. Maria Child.

Looking toward Sunset. 4to, $2.50.

James Freeman Clarke.

Ten Great Religions. 8vo, $3.00.
Common Sense in Religion. 12mo, $2.00.
Memorial and Biographical Sketches. 12mo, $2.00.
Exotics. $1.00.

J. Fenimore Cooper.

Works. *Household Edition.* Illustrated. 32 vols. 16mo. Cloth, per volume, $1.00; the set, $32.00.
Globe Edition. Illust'd. 16 vols. $20.00. (*Sold only in sets.*)
Sea Tales. Illustrated. 10 vols. 16mo, $10.00.
Leather Stocking Tales. *Household Edition.* Illustrated. 5 vols. $5.00. *Riverside Edition.* 5 vols. $11.25.

C. P. Cranch.

Translation of the Æneid of Virgil. Royal 8vo, $4.50.

Richard H. Dana.

To Cuba and Back. 16mo, $1.25.
Two Years Before the Mast. 16mo, $1.50.

Thomas De Quincey.

Works. *Riverside Edition.* In 12 vols. crown 8vo. Per volume, cloth, $1.50; the set, $18.00.
Globe Edition. Six vols. 12mo, $10.00. (*Sold only in sets.*)

Madame De Stael.

Germany. 1 vol. crown 8vo, $2 50.

Charles Dickens.

Works. *Illustrated Library Edition.* In 29 volumes, crown 8vo. Cloth, each, $1.50; the set, $43.50.

Globe Edition. In 15 vols. 12mo. Cloth, per volume, $1.25; the set, $18.75.

J. Lewis Diman.

The Theistic Argument as Affected by Recent Theories. 8vo, $2.00.

Orations and Essays. 8vo, $2.50.

F. S. Drake.

Dictionary of American Biography. 1 vol. 8vo, cloth, $6.00.

Charles L. Eastlake.

Hints on Household Taste. Illustrated. 12mo, $3.00.

George Eliot.

The Spanish Gypsy. 16mo, $1.50.

Ralph Waldo Emerson.

Works. 10 vols. 16mo, $1.50 each; the set, $15.00.

Fireside Edition. 5 vols. 16mo, $10.00. (*Sold only in sets.*)

"*Little Classic*" *Edition.* 9 vols. Cloth, each, $1.50.

Prose Works. Complete. 3 vols. 12mo, $7.50.

Parnassus. *Household Ed.* 12mo, $2.00. *Library Ed.*, $4.00.

Fénelon.

Adventures of Telemachus. Crown 8vo, $2.25.

James T. Fields.

Yesterdays with Authors. 12mo, $2.00. 8vo, $3.00.

Underbrush. $1.25.

Ballads and other Verses. 16mo, $1.00.

The Family Library of British Poetry, from Chaucer to the Present Time (1350–1878). Edited by James T. Fields and Edwin P. Whipple. Royal 8vo. 1,028 pages, with 12 fine Steel Portraits, $5.00.

Biographical Notes and Personal Sketches. 1 vol. 8vo, gilt top, $2.00.

John Fiske.

Myths and Mythmakers. 12mo, $2.00.

Outlines of Cosmic Philosophy. 2 vols. 8vo, $6.00.

The Unseen World, and other Essays. 12mo, $2.00.

Goethe.

Faust. Metrical Translation. By Rev. C. T. Brooks. 16mo, $1.25.

Faust. Translated into English Verse. By Bayard Taylor. 2 vols. royal 8vo, $9.00; crown 8vo, $4.50; in 1 vol. 12mo, $3.00.

Correspondence with a Child. Portrait of Bettina Brentano. 12mo, $1.50.

Wilhelm Meister. Translated by Thomas Carlyle. Portrait of Goethe. 2 vols. 12mo, $3.00.

Bret Harte.

Works. New complete edition. 5 vols. 12mo, each $2.00.

Nathaniel Hawthorne.

Works. "*Little Classic*" *Edition.* Illustrated. 24 vols. 18mo, each $1.25; the set $30.00.

Illustrated Library Edition. 13 vols. 12mo, per vol. $2.00.

Fireside Edition. Illustrated. 13 vols. 16mo, the set, $21.00.

New Globe Edition. 6 vols. 16mo, illustrated, the set, $10.00.

(*The Fireside and Globe Editions are sold only in sets.*)

George S. Hillard.

Six Months in Italy. 12mo, $2.00.

Oliver Wendell Holmes.

Poems. *Household Edition.* 12mo, $2.00.

Illustrated Library Edition. Illustrated, full gilt, 8vo, $4.00.

Handy Volume Edition. 2 vols. 18mo, gilt top, $2.50.

The Autocrat of the Breakfast-Table. 18mo, $1.50. 12mo, $2.00.

The Professor at the Breakfast-Table. 12mo, $2.00.

The Poet at the Breakfast-Table. 12mo, $2.00.

Elsie Venner. 12mo, $2.00.

The Guardian Angel. 12mo, $2.00.

Soundings from the Atlantic. 16mo, $1.75.

John Lothrop Motley. A Memoir. 16mo, $1.50.

W. D. Howells.

Venetian Life. 12mo, $1.50.
Italian Journeys. 12mo, $1.50.
Their Wedding Journey. Illus. 12mo, $1.50; 18mo, $1.25.
Suburban Sketches. Illustrated. 12mo, $1.50.
A Chance Acquaintance. Illus. 12mo, $1.50; 18mo, $1.25.
A Foregone Conclusion. 12mo, $1.50.
The Lady of the Aroostook. 12mo, $1.50.
The Undiscovered Country. $1.50.
Poems. 18mo, $1.25.
Out of the Question. A Comedy. 18mo, $1.25.
A Counterfeit Presentment. 18mo, $1.25.
Choice Autobiography. Edited by W. D. Howells. 18mo, per vol., $1.25.
I., II. Memoirs of Frederica Sophia Wilhelmina, Margravine of Baireuth.
III. Lord Herbert of Cherbury, and Thomas Ellwood.
IV. Vittorio Alfieri. V. Carlo Goldoni.
VI. Edward Gibbon. VII., VIII. François Marmontel.

Thomas Hughes.

Tom Brown's School-Days at Rugby. $1.00.
Tom Brown at Oxford. 16mo, $1.25.
The Manliness of Christ. 16mo, gilt top, $1.00.

Henry James, Jr.

Passionate Pilgrim and other Tales. $2.00.
Transatlantic Sketches. 12mo, $2.00.
Roderick Hudson. 12mo, $2.00.
The American. 12mo, $2.00.
Watch and Ward. 18mo, $1.25.
The Europeans. 12mo, $1.50.
Confidence. 12mo, $1.50.
The Portrait of a Lady. $2.00.

Mrs. Anna Jameson.

Writings upon Art subjects. 10 vols. 18mo, each $1.50.

Sarah O. Jewett.

Deephaven. 18mo, $1.25.
Old Friends and New. 18mo, $1.25.
Country By-Ways. 18mo, $1.25.
Play-Days. Stories for Children. Sq. 16mo, $1.50.

Rossiter Johnson.

Little Classics. Eighteen handy volumes containing the choicest Stories, Sketches, and short Poems in English literature. Each in one vol. 18mo, $1.00; the set, $18.00. In 9 vols. square 16mo, $13.50. (*Sold in sets only.*)

Samuel Johnson.

Oriental Religions: India, 8vo, $5.00. China, 8vo, $5.00.

T. Starr King.

Christianity and Humanity. 12mo, $2.00.
Substance and Show. 12mo, $2.00.

Lucy Larcom.

Poems. 16mo, $1.25.
Wild Roses of Cape Ann and other Poems. 16mo, $1.25.
An Idyl of Work. 16mo, $1.25.
Childhood Songs. Illustrated. 12mo, $1.50; 16mo, $1.00.
Breathings of the Better Life. 18mo, $1.25.

G. P. Lathrop.

A Study of Hawthorne. 18mo, $1.25.

G. H. Lewes.

The Story of Goethe's Life. Portrait. 12mo, $1.50.
Problems of Life and Mind. 5 vols. $14.00.

J. G. Lockhart.

Life of Sir Walter Scott. 3 vols. cr. 8vo, $4.50.

H. W. Longfellow.

Poems. *Cambridge Edition complete.* Portrait. 4 vols. cr. 8vo, $9.00. 2 vols. $7.00.
Octavo Edition. Portrait and 300 illustrations. $8.00.
Household Edition. Portrait. 12mo, $2.00.
Red-Line Edition. 12 illustrations and Portrait. $2.50.
Diamond Edition. $1.00.
Library Edition. Portrait and 32 illustrations. 8vo, 14.00.
Prose Works. *Cambridge Edition.* 2 vols. cr. 8vo, $4.50.
Hyperion. A Romance. 16mo, $1.50.
Outre-Mer. 16mo, $1.50.
Kavanagh. 16mo, $1.50.
Christus. *Red-Line Edition.* 16 illustrations. $2.50.
Translation of the Divina Commedia of Dante. 3 vols. royal 8vo, $13.50; cr. 8vo, $6.00; 1 vol. cr. 8vo, $3.00.

James Russell Lowell.

Poems. *Red-Line Ed.* 16 illustrations and Portrait. $2.50.
Household Edition. Portrait. 12mo, $2.00.
Library Edition. Portrait and 32 illustrations. 8vo, $4.00.
Fireside Travels. 16mo, $1.50.
Among my Books. 12mo, $2.00.
Among my Books. Second Series. 12mo, $2.00.
My Study Windows. 12mo, $2.00.

T. B. Macaulay.

England. *New Riverside Edition.* 4 vols., cloth, $5.00.
Essays. Portrait. *New Riverside Edition.* 3 vols., $3.75.
Speeches and Poems. *New Riverside Ed.* 1 vol., $1.25.

Harriet Martineau.

Autobiography. Portraits and illustrations. 2 vols. 8vo, $6.00.
Household Education. 18mo, $1.25.

Edwin D. Mead.

Philosophy of Carlyle. 16mo, $1.00.

Owen Meredith.

Poems. *Household Edition.* Illustrated. 12mo, $2.00.
Library Edition. Portrait and 32 illustrations. 8vo, $4.00.
Shawmut Edition. $1.50.
Lucile. *Red-Line Edition.* 8 illustrations. $2.50.
Diamond Edition. 8 illustrations, $1.00.

Michael de Montaigne.

Complete Works. Portrait. 4 vols. crown 8vo, $7.50.

E. Mulford.

The Nation. 8vo, $2.50.
The Republic of God. 8vo, $2.00.

D. M. Mulock.

Thirty Years. Poems. 1 vol. 16mo, $1.50.

T. T. Munger.

On the Threshold. 16mo, gilt top, $1.00.

J. A. W. Neander.

History of the Christian Religion and Church, with Index volume, 6 vols. 8vo, $20.00; Index alone, $3.00.

C. E. Norton.

Notes of Travel and Study in Italy. 16mo, $1.25.
Translation of Dante's New Life. Royal 8vo, $3.00.

Francis W. Palfrey.

Memoir of William Francis Bartlett. Portrait. 16mo, $1.50.

James Parton.

Life of Benjamin Franklin. 2 vols. 8vo, $4.00.
Life of Thomas Jefferson. 8vo, $2.00.
Life of Aaron Burr. 2 vols. 8vo, $4.00.
Life of Andrew Jackson. 3 vols. 8vo, $6.00.
Life of Horace Greeley. 8vo, $2.00.
Humorous Poetry of the English Language. 8vo, $2.00.
Famous Americans of Recent Times. 8vo, $2.00.
Life of Voltaire. 2 vols. 8vo, $6.00.
The French Parnassus. *Household Edition.* 12mo, $2.00.
Holiday Edition. Crown 8vo, $3.50.

Blaise Pascal.

Thoughts, Letters, and Opuscules. Crown 8vo, $2.25.
Provincial Letters. Crown 8vo, $2.25.

Charles C. Perkins.

Raphael and Michael Angelo. 8vo, $5.00.

E. S. Phelps.

The Gates Ajar. 16mo, $1.50.
Men, Women, and Ghosts. 16mo, $1.50.
Hedged In. 16mo, $1.50.
The Silent Partner. 16mo, $1.50.
The Story of Avis. 16mo, $1.50.
Sealed Orders, and other Stories. 16mo, $1.50.
Friends : A Duet. 16mo, $1.25.
Poetic Studies. Square 16mo, $1.50.

Adelaide A. Procter.

Poems. *Diamond Edition.* $1.00.
Red-Line Edition. Portrait and 16 illustrations. $2.50.
Favorite Edition. Illustrated. 16mo, $1.50.

Henry Crabb Robinson.

Diary. Crown 8vo, $2.50.

A. P. Russell.

Library Notes. 12mo, $2.00.

John G. Saxe.

Works. Portrait. 16mo, $2.25.
Highgate Edition. 16mo, $1.50.

Sir Walter Scott.

Waverley Novels. *Illustrated Library Edition.* In 25 vols. cr. 8vo, each $1.00; the set, $25.00.
Globe Edition. 13 vols. 100 illustrations, $16.25.
(*Sold only in sets.*)
Tales of a Grandfather. *Library Edition.* 3 vols. $4.50.

Horace E. Scudder.

The Bodley Books. 5 vols. Each, $1.50.
The Dwellers in Five-Sisters' Court. 16mo, $1.25.
Stories and Romances. $1.25.
Dream Children. Illustrated. 16mo, $1.00.
Seven Little People. Illustrated. 16mo, $1.00.
Stories from my Attic. Illustrated. 16mo, $1.00.
The Children's Book. 4to, 450 pages, $3.50.
Boston Town. Illustrated. 12mo, $1.50.

J. C. Shairp.

Culture and Religion. 16mo, $.125.
Poetic Interpretation of Nature. 16mo, $1.25.
Studies in Poetry and Philosophy. 16mo, $1.50.
Aspects of Poetry. 16mo, $1.50.

Dr. William Smith.

Bible Dictionary. *American Edition.* In four vols. 8vo, the set, $20.00.

E. C. Stedman.

Poems. *Farringford Edition.* Portrait. 16mo, $2.00.
Victorian Poets. 12mo, $2.00.
Hawthorne, and other Poems. 16mo, $1.25.
Edgar Allan Poe. An Essay. Vellum, 18mo, $1.00.

Harriet Beecher Stowe.

Agnes of Sorrento. 12mo, $1.50.
The Pearl of Orr's Island. 12mo, $1.50.
Uncle Tom's Cabin. *Popular Edition.* 12mo, $2.00.
The Minister's Wooing. 12mo, $1.50.
The May-flower, and other Sketches. 12mo, $1.50.
Nina Gordon. 12mo, $1.50.
Oldtown Folks. 12mo, $1.50.
Sam Lawson's Fireside Stories. Illustrated. $1.50.
Uncle Tom's Cabin. 100 Illustrations. 12mo, full gilt, $3.50.

Bayard Taylor.

Poetical Works. *Household Edition.* 12mo, $2.00.
Dramatic Works. Crown 8vo, $2.25.
The Echo Club, and other Literary Diversions. $1.25.

Alfred Tennyson.

Poems. *Household Ed.* Portrait and 60 illustrations. $2.00.
Illustrated Crown Edition. 48 illustrations. 2 vols. $5.00.
Library Edition. Portrait and 60 illustrations. $4.00.
Red-Line Edition. Portrait and 16 illustrations. $2.50.
Diamond Edition. $1.00.
Shawmut Edition. Illustrated. Crown 8vo, $1.50.
Idylls of the King. Complete. Illustrated. $1.50.

Celia Thaxter.

Among the Isles of Shoals. $1.25.
Poems. $1.50.
Drift-Weed. Poems. $1.50.

Henry D. Thoreau.

Walden. 12mo, $1.50.
A Week on the Concord and Merrimack Rivers. $1.50.
Excursions in Field and Forest. 12mo, $1.50.
The Maine Woods. 12mo, $1.50.
Cape Cod. 12mo, $1.50.
Letters to various Persons. 12mo, $1.50.
A Yankee in Canada. 12mo, $1.50.
Early Spring in Massachusetts. 12mo, $1.50.

George Ticknor.

History of Spanish Literature. 3 vols. 8vo, $10.00.
Life, Letters, and Journals. Portraits. 2 vols. 8vo, $6.00.
Cheaper edition. 2 vols. 12mo, $4.00.

J. T. Trowbridge.

A Home Idyl. 16mo, $1.25.
The Vagabonds. 16mo, $1.25.
The Emigrant's Story. 16mo, $1.25.

Voltaire.

History of Charles XII. Crown 8vo, $2.25.

Lew Wallace.

The Fair God. 12mo, $1.50.

George E. Waring, Jr.

Whip and Spur. 18mo, $1.25.
A Farmer's Vacation. Square 8vo, $3.00.
Village Improvements. Illustrated. 75 cents.
The Bride of the Rhine. Illustrated. $1.50.

Charles Dudley Warner.

My Summer in a Garden. 16mo, $1.00. *Illustrated.* $1.50.
Saunterings. 18mo, $1.25.
Back-Log Studies. Illustrated. $1.50.
Baddeck, and that Sort of Thing. $1.00.
My Winter on the Nile. 12mo, $2.00.
In the Levant. 12mo, $2.00.
Being a Boy. Illustrated. $1.50.
In the Wilderness. 75 cents.

William A. Wheeler.

Dictionary of the Noted Names of Fiction. $2.00.

Edwin P. Whipple.

Works. Critical Essays. 6 vols., $9.00

Richard Grant White.

Every-Day English. 12mo, $2.00.
Words and their Uses. 12mo, $2.00.
England Without and Within. 12mo, $2.00.

Mrs. A. D. T. Whitney.

Faith Gartney's Girlhood. 12mo, $1.50.
Hitherto. 12mo, $1.50.
Patience Strong's Outings. 12mo, $1.50.
The Gayworthys. 12mo, $1.50.

Leslie Goldthwaite. Illustrated. 12mo, $1.50.
We Girls. Illustrated. 12mo, $1.50.
Real Folks. Illustrated. 12mo, $1.50.
The Other Girls. Illustrated. 12mo, $1.50.
Sights and Insights. 2 vols. 12mo, $3.00.
Odd or Even. $1.50.
Boys at Chequasset. $1.50.
Pansies. Square 16mo, $1.50.
Just How. 16mo, $1.00.

John G. Whittier.

Poems. *Household Edition.* Portrait. $2.00.
Cambridge Edition. Portrait. 3 vols. crown 8vo, $6.75.
Red-Line Edition. Portrait. 12 illustrations. $2.50.
Diamond Edition. 18mo, $1.00.
Library Edition. Portrait. 32 illustrations. 8vo, $4.00.
Prose Works. *Cambridge Edition.* 2 vols. $4.50.
John Woolman's Journal. Introduction by Whittier. $1.50.
Child Life in Poetry. Selected by Whittier. Illustrated. $2.25. Child Life in Prose. $2.25.
Songs of Three Centuries. Selected by J. G. Whittier. *Household Edition.* 12mo, $2.00. *Illustrated Library Edition.* 32 illustrations. $4.00.

Justin Winsor.

Reader's Handbook of the American Revolution. 16mo, $1.25.

A catalogue containing portraits of many of the above authors, with a description of their works, will be sent free, on application, to any address.

www.ingramcontent.com/pod-product-compliance
Lightning Source LLC
LaVergne TN
LVHW021309110826
84515OLV00003B/528